THE *Regency* COLLECTION

VOLUME
—3—

VOLUME
—3—

Dear Lady Disdain

by

Paula Marshall

An Angel's Touch

by

Elizabeth Bailey

All the characters in this book have no existence outside the imagination of the author, and have no relation whatsoever to anyone bearing the same name or names. They are not even distantly inspired by any individual known or unknown to the author, and all the incidents are pure invention.

First published in Great Britain 1999 by Harlequin Mills & Boon Limited, Eton House, 18–24 Paradise Road, Richmond, Surrey, TW9 1SR.

ISBN 0 263 81709 1
106-9907

Printed and bound in Spain by Litografia Rosés S.A., Barcelona

DEAR LADY DISDAIN

by

Paula Marshall

Dear Reader

When I began to write historical romances for Mills & Boon®, I chose the Regency period for several reasons. I had always enjoyed Georgette Heyer's novels – still among the best – and had spent part of my youth working at Newstead Abbey, the home of Lord Byron, one of the Regency's most colourful characters. It involved me in reading many of the original letters and papers of a dynamic era in English history.

Later on when I researched even further into the period I discovered that nothing I could invent was more exciting – or outrageous – than what had actually happened! What more natural, then, than to write a Regency romance and send it to Mills & Boon – who accepted it and started me on a new career.

Like Georgette Heyer I try to create fiction out of and around fact for the enjoyment and entertainment of myself and my readers. It is often forgotten that the Regency men had equally powerful wives, mothers and sisters – even if they had no public role – so I make my heroines able to match my heroes in their wit and courage.

Paula Marshall

Paula Marshall, married with three children, has had a varied and interesting life. She began her career in a large library and ended it as a senior academic in charge of history teaching in a polytechnic. She has travelled widely, has been a swimming coach, embroiders, paints pictures and has appeared on *University Challenge* and *Mastermind*. She has always wanted to write, and likes her novels to be full of adventure and humour.

Other titles by the same author:

Cousin Harry
An Improper Duenna
The Falcon and the Dove
Wild Justice*
An American Princess*
An Unexpected Passion
My Lady Love
The Cyprian's Sister
The Captain's Lady**
Touch the Fire**
The Moon Shines Bright**
Reasons of the Heart+
The Astrologer's Daughter
Not Quite a Gentleman
The Lost Princess
A Biddable Girl?
Emma and the Earl
An Affair of Honour**
Lady Clairval's Marriage+
The Youngest Miss Ashe
The Beckoning Dream
The Deserted Bride
Rebecca's Rogue
The Wayward Heart**
The Devil and Drusilla
The Wolfe's Mate++
Miss Jesmond's Heir++

* linked
** Schuyler Family saga
+ linked
++ linked

CHAPTER ONE

'What! my dear Lady Disdain, are you yet living?'
Shakespeare

'So, Lord Axforde didn't suit?'

Miss Louisa Landen's question came out idly as she applied herself diligently to her canvaswork. It seemed almost to be an afterthought.

But was it? Stacy Blanchard, seated at her desk in the main office of Blanchard's Bank, situated in the heart of London's financial centre, raised her dark head suspiciously.

'Was that a question, Louisa—or a statement?'

'Whichever you please, my dear,' Louisa returned placidly, without taking her eyes from the peacock she was stitching. 'I must say that I wasn't surprised that you refused him—you have refused all offers made to you so far—but. . .' And she stopped, apparently lost in confusion over the important question as to whether the wool she now required was light or dark blue.

Stacy wrote down the date, October 24th, 1818, before flinging down her quill pen, fortunately now empty of ink. 'But what, Louisa? Lately you seem to have developed the most distressing habit of not finishing your sentences.'

Louisa looked over the top of her work at her one-time pupil, now a handsome woman in her late twenties. Not pretty, or even conventionally beautiful perhaps, but something better. She possessed the oval ivory face of the Blanchards, their brilliant green eyes, and their dark, lightly curling hair, even if the curls were severely drawn back into a large knot at the nape of her neck—which merely served to enhance the pure lines of a classic profile.

'But, my dear, Lord Axforde is, after all, such a tulip of fashion, seems to possess a considerable understanding, and is so rich in his own right that one could hardly claim that he was marrying you merely to get at the wealth of Blanchard's Bank. All in all you could scarcely do better. A handsome, reasonably clever man, and a marchioness's coronet—what more could you ask?'

It was no more—and no less—than the answer Stacy had expected. Louisa had, indeed, made something of a litany of lamentation of it, repeating it, with variations, over Stacy's last six offers—except the one made by Beverley Fancourt, of course. Now *he* really had been an open fortune-hunter.

Louisa might be her oldest, indeed, if truth were told, her only friend, but that didn't give her the licence to choose Stacy's husband for her. She was perfectly capable of doing that for herself—if she wanted a husband, that was. She rose from the desk and crossed the beautiful room, more like a great house's salon than an office, a room which her late father had created and which she had left unchanged.

She stopped before the window to pull back deep green velvet curtains, the colour of the dress which she wore, and to stare at the dome of St Paul's, before saying a trifle satirically, 'Really, Louisa, really? D'you know I gained the distinct impression from the manner of Lord Axforde's proposal that it was to the Bank he was making it, and not to me as a woman?' She gave a short laugh, and continued to inspect St Paul's as though she had never seen it before.

'Do not exaggerate, my dear.' Louisa's reply was coolly judicious. 'I told you not to do that as long ago as the nursery. I am sure that Lord Axforde said everything that was proper.'

Stacy's lips thinned, and, unseen by Louisa, her fists clenched. 'Oh, quite proper, I assure you. A regular commercial transaction was taking place—no doubt about it. Why, I half expected that he would ask me whether the Bank's interest rate would continue to remain high if we married!' She shook her head at Louisa's pained expression. 'Worse, from his expression—that of a man taking medicine—I thought that he was prepared to pay any price to get at Blanchard's money to buy himself a dukedom—even if that price included marrying someone as undesirable as myself!'

'Oh, come!' Miss Landen at last looked up from her stitchery. 'You do not do yourself justice, my dear. You misunderstood him, I am sure. Few prospective brides are as handsome and as *comme il faut* as you are.'

'And few lack as much pedigree as I do,' retorted Stacy briskly, returning to her desk and sitting down again. The desk was another of her father's innovations; previously the office had been furnished with an old-fashioned lectern at which one stood.

She looked across at a row of oil-paintings on the opposite wall. The older ones were hack-work, done by travelling colourmen for a few shillings; the last two were fine things, one by a pupil of Gainsborough and the other by Romney.

'My great-grandfather began life as a Huguenot pedlar who turned himself into a prosperous back-alley money-lender.' She waved her hand at the oldest painting. 'My grandfather built up the business until he was able to found Blanchard's Bank, and my father transformed it into the richest bank in England.' Now she waved at the Romney. 'His father sent him to Harrow, and he had the manners and tastes of a gentleman and married a lady of aristocratic birth, but that does not make us gentry. And they do not really accept us, however much they and the nobility fawn on Blanchard's—when they need the Bank to lend them money to carry on their gambling and their follies.'

Opening a large red and gold ledger which stood on her desk, she said almost savagely, 'Would you like me to read to you the loans we have made to the flowers of English society—and tell you how many have reneged on them? No, I am merely the cit's daughter, who has the bad taste to behave as a young man might, and run Blanchard's—successfully, too.'

She closed the ledger again. 'Do you know what he said to me, Louisa, in the middle of his pretence of loving and admiring me? That he expected that once we were married I would give up the foolishness of running the Bank and put in a manager to do it for me, so that I could give my mind to being a wife fit for a person of his station.'

Miss Landen stitched for a moment in silence, before replying, 'Most husbands would expect you to do that, my dear.'

'Yes, I know that, Louisa, and that is why I promise never to marry. Father didn't train me to run Blanchard's in order to stop doing so once some handsome popinjay decides that he might like my money while consigning me permanently to the nursery or to talk nonsense to fine ladies.'

Louisa sighed, before saying gently, holding up her work to inspect it the better, 'I thought you told me not long ago that you would like to have children of your own, my dear. You are leaving it rather late to marry—you are already twenty-eight years old—and husbands do not grow on trees.' And she gave her one-time charge a sideways look.

So even Louisa was full of sententious piff-paff, it seemed, and she, Stacy, was condemned to live in a childless desert because in order to have children one must first have a husband. How much better if one were a plant, fertilised at a distance by a passing bee—with no idea where the pollen came from!

This ridiculous notion was enough to restore her good humour and bring a wry smile to her face. It was the kind of nonsensical idea which she could never share with kind Louisa but which would have amused her father. Tears pricked at the back of her eyes. Hardly a day passed but she missed him—her father, her tutor, her mentor, her friend, the parent with whom, improbably, she had shared her jokes.

It occurred to her that it was too long since she had made one, or heard one, and meantime Louisa deserved an answer. But she would not like it.

'Oh,' she said, the hint of unexpected laughter in her voice bringing Louisa's head up, 'never fear, my love. When one is as rich as the heiress who owns Blanchard's Bank, husbands forsake the trees and spring out of the ground! There will be no shortage of offers for the richest prize in England! The shortage lies, Louisa, in men whom I might wish to accept. And that is enough of that. I have work to do.' And she opened another ledger and began to write as briskly as she had spoken.

If Miss Landen was thinking sadly that her one-time charge was such a strong woman, both mentally and morally, that it would need a man of equal strength to contain and perhaps tame her, she did not say so. It was all her stupid father's fault, she thought ruefully as she watched Stacy's quill drive across the paper, bringing her up as he had done.

It had been the failure of Louis Blanchard's wife to give him boy children who could survive birth which had done the damage. He had married Lady Rachel Beauchamp, of a poor and noble family, and he had loved her in his aloof fashion, but constant childbearing and miscarriages had made her sickly and ailing.

It had been a miracle that she had carried her one

girl child to term—another miracle that the child had been born large and healthy—but the birth had killed her mother, and left her father, for a time, resentful of the child who had taken his wife from him.

And then, as she grew up, her bright intelligence had begun to impress him. The child was christened Anastasia, but he had early shortened her name to Stacy, not Anna, because Stacy sounded more like the boy he had wanted to continue the Blanchard dynasty. Louisa remembered the first time she had met Louis Blanchard and Stacy.

'I'm not hiring you as a governess,' he had told her bluntly in the rich study of his home in Piccadilly. 'I want her to have the manners and appearance of a fine lady, even if she has the brains and mental accomplishment of a clever man. I have hired male tutors to educate her. 'Why,' he boasted proudly, 'she can calculate a percentage and draw up a bill better than any of my clerks, and she still but a child.'

Louisa had risen from her chair, said severely, 'I do not wish to undertake this task, Mr Blanchard. You are doing the poor child no favour and I ought not to abet you.'

He had given her the smile which transformed his hard face, and which immediately won him Louisa Landen's heart.

'And that is exactly why I am hiring you,' he had told her warmly, 'to keep her still a woman, and a modest one, for all her accomplishments.' He had seen Louisa hesitate. 'I will send for her,' he had said, and had rung the bell, 'and you may see that I am not asking you to care for a hoyden or a female pedant.'

What Louisa had seen when a lady's maid brought Stacy in was a shy, dark little girl, the image of her handsome father, who, for all her shyness, was thoroughly in command of herself, and who took one look at Louisa Landen and thoroughly approved of what she saw.

'My dear,' her father had told her, as coolly as though he were addressing an equal, 'this is Miss Louisa Landen, who I hope will agree to become your companion and teach you the conduct and etiquette of a lady.'

Stacey had looked at the ladylike figure before her, and had seen through Miss Landen's modest exterior to the kind heart beneath it. She had made a short bow and said in a pretty voice, quite unlike anything which Miss Landen might have expected of the child prodigy whom her father had described, 'Oh, I do so hope, Miss Landen, that you will become my companion. I really do need someone to talk to and tell me exactly how a young lady should behave.'

Such composure in a ten-year-old Miss Landen had not met in her long career as a governess. She had bowed in her turn and murmured gently, 'And I shall be pleased to do just that, my dear,' and had begun her long association with Stacy and Louis Blanchard.

And if she had fallen a little in love with Louis Blanchard on the way, no one was ever to know. Occasionally she had remonstrated with him over his daughter's odd education, telling him in no uncertain terms that it was quite improper and that he was doing her no favour by insisting on it.

He had smiled at her and announced, 'I am not here to do her favours. I am here to secure for Blanchard's someone of that name who can run it when I am gone, and if that someone is a woman, then I must make do with what the Creator of us all has sent me!'

And that had been that. Louisa had never raised the matter again and here was the end of it, Louis Blanchard having died suddenly at a comparatively early age, leaving Stacy, still unmarried, to run the Bank, and waiting now for her right-hand man

Ephraim Blount to come in to discuss the day's news and doings with her.

It grew increasingly likely, was Louisa's last sad thought, that Stacy would never marry now, and her unlikely situation was the cause of it!

Stacy didn't feel sad, however, and the arrival of Ephraim Blount, carrying a pile of papers and demanding some immediate decisions, served to invigorate rather than depress her.

He bowed to her, before he stood and presented each problem to her—he never consented to sit by her while they worked together, for Ephraim, although only in early middle age, was a man of the old school. Everything must be done exactly so, as Louis Blanchard had taught him, which was sometimes a disadvantage rather than an advantage, as Stacy had often found. Imagination was not his strong suit. He was often mournfully depressed, rather than happy, when some of her wilder innovations proved to be fruitful. 'So daring for a young woman,' he was given to murmuring to his own assistant, the young Thomas Telfer, who worshipped Stacy from afar, 'but I have to admit that up to the present Miss Blanchard's judgement has never let herself, or the Bank, down.'

Prim, starched, his thinning yellow hair brushed stiffly over his forehead, he was the perfect right-hand man. Now he was saying, his voice melancholy, as though announcing a death, 'Things are not going well at the York house, madam. All seems to be at sixes and sevens since Poxon was appointed. I fear that he is not up to snuff. Something needs to be done, or Blanchard's reputation will suffer. May I suggest that, given your agreement, of course, I myself go there to try to put matters straight?'

Stacy propped her chin in both hands—a gesture of her father's which always brought that formidable thruster to Ephraim's mind. She looked steadily past him at the opposite wall, to where, before the blazing fire, Louisa was now gently sleeping. She no longer took her chaperonage of Stacy, when the latter was entertaining the Bank's employees—all male—seriously.

'D'you know, Ephraim, I have my doubts about the wisdom of that? I think that one of the things which may be wrong at York is that no Blanchard has visited there since my father died. I wish to remedy that. My aunt and uncle Beauchamp have asked me to spend Christmas with them at Bramham Castle, which is only a few miles from York. We have not met since Father's death, and to agree to their wishes would mean that I could combine business with pleasure—and leave you here in sole charge. You would like that, I think.'

If such a dry stick could be said to glow, Ephraim glowed. Stacy noted with amusement that he thought it politic to demur.

'Are you sure, madam? Think of the time of year. To travel to Yorkshire in mid-winter—is it wise?'

'Before the snows, I think,' Stacy murmured gravely. 'It is what my father would have done, I am sure.'

She had struck exactly the right note. Louis Blanchard had been Ephraim's god, and he bowed down before his very name. 'Oh, indeed, madam, yes, madam. Of all things the most suitable. You will take one of our senior clerks with you, I trust, to act as a secretary and aide?'

'Greaves, I thought,' murmured Stacy, happy to have got her own way so easily, 'unless you have any objections?'

'None at all, madam. The very man.' He was trying to contain his pleasure at the prospect of taking sole charge of Blanchard's for at least two months—something which he had longed to do since his late master's death. 'I will write at once and set all in train.' And he bustled importantly out of the room.

Stacy lay back in her chair and contemplated the prospect of a few weeks' freedom from the daily grind of running Blanchard's. Lately she had begun to feel strangely restless, rewarding though her work was, and the power that came with it. A change of scene, the challenge of putting York straight would renew her spirits, she was sure. All that remained was to waken Louisa up and shock her with the news.

'God rest you merry, gentlemen,' she hummed to herself. Perhaps I may hear the waits singing in the northern snows, she thought, and perhaps. . .perhaps. . . I might meet someone more interesting, more to my taste, than Lord Axforde and his not so merry gentlemen-friends!

She walked across the room and bent to kiss Louisa gently on the cheek. She was sure that after her first shock was over Louisa would approve of what she was about to do—and would start to wonder what handsome and eligible young men, of whom her charge might approve, lived in and around York!

'Damn my father,' said Matthew Falconer violently to the lawyer who had been speaking of his parent's wish to be reconciled with his long-estranged son. 'I haven't crossed the Atlantic in order to please him—simply to end my associations here by disposing of all that I own, including this estate which my great-aunt has thought fit to leave me.'

'But, m'lord——' the lawyer began, in a feeble attempt to pacify the massive man who stood opposite him. Matthew Falconer was over six feet tall, and gave the appearance of being nearly as broad. His harshly handsome face, leonine beneath tawny hair., with matching golden eyes, bore the marks of his having worked in the open. His hands, Lawyer Grimes had already noticed, were those of a man who did much physical work with them. His nails were cut short, and there were calluses on his long fingers and on his palms. He was dressed like a farmer—plainly—with nothing of the man of fashion he had once been remaining to hint of his lineage, or of his newly acquired title.

Which he didn't want. He hadn't come to England to be called by his detested brother's name. He interrupted Grimes to say, 'I will not be addressed as Lord Radley—nor will you call me m'lord or sir,' he added as he saw the lawyer's mouth shaping to say it. 'You will address me as Matthew, Matt, Mr Falconer, or Falconer, as you please, or earn my instant displeasure.'

He saw Grimes close his eyes before he replied in a long-suffering voice, 'I will do as you ask, Mr Falconer, but that does not make you less the Viscount Radley, your father, the Earl Falconer's heir, now that your older brother has died so prematurely.'

The man standing by the window, staring sardonically at both Matt Falconer and the lawyer, gave a rolling chuckle before saying in a thick American accent, 'Y'all better learn soon, Mr Lawyer, sir, that what Matt Falconer wants Matt Falconer usually gets. That so, Matt?'

Matt noted with grim amusement the lawyer's wince away from them both, particularly from Jeb Priestly, who, in his determinedly Yankee garb of black and yellow checked trousers, tight at the knee, flaring at the ankle, his black frock-coat extravagantly cut, and his battered black top hat, which he had refused to remove in defiance of all English custom, stood for everything which Benjamin Grimes deplored. A mannerless rebel come to mock his late masters.

Worse, Matthew Falconer was allowing this creature, who was merely his valet-cum-secretary-cum-man-of-all-work, to address him as familiarly as though they were both of the same rank, and made no effort to check his rudeness to Grimes himself.

'I say again, Mr Falconer, before we even begin to dispose of your late great-aunt, Lady Emily Falconer's estate in Yorkshire, that you ought to consider the olive-branch which your father is holding out to you. You are, after all, his only remaining son. . .'

Matt found all this boring beyond belief. 'Why, sir, do you persist in telling me things I know? I am well aware of my position *vis-à-vis* both my father and Lady Emily. So far as the Earl is concerned you may tell him, with my compliments, *timeo Danaos et dona ferentis*. I am sure that he will know what I mean.' This last came out in a mocking drawl reminiscent of the young rattle-pate about town he had once been, so different from the large and sombre man he now was. He could see the lawyer registering shock again.

Priestley saw fit to put his oar in once more. 'Well, your pa might know what you mean by that gibberish, Matt, but, sure God, I don't. Try translating it into good American, would you?'

Matt knew that Priestley was, in his words, twisting the lawyer's tail. Uncouth he might look and sound, but his knowledge of the Classics equalled Matt's own, he being an alumnus of Harvard. Nevertheless, Matt decided to join in Jeb's game.

'It translates, Jeb, being said by a Trojan with whom the Greeks were fighting, into, "I fear the Greeks even when they bring gifts", or, in other words, It is dangerous to accept presents from an enemy.'

'Tro-jans,' drawled Priestley. 'An' which are you, Matt?'

'A Trojan, of course,' smiled Matt, 'ever since I was born to be my father's curse. Isn't that right, Mr Grimes? How many ultimatums had you the honour to face me with until the final one before I left England?

No, don't answer; it would tax your memory to recall them all.'

Grimes' face flamed scarlet. He looked away at the shelves of law books on the wall behind his desk, and said in a low voice, 'I suppose it is useless to tell you how much I regretted m'lord's treatment of you, Mr Falconer, but I must also tell you that your father is a broken old man. . .'

'Only that, I suppose,' returned Matt, his eyes wicked, 'could bring him to wish to see me again—and Rollo's death, of course. That must have been the final facer.'

'You are pleased to be heartless. . .'

'My father cut my heart out long ago,' returned Matt carelessly. He was suddenly regretful of his baiting of the old man who had been the scourge of his childhood, youth and young manhood, until he had finally left England nearly twelve years ago, and added, a trifle stiffly, 'I am wrong to allow my dislike of my father to take the form of tormenting you. You were kind to me, I remember, when I was invalided out of the Navy after Trafalgar, and no one else was.'

'You brought your own doom on you,' Grimes could not help retorting, 'when you ran off with your brother's wife. My sympathy for you died on that day.' He saw Priestly's face change, and knew that here was something Matt Falconer's impertinent shadow had not known.

Matt Falconer was not nonplussed. He was no longer the eager boy who had yearned for his father's love and whom his father's lawyer could patronise.

'Leave that,' he ordered in his quarterdeck voice. 'It has nothing to do with you, or with the business I have come to settle.'

But Grimes must have thought he had found a chink in Matt's armour, although Matt was not conscious of possessing one, for he continued, although in a lower tone, 'And her death does not lie on your conscience, Mr Falconer?'

Oh, the old man did have weapons to fight with after all! Matt closed his eyes, only for a sad and beautiful long-dead face to swim before them. The memories that face recalled had him swinging away from both men. For the first time in the interview he was struggling for self-control.

'I lost my conscience with my heart,' he asserted stiffly. 'And if you refer to my late sister-in-law again, I shall leave this office and England within the day, and you, my inheritance from Lady Emily and my father may all go to the devil. Is that plain enough for you, sir?'

Matt was himself again—cold, strong and unshakeable, the man whom Jeb Priestley had always known, and whom the lawyer had never met. After that they returned to the business at hand, Grimes recognising that the man before him would never agree to any of his father's demands, and consequently now wishful to settle the matter of the inheritance as rapidly as possible.

Pontisford Hall, his late great-aunt's home on the borders of Nottinghamshire and Yorkshire, was the last reminder of Matt's childhood, and the only happy one. He had a sudden burning wish to see it. He remembered warmth and love, and a place where he, as well as his older brother, had been welcome. Before he had reached England, on the boat over, re-reading the letter which told him of his great-aunt's death and his inheritance, he had resolved to sell the Hall and its contents, to raise capital to enlarge his Virginia plantation, and partly rebuild and beautify the stark house which he called home.

But stepping ashore in England, travelling to London, seeing that great city's sights, smelling its unique smell, had reminded him agonisingly of his past, of his youth, before the world had fallen in on him. He had a sudden yearning to revisit the scenes of his childhood—if only to say goodbye to them before he parted from his homeland for the last time.

He said nothing of this to Grimes, merely, 'I shall travel to Yorkshire, sir, to pay my respects to Lady Emily's tomb in Pontisford church, and to visit the Hall for the last time. She was kind to me, and I must not let her go without a proper farewell. You will inform the staff there of my proposed arrival. I shall set out as soon as I have completed other urgent matters here.'

Matt could imagine Jeb's raised and mocking eyebrows at this rare display of sentiment, and the silent cynicism of the old lawyer, but damn that for a tale. When he had reached his middle thirties a man had the right to say goodbye to his youth.

And so it was settled. Mr Grimes did not pry into his client's life. He assumed that Matthew Falconer had not married while in the United States, for there was no talk of a wife. He assumed that he had had some success as a plantation owner, but made no move to discover how much of a success. If the grim man before him wished him to know these things he would have told him. Once or twice he sighed for the carefree young man he had once known, who had faced life with a smile despite his father's displeasure, but it was plain that that man was long gone.

Business was done, and done quickly—after the fashion of Yankees, Grimes presumed. The old Matt Falconer had never been businesslike, or hard. Now he was both. He even kept his insolent man on a tight rein while he and the lawyer went through the necessary business of establishing identity, examining Lady Emily's will, and signing and witnessing the necessary documentation.

It was soon all over, and Matt and his man were in

the street, holding their top hats on, braving the keen wind of early November, before Jeb spoke again.

'Well, there's a fine tale, Matt. Did you really run off with your brother's wife?'

'Yes, but not for the reason you might think.' For once he was short with Jeb. Revisiting England must have made his memories keen again. He thought he had been rid of that old pain long ago.

'Why, what other reason is there?'

Which, of course, was what everyone had said at the time. Matt replied, in what Jeb always thought of as his 'damn-your-eyes' aristocrat's voice, which he had rarely used in the good old United States, 'Nothing to do with you, Jeb. You may have the rest of the day to yourself. I shall meet you for supper at Brown's this evening. We shall set out for Yorkshire as soon as I can organise suitable travel arrangements.'

There was no brooking him in this mood. Jeb rearranged his face, pulled a servile forelock, bowed low, mumbled, 'Yes, massa, certainly, massa,' a ritual which usually drew an unwilling grin from Matt. But not today. Today he was unmoved, immovable, and his shadow, wondering where his master was going, would have been surprised to learn that he ended the afternoon in a church, before a marble memorial consisting of an urn held by a weeping Niobe whose inscription simply read, 'To the memory of Camilla Falconer, Lady Radley, 1785–1806, cut down in her youth. . . "Cometh forth like a flower".'

Naturally there were no pious words chiselled into the marble about loving wives or grieving husbands, and she was buried far from her home and friends, forgotten, probably, by everyone except the grieving man who had come to pay her his last respects too.

CHAPTER TWO

EVERYTHING, but everything, had gone wrong from the moment they had left the confines of the Home Counties. Stacy thought that there must be a curse on the journey, her first of any length since her father had died.

And it had all gone so beautifully right at first—inevitably, with Ephraim and herself arranging things. She was to travel incognito; it would not do to let possible men of the road know that the enormously rich owner of Blanchard's Bank was travelling nearly the length of England in winter. Safety lay in anonymity. She was to be Miss Anna Berriman, to match the initials stamped on her luggage and entwined on the panels of her elegant travelling coach. Polly Clay, her personal maid, and the other servants had been carefully coached for the last fortnight before they set out to address her as, 'Yes, Miss Berriman', 'Indeed, Miss Berriman', 'As you wish, Miss Berriman', until Stacy had almost come to believe herself Miss Berriman in truth.

They were taking two coaches to accommodate Stacy, Miss Landen, Polly, James the footman, young Mr Greaves and his man, a coachman, and a spare footman, Hal, a big strong man, to act as yet another guardian to the party. It occurred to Stacy, as she watched the two post-chaises being loaded with luggage and impedimenta, that throughout her life she had rarely been alone, and for a moment she wondered what it would have been like truly to be not-so-rich Miss Berriman, who was no more and no less than an ordinary, unconsidered spinster. She decided that the uncomfortable truth was that on the whole she would not have liked it. She had grown used to being in command in exactly the same way as a man would have been.

It was while they were crossing from Lincolnshire into Nottinghamshire through heavy rain, after an unpleasant night in a dirty inn, that Greaves' cold, which had been merely an inconvenience to him, became much more than that. From her seat opposite him Stacy watched his complexion turn from yellow to grey to ashen, tinged with the scarlet of heavy inflammation round his eyes, nostrils and mouth. Her concern grew with each mile that they jolted forward, until she ordered the coach to stop when they reached Newark.

'Greaves,' she said, genuinely troubled, 'I do not think that we should go further today. You look very ill.'

Louisa nodded her head, agreeing with her, while Greaves muttered in a hoarse voice—his throat was badly affected—'I feel very ill, madam, but. . .'

'No buts. . .' Stacy was both brisk and firm. 'We shall stop at the first good inn in Newark, put you to bed and send for a physician. I do not think that you are in any condition to continue.'

He didn't argue with her, nor, a day later when the physician had said that his fever was a severe one and he must not rise from his bed, did he or Stacy argue that anything other was to be done than leave him at the inn, with sufficient funds, one of the coaches, his man and James, the senior of the two footmen, to follow after Stacy's party as soon as the physician pronounced him well enough to travel. 'Which will be some days yet, I fear,' he said.

So now the single coach toiled onwards towards York, through the East Midlands counties and beyond—land which Stacy had not seen since she was a small girl. Alas, the further north they went, the worse the weather grew. The rain turned into an unpleasant sleet, and even the stone hot-water bottles and travelling warming-pans, wrapped in woollen muffs and kept on all the travellers' knees, were hardly enough to keep them warm as the temperature continued to drop.

Ruefully Stacy privately conceded that Ephraim Blount had been right to worry about her going north in winter, until, at the beginning of the stage where they were due to pass from Nottinghamshire into Yorkshire, her party woke up to find a brilliant sun shining and the sky a cold blue. Everyone, including Stacy, felt happy again.

Everyone, that was, but Louisa Landen, who had endured a bad night and suspected that she had caught Greaves' cold, but, being stoical by nature and knowing that it was necessary to make up the time lost in caring for Greaves, decided to say nothing of it to Stacy. The cold might not grow worse—and besides, the day was fine.

Except that the landlord of the Gate Hangs Well had shaken his head at them, and before they set out had said gloomily to John Coachman and the postilion they were taking on to the next stage, 'Fine weather for snow, this, maister.' John Coachman, however, who wished to press on to make up for lost time, had decided that such country lore was not worth the breath given to offer it, and that he would ignore the warning.

It was a decision that he would come to regret.

Stacy was already regretting her ill-fated winter journey to York. She was to regret it even more as, towards noon, when they were still far from journey's end, the weather suddenly changed; the sun disappeared, it became cloudy, dark and cold, and the bottles and warming-pans grew cold too. Louisa began to cough, a dry, insistent cough, which had Stacy at last registering her companion's wan face, with a hectic spot on each cheekbone.

'Oh, Louisa, my dear!' she exclaimed, taking her companion's cold hand in hers. 'I have been so selfish, wishing to make good time and not thinking of anything but my own convenience. You have caught Greaves' cold, and we ought not to have journeyed on today. You should have told me.'

Louisa shook her head and croaked, 'My fault—I said nothing because we are not so far from our journey's end, and I knew you wished to make good time today since the weather seemed to have taken a turn for the better. I must confess I did not think that I would feel so ill so soon.' She had begun to shiver violently, and it was plain that she was in a state of extreme distress.

The shivering grew worse, almost in time with the snow which had begun to fall, turning into a regular blizzard. By the early afternoon they were making only slow progress into territory where it was plain that snow had fallen during the night, and only the fact that a few carriages had passed earlier, leaving ruts for them to drive in, kept them going at all.

John Coachman had consulted his roadbook, and had already told Stacy bluntly that they would be unlikely to find a suitable inn to stop at before Bawtry, which they had originally planned to make for. They were now, he said, in an area where hostelries with beds were few and far between. 'We'd best be on our way, madam, or night will fall or the road become impassable before we reach the inn.'

The prospect of being trapped by the snow and spending the night in the coach was not a pretty one. Polly's lip trembled, but the sight of Louisa lying silent in Stacy's arms kept her silent too.

Night fell early, and John Coachman was now gloomily aware that he must, in the dark among the snowdrifts, have taken a wrong turning, for he had no idea where they were, only that they were lost—something he didn't see fit to tell his mistress. He called for directions to the postilion who was riding the near horse, who shouted back, 'I'm as lost as you are, maister. Mayhap we're nigh to Pontisford,' which was no help at all, as there was no Pontisford in John's book.

Worse, the road was growing impassable, and only the sight of the lights of a big house, dim among trees, gave him some hope that he might be able to drive them all there safely—perhaps to find shelter for the night.

He had no sooner made this decision, and told the postilion of it, than the horses, tired by their long exertions, slithered into a ditch which had been masked by the drifting snow. The coach tilted and was dragged along for a few feet before toppling slowly on to its side.

Hal, the footman, who was riding outside, was thrown clear. John, less fortunate, was caught up in the reins, and before he could free himself completely one of the falling boxes of luggage which had been stowed on top of the coach struck him a shattering blow on the arm, fortunately not breaking it.

Somehow avoiding the plunging horses, he fell across poor Hal, who was trying to rise, winding him all over again. The postilion had also been thrown clear, only to strike his head on a tree-trunk and fall stunned into the freezing ditch-water. They were later to discover that one of the horses had been killed in the fall, breaking its neck instantly.

The three passengers inside were flung from their seats to land half on the floor, half across the door next to the ground. Stacy, when everything had subsided, found herself with Louisa still in her arms and Polly, on top of both of them, gasping and moaning, her wrist having been injured in the fall.

Stunned and bruised, but happy to be alive, Stacy could only register that their ill-fated odyssey was at an end, and that she was somewhere in North Nottinghamshire, but where she had no idea. . .

Matt Falconer was wishing himself anywhere but in North Nottinghamshire. He and Jeb had arrived at Pontisford Hall two days earlier, after a hard and uncomfortable journey in a hired post-chaise which had stunk vilely of tobacco and ale.

All the hard and jolting way to North Nottinghamshire he had sustained himself with the thought of the comfortable billet which was waiting for them at journey's end. The sardonic mode which ruled his life these days had told him later that if it were better to travel than to arrive then he might have guessed what he would find!

He had dismounted from the chaise in the dark of the November afternoon, the first snow of winter beginning to fall, to be greeted by an ill-clad bent old man whom Matt, with difficulty, had identified as Horrocks, the butler, whom he had last seen fifteen years ago as a man still hale and hearty.

'And who the devil may you be, sirs,' he had quavered at them, 'to stop at Pontisford? There are none here to entertain you since my mistress died—only a few of the old retainers who cared for her are still living at the Hall.'

Matt had blinked at him. 'Don't you recognise me, Horrocks? It's Matt Falconer. My aunt left me the Hall and I have come to claim my inheritance.'

The old man lifted the lantern he was carrying to inspect his face. He shook his head. 'Master Matt, is it? Lord, sir, I would never have known you. You've changed.'

'So have we all,' Matt told him gently. 'Are you going to let us in?' He pointed at Jeb and the shivering driver.

'Aye, but I warn you there's little to eat and little to warm yourselves with,' mourned Horrocks as he led them indoors. 'No money's come in since Lady Emily died, and we had little enough before that.'

Grimes had said nothing of this. Matt asked urgently, 'And Lady Emily's agent, where is he?'

'Gone, Mr Matt. With the money. He upped and left two months ago, his pockets well-lined with all he'd stolen from the estate. But Lady Emily wouldn't hear a word against him. Wandering in her mind, she was. I wrote to Lawyer Grimes, but by chance the letter went astray.'

Matt could only suppose that it had. He didn't suspect Grimes of wrongdoing, only carelessness about matters taking place so far from London. He heard Jeb giving suppressed snorts of laughter as they entered the derelict house of which Matt had talked with such enthusiasm on the way north. It was plain that Lady Emily must have fallen into her dotage unable to control her life, for Horrocks' lantern showed the entrance hall to be dank and cold, the statuary and furniture covered in filthy dust-sheets, the chandeliers empty of candles, the smell of must and mould everywhere. And the whole house was the same. There was a scuttle of rats in the wainscoting of an unheated drawing-room which Matt remembered as full of warmth and light and love.

His aunt had died earlier in the year in her late seventies, and, by what Horrocks had said, having been pillaged by her agent. Her mind wandering, she had seen Pontisford as it had been, and not as it was.

'Turned nearly all the servants away, didn't he?' quavered Horrocks. 'Only left enough to keep m'lady fed and bedded. Short commons, we was on, while he lived in comfort in his cottage with his doxy—you remember miller's Nell, Master Matt?'

Yes, Master Matt remembered miller's Nell. She had educated him in the coarser arts of love the year he had reached fifteen, on the edge of the park not far from the ford in the Pont from which the Hall and village took its name. He shook his head, avoided Jeb's eye, and asked to go to the kitchen. Which was, as he had expected, the only warm room in the house.

The cook, a blowsy fat woman, stared coldly at him, bobbed an unwilling curtsy when told who he was, and grudgingly hung the big cauldron, which he remembered from his childhood visits, above the fire to make them tea. Bread was fetched from a cupboard, and a side of salt beef from which she carved coarse chunks of meat to fling at them on cracked plates. It was all as different from Matt's memories as anything could be.

A thin-faced serving-girl peered at them before being bade to 'Take the master's food into the drawing-room as was proper'.

Jeb finally broke at this point, spluttering with laughter, and said, 'By God, she'd better not do any such thing. I've no mind to freeze to death while sharing my meal with the rats.'

Matt would have joined in his laughter except for the agonised expression on Horrocks' face—he shamedly remembering other, better days.

'Right, Jeb, we'll eat before the fire. At least this room is warm.'

The kitchen door was flung open and a hard-faced woman bounced in. 'What's going on in here, Cook? Entertaining chance-met strangers, are we? Not in my house.'

It was Matt's turn to break. Bereft of his childhood's dreams, unknown in the house where he had been known and loved, he said as coldly as he could, 'Your house, madam? You are, then, Lady Emily Falconer?'

The woman drew herself up. 'I was the late Lady Emily's housekeeper, I'll have you know, and as such it is my duty to see that the servants here do their duty. I'll thank you to leave.'

Matt walked to the window to pull back the ragged curtain and reveal the snow falling relentlessly outside, 'No, madam. It is you who must leave. Were it not for the weather I should turn you out this instant, for it is all you deserve if you say that you are responsible for the state which the Hall is in. I am Matthew Falconer, Lord Radley, and my aunt has left me this house and her estate.'

He was aware of Jeb staring at him, jaw dropped, aware that he had never sounded more like his stern and detested father, and that, for the first time, he had laid claim to the title which he had vowed he would never assume.

The woman before him clapped her hands to her mouth. 'M'lord, if I had known who you were. . .'

'You had no need to know,' Matt returned savagely. 'On such a night as this it was Lady Emily's habit to care for any lonely travellers who might need shelter. The fact that I am your master is neither here nor there. You will see, at once, that beds are prepared for Mr Priestley and myself, and a fire will be lit in the drawing-room and candles provided, and if there are any able-bodied men about they will begin to clear out the rats which have invaded the house. You will work until the weather allows you to leave, madam, taking your wages for the present quarter with you. See to it.'

He had turned his back on her as she'd run to do his bidding, but as he was saying now to Jeb, two days later, 'It is of no use. Cut off by the snow as we are, with only one half-witted boy besides Horrocks and the cook, and two young girls as maids, and little in the way of food and means to make fires and warm the place. . .' He shrugged. 'There is little that can be done to improve the condition of Pontisford Hall. It needs time and an army of workers, and I have no mind to organise it. Sell up and go back to Virginia, I say.'

The shivering Jeb nodded agreement. They were huddled over the drawing-room fire, with two small tallow candles to give them light, wax ones being unknown at Pontisford. Matt had insisted on using the room for part of the day, carrying wood and coals through himself to light the fire to ease the burden on Horrocks and the half-witted boy, Jake.

'We shall leave when the snowstorm stops, and I shall put the Runners on the track of that damned agent, and see him swing before I leave England.'

Jeb said, his teeth chattering, 'And then you can turn back into cheerful Matt Falconer again. I can't say I care much for Lord Radley.'

'Nor do I,' returned Matt. He walked restlessly to the window to look out at the grim scene. The snowstorm had abated and the moonlight showed a white and icy world. 'I'm sorry for anyone out on a night like this. . .' And then, 'What the devil's that?' For someone was beating a tattoo on the big front door and shouting above the noise of the gale.

He seized the second candle, said, 'I'll go. Poor old Horrocks will take an age to answer the door and the poor devils outside will be dead of cold before he gets there. You stay here and try to warm yourself.' He crossed the dim entrance hall, shouting, 'I'm coming, I'm coming,' as the knocking redoubled, and then as those outside found the bell it began pealing vigorously—as Horrocks said in the kitchen,

'Enough to wake the dead.'

Afterwards Stacy could hardly remember how her small party had made its way from the fallen coach to Pontisford Hall. One horse was dead, and another, which Hal and John released from its traces, escaped from their numbed hands and bolted into the distance.

They were more careful with the other two, and they and the recovered postilion put John and Louisa, now barely conscious, on the third horse, and Hall, with the injured Polly riding precariously sideways behind him, on the fourth. Stacy, oblivious to Polly's wails that it wasn't fitting for her to walk, helped the postilion to lead them along the lane and up the winding drive to the Hall, trying to avoid ditches and other obstacles, unseen because of the blanket of snow.

Fortunately the snowstorm was gradually abating and a wintry moon came out, which seemed to make the cold worse. None of the party was dressed to be outdoors in such cruel weather. John had put a horse-blanket around Louisa and had covered Stacy with the blanket from the box, which, even if it smelled dreadfully of horse, gave her a little warmth.

The one thing which kept Stacy on her feet and walking was what awaited her at journey's end. A warm house, a comfortable bed, food and succour, perhaps even some inspiriting conversation after the trivialities of the past few days. The very notion made her blood course more rapidly, kept her head high and her spirits from flagging.

Hal slid off his horse as they reached the steps leading up to the entrance of the Hall, which the moon had already revealed to be a massive and brilliant structure, built in the Palladian style. It was a smaller version of the Duke of Devonshire's villa at Chiswick, although by now Stacy was incapable of registering such architectural niceties.

She followed Hal up the steps, leaving John still cradling poor Louisa in his arms and trying to keep her out of the wind. It seemed to take ages for the door to open, and when it did she eagerly walked forward to say to the butler who had answered it, 'My name is

Miss Anna Berriman. The chaise taking us to York has broken down and we are in need of shelter and succour for the night, and men to rescue the chaise tomorrow morning, check the damage and arrange for it to be repaired. Please inform your master of our arrival.'

All this came out in her usual coldly efficient manner, the manner which set everyone at her home and at Blanchard's Bank scurrying about to do her bidding without argument. For a moment, however, the man before her did and said nothing. By the light of the dim candle he was holding she could merely see that he was very large, and only when the moon came from behind a cloud was she able to see him fully for the first time.

He was not wearing any sort of livery but a rough grey country coat and a pair of black breeches. His cravat was a strange loose thing, black, not white, made of silk, with a silver pin in it. The only immaculate thing about him was his boots. A butler wearing boots! His whole aspect was leonine; tawny hair and eyes, a grim, snapping mouth—she was sure it was a snapping mouth. Who in the world would allow a servant to dress like this?

He seemed about to say something, and his mouth quivered, but he simply waved a hand and enunciated—there was no other word for it—curtly, 'Enter. We have little enough to help you with, but what we can do we will do.'

Well, on top of everything else he was certainly the most mannerless churl it had ever been her misfortune to meet! His harsh voice was as strange as the rest of him. There was an accent in it which she had never heard before. Now he was turning away, without so much as a by your leave to her, and motioning them in.

For a moment Stacy had a mind to reprimand him,

but then she remembered poor Louisa. It was no time to be training servants.

'My poor companion has a bad fever,' she told the broad back before her, making her voice as commanding as she could—she was not used to being treated in such a cavalier fashion by anyone, let alone a servant—'and I think she ought to be put to bed in a warm room immediately.'

The butler turned around, to show her his leonine mask again. He really was the most extraordinary-looking creature, strangely handsome, almost. 'That may be a little difficult, *madam*.'

Was it her imagination, or had there been something unpleasantly sneering in the way in which he had said the last word? Stacy, followed by her small party, who were looking about them in astonishment at the decayed state of the entrance hall, continued to walk on until she said, 'I find it difficult to believe that your master would refuse warmth and shelter to forlorn travellers. . .' She stopped, indicating that she wished to know his name, and as he turned around just as they reached a large baize-covered door he apparently read her mind for he said, head bowed, almost in parody of a servant, 'Matt, madam. You may call me Matt.'

May I, indeed? was her inward angry thought, but, about to say something really sharp, she was stopped by Matt—could that really be his name?—checking his stride to say to John Coachman, who was carrying Louisa and was staggering with weariness, 'You're out on your feet, man; give me the lady,' and he lifted poor Louisa out of John's arms to carry her himself.

He waved at Hal to open the door. Hal was nearly as shocked as his mistress by this strange ménage and even stranger servant—as he was later to say to the assembled staff at Bramham Castle, when Stacy finally reached there, 'I were fairly gobsmacked by it all, and no mistake.'

At last, Stacy thought, comfort and succour. The whole party felt as though their life had been suddenly renewed—but what was this? They were in the kitchens, where, although they didn't know it, for the first time in years the great fireplace had been properly cleaned. Jeb had retreated to its comfortable warmth when Matt had left the drawing-room.

Behind her Stacy felt her party shuffle their feet and begin to hem and haw. The butler laid Louisa gently down on a settle in the corner of the huge, high-vaulted room, and, taking a blanket from a cupboard, put it over her. She surfaced for a moment to say blindly, 'Where are we?' before lasping back into semi-delirium again.

'You have brought us to the kitchens,' announced Stacy dramatically. 'Kindly inform your master of our arrival. I am sure he will order you to prepare somewhere more suitable for us.'

She was uncomfortably aware that not only were her feet frozen, but that her light boots were soaked as a result of her long trudge through wet snow. Approving of being shown into the kitchens or not, she found herself holding her skirts before the huge fire in an attempt to dry them. She would wait to remove her boots until she finally reached a comfortable bedroom. The rest of her party were clustering round the fire, which was large enough to heat even this most cavernous of kitchens. Steam was beginning to rise from their wet clothes.

Jeb, who was finding life in the frozen wastes of northern England even more amusing than he had anticipated, if not exactly comfortable, gave a snort of laughter on hearing Stacy's orders. Horrocks, whose wits seemed to decline daily, began to speak, caught Matt's stern eye, and thought better of it.

Matt Falconer offered the stone-faced termagant who was speaking to him so brusquely his hardest stare. All the pent-up anger created by this wretched visit to England, compounded by what he had found at Pontisford Hall, was making him behave in a manner totally unlike that of his usual good-humoured self.

Oh, yes, he's Lord Radley to a T, thought Jeb gleefully, guessing what was passing through Matt's mind as he was addressed so peremptorily, and this icy-faced bitch had better watch her step. He's had a hard time lately, has our Matt, and someone is going to pay for it.

Matt was thinking the same thing. What a shrew! She hadn't even the decency to enter the house before she was throwing orders about like confetti. She deserved a few lessons in good manners, if not to say due humility. Never mind if she had had to endure the storm and a wrecked coach—that was no reason for her to carry on like a mixture of the Queen of Sheba and Catherine the bloody Great rolled into one.

'There are no warm rooms other than this one,' he announced, his voice as cold as the snow outside. 'We shall all have to sleep down here tonight. By tomorrow some of the bedrooms may be fit for habitation, and if so I shall arrange for them to be made ready for you. Kate,' he told the little maid, who was helping Polly into a chair and exclaiming over her damaged wrist which Stacy had bound up with a length torn from the bottom of her petticoat, 'go and fetch Mrs Green from her room. And Cook, the soup left over from dinner can be heated up to stop these poor folk from dying of the cold.'

He stretched out a booted foot to kick one of the logs on the fire into a more useful position. 'And you, madam,' he added, drawing up a tall Windsor chair, 'may sit here—unless, that is, you care to make yourself useful. You seem to have come out of this accident more fortunately than the rest of your party. Instead of shouting the odds about what we are all to do, you would be better employed doing something yourself.'

Matt watched with a wicked delight as the shrew began to say something, then bit her tongue before the words could fly out. Stacy wanted to scream at him that she and the postilion, who was now on his knees before the fire with his frozen hands held out to it, had trudged more than a mile through the snow while the rest of the party had ridden, but her pride forbade it. She would not bandy words with servants; she would not.

If the half-conscious Louisa Landen had ever wondered how her wilful charge would fare when faced by someone with a will as strong as her own, and who did not give a damn for her name and fame, which he didn't know in any case, she was soon to find out.

Hal walked up to her, his face worried, to say in a low voice before she sat down, 'He should not speak to you as he does, mistress. Let me tell him who you are. That should silence his impudent tongue.'

'No, I forbid it,' Stacy whispered fiercely at him. 'On no account—and you may tell John Coachman and Polly the same. We shall not be here long, I trust, and I do not bandy words with servants.'

Hal was doubtful. 'As you wish, mistress.'

'I do wish, and now go and sit down. You have had a hard day.'

She sat down herself, in the chair which the butler had earlier offered her, and began to pull off her ruined boots, seeing that she was not going to be offered a decent room of her own in which to do so, only to discover that her stockings were as wet as they were. Which did not improve her temper, for she could see that there was no way which she could pull them off surrounded as she was by staring underlings, some of whom seemed to be taking a delight in her discomfort. She put her boots before the fire to dry after first helping Polly to remove hers; her damaged wrist was making life difficult for her.

The little maid had set out coarse pottery soup bowls and an odd assortment of servants' hall cutlery on the big scrubbed table, and presently the cook ladled out a thick vegetable soup for them all. Stacy's party set to work with a will, being hungry as well as tired. Even Stacy swallowed the greasy stuff, although it nearly choked her. Matt had left the kitchen for a short time, to return with blankets and pillows which he put to warm before the fire before making up an impromptu bed for Louisa.

Jeb had accompanied him, saying with a grin as he helped to collect bedlinen, 'Come on, Matt, put the poor bitch out of her misery and tell her who you are. She's in an agony about having to argue with a butler.'

'Not. . .likely,' Matt had sworn. 'She's just the kind of useless fine lady I thought that I'd left behind for good. Full of her own importance and fit for nothing but embroidery and spiteful gossip!'

He had said this with such venom that, not for the first time since he had heard of the scandal in which his master had been involved, Jeb had been curious about the details of it.

'You'll have to tell her some time—and soon,' he had argued.

'But not yet. Let the shrew sweat.'

Jeb had shrugged, and later he was a little surprised to discover that it was the fine lady herself who fed Louisa, whom the kitchen's warmth had restored to consciousness, sitting by her on her impromptu bed and spooning the soup gently into her unwilling mouth. 'Come on, my love. You won't help yourself by starving,' she coaxed, to be rewarded by a watery smile.

After that Stacy insisted on looking after Polly's wrist, rubbing goose-grease salve on it which the cook had grudgingly fetched from her store-cupboard. Matt watched her with a puzzled expression on his face—he had not expected so much practical compassion from such a proud piece—only for him to lose it when Stacy said curtly to him, 'I would like to speak to your master now. At once, if you please!'

What on earth was the matter with the man? This perfectly ordinary request produced such an answering spark in his golden eyes, and such a savage twist to his lips, that it almost had Stacy stepping back in fear. She was trying to imagine what kind of master would tolerate such a. . .wild animal. . .as a butler. A dilatory one, obviously, who in his idleness let his servants do just as they pleased, for after a second's hesitation this most unlikely butler came out with, 'Oh, I daren't disturb him just now, madam. More than my job's worth, I should say.'

For some reason, after he had offered her this piece of insolence, the uncouth and strangely dressed Jeb—and what was his position in this zoo, if not to say menagerie, which apparently comprised the Hall's staff?—saw fit to fall into a fit of the sniggers. He had previously been engaged in flattering Polly, who was simpering and grinning at him in the most unseemly fashion. Were her own servants becoming infected by this disorderly crew?

Not Hal, who said bluntly to the butler, who had turned away to begin placing the used pots on the massive board by the large stone sink preparatory to beginning to wash them, 'Have a care how you speak to my mistress, man. What your master requires of you is one thing. What she deserves in respect from you is quite another.'

The butler turned to stare at Hal, who was belligerently squaring up to him. Big though he was, he was by no means a match in size for the butler who, now Stacy came to think of it, resembled a prize-fighter rather than an indoors servant.

'Oh,' he came out with, a faint smile on his face, 'but she doesn't pay my wages, does she?'

Which produced another snigger from Jeb, who, to stir this delightful pot even more, added, 'I doubt whether she could afford them.'

Hal turned on Jeb, enraged by his attentions to Polly, on whom he was sweet himself. 'Oh, and who the devil are you to tell me anything? And as for my mistress's ability to pay this yokel. . .'

'Hal!' Stacy used her very best voice on him, not loud but stern and compelling, the voice with which she had dragooned the employees of Blanchard's Bank into realising that here was no girlish and innocent chit to be ignored, but Louis Blanchard's true heir in person. 'Be quiet. I will not have any brawling here on my account.'

'What a wise conclusion,' the yokel—and what a splendid description of him that was—drawled amiably, beginning to wash pots with what even Stacy could see was exemplary speed and precision. 'Hal shouldn't begin on an enterprise which he can't win.'

This had the desired effect on Hal, of starting him off all over again. He had begun by defending his mistress from discourtesy, but he was now defending his own prowess. He advanced on the smiling butler with his fists raised. 'I'll have you know I work out at Jackson's gym. I've never seen you there, and that's a fact. Put up your dukes—or shut up.'

The only things the butler raised were his wet and soapy hands, which didn't stop Hal. 'Any excuse to dodge a fight,' he sneered, and threw a punch in the butler's direction.

For a moment Stacy was frozen by the unlikely revelation that Hal was not only her loyal servant, but also saw himself as her champion. At all costs she must not allow him to fight with the butler. Desperately she threw herself between the the two men to expostulate with them, to do anything which might stop the coming brawl.

All she stopped was Hal's fist. By good fortune she was struck only a glancing blow, but it was enough for her to see stars before she sat down, ignominiously and humiliatingly, on the kitchen floor. Through her swirling senses she heard Hal's cry of distress. 'Oh, mistress, God forgive me.'

She also heard the butler cursing under his breath, 'Oh, hell and damnation, what next?' as he put his soapy hands under her armpits and hauled her to her feet again.

Oh, God, what next, indeed? Would this dreadful evening never end? All that Stacy wanted was to be in her own comfortable bed, Polly in attendance, kind Louisa well and on her feet again, somewhere near by in loving attendance.

But what she got was something else entirely. The kitchen door opposite her opened abruptly to reveal to her dazed eyes a tall woman with a thin, hard face, decently dressed in black. The housekeeper presumably.

The woman took one comprehensive look at them all. At Stacy, white-faced and trembling. At Hal, now on his knees, agonised, begging forgiveness of her for his unintended blow. At Jeb, leaning against the wall, convulsed and chortling, 'Oh, Matt, boy, this is your finest turn ever. Better than a play.' At the assembled servants, both the Hall's and Stacy's, all either shocked or amused according to their preference, and lastly at the butler, a canvas apron round his waist, his soapy hands just releasing the now furious Stacy.

'And what,' the woman roared, happy to have a chance at getting back at the uncouth monster who had disrupted her easy life, and knowing that now she was under notice to leave she had nothing to lose by saucing him, 'is the meaning of this, m'lord? And why are you wearing Cook's apron and doing the washing-up?'

CHAPTER THREE

EVERYTHING, but everything, went into a weird kind of paralysis, as though time itself had stopped. For a long moment no one moved and no one spoke.

M'lord? Thought Stacy and all her party. *M'lord*? She must mean the butler. She can't mean the butler, can she? Can she?

But she did.

Stacy turned to face him. M'lord. Of course, she should have known. Everything about him radiated authority—which she had mistaken for insolence. For whatever goddamned reason—and really, her internal language was growing more impossible by the minute—the coarse brute had chosen to lie to her from the first moment that he had spoken to her.

She did something which she had never expected to do, something which no lady should ever have done—but then, she told herself grimly afterwards, I am no lady, and for sure, for all his title, he is no gentleman! She slapped him across the face with all her strength.

Her blow broke the paralysis which had afflicted them all. Hubbub ensued. Hal rose slowly to his feet, staring at this unlikely lordship. Jeb gave a whistling roar into the silence which followed Stacy's blow, and then began to clap his hands slowly. 'Well struck, madam,' he called to her from his post by the wall.

For his part Matt Falconer held his flaming cheek, and slowly admitted to himself that he should never have allowed his hot temper, long reined in during his years in the United States, to take him over now that he was back in England again and incite him to taunt this heastrong shrew—however much she had deserved it. And now least said, soonest mended. He picked up a towel and began to dry his hands.

He didn't immediately address Stacy but said, almost mildly, to the triumphant woman who was defying him, 'I told you not to call me m'lord, and I meant it. I am Matt, Mr Matt, or Mr Falconer to you.'

Stacy, overwhelmed by her own unladylike behaviour, conscious only of poor, sick Louisa's reproachful stare, murmured hollowly to him, 'She called you m'lord. Was that another lie in this house of liars, which you, the biggest liar of them all, are supremely fit to head?'

Matt held on to his temper. A hard feat, since he could see that the cross-grained bitch in front of him now had the upper hand, the moral hand, and would use it to provoke him further. She had a tongue like a striking adder, and no mistake.

'Strictly speaking, madam. . .'

Stacy, lost to everything, resembling, had she but known it, her father in one of his rare and formidable tempers, raged at him. 'You *can* speak strictly, then? I had thought insolence was more your line. But pray continue,' she added, poisonously sweet, as she saw him open his mouth. To explain presumably. But what explanation could mend this?

She no longer wanted her bed. She wanted to see m'lord whoever-he-was grovelling before her. Nothing less would do.

Matt decided not to bandy words with her. They had an audience, fascinated by the sight of their masters engaged in a ding-dong, knock-down quarrel in front of them, instead of it taking place decently in private. What a rare treat! And all the time in the world to enjoy it, since it was plain that they were all, except possibly the housekeeper, trapped in the kitchens for the night.

'Strictly speaking,' he said between his splendid

teeth, his eyes still defying her whatever his tongue might say, 'I am Matthew Falconer, Lord Radley—Earl Falconer's heir. I prefer, however, to be known as Matt Falconer.'

'Oh, I thought your preference was to be known as the butler,' returned Stacy nastily, green eyes flashing, while inwardly she said to herself, Matt Falconer—now wasn't he involved in some massive scandal when I was barely out of childhood? And no wonder, carrying on as he does.

'Something wrong with butlers, is there?' gritted Matt, his own eyes shooting fire as he immediately forgot the resolution which he had just made, that he would be unfailingly polite to this icy hellcat—could hellcats be icy?—and giving her what his old nurse had used to call 'what for' again. 'Unconsidered serfs, are they? I had sooner be a good butler than a bad nobleman any day.'

'And, of course, being who you are,' Stacy shot back, all discretion, all decency gone, now completely the true descendant of the rampantly outrageous pedlar who had made the Blanchard fortune, '*you* know all about bad noblemen, I'm sure!'

Jeb, who was busy counting the score for each side as though he were the referee at a boxing-match, saw that red rage was overcoming his employer. He had experienced it rarely, but he knew the signs. And for once Mad Matt had met his match in a woman whose icy deadliness equalled his fiery temperament.

How he mastered himself Matt never knew. Each fresh insult she offered him had him wishing that he could teach her a lesson, put her across his knee. . . Added to his rage was his sudden shocked horror at the knowledge that, of all dreadful things, he was becoming sexually roused.

What he really wanted to do was to take her in his

arms, bear her to the floor and show her who was master. . .

He shook his head to clear it, rebuked his misbehaving body, and ground out, 'No useful purpose is served by our being at odds in this situation, madam. I apologise to you for my deception.' Which, had he ended there, might have done the trick, but the sight of her small contemptuous smile had him adding, 'Although you must admit that you did come on too strong from the beginning.'

Behind them Jeb gave a groan, and Hal, forgetting his mistress's orders, grew angry with the arrogant swine all over again. Lord he might be, but his mistress was right. He was no gentleman.

Stacy was also ready to restart the battle. Just because he was a man, an aristocrat, was big and strong, and, it must be admitted, in an odd way handsome, that was no reason for him to think that he could speak to her as he pleased, but as she opened her mouth to deliver another broadside she was stopped by her companion.

Louisa Landen had watched the affray with growing horror, and total surprise at seeing Stacy, who was usually so cool and controlled, so completely and utterly lost to all ladylike as well as decent behaviour. At first she had felt too weak to intervene, but was now so shocked by the behaviour of both parties that she cried feebly, 'Stacy, oh, Stacy. I feel so ill! Do leave off wrangling, my love, I need you.'

This had the effect of Stacy exclaiming remorsefully, 'Oh, Louisa, forgive me! I had quite forgot how ill you are.'

While Matt Falconer remarked nastily, 'Stacy? I had thought that you had informed me that your name was Anna!'

Stacy dodged this question, which proved that he was not the only liar in the kitchen, by running over to

Louisa, putting a hand on her hot forehead and murmuring, 'Oh, dear, you have a strong fever.' She looked across at the housekeeper, who, amused by what she had provoked, was standing there mumchance, being, like the rest of the servants, content to leave her betters to their quarrel. 'Have you no willow-bark, madam, which we may infuse to break my companion's fever?'

A learned shrew, was Matt's grim inward comment as he turned his attention to the cooling water in the stone sink—to have the little maid twitter at him, 'Oh, you should not be doing that, sir. Allow me,' and try to push him to one side.

'Nor he should,' drawled Jeb. 'Even if you were the butler, Matt, you wouldn't be washing up. Most remiss of you. Should have given you away immediately—if everyone was in their right mind, that is.'

Taking this remark as a reflection on herself, Stacy, her language deteriorating further, pronounced in her most deadly manner, calculated to bring idle clerks to heel, 'And who the devil may you be, to speak to both me and Lord Radley so impudently?'

Before Matt could answer Jeb executed a low bow. 'Matt's man, ma'am, right hand and factotum. Adviser, too, as you may have gathered.'

'Your man, m'lord!' Stacy was all indignation. 'And you allow him to speak to you so insolently? Did you learn your manners from him, or he from you? No matter,' she added hastily, as Matt flung down his washcloth and began to advance on her. 'Pray do not disturb yourself; you will never finish the washing-up at this rate!'

Only Louisa Landen, throwing a conniption fit—Jeb's words—at this point, stopped both Matt and Stacy from prolonging their slanging-match into the night's watches.

As Stacy, remorseful again, bent over Louisa, that good lady hissed at her, 'For shame, Stacy, and use your common sense if it hasn't quite flown away. You do no good bandying words with him. He has an answer for everything.'

'And so do I, madam,' retorted Stacy between her excellent teeth, 'so do I.'

'Quite so, and that is what I complain of. He is a dangerous man, and, for him, you appear to be a dangerous woman. A quiet, ladlylike refusal to join in his games would end all.'

His games! Was he playing with her? Perhaps so. He had returned to his duties, to fling over his shoulder at her, 'I am late from the United States, Miss Stacy, or whatever your name is, and we have no masters and servants there, only equals working together.'

Forgetting all her resolutions and Louisa's wise advice, Stacy shot back at him, 'Which country, sir, since you are no gentleman, must be an eminently suitable place for you to live. I recommend that you return there.'

'And by the same token, madam, since you are no lady, you should surely accompany me. Except that in the States your haughty manners would soon earn you a reprimand from everyone unfortunate enough to meet you.'

Behind her, Stacy heard Louisa wail her name, and how she refrained from answering him back she never knew. She knew only that her common sense, which seemed to have taken flight from the moment she had set foot in this accursed place, told her that she must consider poor, stricken Louisa, and try not to disgrace herself before her own people, who, apart from Hal, were staring open-mouthed at her. Who would have thought that their cool and haughty, if kind mistress could behave so wildly?

Astonishingly, bending over Louisa again, Stacy found tears pricking at her eyes. No, I will not cry, she told herself. This vile bully, who, as I recall, is no better than he should be, shall not make me cry. I will see him in hell first! And what on earth was happening to her that she should think such dreadful thoughts, use such language?

She straightened up, turned towards her tormentor, and said in a more normal voice, 'You have said that we must sleep here tonight, sir. Are you sure that you have no rooms in this vast house sufficiently warm for us to sleep in them?'

That's more like it, madam, thought Matt grimly. A little due humility works wonders. He forgot that he hadn't been humble either. But he replied more gently, 'I arrived here only two days ago, and no one has lived in most of the Hall's rooms for the past fifteen years, nor, I fear, have they been heated during that time. We also face a shortage of fuel, so I am afraid that we are all doomed to spend the night in the kitchen—where it is at least warm—or die of cold in one of the bedrooms. I have already moved the servants from their attic bedrooms—I wouldn't stable beasts in them.'

Jeb was nodding agreement, as well as old Horrocks, who, by what was being said among the servants, really was a butler. But what a butler! Physically frail and in his dotage, he was nearly as unsuitable in his way as Matt Falconer had been in his.

That gentleman was now asking Hal to accompany him and Jeb into the linen-store, which was kept upstairs, to fetch down sheets, more blankets, pillows and pillow-cases, and air them before the fire, which he kept going by fetching logs from a store in a lean-to against the kitchen's outer wall. It was plain that 'm'lord' he might be, but he was performing menial tasks to the manner born.

It wasn't only the logs which were almost in the open, but also the very necessaries of life. And, since the earth closet used by the servants had become frozen, Stacy was soon to discover that relief was only to be obtained by using the buckets and pails in a small storeroom with a door which didn't shut properly and a broken window through which the keen wind whistled.

Trying to keep her voice reasonable, a difficult task, Stacy returned indoors after she had visited it to address Matt Falconer, who was now using blankets to rig up impromptu partitions to separate the women from the men during the hours of sleep. 'I would like to wash myself, and Louisa would probably benefit from being sponged. Where shall I do so. . .please?'

To Matt's grim amusement he saw that it almost choked the haughty bitch to be polite to him. And well might she ask. 'The kitchen pump,' he told her agreeably, 'will supply you with cold water. Use the big iron cauldron which stands by the fire to heat it. Cook will help you.' And then, seeing that Cook was already engaged in making up beds on the floor, he added, 'No, allow me to assist you.'

Never in her life had Stacy ever contemplated having to do any such thing as haul buckets and pails about, or to wash herself in the full view of Cook, the little maid and Polly, whose right wrist Jeb had placed in a makeshift sling. It was quite plain that anything she needed she would have to supply herself! And the beast knew that, and was waiting to see her throw a tantrum at the prospect of having to be her own servant, as it were. Well, damn him, and his ready sneer too. If Stacy Blanchard couldn't learn how to do the simple menial tasks which so far others had performed for her, she wasn't worth the signature she wrote on the cheques and accounts of Blanchard's Bank.

'Very well,' she replied crisply, avoiding his satiric eye, and walked across to the cauldron, which she lifted with some difficulty before placing it beneath the pump which stood by the sink. Not only was Jeb watching her, but also her servants, their jaws dropped at the sight of madam being so meek and obliging.

But, alas, when she came to try to lift the cauldron with water in it it was too heavy for her, and presently, as she struggled, she found a large hand pushing her own smaller one to one side, and Matt Falconer was lifting it with ease to hang it from the great hook above the fire.

His hands, Stacy noted, were long and shapely, but the strange thing about them was that they were the hands of a workman, not a gentleman. They were brown and scarred, with calluses on them, like Clem's, her gardener, and his nails were cut short, quite unlike those of the men who had danced attendance on her since her first season, begging her to marry them.

Matt saw her eyes on them, smiled wryly, but said nothing. Later he ladled warm water for her into a bowl, and she retired behind one of the screens to give Louisa and herself what passed for a wash.

'Oh, my dear, you shouldn't be having to do all this,' murmured Louisa ruefully, after Stacy had draped blankets round her and helped her outside to what they all referred to as the conveniences, although John Coachman forgot himself once by asking loudly before all the company, 'Where are the jakes?'

'Well,' replied Stacy incontrovertibly, 'Cook can't do everything, the maid is useless, Polly's wrist prevents her from assisting us, all the able-bodied men have gone outside to shovel the snow away from the fuel-store and the path to the conveniences—such as they are—so who else can help us, I should like to know?'

Louisa patted her hand. 'You are a brave girl, my dear. Try not to mind too much the pickle we have found ourselves in. After all, we might be freezing to death in a ditch, or killed or maimed for life in the accident. And I am beginning to feel so much better after your ministrations.'

Which was no lie. The willow-bark had broken Louisa's fever, and presently Stacy tucked her up for the night before going back into the main part of the kitchen to find the men all sitting round the scrubbed table drinking good ale. The other women were already in their beds behind the hanging blanket.

Jeb waved a hand holding a pewter pot at her.

'Ah, Miss Berriman, what can we do for you?'

There was bread and cheese on the table, she saw longingly, and from somewhere Horrocks had found bottles of port as well as the ale. Matt, who was seated at the head of the table, stared coolly at her and said, 'There's food here if you want it.'

Did she want it? Of course she wanted it. She had been too strung up to eat much earlier, but she had done a lot of unaccustomed physical work during the day, and hunger gnawed at her. Pride as well as etiquette said, No, it is not possible for you to sit here, the lone woman among a pack of men, all but one your social inferiors, and tope with *him* and Hal and the rest; it wouldn't be proper. They had already unwillingly dragged themselves to their feet on her arrival.

'Sit, sit,' she said imperiously, meaning to tell them that no, of course she wanted nothing.

Then *he* said mockingly, 'I think that the fare here is too coarse for m'lady, perhaps.'

Was it, indeed? And was she to starve because she was too finicking to sit down with them on the worst night of the year, and please *him* by starving herself?

'No, indeed,' she shot back. 'I find myself ravenous, and ale and bread and cheese, after a day spent in the snow, seem just the thing!' She sat down by the amused Jeb and stretched out a hand for the loaf and cheese, to cut herself a good share of them and place them on one of the pewter plates which Matt had set out.

And if that broke up their damned masculine drinking-party, so much the better. They would have clearer heads in the morning, when, with luck, the storm would have abated, the coach and their possessions would be rescued from the ditch, and she could be on her way again.

A pewter pot of ale was pushed in front of her by Jeb, who, she could see, now that she was close to him, was quite a personable man despite his strange accent and even stranger clothes. She took a defiant swig from the pot and said, as though she were conversing at dinner with Lord Melbourne himself, or perhaps the Duke of Wellington, with both of whom she was on terms of friendship, 'Pray tell me, sir, how do you find England after the United States?'

Jeb nearly choked into his ale at the sound of such ineffable condescension. He surfaced to say, 'Cold, ma'am, damned cold. Nigh as bad as a Virginia winter, eh, Matt?'

Matt drawled, his lion's eyes hard on her, 'Oh, I don't think that Miss Berriman really wishes to know about the States, Jeb. She is merely making dinner-party small talk, to put you at your ease.'

His man—or whatever he was—considered this unlikely possibility solemnly. Since Jeb was always at ease, whatever the company, high or low, the notion of a spinster lady putting him there seemed rather odd. He was about to reply, but was unable to do so, for Stacy put down her pot of ale with a defiant bang and threw loudly down the table in Matt's direction, 'When did you take up mind-reading, sir? Recently, I hope, if your present failure to perform it correctly is any guide. I am most intensely interested in. . . Jeb's. . . impressions of his ancestors' country.'

'So there', would have been a nice ending to that piece of defiance, but Louisa had long cured her of that trick. Now let him trump that ace, if he could!

But of course he could. He threw back his head and

laughed, and damn him, why did he have to look exactly as she had imagined the dashing hero of every delightful Minerva Press novel which she had ever read, when she disliked him so? 'Tell her why your ancestors found themselves in Virginia, Jeb, and then Miss Berriman will understand why your impressions of the old country are hardly likely to be favourable ones!'

Ever willing to oblige, and putting on his best smile, Jeb offered a trifle tentatively—for, while he was not ashamed of his ancestors' behaviour, he was not exactly proud of it either—'Why, Great-granfer Priestley was transported to Virginia as a convict, ma'am, having taken part in the Monmouth Rising, when his sentence of hanging was transmuted to penal service in the colonies.'

Stacy, overcome by what she had provoked, and angry with herself as well as with Matt, said as firmly as she could, 'Well, Mr Priestley——' for she now knew his name '—a man is not to blame for what his ancestors did. I own that if I had to answer for my own great-grandfather's actions I should be hard put to it to excuse them. And Mr Falconer should not have compelled you to answer me thus, but that doesn't surprise me, since he obviously gave up the pretence of being a gentleman long ago.'

Matt, who was a little surprised by this generous offering to Jeb from someone whom he had thought was steeped in pride of birth, still could not prevent himself from asking, 'And what, pray, Miss Berriman, did your ancestor do which was so scurvy? Entertain us, please.'

She had entertained them enough, Stacy thought. She had behaved like a vicious termagant in the stews or in an alehouse, and in front of her own servants too! What Louisa would have thought of her sitting at a kitchen table with a gang of men swilling drink she couldn't imagine. At least she had avoided the port, of which Louisa always spoke in shuddering horror as the corrupter of men. But she had drunk heavily from the pot which Jeb had mischievously refilled several times, and the effects of the ale, tiredness, and the increasing warmth of the kitchen were beginning to overcome her.

'Certainly not,' she told him firmly. 'I will now retire.' And she stood up, to find the room going around her. Her face paled, and Matt Falconer, moved by an impulse he refused to recognise, swore to himself and as swiftly as he could ran round the table to catch her and prevent her from falling. Cold bitch she might be, but she had had a hell of a day, and behind the autocratic and imperious manner was a woman with a lot of guts—he had to grant her that. She had cared for the welfare of all her people before she had so much as sat down herself.

He picked her up, to find her strangely light for such a tall female, said softly, 'Allow me, madam. I think that you are not accustomed to drinking strong ale,' and carried her, unprotesting and already half asleep, to her bed, which was made up between those of the sleeping Polly and Louisa.

Stacy, unaware of anything but that she was in someone's strong arms, was back in her childhood again, being carried to bed by her father. Without thinking, eyes closed, she kissed the man carrying her, on the cheek which she had earlier struck, murmuring drowsily, 'Goodnight, Papa,' and by the time the surprised Matt had lowered her to the bed she was soundly and sweetly asleep.

CHAPTER FOUR

STACY started awake as a dim early light began to steal into the kitchen. She had been dreaming that she was on a wide plain, quite alone, no friend or companion with her. There was a brilliant sun overhead, and on the far horizon there was a stand of strange trees, quite unlike anything which she had seen before.

On impulse she looked down at herself, to discover that she was most oddly dressed—or rather undressed, since she was wearing nothing but a short garment made of skin, which left her arms and her legs bare. Her hair streamed, long and unruly, down her back.

Where can I be, and whatever am I doing here? she thought rather than said, looking around for help and succour. But there was no one in sight. A strange terror seized her, which deepened when from out of the stand of trees a male lion emerged, his back rippling as he moved slowly towards her, his mask inscrutable, his golden eyes blazing.

Paralysed with fear, Stacy could neither run nor speak, but stood there, staring back at him, waiting to be eaten, she supposed.

Only. . .only. . .something weird happened. The nearer the lion drew, the more he began to change, his shape shimmering, so that when he reached her it was not a lion who stood before her but a man, dressed in skins like herself; his tawny hair, like hers, flowed down his back, his strong jaw was bearded like the lion's, and his eyes, a golden-brown, were lion's eyes. . .

The lion-man gave her a brilliant smile, revealing his splendid white teeth, his eyes flashed, and, before she could register anything, whether fear or desire, she was in his arms, his mouth was on hers, his hands about her body. . . And she was sitting up in bed awake, panting, sweating. An ecstatic sensation which she had never before experienced was sweeping through her body, its passing leaving her weak and shuddering, as though she had run a race.

A fever! I must have caught Louisa's fever! she thought. But when the shudderings had subsided they left no sensations of illness behind, only those of shock. It was *him* she had been dreaming of, and in her sleep she had allowed him to begin to make love to her.

She must be going mad. Or had gone mad the night before, for she was wearing all her clothes except her shoes, and she had no memory of how she had reached her bed. And what a bed! Memories of the previous day came flooding back, all of them unpleasant.

The kitchen was quiet except for the occasional groan, cough or snoring of the humans who occupied it. She had a strong desire to relieve herself—all the ale she had drunk, doubtless—but she had to drive herself to visit the outhouse, only dire necessity compelling her to do so. She must try not to wake the sleepers on her way there and back.

Stacy found her shoes on the floor beside the bed—who had taken them from her feet and placed them there? Was it. . .*him*? Her memory failed her again, but as she picked her way cautiously out of the kitchen it came back. Yes, *he* had carried her to bed, and had stopped short of stripping her of everything, had merely removed her shoes.

It had begun to snow again, and the wind had risen during the night, so that using the inadequate convenience was even more of a pennance than she had feared, but needs must. She pulled the blanket she had thrown about her shoulders more tightly around them before making her way back. With luck she would be in her bed again before anyone was up and stirring.

But the kitchen door opened even as she put a hand out to open it, and, of course, it was *he* who was up and about. He would be. Matt closed the door carefully behind him before he saw that she was there, and for a heart-stopping moment they stared at one another in silence.

She was right: he *had* been the lion-man. He was carrying a heavy greatcoat and his perfect boots, the only dandified thing about him. Otherwise he was, all things considered, lightly dressed, wearing only his shirt, unbuttoned almost to the waist, to show a tawny pelt extending from his neck to his middle, and his black breeches, with his legs and feet in black silk socks. If anything, he looked even larger and more massive than he did when he was fully dressed. And she had been right about him looking like a prize-fighter: he was fully as muscular as she had imagined him to be.

His firm jaw showed a light, tawny stubble, and a pang shot through her. She had a dreadful, insane desire to run her fingers along the strong line, to feel his growing beard's roughness. His eyes, the most compelling thing about him, were on her, as avidly as hers were on him. Yes, this place was driving her mad to make her think such thoughts.

Matt Falconer, for his part, saw a transformed woman. The softness of sleep was written on Stacy's face; all the stern lines, together with the strong set of her mouth, were quite gone. She looked like a woman ready to entertain her lover. Did she know, or was she quite unconscious of what she looked like when she wasn't playing Lady Disdain? Her black hair had come loose during the night so that it was no longer strained away from her face, sharpening it, but tumbled in soft, curling waves almost to her waist, adding to the impression of soft abandon which the rest of her gave.

The stasis which held them both paralysed passed.

Stacy said in a whisper, 'You are out and about early, sir.'

Matt shrugged, replied prosaically, 'Someone must look after and feed the horses.'

The horses! She had quite forgotten about the horses in worrying about everyone and everything else. Matt was now sitting down on a low stool which stood by the door and was beginning to pull his boots on. *He* was going to feed the horses. How odd. Why not Jeb, or one of the other menservants—Hal or John Coachman, for instance, or even the postilion? She could not think of one of the many men who had passed through her life, offering for her hand—no, for the Bank—who would have gone to the trouble of caring for and feeding the horses when there was a kitchen full of menservants who could be ordered to do so.

The wind struck her keenly and she began to shiver, with cold this time. 'I ought to help you,' she offered.

Matt, now booted, stood up and began to pull on his heavy many-caped coat. 'No,' he told her curtly. 'Not that I couldn't do with your assistance, but you are not properly dressed for the task. If it becomes too much for me I shall fetch that tall footman of yours, the one who is so keen to defend you, to help me. He will probably be awake by then. Now go indoors before you die of cold, and if you really want to be useful make up the fire and put water on to boil for the breakfast porridge.'

His coat was on and fully buttoned, and without further ado, and certainly without any of the usual empty politenesses with which gentlemen usually favoured ladies, he was gone, struggling through the driving snow to the stables. What a strange creature he was! One moment insulting her by talking so of Hal, the next off to save Hal and the others trouble, after speaking to her as though she were a servant!

Anger flooded Stacy as she made her way to the big

kitchen fire, to find Cook there, already beginning to work, but grateful to the fine lady who insisted on helping. In the daylight she could see how large the kitchen was, and also that, over the years, it had been allowed to deteriorate. The walls were black, the copper pans were dull, overgrown with verdigris, and the tables looked as though they had not been scrubbed since the Domesday Book had been written.

Which was probably due, thought Stacy disgustedly, to Matt Falconer's easy way with servants. No wonder he orders me about as though I were a kitchen maid if he is so willing to do the menial work himself—but how can he bear to live in such a pig-sty? This was a puzzle which occupied her until the next time she crossed swords with him.

Matt Falconer, feeding the horses, throwing extra blankets over them, was occupied in trying to solve another problem—that of Miss Anna Berriman, known to her companion and servants, when they weren't thinking of what they were saying, as Miss Stacy.

He had met many women in the United States who carried themselves with a frankness usually reserved for men, and who often, out in the fields of Virginia in the poorer plantations, did the work of men. But Miss Berriman was another thing altogether. It was plain that all her people were, if not frightened of her, ever-ready to jump to her orders. She had an unconscious arrogance, giving her orders as though it were the only thing in life she existed to do. But she was, he was coming to see, much more than your usual domineering fine lady, who took her rank as *carte blanche* to be as unpleasant as she could to all around her while doing nothing herself.

She organised her affairs in a wholly practical way. There was nothing frivolous about her. And she was ready to do things herself. She had helped to feed

Louisa and had bound up Polly's wrist, and although she had bridled and tossed her head at his orders she had carried them out once she saw that her assistance was necessary if they were going to get through the night without undue distress.

And Hal, the young footman, once the ale had begun to work on him the night before, had roared belligerently at Jeb, who had said something deliberately provocative about Miss Anna Berriman, calling her 'your typical idle fine lady', and suggesting that she was more decorative than useful. 'You just watch your manners, sithee. Miss Stacy ain't no useless fine lady. Why, tonight she not only took the lead in getting us all out of the pickle we were in when the coach overturned, but she walked more than a mile through the snow herself, helping the postilion so that poor Polly, who was injured, could ride pillion with John Coachman, when by rights *she* ought to have been sitting there with him.'

Well, now, that was a surprise. Eager to discover more about this odd young woman, who annoyed him every time they met—and partly, he acknowledged, by not conforming to any of the expectations he had of women—Matt had commented sardonically, 'And is that her sole claim to not being a fine lady? If so, it's little enough.'

Hal had just been about to retort hotly, Well, she runs Blanchard's Bank as well as any man, when he had belatedly remembered Miss Stacy's injunction that no one was to reveal who she was until they reached York.

So he had consoled himself by sulking until Matt, still pushing at him, had asked, apparently inconsequentially, 'And what is her real name, Hal? She says she is Miss Anna, and you and the rest sometimes call her that and sometimes Miss Stacy. Which is it?'

Hal had muttered sullenly into his ale, 'Her pa used

to call her Miss Stacy, and it stuck. Something to do with her ma, I think.'

'Oh, and who and what was her pa when he was at home?' asked Jeb, who, like Matt, found Miss Berriman intriguing as well as annoying.

'A gentleman.' Hal had enough sense left to be evasive. 'His pa left him money, they say.'

One of the *nouveaux riches* created by the late wars, then, thought Matt. Which might explain the hauteur as a form of defence, in a society which tolerated rather than approved of them, although the explanation seemed thin. He wanted to ask, How much money? but he thought that any more questions and Hal would be waving his fists at him again, and the last thing he wanted, with the women sleeping at the other end of the kitchen, was a brawl.

Just before they finally retired for the night Jeb came up to him and muttered, so that the others couldn't hear what they were saying, 'Hot for her, are you?'

Matt drew back, almost assuming the aristocrat again. He stopped abruptly. He didn't like the effect being back in England had on him. The very air breathed social difference and unwanted deference. He was used to being a man among men, not a demi-god among men.

'Now what should make you think that? I don't even like the woman, as you must see.'

Jeb shrugged. 'Liking has nothing to do with it, as well you know. Wanting to wipe that don't-touch-me expression off her face by having her on her back was more what you were thinking of by your own expression, I should say.'

There was such a grain of truth in this that Matt turned away, saying irritably, 'For God's sake, Jeb, have you nothing better to do than try to talk me into bed with a noisy termagant? And now off to your own bed before I lose patience with you.'

Well, he hadn't convinced Jeb that he didn't want Miss Anna Berriman, if that was her name, beneath him, that was for sure, if the knowing expression on his face when he crawled into his makeshift bed was any guide.

And what did he think of her? Nothing, of course, only that she was someone chance-met and now in his house, and he wanted her out of it.

Which, he now recognised wearily, wasn't going to be soon. If the worsening weather was any guide, they might be penned in the Hall for days. The sooner they could warm up some of the bedrooms so that they were all spared her dictatorial presence the better.

Later on in the day he found that trying to heat some of the many bedrooms was a mammoth task, and no mistake. Matt, Jeb and all the able-bodied men lent a hand, including the postilion, who, when he moaned that this was no business of his and he wasn't paid to lug coals and logs about for free, was rapidly informed by Matt that to do so was some part of his payment for his board and lodging.

On his second trip upstairs Matt found Lady Disdain, as he was coming to think of her, toiling along the landing with a full scuttle of coal.

'Come, madam,' he told her roughly, 'allow me to take this from you. Carrying coals is men's work. What are you trying to prove?'

Stacy looked him firmly in his blazing amber eyes. Her eyebrows rose, and she evaded his reaching hand, swinging the scuttle away from him. 'Men's work, you say? How many maidservants have carried scuttles full of coal up and down these stairs, do you think? That poor child in the kitchen can barely lift a pan on to the fire, and Horrocks was commanding her to see that this was taken up to the master. You mean, I think, that ladies don't carry coal. But you have already informed me that I am no lady, so have done, I pray you.'

There was no telling her anything.

Stacy saw that she had scored a hit, a palpable hit.

He shrugged. 'As you will, but remember that the servants are trained to do this work, and you are not.'

'Then I collect that I must learn, m'lord,' was her smart riposte to him, and she swept by him, a slow and laboured sweep, she thought afterwards ruefully, for it was true that her whole body was beginning to protest at the back-breaking work she had been doing since she had arrived at Pontisford Hall.

The coals were for her bedroom, one of the smaller and less well-appointed ones, since its size would make it easier to warm up quickly. The fire was alight, but there was more smoke than flames rising from it, and Jeb was poking at it in an uninformed way, she saw. Doubtless he was more used to squatting half-naked in a wigwam and nursing a few sticks to life, was her acid inward commentary.

'Allow me,' she said briskly and, wrenching the poker from his astonished hands, she stirred the fire vigorously, producing a blazing flame which she presently fed with a few coals, before standing back to look at her room.

And what a room. No lady's bower, this. The dust-sheets had been ripped from the bed and the furniture and were lying discarded in the corner. Grey fluff and cobwebs were everywhere. Clean linen, ready for the bed, and a great quilt had been placed on a chest under a window whose only view was of snow, and yet more snow.

'I can't sleep in this,' she told Jeb. 'The room needs a thorough cleaning before it is habitable.'

'So it does.' Jeb's grin was sly and he lifted his shoulders in a massive shrug. 'Poor Polly's wrist is worse than ever this morning, the cook isn't paid to clean bedrooms and the little maid has woken up with a fever. So, who's to do it?' He was being particularly insolent because he wanted to see how far the woman opposite him would go if provoked. A long way, it seemed.

'If there is no one else able to clean this room, and the one which is being prepared for Miss Landen,' Stacy told him, wondering how long she could keep up her iron determination to show him, and his impossible master, that there was nothing, but nothing this fine lady would not do to prove herself as willing as any high-nosed man, 'then I shall clean them myself.'

Jeb bowed to her, and whether he meant the bow to be one of admiration or derision he wasn't sure. 'Ma'am, I think that you may be ill-prepared for such a task.'

Up went Stacy's eyebrows again. 'Oh, you are an expert on housewifery, Mr Priestley? It seems to me that nothing but diligence, common sense and a strong back are needed to carry out most of the duties I see done around me. But if I fail in the doing, be sure that I shall come to you for advice.' And this time she did sweep out, a real sweep, not an arthritic one, since she had no bucket of coal to discommode her.

'Oh, Miss Landen,' wailed Polly, later in the day, 'I wondered what Miss Stacy was doing, running in and out all the time, and now Jeb tells me that with the maid's help she has been scrubbing, cleaning and dusting the bedrooms which are being warmed for us. On her knees, Miss Landen. It cannot be proper. She should not be doing that. What would her late pa have said to such goings-on?

'And he,' she added, nodding at Matt, who was falling asleep after a hard morning moving furniture, feeding horses, hauling logs and coal and ashes up and downstairs, and trying to keep a pathway cleared to the back door, 'he don't make no effort to stop her.

"Do her good to do a bit of hard work," he said to Jeb and me.'

'Good God, Polly,' murmured Louisa faintly, 'you cannot be telling me the truth.'

'As God's my witness, Miss Landen, I would not lie to you. And he's as bad,' she moaned, waving a hand at the semi-conscious Matt. 'He does more work than his man or his butler. He's the strangest lord I ever met.'

And Miss Stacy's the strangest mistress, was her unspoken gloss.

Stacy, her colour high, her back aching, her hands like coarse crêpe from being constantly immersed in water, entered, carrying a bucket and a scrubbing-brush in time to prove the truth of Polly's unlikely tale. Louisa sat up in bed, and, using the voice which had brought the childish Stacy to heel, called to her, 'Anastasia! Whatever do you think that you are doing?'

Her first word was so loud and shrill that it woke the dozing Matt in time to hear the rest of the sentence.

Stacy sat down plump on one of the Windsor chairs to rest her protesting body and replied as cheerfully as she could, 'I don't *think* that I'm doing anything, Louisa. I have been making our rooms habitable. But, of course, if you would prefer to remain in the kitchen until the weather changes, then I will stop.'

'It is not fitting, it is not proper,' the agitated Louisa wailed. She turned to Matt, a useless ally, she was to find. 'Tell her m'lord, tell her that it is neither fit nor proper for a young lady of her great position to be carrying out menial tasks.'

'Oh, no,' returned Matt placidly, sinking even further into his chair and putting his booted feet up on to a bench. 'I shall tell her nothing, for she never takes the slightest heed of anything I say—or of anything anyone else says, for that matter.'

Jeb gave another of his snorts of laughter, and Hal, aware that his mistress was being criticised again, sat up straighter, ready to do battle on her behalf.

Stacy, rising and carrying the bucket to the sink to empty it, to wring dry the swab she had been using and to clean the scrubbing-brush, merely said over her shoulder in the general direction of everybody, 'I shall always listen to anything of sense which is proposed to me, Louisa, as you well know. But I take no note of nonsense, however great the station of the person who offers it to me. Lord Radley would do well to keep his opinions to himself—the neglected state of his home is no testimonial to the soundness of his judgement or of his organisational abilities.'

Louisa, by now deprived of any ally, told herself miserably that she might have known that if Stacy was uncontrollable in her own home and at the Bank, then it was not to be wondered at that, given the circumstances at which they had arrived, she should be uncontrollable here too. Only the prospect of a comfortable room where she might be ill in private could console her for Stacy's total abandonment of all the decencies which made up a genteel female's life.

'And when,' Stacy queried briskly, drying her poor damaged hands on a coarse towel, 'will luncheon be ready? All this hard work is making me feel uncommon hungry.'

Cook looked up from the fire to announce that if madam cared to bring over one of the crockery soup plates she might have a couple of ladlefuls of vegetable broth. As for the bread, butter and cheese, that was laid out on the table, and she could help herself to them.

This was so unlike her normal life, where a deferential butler served her exquisite and delicate food in fine porcelain on a damask tablecloth, offering her a noble French wine to go with it, that Stacy almost laughed aloud. Instead, she said, without thinking, 'You see, Louisa, you always said that I worked too hard, but I assure you that a morning spent in cleaning is harder than a week spent in figuring. Never reproach me again. But, as you only live to reproach me, I fear that that is probably a vain hope.'

And she carried over Louisa's bowl to hand to her before fetching her own share of the soup and sitting down at the table with Hal and the rest to eat it.

Figuring? A week spent in figuring? Now, whatever could be meant by that? was the thought which crawled like a maggot through the brains of both Matt Falconer and Jeb Priestley. What figuring could Miss Anna Berriman possibly be doing? And what did Louisa Landen mean by Miss Anna—or Anastasia—Berriman being a lady of great station? Who and what was her family? Berriman was not a name which sprang to Matt Falconer's mind as carrying a great weight in Society!

Only too well aware that she had made a slip of the tongue, Stacy decided to say nothing further, but instead to eat her luncheon as quietly as she could, avoiding the sardonic gaze of Matt Falconer and his shadow.

Later, going over to take Louisa's empty soup bowl from her, she said quietly and reproachfully to her, 'You must understand, Louisa, that without my active help we are both condemned to live here in public until we leave. May I also remind you that your comfortable life with me is built upon the daily work which I do at Blanchard's and which brings us our profits? I don't think that you quite understand that Papa left Blanchard's to me to run because he didn't believe that, faithful though they may be, either Ephraim Blount or any of his associates possess either the skill or the foresight to steer Blanchard's Bank in the direction in which he thought it ought to go. That is my last word on the matter, Louisa. You may advise me, but you will not issue orders to me. Now I will give *you* an order. Rest a little, I beg of you, before we carry you upstairs to your room.'

She had never spoken so to Louisa before, although occasionally she had spoken even more sternly to members of the Bank's staff who had failed to carry out her orders efficiently. It was not a tone which Louisa approved of or liked, but it was one which she had heard before—when Louis Blanchard was alive. She was truly her father's daughter, thought Louisa sadly, and as she had loved the father, for all his faults, so she loved the daughter. But from now on she knew that their relationship would have changed. Stacy had cast off the last bonds of her childhood.

She wondered what Matt Falconer would have made of Stacy's little speech if he had heard it. That gentleman was now fully awake, eating his luncheon, and directing a quizzical stare at his most unwanted guests as he did so. He was wiping his mouth with a much darned napkin which Horrocks, who was trying to carry out what his poor old brain hazily told him were the duties of a good butler, had given him a few moments earlier.

His meal finished, he walked over to Louisa and said in a kind voice, 'My dear Miss Landen, I trust that you will be delighted to learn that in a short time we shall be able to carry you to a warm bedroom, where you may recover from your malaise in peace and comfort.'

He finished this pretty speech with a short bow, bringing a blush of pleasure to Louisa's wasted cheek, and also bringing a sardonic curl to Stacy's lips. But she said nothing—safer so.

Nor did she speak again to any of the company while the arrangements to move herself and Louisa to their new rooms went ahead, but contented herself with sitting comfortably before the fire, falling into a doze which eased her aching back and legs. It might be true that the hard menial work of servants was not difficult, but oh, it was exhausting.

Jeb watched her with amusement, whispering to Matt, 'Looks a proper gentle fine lady when she sleeps, don't she? Nice and quiet! Pity she don't sleep all the time!' To which Matt said nothing. He too had come to the conclusion that least said was soonest mended.

Stacy's sleep was a happy one. She was dreaming again of the lion-man, although this time it was not bright day but dark night, with a big moon and stars overhead, and the lion-man was sitting opposite her, tending a fire. A bird was calling somewhere, and she was lying on skins.

The lion-man was looking at her, the firelight making his amber eyes glow, and presently he rose in one lithe movement and walked over to her, to sit beside her. She knew that he was going to embrace her, and delight shuddered through her.

Alas, as before, even as he touched her she was sliding awake, a smile on her face—to hear Matt Falconer's taunting voice in her ear. 'At least, madam, I see that you are happy in your dreams—if nowhere else.'

Stacy looked up at him, and knew at once that he was the lion-man of her dreams—indeed, momentarily she didn't know whether or not she was awake, or whether she was still lost in her dreams.

She was now awake, that was for sure, and why should she dream of *him*? Simply to think of her dream caused a hot and betraying colour to flood her face. Jumping to her feet and turning away from him to avoid his mocking amber gaze, she muttered in a stifled voice, 'The warmth made me sleepy, I fear. Does it still snow?'

By asking the last innocent question—anything to take her mind off what her dreams might be telling her—Stacy hoped to turn the conversation into channels which would neither embarrass her nor cause him to attack her. This ploy seemed to work, for he told her mildly, 'Yes, I'm afraid that the storm shows little signs of abating as yet. Jeb and I have carried Miss Landen upstairs to the room we prepared for her earlier, and where Polly will be able to look after her during the day—if that is agreeable to you?'

'Of course. And my room—is that ready too?'

Matt nodded gravely. 'Jeb and I are agreed that it is sufficiently warm for you to retire there as soon as you wish. Supper will be served at six of the clock. Cook is making tea for us all, and you might like to share a cup with us before you go—if you don't object to being without either your companion or your maid, that is.'

Was he offering her an olive-branch by speaking to her so steadily and calmly? If so, she must try to respond in kind, and accept the offered tea before she took herself out of his disturbing presence. She seemed to have taken leave of her senses since she met him, and as for dreaming of him in such a dreadful fashion. . . She was only too happy that dreams could not be shared. Who knew what might happen if he knew that he walked so intimately through hers?

For in the last dream he had been stripped to the waist, and how could such an innocent maiden lady as herself know that the rough pelt of tawny hair which covered his chest would arrow down into his stomach? It must be the Greek statuary which Papa had purchased for the gallery in their country home outside London which had produced such immodest thoughts!

'A cup of tea would be most welcome,' was her even reply, eyes downcast so that she could avoid looking at him, and she took from him the porcelain cup and saucer, two fine and delicate pieces, which Matt told her had been rescued from a glass case in the anteroom off the dining-hall.

For a moment Stacy considered asking him how he could have allowed such a splendid place as Pontisford Hall must have been to fall into neglect and ruin, but prudence said, Do nothing to provoke him, and after she had drunk her tea in silence she allowed Matt to take her arm and escort her upstairs. And that was worse than ever, for his very touch seemed to scorch and burn her skin as the lion-man's had done in her dreams. But no matter; she must control herself. They walked upstairs as decorously as though all the fierce words they had so recently hurled at one another had never been uttered. On the way to her bedroom they passed through what had once been a noble gallery hung with portraits, now hidden in canvas bags, and in which statuary of all periods stood, also hidden away under dust-sheets.

Matt felt her arm stiffen beneath his hand and, because touching her was affecting him almost as strongly as his touch was affecting her, with the difference that Matt Falconer knew what the spark which was being lit between them meant and was determined to stifle it, remarked coolly, 'You are strangely quiet, madam.' He couldn't be attracted to such a strong-minded, strong-willed termagant; he couldn't. She was everything which he most disliked in women, so he made his tone as cold as possible to demonstrate that he tolerated her only—which was a damned lie if ever there was one! Every moment he spent with her only served to magnify his growing and unnatural desire to have her in his arms, or in his bed.

His tone undid Stacy's resolution not to provoke him. She replied, her voice sharp, 'You have given me the distinct impression that you prefer my silence to my speech, so I was duly obliging you. If, on the other hand, you wish me to say what I think without fear of offending you, then I will cease to keep my thoughts to myself.'

They were by now at her bedroom door. Matt threw it open with an elaborate gesture. 'Your bower, madam. I regret that I cannot deck it about with the nettles which your mode of speech deserves.'

Stacy walked by him into the room, turned, and hurled at him, 'And I regret that I have to be in this benighted hole at all. You will forgive me if I don't come down to supper. I would rather not eat at all than owe my bread to someone whose only wish appears to be to insult me.'

That's better, madam, was Matt's unholy thought. Nag at me like that and I shall soon lose all desire to teach you what men and women can do together besides talk! But again he was lying, for he was beginning, unwillingly, to understand that what attracted him was not only her fiery spirit but the wit and intellect which fuelled it. She was gradually destroying all his easy expectations of women and their behaviour. He had always told himself that he was attracted only to women like poor Camilla had been—small, delicate, shy and—yes, admit it, Matt—innocently worshipful of any man they might love.

There was nothing of any of that about Miss Anastasia Berriman. She was certainly not ready to worship any man! He almost resented her for it, for she was beginning to tell him something about himself which he was not sure that he wished to know. That he had changed fundamentally over the years since Camilla's death. He pushed the thought away from him, to say curtly to his tormentor, 'I cannot allow that. The cold is such that you must eat, madam. I have no desire to nurse you on a sickbed. If you are as demanding as this in rude health, I can scarce imagine what you would be like when ailing.'

Stacy turned. 'I shall not,' she blazed at him, 'come down if I do not wish to.'

'Madam, if I have to carry you down by main force

to compel you to eat, I shall do so. Do not provoke me to act thus, I beg of you. It is for your own good, I assure you.'

They were face to face now, like two duellists. Stacy knew that he meant it. That he would do as he said. The lion's eyes told her so. His whole demeanour told her so. A strange excitement coursed through her. She would defy him! And then, dismally, she asked herself, Is that what I want? For him to manhandle me, lift me up, carry me down, while I try to stop him? Does the notion excite me?

Dreadfully, only the thought of what the servants downstairs would think if she were to allow any such thing stopped her from trying Matt Falconer to the point where he would physically overcome her.

'You leave me no alternative,' she muttered. 'I will come down at six, but under duress, mind. It is not my wish.'

'With or without duress, it is all the same to me, so long as you do as I wish,' he told her arrogantly. And if, thought Stacy after he had gone, he sees me as Kate in *The Taming of the Shrew*, then, damn him, he's as cross-grained as Petruchio!

She sank on to the bed, clutching her hot cheeks. How can I think such things, for how did Kate and Petruchio end? In one another's arms, and she agog to please him. I must be going mad. I'll be damned before I let the unnatural circumstances in which I find myself lead me to believe that I could ever have developed so strong a *tendre* for such a damned domineering oaf as to wish myself in his arms.

On his way downstairs Matt was thinking similar thoughts. But the play of Shakespeare's which he appeared to be trapped in was *Much Ado About Nothing*. My damned Lady Disdain, was his fiery thought, and then, But by God I'll not be Benedick, for he ended in his lady's arms, and I'll see her in hell before I give way to such a ridiculous impulse. She's just another woman, after all.

But he knew that he lied.

CHAPTER FIVE

'No sign of a thaw, my poor Louisa,' announced Stacy on the fourth morning of their stay, looking out of the window at the featureless white world which was Pontisford Hall's park. 'But even if there had been I do not think that we ought to have attempted to continue our journey today—you still look a trifle wan.'

'For all that,' returned her companion, pleased to see Stacy more like her usual equable self, 'I shall rise from my bed today. My fever seems to have broken during the night.'

'But you must promise me not to overdo things. We shall leave Pontisford instanter the thaw does begin and the coach is rescued. Even if it proves to be too damaged for us to continue in it, I shall arrange either for Mr Falconer to allow us to borrow his, or send to the nearest inn for a post-chaise to speed us on our way. I have quite taken this place in disgust. I find Mr Falconer and his impudent servant to be intolerable beyond belief.'

Louisa held her tongue. She thought that Stacy's behaviour had also not been beyond reproach. But Stacy had also made it plain that she was not in Louisa's charge any more, so caution in speech must be the rule.

Polly came in while Stacy was helping Louisa to dress to tell them that breakfast was ready—did Miss Stacy wish to eat it in the kitchen, or should she bring it to her room?

Louisa said briskly, before Stacy could reply, 'I should prefer to eat in the kitchen. I must recover my sea-legs and my strength.'

Stacy would have preferred to remain where she was. Her room was now sufficiently aired and warm for Matt Falconer to be unable to demand her presence in the kitchen, and to go there might now look like conceding him some right to dictate what she did. But Polly's wrist was still painful, and she couldn't have her carrying trays several hundred yards through all the long corridors and up the great winding staircase of Pontisford Hall.

'I shall eat in the kitchen too,' she announced. 'Come, Louisa, give me your arm. We must not keep the company waiting.'

But, of course, when they reached the kitchen no one had waited for their arrival and breakfast was in full swing—Matt Falconer, indeed, had already finished, and was shrugging himself into his big coat preparatory to taking buckets of mash to the horses.

'Good morning, madam. You have condescended to breakfast with us, I see.'

Trust him to come out with some disparaging remark. Well, she had a suitable answer for that. 'Good morning, sir. I had hoped that a night's sleep might improve your manners, but I see that I was wrong!'

Louisa closed her eyes at this. Stacy, head high, having reproved insolence, picked up two pottery bowls and went over to the cauldron of porridge hanging over the fire and ladled the steaming oats into them. Carrying them back to the table, she looked for milk to put in her tea and over the porridge but found none. Matt Falconer, who had ignored her cutting response to his curt welcome, remarked drily from the door, 'We have run out of milk, I fear, but there is plenty of honey, Cook says, so you may use that instead.'

No milk. Well, she could not reprimand him for that. In all fairness, it was the sudden arrival of Stacy and her party which had depleted Pontisford's supplies so rapidly. Jeb had told her the day before that most of their store of fresh food came from the home farm from which they were now cut off.

She spooned honey over the oatmeal and began to eat it. She was so hungry that the coarse stuff tasted good, and she said so.

Jeb, who sat astride a bench mending tack, said brightly, 'Well, that's a good thing, madam, seeing that we have run out of bread, butter and smoked bacon too, and shall be reduced to eating oatmeal and vegetable soup at alternate meals.'

'Better that than nothing,' she riposted. Louisa gave a faint groan, porridge not being her favourite food. Jeb offered Stacy his impudent smile as a reward for her stoicism—never say the haughty bitch had other than a gallant spirit. If Mad Matt hadn't set his heart on having her—for Jeb had no doubt that he had, even if he refused to acknowledge it—he might have tried to give madam the time of day himself. Such spirit augured well for her performance in bed.

Something of this showed on his face, so Stacy gave him her most haughty and repressive stare before she carried the bowls over to the sink. Jeb put his tack down and followed her there. 'My dear Miss Berriman,' he murmured, 'pray do not be over-hard on Matt. We had a difficult journey here from Virginia, unwelcome news for him when we reached London, and another long haul before we arrived at Pontisford. Now, as to the Hall's condition. . .'

'I should worry about your condition, Jeb, if you choose to gossip about my affairs,' Matt Falconer's hard voice ground out. He had returned earlier than expected from his task, having taken Hal and John Coachman with him to finish examining the horses to see how they were bearing up under the cold.

Jeb turned an unrepentant face on his master and friend. 'Why, Matt, I but thought to put Miss Berriman wise about our reason for being here. . .'

Matt said harshly, throwing down his wet greatcoat before the fire, 'I shouldn't trouble yourself overmuch. I doubt whether Miss Berriman thinks that anyone could put her wise about anything.'

'Oh!' Stacy rose to her feet to excoriate him. 'Enough, sir. I shall retire to my room at once, where I may read in peace.' Yesterday she had found and explored the dusty library, and had discovered there Sir William Blackstone's great treatise *Commentaries on the Laws of England*. Just the right corrective, she thought grimly, to the lax goings-on at Pontisford Hall. In any case, the owner of Blanchard's would do well to be *au fait* with her country's legal system.

'As you wish,' was Matt's curt answer, while Louisa closed her eyes again. Her eyelids were going up and down like a shop's awning on a showery day, but what could be wrong with Stacy? It was not like her to be so cross-grained and downright rude. Why, she'd even flounced like a reprimanded parlour-maid when she'd walked out of the kitchen.

Blackstone, Stacy found, might be useful, but was hardly riveting. She visited the kitchen again for luncheon: soup without bread. Cook had unearthed some withered potatoes and had roasted them in the front of the fire, and Stacy found herself eating them as though they were manna, trying to avoid Matt Falconer's satiric eye while she did so. Later, after several more stunningly dull, if instructive, pages of Blackstone, she found herself supping off porridge, with more honey than seemed advisable.

Her ill-temper, something which she had never known that she possessed before she had arrived at Pontisford Hall, was not improved by having read Sir William's pompous dismissal of the Rights of Women, who were, he wrote, fit only to be the handmaidens of men, and who, once they were married, were dead to law and lost all the rights which they had possessed as single women!

Worst of all, Blackstone solemnly asserted that this proved how favourably the law regarded women! At this point Stacy had closed the book with a bang, sending dust flying about her room and making her sneeze. 'The man is a fool,' she had announced in ringing tones to no one at all, 'if he can believe anything as stupid as that.'

After enduring Sir William Blackstone's vapourings it was the outside of enough to watch Matt Falconer striding about the kitchen, giving orders to all and sundry and doubtless regarding her as a member of an inferior species. Papa had not brought her up to be the instrument of fools. No, she would never marry—to be the appendage of a husband, no more than his tail. . .

This unlikely thought brought on a fit of the giggles, so that she almost choked over her porridge. Louisa clapped her on her back and the whole table, masters and servants, admired her scarlet face. Matt Falconer seemed particularly to enjoy her discomfiture. For some reason this enraged Stacy so strongly that a red mist rose before her eyes, a response out of all proportion to the offence. Later she dismally conceded that it had been reading Blackstone which was responsible for her anger, but, whatever the cause, she was lost to everything.

'Laugh on, sir,' she threw at him furiously. 'It becomes you, who, I collect, have little care or respect for women so to enjoy a woman's discomfiture. I seem to remember that Society cast you off for your disgraceful conduct. It has seldom made a better judgement. You had done better to remain in the savage country you chose to settle in, where you might exploit women as you pleased, rather than return to these more civilised shores.'

The silence which followed this public denunciation

could almost be felt. Matt's face became truly a lion's mask of fury, as Stacy's was a Medusa's, all hateful condemnation. Then Louisa gave a wailing cry. 'Oh, Stacy, Stacy, you forget yourself.'

'On the contrary, madam, I have never remembered myself more. I bid you all goodnight.' And for the second time that day she flounced out of the kitchen.

Jeb read the signs on his master's face. He had risen, stood with his hands flat before him on the table, his expression a rictus of anger. Oh, madam had tried him beyond endurance—and what delightful consequences might flow from this to entertain a man of sense! Which Matt Falconer at that moment plainly was not. He was all Lord Radley, with a vengeance. And vengeance was what he wanted.

He snarled at Jeb, 'See to the horses for me, man,' and strode out of the kitchen after the shrew who had at last succeeded in smashing his fine control. 'I shall be down presently.'

The door banged shut behind him; the company all let out its collective breath, and began to talk frantically about anything but the conduct of their betters—although later, when Louisa and Polly had gone to their beds, speculation and sly amusement ran rife among the men—except for poor Hal.

Stacy reached her room, shaking at the enormity of her behaviour. Louisa was right. Of course she was right; never more so. What would Papa have thought of her? She had always been, until she had reached Pontisford Hall and met Matt Falconer, absolutely in command of herself—icy cool, reserved, correct at every point of her behaviour, almost a joke in the eyes of Society for her determined rectitude. And where had it all gone? And how could she have behaved so dreadfully? Whatever would the servants think of her? What did *he* think of her?

She was soon to find out. The door to her room flew open, and he stood there, either an avenging archangel or a demon come from hell to devour her, whichever version of him you preferred.

He kicked the door to behind him and advanced on her, the amber eyes shooting sparks at her. Stacy almost expected to see a lion's fangs appear when at last he spoke. She found herself retreating before him, until the wall stopped her from retreating further.

'Damn you, madam, who gave you leave to speak to me thus so publicly? You are exactly the kind of high-nosed bitch I most detest.'

Shivering and shaking at the sound of him, Stacy said through her teeth, all her recent remorse flown away in the face of his insults, 'And you, sir, are the most boorish oaf it has been my misfortune to meet.'

'Then it seems, madam, that in terms of dislike we are quits.'

'Quits, sir, quits? Indeed not,' she flashed back at him. 'We can never be quits, nor do I wish to be so. You are beneath my consideration, sir. I beg leave to continue disliking you more intensely than you dislike me.'

'On the contrary. I shall make it my good fortune to be the winner in this contest.'

They were eye to furious eye now. Stacy, who was standing on tiptoe in an effort to be level with him, was trembling, and so, she saw, with fascination and trepidation equally mixed, was he.

Matt's jaw was clenched, the muscles standing out on it. His eyes devoured her, as a lion by doing so might hypnotise its prey before sinking its jaws in it. The whole room was warmed by their wrath. He began to speak again, hissing at her through his clenched teeth, causing Stacy to walk sideways along the wall to try to escape him as he stalked her, step by ruthless step. 'What unkind God sent you here to plague me? A woman lacking in all the womanly arts which give your sex grace. A disputatious, loud and unlovely shrew. By God——' and he raised his hands '—I have a good mind to give you a lesson in decent submission, a lesson which your father should have given you long ago.'

Stacy found herself, improbably and to her complete astonishment, to be in a condition of intense and quivering excitement. Her whole body hummed and throbbed, and, far from fear at the sight of Matt's ferocious mask so near to her own, a mask which resembled the face of the battered Hercules which she had seen in the gallery, she felt a strange exhilaration.

She felt more alive than she had ever felt before. His anger and fury, added to her own, had broken the icy shell in which she had been living since her father had made her his aide and his confidante at Blanchard's.

'Touch me, sir,' she panted, 'and I promise you that you will live to regret it sorely.'

'Touch you? Why should I touch you, other than to chastise you? What man in his senses would wish to touch you?' But he continued his slow pacing alongside her, and now Stacy had reached the wardrobe and could move no further—other than towards him.

From eye to eye they were breast to breast. Green eyes met golden-brown ones, flashing an equal fire. The whole world had shrunk down to the pair of them. Matt stood back a little and Stacy slipped by him, only to have him catch her by the shoulders and turn her, so that now she was trapped against the bed curtains, and to retreat further was impossible—unless she wished to take him with her on to the top of the bed.

Excitement made her reckless—she felt that she lived only to provoke him. To do what. . .? She put up her hands against his chest to push him away from her. Immediately the strong and rapid beat of his heart, matching his breathing, assaulted her. Her touch, light though it was, served only to excite him. His heart beat more rapidly still, his breathing grew shorter, the very pupils of his lion's eyes dilated.

'You challenge me with your body, madam, after challenging me with your tongue. Is that it? Is this what you have wanted all along, the cause of your provocation? To be beneath me, in my arms? If so, I accept the challenge!'

So saying, he grasped her wrists to pull her to him so that she could feel the power of him, to feel—for Stacy was not so ignorant that she was unaware of what a roused man might feel like—the hard evidence of it stark against her stomach.

Stacy gave a tiny sob, quite unaware that her own face betrayed to her enemy, who was rapidly becoming her lover, the strength of the arousal which their mental and physical struggles had created in her.

His mouth was hard on hers, his hands clasped her head, and now that she was free to fight him off Stacy made no attempt to do so. Rather, she clutched him to her, and was returning his kiss with interest, finding his mouth again when for a second he raised his away from hers for very breathing's sake.

They stood like this for a long moment before he whispered into her ear, 'And this too, madam, this too,' and he was lifting her on to the bed before joining her there, where her hands became as purposeful as his as they continued their busy work about her body.

He was unbuttoning the bodice of her dress, to find her breasts fashionably unbound, to release them, to stroke them, to take them in his mouth, while she moaned and whimpered in his arms, before imitating him by unbuttoning his shirt and stroking the tawny pelt which she had seen before only in her dreams. It was as though her body, quiescent and dormant for so long, had been released from a long sleep. Each touch of his lips, hands and body stoked the fire of passion which was rising within her.

She was on her back, her arms around his neck; his mouth was now on hers again, his tongue found its teasing way inside, and they were touching there too as her tongue learned what to do from his. The acute pleasure this created in them both had Stacy half lifting herself off the bed and Matt pulling away to groan fiercely, 'And this, madam, and this?' and his hands were inside her skirts and were stroking her inner thighs. Oh, God, such sweet delight!

And where, in all this maelstrom of lust, was icy Miss Anastasia Blanchard? Disappeared quite in the gasping maenad on the bed. And when, finally, Matt lifted his body above hers, it was her hands and body which helped him, rather than repelled him, on towards the final act of love.

Above him, for a fleeting second, Stacy registered the grimy and cracked plasterwork of the ceiling, before her eyes closed, to seal the sensation of being apart from her body; Stacy Blanchard had disappeared from the moment she had surrendered her will and her reason in her desire to be one with the man who was rapidly fulfilling that wish.

He was pulling up her skirts and she was unbuttoning his breeches' flap to stroke him—or was it the other way round, and she was taking the lead. . .? Her principles seemed to have disappeared with her clothing and his—she was too busy enjoying the new sensations which coursed through her to trouble about them. Afterwards she was to ask herself how in God's name they could have changed from blistering hate to an equally blistering passion in the blinking of an eye. So blistering that the only thing which mattered was their ultimate union, as though all their life had simply been a preparation for what was happening upon the bed. . .

In this, in passion, as in all else between them, they were equals. In no way afterwards could Stacy excuse herself, call what had happened between them rape.

She had connived at her seduction—nay, asked for it, by provoking him until he had lost his self-control. Afterwards she was to ask herself from what depths of womanly knowledge, untaught, never before plumbed, she had fished up the skills which had enabled her to pleasure him as he pleasured her.

Strangest of all, although they had begun by making love with the same ferocity with which they had warred, gradually, as they lay naked together, tenderness followed, and although desire never slackened it became channelled into softer kisses, gentler stroking, so that when, with a groan, Matt entered her, there was nothing violent in his actions. The only pain which Stacy felt was the momentary tearing pang which told of virginity gone.

And if for a moment Matt hesitated at the enormity of what he had done, was doing, it was lost in Stacy's cries as she clutched him to her, tighter than ever, until the ecstasy took them both higher and higher, to deposit them, satisfied, on the further shores of love, where they lay quiet in one another's arms.

Downstairs, as time passed and Matt did not return, Jeb began to whistle thoughtfully. Hal sprang to his feet, shouting, 'I shall go upstairs to protect the mistress' but Louisa pulled him down, saying gently,

'I think that Miss Stacy can protect herself.' But what she really thought was, I dare do and say nothing, for if I do she might cast me off, with a pension, no doubt, and I shall die alone and friendless, which I do not want—and nor, I think, does she. She has made her bed and she must lie on it, which, I fear, is exactly what she is doing.

She looked around at the assembled company and defied them to say anything as the clock ticked on and they were all left masterless. . .and mistressless.

CHAPTER SIX

THE inhabitants of Pontisford Hall slept on until the dawn. Jeb, imitating his master, though unable to sleep with the woman he had—against all the odds—begun to admire, contented himself with Polly in his bed instead.

Louisa passed Stacy's closed bedroom door, wondering whether she and Matt Falconer were still together, before resignedly shrugging and retiring to her own empty bed—to enjoy the first peaceful night since she had arived semi-conscious at Pontisford. Stacy had declared her independence of all restraint, and she must live with that decision.

Inside Stacy's bedroom the strong man and the strong woman slept in one another's arms. Shortly after their first coupling, while Stacy had lain temporarily replete, in the dim light from the dying fire, Matt had slipped from her bed to renew it. She had watched him walk naked through the shadows, a Greek statue come to life, and instead of feeling shame or regret had felt only admiration of the superb body which had so recently pleasured her.

His return had found her slipping her arms and body around him to warm him, so that presently they were making love again, slowly this time, Stacy exploring sensation while Matt explored Stacy.

After that sleep had claimed them. They had defied winter by celebrating the renewal of life, and outside a steady dripping sound told them, had they been inclined to listen, that winter had been temporarily routed and the Blanchard party's forced occupation of Pontisford Hall would shortly be at an end.

Matt woke first. Momentarily he wondered where he was and whose head it was which lay so confidingly on his broad chest. Memory revived, to have him sitting up, his heart hammering again, but not with passion. In the cold light of early dawn the euphoria of bliss which he had shared with Stacy was dissolved, and all that he was left with was a strong and strange sensation of shame.

What in God's name had he done? And why had he done it? To put it bluntly and brutally, in the plainest terms, he had lost his temper to such a degree that he had set upon and ravished a maiden lady of mature years. He was at last worthy of all the reproaches and insults which had been heaped upon him at the time of poor Camilla's death. If he had been innocent then, he was assuredly guilty now.

He looked down at Stacy's sleeping face. It was soft in the harsh light; all the lines of strain, of hauteur, which he had seen upon it since he had first met her, had vanished. Peace surrounded her like a halo.

This almost made matters worse, not better. He remembered the passion with which she had so freely offered herself to him throughout the long night, and closed his eyes at the memory of it. He wanted to deny what he had done, what their loving meant. He wanted to deny that he had been strongly attracted to her, for he had long told himself that after Camilla he could give himself to no woman other than as a temporary lover.

He put out a hand to stroke her into life—then drew it back. Shortly, when she awoke, she would remember too, and, being what she was, she could only do so with the deepest regret for what she had done. She would hate him for being the cause of her ruin, her surrender of virginity, honour and chastity, all things which a virtuous woman would hold most dear. He put his head in his hands; what to do?

He could ask her to marry him—but what would that mean to her? She didn't even like him, and he certainly didn't want to lose his freedom, or so he told himself. No, the best way was for him to leave her bed, and by his actions help her to pretend that last night had never happened. That she was still untouched icy Miss Anna Berriman, who would leave Pontisford Hall as chaste as she had been when she had arrived.

But the servants must know what had passed, surely? He hadn't returned, and Jeb at least would be aware that Matt Falconer had not slept in his own bed that night. No, they could not *know*, they could only suspect. Let him return to his room, to be found there later, and there could be no certainty attached to their suspicions.

So thinking, he gave his sleeping love one last gentle kiss, pulled on his shirt and breeches, picked up his other clothes and walked to his bedroom. To find Jeb already there.

The two men stared at one another. Matt said violently, as he saw Jeb begin to speak, 'Not a word, you understand. Not a word. I spent the night in this room, and you must bear me out. Whatever happened last night was my fault, no one else's, and no one else must pay the price.'

'If you say so, although I find difficulty in believing that whatever you got up to was not most vigorously consented to by the lady in question. I am certain that she knew her own mind, and exactly what she was doing.'

Matt flung his clothes on the bed. 'Damn you, Jeb, be silent. I gave you an order. Obey it. She deserves your consideration as well as mine.'

'And shall surely have it. I take it, then, that officially nothing happened? Is that what she wants?'

'How the hell do I know?' groaned Matt. 'I left her

sleeping. And why am I discussing this with you? I said silence, and I meant it.'

'Ah, but can you guarantee her silence? No, don't strike me——' as Matt raised his fist '—it is surely a consideration. Is she likely to come after you, through a relative, with a pistol, to redeem her honour—or does she want a permanent mate, not a fly-by-night?'

There was no silencing him. 'You are not my conscience,' snapped Matt. 'Look to your own. Whose bed did you spend last night in?'

'Oh, "a hit, a very palpable hit"!' quoted Jeb. 'But I have never claimed to possess a sense of honour—you do. What made you lose it?'

Matt closed his eyes, turned his back on Jeb who had, strangely and uncharacteristically, apparently constituted himself Miss Anna Berriman's defender.

'Go and join Hal,' he said as he pulled off his shirt to change into a fresh one. 'The pair of you are lost in the wrong century. Chivalry is not dead while you and Hal still live!' After which unkind remark he refused to speak again. But he thought a great deal, and none of his thoughts was pleasant, and all of them reproached him.

Stacy awoke, her right hand questing to find Matt's. Unlike him she had no doubts about where she was, or with whom she had shared her bed and spent the night. Nor had she any regrets—as yet. The first of them surfaced when she found him—and all his clothing—gone.

It was only when she sat up and full consciousness had returned that the full enormity of what she had done struck her. Her hands rose to clutch her flaming cheeks. How could I? No, I must have dreamed it, she thought. But the hard evidence of a night spent in loving was all about her: her swollen mouth, her face reddened where his beard had caught it as they had kissed and clutched at one another. Her nipples were sore and tingling, and the very thought of what he had done to them brought them erect again.

She had been shameless, quite shameless, and whatever would he think of her? Simply, of course, that she was as loose as any whore, not even offering him a token resistance. When he had come to his full senses he must have been disgusted by her, and that was why he had crept away without so much as a kind word or a last caress.

It had never happened. Yes, that was it. If she thought and said so, then it must be so. Had not Bishop Berkeley, whom her father had admired, said that nothing existed except in the mind of the beholder? If so, then all that she had to do was wipe last night's madness from her mind until it no longer existed. There was no beholder. He was only a part of her mind, not she of his.

The boldness of this notion brought a sad smile to Stacy's lips. And if he tried to pretend that something had happened, then she would deny it, firmly and truthfully, since such an unlikely happening as Stacy Blanchard taking a man to her bed was, of course, unimaginable.

But it had happened. Worse, not only had she enjoyed it, but she had found inside herself a cauldron of passion like the one which boiled and bubbled above Cook's fire. Which reminded her that she was hungry, and she must go downstairs and face the assembled servants, persuading them by her iron control that nothing, absolutely nothing had happened and that she was indifferent to him.

But inside herself, as she was dressing, something shrieked and wailed, Oh, but I am not indifferent to him, and I want him back in my bed and in my life, and without him I am but of a barren stock, and always will be!

A timid knock came on her door. She called, 'Come in,' as she brushed her hair back into its most severe mode, having smoothed down as best as she could the deep green woollen travelling-dress in which she had been living since the coach had broken down five nights ago.

It was Louisa, looking better, but also looking timid, bleating anxiously, 'I trust I see you quite well this morning, my dear?'

Her brush still battering her curls into smoothness, Stacy lied boldly back, 'Of course, Louisa. Why should I not be?'

'I thought Mr Falconer seemed rather annoyed by what you said to him last night, Stacy. I feared that he might reproach you.'

'Oh, he did, Louisa, he did. But you know me, I trust. I gave as good as I got.' Which was the literal unspeakable truth, was it not?

'I fear that you are too bold with him. He is not one of your bank clerks, my love, nor does he take kindly to strong-minded women. Most men don't.'

She couldn't resist speaking out after all, only to have Stacy reply briskly, 'Which doesn't worry me in the slightest, seeing that I have no interest in what any man, let alone most men, think of me. They must take me as I am.'

Which he had last night, even if he apparently regretted it afterwards. But it had been lovely while it lasted.

'All the same——' began Louise.

'All the same, Louisa? Nothing has been the same since we arrived at Pontisford.' And that is telling the truth with a vengeance, she added silently.

She swept downstairs in what Louisa was dismayed to see was her haughtiest mode. She made Jeb a languid bow as he emerged from the drawing-room, also on his way to breakfast; she wondered what he had been doing there. She missed the admiring glint in his eye as he watched madam brazenly throw open the kitchen door to sweep in and equally brazenly carol, 'Good morning all,' as though she were the town crier wishing everyone well.

Sure God, Matt had pleasured madam last night to the top of his and her bent—she was on even higher ropes than usual. It was to be hoped that she didn't fall off them.

Louisa was thinking the same thing in slightly different terms.

All the servants gave her a slightly stunned, 'Good morning, madam,' including Hal, who was relieved to see that his lady, far from looking subdued and downtrodden after a rating from that unpleasant bastard Matt Falconer, or Lord Whoever-he-was, was, on the contrary, more pleased with life and herself than he had ever seen her. Unlike Jeb, he and the rest of her servants did not draw the correct conclusion from this.

The cauldron supplied her and Louisa with porridge. Ten minutes of time supplied her with Matt Falconer, who entered the kitchen after having overseen the horses, feeling that he was either about to be beheaded or would behead. He wasn't sure which.

All his expectations were confounded when his late bed-mate looked up from her porridge to announce briskly, 'Good morning, sir. I trust that you spent a pleasant night? It was my first comfortable one since arriving at Pontisford, and I do believe that a thaw is setting in, which will be a great relief to all of us.'

So that was to be the way of it. Nothing had happened. She had made the same decision as himself, so all would be well, and all manner of things would be well.

So why was it that, far from being happy, his own spirits took a nosedive? Could madam dismiss him so easily, then? Why, had he not pleasured her as few women had been pleasured, and had she not screamed beneath him in ecstasy, not once but several times? It almost demeaned a man that his doxy could be so airily non-committal after such a night of bliss.

'Middling,' he growled back at her, 'middling. I have known better.' And there, that should hold you, madam, if nothing else does.

Jeb was enduring another fit of the chokes, a real one this time, as the late lovers' double-edged conversation flew above his and everybody else's head. Stacy pounded his back vigorously. She had begun to have her suspicions of Jeb, and if she couldn't strike his conniving master, who had loved her and left her, why, then, she would strike his man—hard.

She took Matt's dismissive comment in her stride. 'I am sorry to hear it, sir. Such hard work as you indulge in deserves a better reward. You will, I am sure, be relieved to find that the weather has changed. I trust that as soon as possible labourers may be fetched to lift our coach from the ditch into which it has fallen, and, if it prove unroadworthy, that we may hire—or borrow—a post-chaise so that we may soon be on our way? You may rest a little easier then.'

The bitch, the magnificent bitch! She was taunting him before them all. What a nonpareil she was, to lose what no woman should lose before marriage and then to dismiss so casually the man who had done it, and defy him, publicly, to say or do anything which might betray both him and her. He was in no doubt that it was her behaviour which had caused, and was still causing, Jeb's splutterings.

Stacy rose, to recommend sweetly that Jeb consult a physician. 'You have these spasms far too often for your own good,' she informed him, and said to Matt, 'I'm sure that I need hardly remind you to act with all speed to arrange our departure. "Welcome the coming, speed the parting guest" is a maxim that I can recommend to you. It is one which I have always followed.' And this time she didn't flounce out of the kitchen, but moved like a Spanish galleon, carrying all before it in state and majesty. My dear Lady Disdain in person. Nothing, but nothing, anyone could do would ever be able to overset her.

Even Louisa was open-mouthed. Jeb was having convulsions again. Matt Falconer looked at them and the smirking servants with exasperation. 'For God's sake,' he bawled in their direction, not being able to vent his anger on Stacy, 'rattle your hocks. The sooner Pontisford is rid of you all, the happier I shall be.'

Which was just about the most curmudgeonly thing that he could think of to say, when all that he really wanted to do was to pelt after madam and have her on her back again, welcoming him, but where in the world that would lead to scarcely bore thinking of!

What *did* bear thinking of was the rapid thaw, and the arrangements for Pontisford Hall's unexpected guests to leave. Matt, Jeb, Hal, John Coachman, the postilion and the dull boy, the last two having watched all the goings-on open-mouthed and uncomprehending, trudged through the slush to rescue the luggage from the coach. They were watched by Stacy from the window of her room. She had resolved to remain there until they left. She would have nothing to do with him ever again. Nothing! He was a vile seducer, that was all.

Louisa had come to her, later in the day, when it was decided that Matt would lend them his post-chaise to take them on the final stages of their journey to York, their coach being beyond immediate repair. Louisa's face was grave. 'I believe that we may be able to leave tomorrow, my dear, or so Mr Falconer seems to think.'

Stacy looked up from reading Blackstone to say

coldly, 'He has not the good manners, then, to come to tell me himself?'

Louisa hesitated, and said placatingly, because she had rarely seen Stacy's face set in such uncompromising lines, 'I think that he will, my dear, when all the arrangements are made and it appears that the present milder weather will hold.' She hesitated again. 'I have remembered a little about what the scandal in which our host was involved consisted of. Your own remarks to him, in the circumstances, could scarcely be more unfortunate.'

'Indeed. And am I to be allowed to know?'

No, Louisa had never known her so icy, so withdrawn. 'I think that you ought. You will then be able to guard your tongue a little.'

The cauldron inside Stacy almost boiled over. Somehow she controlled herself, said, 'Continue, pray. I am agog.'

Louisa sighed. 'It seems that when he was a very young man he fell in love with and ran away with his brother Rollo, Lord Radley's wife. She died shortly afterwards, while quite young. The details of what happened were hushed up.'

'And that's it?' Stacy's voice was stifled. She had tried to keep it level, but could not.

'Isn't that enough? To run off with his brother's wife? He was cast off by his family, as you may imagine, and fled England to farm, his man Priestley tells me, in the Virginias on some land settled on him by his mother—her mother was an American. He worked alongside his men, I collect, which perhaps explains his strange behaviour here, working alongside the servants. . .'

'And expecting me to do so. Thank you, Louisa; I wish that you had told me the details of the scandal before.'

Louisa nodded. 'It was remiss of me, I own. But I

thought... I don't know what I thought... That it would not be helpful. I was wrong.'

Stacy sat on the bed. 'Leave me, I beg of you. I wish to make ready for the journey.'

Which was a monstrous thundering lie. She wanted to face the fact that she was not the first woman he had ever seduced—as though she had ever thought that she was. But worst of all was that he had dishonoured his brother.

And I? Stacy suddenly thought, springing to her feet to put her hands to hot cheeks. Suppose I have been left pregnant? And what has possessed me that I should never think of such a possibility, either before, during or after what we did? Yes, I have truly run mad ever since I set foot in Pontisford Hall. God help me, but I must leave as soon as possible, and also trust in God that I may not pay a price for what I have done. What could I have been thinking of or, rather, not thinking of? How could my wits have gone so far astray?

And he? Should he not have considered what might be the inevitable end of...last night? And I was a virgin, too. Oh, yes, after our night together nothing was left of any maidenly modesty I might once have possessed.

Stacy's whole body was burning and shivering as though a fever afflicted it. The knock on the door in the middle of her torment had to be repeated before she pulled herself together and called, 'Come in!'

It was Matt Falconer. He had the effrontery to look and speak as though nothing untoward had passed between them. He bowed, said, 'Madam, I am come to inform you that with luck, and the thaw holding, you and your party should be on your way by first light tomorrow morning. Your luggage has been brought from your coach. Hal will be carrying your boxes up so that you may change for the journey should you wish to do so.'

Stacy inclined her head graciously, looking away from him as though the sight of him hurt her. 'I thank you, sir, for your consideration and the hospitality which you have shown to me and mine.'

Matt could not help himself; he started forward, said impetuously, 'Do not look at me so, madam. I do not know how to express my regrets for what occurred here last night——'

Her smile was frozen. 'A little late, wouldn't you say, sir?' And then putting up her hands as if to ward him off, 'No, do not say anything further, sir. Your departure this morning, without a word, tells all. I do not wish to dwell on what should never have happened. I pray that we do not meet again.' And she gave him her back.

'Miss Berriman,' Matt found himself saying hoarsely to that forbidding sight, 'I can only ask your forgiveness, and ask you to marry me. That is the least a man can do who behaved as I did.'

So, 'the least a man could do' was all that he had to offer her! And why not, pray, the most? Had he, then, felt nothing of the burning passion which had overwhelmed her, allied to the feeling afterwards, as she'd lain in his arms, that she had come home, had found the lost half of herself?

Apparently not, so coolly had his proposal been made. A proposal plainly made to salve his conscience rather than because he had felt anything but a passing lust for the woman he had bedded so casually. Desolation, followed by rage, overcame her.

'Marry you, sir? Marry you? I had as lief marry one of the apes from the zoo at the Tower. Or lead them in hell, as our forefathers said spinsters did! Marry a man, chance-met and chance-bedded? Indeed not.

Take your proposal away, to offer it to someone less discriminating than I!'

Face on fire, he was almost on her again. Mastering himself, he stopped without touching her. 'That was not what you felt last night, madam, when you sighed and moaned in my arms. Where was your discrimination then?'

'Lost, with my wits,' she hurled at him, near to tears, near to breaking down, to clutching at him and howling, Say that you care for me a little. That what we felt in our transports was more than mere pleasure, was an identity shared.

Pride forbade it. And he, conscious of the enormity of what he had done, and that, excuse himself as he might, he deserved no more of her than the scorn which she was pouring over him, could not believe other than that was all that she felt for him.

She was splendid in her anger, splendid in her straight-backed independence, which offered neither him or any man quarter.

'Think again, madam. I have a title to offer you, if that might please you. And a good name, even if I have done little to cover it with glory. . .'

'I would not have you,' lied Stacy, 'if you offered me the Crown of England.' But oh, if you offered me your love, I would have you though you had not a penny, and I not a sou to my name, and we walked ragged through England.

No, he was not about to offer her that. He was backing away, saying as he reached the door, 'You will not reconsider?'

'You have had my answer, sir. I am accustomed to my yea being accepted as my yea, and my nay as my nay. Nay it is. You should have considered what you were doing when you set upon me.'

For the second time in two days she had broken through his usually iron control.

'Oh, madam, do but you consider. I may have begun our bout of love but, by God, you joined in it so lustily that you had my breeches off before I had your skirts up!'

She should have fainted, died away, at having anything so gross thrown at her, but dreadfully Stacy had only one impulse overcome. . .and that was to laugh. She was hard put to it to stifle her giggles at the picture this conjured up, which was unfortunate, because had she laughed things between them might have been mended immediately, they being so equal in all that mattered between a man and a woman—in humour as in everything else.

Instead, she lifted her hands primly before her face and said in a fainting voice, 'Oh, for shame, sir, for shame! I did not know what I was doing I was in such shock.'

'But I think you did, madam, I think you did—to succeed in your objective when so stricken! But no matter I will leave you with my apologies, and with my offer. It stands, madam, it stands. Remember that.'

She shook her head at him, and he was fain to take her in his arms, to say, For God's sake, woman, for no reason on earth you attract me, sharp-tongued though you are, as no woman has ever done, not even my poor Camilla. We should deal well together, you and I, so let us deal well for life.

But, like Stacy, life had made him fearful of expressing himself, of betraying his emotions. If she distrusted men because all that they had ever wanted of her was Blanchard's Bank, then he distrusted not women, but the wretchedness which loving one woman had caused him. Better not to love them but simply to enjoy them. What distressed him over his treatment of Miss Anna Berriman was that he had taken her into his bed at first without her consent, even if by her conduct she had freely given it to him afterwards.

Stacy turned away from him. The word 'remember' rang in her head. She would always remember him, but she dared not trust him. Besides, duty and Blanchard's called, York awaited her, and she would not exchange her free life to be a man's slave, not for all the love he might have offered her but hadn't, and certainly not for his title—which he apparently didn't value anyway.

It was over. Useless to continue. He said, 'Remember,' again, and stalked out of the room, having bowed to her. Nothing was left to her but to open her boxes, change into clothes which she had not spent five days a-wearing, and leave for York. To resume her character as the passionless owner and ruler of Blanchard's Bank, her father's true daughter.

Matt walked downstairs, and only later, when the chaise was being driven through the slush of the drive on its journey to York, did he think to rebuke himself for not taking madam in his arms and convincing her that, chance-met or not, he and she could make a pair to withstand the world.

But by then it was too late.

CHAPTER SEVEN

'THANK goodness it's behind us,' sighed Stacy dramatically as the turning road, which for a fleeting moment had offered them one last glimpse of Pontisford Hall, took it away from them.

She had to admit, inwardly—not outwardly, that in the distance, beneath the clear blue of the November sky, Pontisford Hall, set in a landscape which was rapidly changing from an engraving in black and white to a dramatic oil-painting, looked singularly lovely. Its severe classical façade gave no hint of the horrors within.

Louisa nodded. 'So neglected,' she sighed, 'I wonder at Lord Radley allowing it to fall into such decay, I really do.'

Polly, sitting opposite them, not sure whether she had been using her common sense in allowing Jeb Priestley into her bed with her two nights ago, interrupted her betters pertly.

'Not Mr Falconer—I mean Lord Radley's fault,' she announced knowingly. 'He and Jeb—I mean Mr Priestley—only arrived there a few days before we did. Inherited it from his great-aunty, Lord Radley did, who was too old to care what condition she lived in. They were as shocked as we were by what they found.'

Which only goes to show, thought Stacy resignedly, that the servants often know more than we do. And, of course, Jeb was trying to tell me so that time when Matt came in and stopped him. She wriggled a little—she had misjudged him over that at least, but it was his own fault that she had done so. But I won't think about him, I won't. With luck I shall never see him again, she told herself.

Then why did she give an odd little shiver at the very idea that he had passed out of her life for good? She shook her head to clear it, and remarked briskly to Louisa, 'It is to be hoped that we reach York without further delay. They will be wondering what has detained us—unless, of course, they shared our bad weather.'

As if to make up for the disasters inflicted on them in the earlier part of their odyssey, Stacy's party reached York without further trouble, to find that the rooms taken for them in a house in the shadow of the great Minster were as warm and comfortable and as unlike Pontisford's filthy splendour as rooms could be.

The landlady welcomed them with open arms—pleased that her lodgers had taken over the whole house, saving her the trouble of looking for more—exclaiming, 'At last, madam! I had quite given you up. The weather here has been atrocious.'

There was a splendid meal soon made ready for them, comfortable beds in warm bedrooms, a footman of the landlady's own to help poor Hal carry in their boxes and other impedimenta, and maidservants to assist Polly, whose wrist still pained her. Louisa, face grey, was helped to her room where her dinner was sent up to her, daintily laid out on fine porcelain on a silver tray, while Stacy dined in lonely splendour off food which she had only dreamed of while half starving at Pontisford.

So why did she feel so desolate, so full of ennui at being, as she usually was, alone? At Pontisford she had been compelled to share her life with others, to sit at table with a pack of dependents, to listen to Matt and Jeb and the others laugh and talk companionably when she had retired to her bed behind the makeshift partition. And she surely couldn't be missing the rough fare which was all that Pontisford had supplied.

But she had never felt so lonely, she who had never felt lonely before. And could she also be missing the sound of masculine voices in this house of women?

Enough of that, she told herself briskly. Tomorrow she would visit the York branch of the Bank, to discover what had been going wrong there and try to put it right. She would have preferred to have Greaves with her, not because she wanted him to assert authority over the men whom she would have to face, but because he would have been an ally, and she might need an ally.

Poxon, the manager, when he finally met her, thought that she not only needed an ally but a keeper, she having evidently escaped from a madhouse. . .

Remembering her father's wise advice, Stacy had given the staff at Blanchard's, York no warning that she was immediately to descend on them. Oh, they knew that a party from the London headquarters was on the way, and that it would include Miss Blanchard herself, but they had no idea of exactly when that party would arrive—or that, improbably, it would be Miss Blanchard who would head it.

Stacy dressed herself carefully in a black gown of sober cut, with small Mary, Queen of Scots-style fine linen ruffles discreetly edged with lace at her throat and wrists, and a black leather belt with a silver buckle and a small chain hanging from it, to which was attached a tiny notebook and a pencil. Over this she wore a long black coat, caped and cut like a man's. A black fur busby completed the ensemble. The impression of cold and competent austerity was completed by her hair, which had been pulled straight back into a giant knot; a black velvet band was wound round her head and across her forehead to restrain any curls which might wish to spring loose. A single pearl depended from its middle.

The whole effect was formidable in the extreme, as was intended.

Thus accoutred, with Louisa and Hal in attendance, Stacy set off on foot to the Bank's premises, situated not far from the house which she had taken. All seemed fair outside, and inside too, as she entered, her acolytes a little behind her.

The clerks behind the gilt grilles and the mahogany counters stared a little at this procession, particularly as no gentleman seemed to be in attendance. Hal, wearing the green and gold of the livery which Louis Blanchard had designed in one of his more creative moments, was the only male in the party. He was carrying a large leather bag which held all the business papers relating to the York branch which Stacy had brought with her from London.

The clerk whom she approached stared the hardest of all. She stripped off her long black gloves and said, without giving the man behind the counter the slightest notion of who she was, 'I would like, sir, to speak to your manager—as soon as possible.'

The clerk bowed and said, 'Oh, madam, I am afraid that might be difficult. Perhaps you could inform me of what business you wish to transact? Although, forgive me, it would perhaps be better if I, or the manager, spoke to your brother or to your husband about financial matters.'

'Now that would be difficult——' Stacy smiled at him '—seeing that I have neither. Pray escort me to your manager. The business which I have with him is serious in the extreme.' And as she saw him hesitate, 'Come, sir, I have my companion with me, and my footman; it will be quite proper for him to see me with them as chaperons.'

The clerk gave way; he came from behind the

counter, bowed again, and asked, a shade of insolence in his expression, 'What name shall I give to him, madam?'

'Why, sir, I prefer to name myself to him.' And as he prepared to argue with her Stacy added lightly, 'Come, I have a deal of money to dispose of, and your bank has been recommended to me as a sound one. You would not wish to lose my account, surely?'

'Indeed not,' sighed the clerk dubiously, beginning to lead the way to the bank parlour, watched with intense interest by the rest of the staff, business obviously being poor at Blanchard's that morning. By the papers in Stacy's bag, it was never other than poor.

The clerk knocked on the door, heard the answering, 'Come in,' before bowing and escorting Stacy through it, saying, 'A lady to see you, Mr Poxon, sir.' He walked by Stacy to stand at the rear of the room, his master's aide, it would seem.

'A lady?' The manager, a gross man, with the signs of heavy drinking about his face and body—he was so red-faced and barrel-stomached, put down a large glass of port and said, 'Good morning, madam. You wish to do business with me? Forgive me, but——'

'You would rather do it with my husband, father or brother,' Stacy finished curtly, refusing the chair he was offering to her. 'No, I prefer to stand.' Perforce that left him standing too, but she was unable to prevent him from seizing her hand and planting a wet kiss on the back of it. Unattended ladies—for he obviously regarded Hal and Louisa as non-existent—were fair game.

'Yes, thank you, I should care for a glass of port,' she intoned in response to his lack of an offer of it, 'seeing that you appear to be out of Madeira,' and, when he stared at her nonplussed, added sweetly, 'I will have the one which you would have offered my father, brother or husband. It is, I understand, the custom for managers to offer those who visit the bank parlour a glass of something or other and a sweet biscuit. I see that you have anticipated my arrival and favoured yourself with one. On examination you seem to have a deal of liquor and a marked lack of sweet biscuits!'

Behind her Hal gave a curious snort, rather like the ones which Jeb Priestley had been accustomed to give when his betters were entertaining him. The clerk looked as though the sky had fallen in on him.

'I had not thought. . .a lady. . .' stammered the manager, beginning to pick up a decanter, to pour a hefty share of port into a large glass. 'But if madam wishes. . .'

'Madam wishes,' returned Stacy. She was beginning to enjoy herself. After five hard days of battling with a man whose wit was as ready as her own, to cut this poor fool down to size was a pleasure. It might be cruel of her, but perusal of her papers back in London, Ephraim assisting, had proved to them both that if the manager was not on the take his incompetence bordered upon genius! Seeing him, Stacy didn't think that he displayed genius in any department; he was most likely a crude swindler.

'You would care for a glass too?' she asked Louisa, who shook her head determinedly.

'Not in the morning, my dear.'

'Very wise of you,' commented Stacy, draining her glass at one go, in imitation of all the men she had seen doing the very same thing when business was under discussion. 'A clear head is most necessary when one talks business. I'm sure you agree, sir.' And, as he picked up the glass he had refilled, 'Oh, no, I couldn't possibly advise you to drink further. I fear that you will need all your wits about you in the next few hours.'

She placed her glass on his leather-topped desk, walked around it and, before he could remonstrate, took his glass from his astonished hand and sat down in his high chair.

'I think that we ought to begin our business immediately. I have little time to waste,' she informed him sweetly.

The manager stared at her as if she had lost her wits. Louisa, used by now to Stacy's methods, designed to destroy confidence even before she began a merciless interrogation, sighed internally. She should have been a man, that was plain. The manager, poor fool, reached for the bell standing on his desk, to ring it to summon help. 'I will have you removed, madam. The madhouse is your proper destination, not the parlour of a bank!'

Stacy put her hand over his before he could use it. 'Not so, sir. Now, were I to be here to open an account, I should require a full and frank statement from you as to the solvency or otherwise of this branch. But, seeing that that is not my business with you, we shall come to that which is. Hal! Pray hand me my bag, if you please.'

'Certainly, madam.' Hal placed the bag on the desk before her.

The manager, face now purple, went to pick it up, to remove it. Stacy looked at him and said, her voice cool, 'Pray leave the bag where it is, Mr Poxon, or I shall ask my man to restrain you.'

'Burtonshaw!' thundered the manager at the stupefied clerk. 'Either assist me to dispose of this madwoman or fetch a constable to do so!'

'Oh, I shouldn't do that,' smiled Stacy, all deadly charm. 'Were you so unwise as to summon a constable, I should feel compelled to ask him to charge you with fraud and embezzlement, for the papers in my bag seem to suggest that you have been engaged in both, and I wouldn't like to do that until I had given you a chance to defend yourself. Besides, I wouldn't want Blanchard's to have an open scandal which might cause a run on the bank in York and damage the London house too. No, Mr Poxon, let us keep this in the room for the time being.' She paused. 'Oh, I forgot. I didn't inform you of my name, did I? Most remiss of me. I am Miss Anastasia Blanchard, come from London to discover what has been going wrong in York.' She eyed the decanter before her with distaste. 'I think that I may already have discovered part of the reason.'

She began to pull papers out of her bag, fixing the stunned manager with a basilisk eye before handing him the letter of intent which she and Ephraim had jointly signed. He took it with a nerveless hand, and collapsed into a chair as though his legs had failed him.

'And now,' Stacy contrived, holding up the first of the papers from her bag, 'we shall begin to discuss your last balance sheet, and you may endeavour to explain to me how you have managed to achieve these remarkable figures. . .'

'You've never seen anything like it,' a grinning Burtonshaw told the rest of the clerks in the alehouse that evening. 'She had it all off pat. Knew more about how the house ran than he did! Sat there figuring away in her head, as though she had worked in a counting-house all her life, catching him out whenever he tried to fudge an answer. *And* she did something I've never seen afore—added all three columns up at once, pounds, shillings and pence in one go—*and* got it right—while poor old Poxon was still stumbling over the pennies! Like a trick in a fair.' He mimicked a woman's voice. '"But oh, pray, Mr Poxon, how can that be? Your figures distinctly prove otherwise, unless you are keeping a second set of books for your own pleasure, of course."'

He took an almighty swig of his ale. 'Never thought I should ever see old Poxon done down by a lady who looked as though butter wouldn't melt in her mouth. Halfway through he started some tale of it not being proper for a *real* lady to be adoing all this, and why hadn't she sent Ephraim Blount to see to things? So then, so then,' he went on, relishing his tale, 'she snaps the ledger in front of her tight shut—did I tell you she had all the ledgers in *and* mastered them before you could say knife?—and says, as sweet as pie, "Very well, Mr Poxon, if you prefer not to deal with me, and seeing that Ephraim has more to do than tour Yorkshire in winter, let me go to the magistrates this afternoon and swear a warrant for your arrest." And *then* she says, "And if you can't see that I'm saving of you from being transported, and saving Blanchard's name too, then you are an even bigger fool than I take you for!"

'That finished him, I can tell you. And she's a-going to speak to us all tomorrow morning, afore the bank opens. I ain't never seen such a high-stepping goer in my whole life, I ain't.' In his excitement he had reverted to the coarse speech of his youth, before he had gone to the grammar school and had become one of Blanchard's clerks aspiring to be a manager himself.

One of the younger men said, 'What right has she to behave like that, though, eh?'

'Owns the bank, don't she? And she told Poxon that while he had been making a loss in York she had been making a handsome profit in London, and so he ought to attend to her, and not the other way round. . .'

That silenced everyone, for the time being at least, and not forty-eight hours had gone by before all York laughed and buzzed over the doings at Blanchard's, and a small crowd gathered outside the bank each morning to see the forward hussy who had had the temerity to tell Bob Poxon what was what, and turn him off as well, before the week's end.

Even the drawing-rooms of the Minster's clergy hummed discreetly, Mrs Canon Gunter saying to her husband, 'Pray, my dear Alberic, can it conceivably be true that some unsexed creature came down from London to dismiss poor Mr Poxon and publicly address the bank clerks in the bank's parlour?'

The Canon nodded his grey head, adding mildy, 'Although you might be surprised if you met her, my dear, as I was, when she discussed with me Blanchard's loan to the Cathedral of a sum of money to repair the stained-glass window broken in the recent storm, to find that she appears to be a perfect lady.'

'My dear Alberic, I have not the slightest wish to meet her.'

But the very next day, while she was dining with the Bishop, there was the Bankeress, as York society had begun to call her, being introduced to her! It appeared that she was a relative of the Beauchamps of Bramham Castle, in whose company she had arrived, and, after her work in York was ended, was to stay with them over Christmas, her mother having been Lady Beauchamp's late sister!

'It was a wonder,' Mrs Canon announced later, 'that she wasn't turning in her grave, her daughter's conduct being so unladylike.'

York society at the dinner was all agog. The more so because of the remarkable cold beauty and composure of the woman who had set the town's gossips a-roaring. If Stacy was aware of the impression she had made, she gave no sign of it. Inwardly she was less sure of herself than she had ever been.

Earlier that day she had dismissed Poxon, with the pay owing to him. Her work with the bank's ledgers and her discussions with the clerks involved had made it apparent that he had, in addition to running the bank into the ground financially, been looting it for years. Greaves, who had at last arrived in York, cured of his malaise, was in full agreement with her.

Poxon had first paled, and then gone purple. His chief clerk, Robson, who had always disliked him and had remained honest—although many had not—was, at her order, standing by, waiting to be appointed in Poxon's place, with Greaves to help him during his first few weeks.

'You hard-hearted bitch!' Poxon had ground the words out between his teeth. 'I might have known this would be the end of it when I first met you—a woman who doesn't know her place in the world. But, by God, what place can you have, other than to turn men away from their rightful employment? What man worth his salt would want to touch you, I ask myself, other than to get at your money? What mercy could I expect from such an unsexed creature as you are?'

She had heard Louisa gasp as, ruined and frustrated, the wretched Poxon had continued to pour verbal filth over her, even as Hal began to draw him away and young Greaves started forward, thinking that she might need his protection as well. But, by God, madam had courage, one had to grant her that! She never moved, her colour never changed, and when Hal had wrestled Poxon to the door, preparatory to throwing him out of the office he had once ruled, she said, her voice peremptory and as impersonal as she could make it, 'Wait!'

He fell silent. Stacy rose to her feet and, disguising her inward tremblings, said coolly and clearly, 'The mercy I have offered you, Mr Poxon, is that I have not called on the magistrates to arrest you for offences for which you might either hang or be transported to New South Wales. It might be what you deserve, but would neither benefit your poor wife, who would be thrown upon the parish, nor Blanchard's Bank. Be thankful that I have spared you that.'

He made her no answer, but allowed Hal to drag him from the room. Once the door had closed behind him, Louisa rose, went over to Stacy, whose self-control was on a knife-edge, and cried forcefully, 'You see how wrong you are to try to take your father's place. No lady should have to endure what you did just now.'

Stacy closed her eyes. 'You are more troubled than I am by it,' she said severely, which was not quite the truth. 'Allow Hal to escort you home when he has finished with Mr Poxon. Send him and Polly back for me—I have more instructions to give Mr Robson before I leave.'

Later, after she, Robson and Greaves had gone over the changes which she had ordered in the Bank's administration, she walked out of the York branch's big mahogany front doors into the narrow street. Her feet took her towards the Minster, whose towers dominated the little town which was barely changed from what it had been in medieval times.

None of the Blanchards could ever have been called truly religious, even though the founder of the line had been compelled to flee Paris because he was a Huguenot, but Stacy suddenly felt that she needed more than mortal help. She realised that during her reign at the London bank she had been cushioned from the stark unpleasantness of dismissing those who had behaved criminally. Louis Blanchard had run his business on a tight rein, overseeing everything, leaving little chance for dishonesty to flourish, so she had not encountered the more distressing aspects of business life. For the first time she understood what Ephraim Blount had been trying to tell her on the day before she had left London.

'You must be strong, madam,' he had said, blinking at her over his gilt half-moon spectacles. 'You must be aware that the York branch's poor performance is due to more than simple neglect and idleness. Dishonesty is involved, and you must deal with it as firmly as your father would have done. The Bank expects it of you.'

'Oh, never fear,' she had told him impatiently, 'I am

ready for anything.' Which had not, after all, proved quite true. Worse, Poxon's accusations that she was unsexed had touched a nerve which Matt Falconer had touched before him.

It was growing dark as she walked along. Hal was carrying a flambeau on a pole before her and Polly walked by her side. 'Wait for me here, if you please,' she told them, before she entered the Minster's porch which gave access to the nave. 'I shall not be long, I trust.'

There was a brazier burning in the street before the porch, and a man was stirring the coals into flaming life. Hal and Polly warmed themselves at its welcome heat, but the Minster struck cold as Stacy entered it—to hear the choir singing and find just sufficient light for her to glory in the sight of the great window, The Five Sisters of York, of which she had often heard tell.

Alone in the all-enveloping gloom, Stacy had never felt so lost and isolated. Every rule by which she had lived since her father's death seemed to be under challenge, not only because of what had happened to her at Pontisford Hall—and what she had done with Matt Falconer—but also because of what loyalty to the Bank had compelled her to do in York. Poxon had earned his dismissal, but she could take no pleasure in her part in it, even if, at the end, she had shown him a mercy which neither her father nor Ephraim would have done. They would have had him before the magistrates and on his way to Botany Bay without a second thought.

She needed grace. She needed to feel that what she was doing, to others as well as to herself, although harsh, was just. Most of all she needed to come to terms with her own passionate nature. Until she had met Matt Falconer she had not known passion, had, indeed, denied that she could ever experience it. A few short days had shown her how wrong she was. The memory was with her still, and to her horror, instead of being remorseful for what she had done, she was waking each morning to regret that he was not in her bed. Instead, in his guise as the lion-man, Matt Falconer visited her nightly in her dreams. Dismayingly she also knew that her body burned, not with shame but with frustrated desire.

Kneeling down, hands covering her face, Stacy prayed for help, for guidance. For the first time she—a Blanchard—almost wished that she were a Roman Catholic, so that she might confess her sins and receive absolution. Perhaps after that the memory of his lips and hands would fade away and disappear.

After a little time she rose, to see Canon Gunter standing in the aisle, dressed not as he had been in the bank's parlour but in his robes. He spoke hesitantly to her. 'You are not ill, I trust, Miss Blanchard? You are alone. Do you need help?'

What to say? Simply, 'Is it enough for us to try to do good, sir, even if our frailty means that we not only find it hard, but sometimes impossible? And if we backslide, may we be forgiven, however gross our sin?'

'If we truly repent, my dear. Yes.'

Stacy closed her eyes. How could she truly repent her night of love with Matt Falconer, however much she ought to do so?

'Repentance is hard, sir.'

'Oh, but consider, to do right and to repent is never easy. To be easy is the way of the sinner.'

That, at least, was true. She had fallen into bed with Matt Falconer with such consummate ease, but to repent of her sin seemed impossible. She tried again to discover whether the Canon had an answer for her, but since she could not tell him why she needed absolution she doubted whether he could help her.

'And does God forgive us our sins, even if we find it

hard—nay, impossible—to repent?' Stacy heard her voice shake as she spoke.

The Canon considered her for a moment, doubtless, she later thought wryly, wondering what improbable sins Miss Anastasia Blanchard might have committed that she should so desperately ask him for help and absolution.

'I think that He would prefer us to repent, but I believe that, knowing our weak natures, He might be inclined to forgive us if we had tried to do so, even if we found it difficult.'

It was plain that he was not one of the new Evangelical clergy, who would have thundered at her about hellfire and damnation lying in wait for those who sinned and did not repent. Would she have preferred him to do so? Stacy wasn't sure. As though he had divined her thoughts he added gently, 'I can only advise you to throw yourself on the infinite mercy of God if you are troubled, my dear Miss Blanchard.'

She bowed. 'I will remember that, sir, and I thank you for your help.' And she walked on, aware that he was gazing thoughtfully after her as she moved away from him to rejoin her waiting servants.

Polly said to her as they crossed the deserted road, 'Only think, madam, we thought we saw Jeb Priestley while you were in the Minster. Hal and I went a little way down the road—keeping an eye on the porch, a-course, in case you came out—and we thought we saw him going into an ale-house.'

This confidence had the improbable effect of cheering Stacy up. 'Well,' she said briskly, 'I can imagine that if you did see Jeb Priestley he would most likely be making for an ale-house, but I also think it is highly unlikely that either he or his master is here in York. I distinctly remember Mr Falconer saying that he intended to return to London as soon as his business was ended at Pontisford, and that he did not wish to remain there any longer than he needed.'

'Hal thought it might have been him,' offered Polly pertly.

Doubtless Polly's wish to meet Jeb again was father to the thought! Well, she, Stacy, didn't want to see him or his arrogant master again.

But what if, said a little voice in her head, he has made you pregnant? What then? To which the only possible internal answer was, I'll think about that if it happens, which, pray God, it won't. After all, we only spent one night together, and I am constantly hearing tales about persons who have been married for years failing to have children when they most desperately need them to provide a succession for a title or for estates, so one night's madness would surely not be enough. Would it?

The truth is, she admitted to herself, and it was something which she could never have confided in Canon Gunter, I might repent of the possible consequence of the sin of becoming Matt Falconer's mistress for one mad night, but I don't repent of the night itself, even if I wish that it had never happened—especially seeing that I don't even like the man!

And what did such an admission make of the once virtuous Miss Anastasia Blanchard?

CHAPTER EIGHT

'YORK?' queried Jeb Priestley, thunderstruck. 'We are going to York? I thought that you said when we reached Pontisford that we should return to London as soon as our business here was done, which it is, and take a passage back to Virginia post-haste. What are we going to York for?' And then, staring at his master, 'Oh, never tell me! You are haring after Miss Anna Berriman.'

'Not at all.' Matt made his voice as rough as he could. He was standing in his bedroom at Pontisford Hall, packing his bags, a task which was, by rights, Jeb's, only somehow he always managed to avoid doing it. 'I had quite forgotten the woman existed.' Which was a thundering lie; he thought about her every time he went to his lonely bed, and frequently in the day-time too. Which was a nonsense, considering what a cold-hearted bitch she was—except when she was in his bed. He would never have thought that a woman could show him two such different faces—as well as such a splendid body.

He swore at a recalcitrant shirt before stuffing it any old how into his bag. 'I need to see the lawyers there about some property in the town which my great-aunt owned—or so some papers I found seemed to hint—something which that ass of a lawyer in London appeared to know nothing of.'

Which was the truth. Or part of it. The real truth being that he would have taken the papers back to London with him, told Grimes to get on with sorting the whole business out, had they not provided him with the most splendid excuse for 'haring after Miss

Anna Berriman'—Jeb's words—but he had to admit the truth of them. The woman haunted him. And, after so many years of loving them and leaving them, that was almost a bad joke.

'Well, I must say, I don't mind seeing Polly again, and for God's sake, m'lord, Mr Falconer, sir, or Mad Matt, whichever you prefer today, allow me to pack your bag for you before you ruin everything. You're showing a rare impatience to be off, I must say. Good in bed, was she?'

Even for Jeb this was insolence indeed. But how could you rebuke a man who had once saved your life for you, albeit you had already saved his? And who, despite his wagging tongue, was as faithful a friend as a man could have?

'Matt will do,' he told Jeb mildly, 'as I've informed you often enough before.'

'They don't like me to call you Matt here, though,' mourned Jeb, folding m'lord's fine cotton underwear. 'That poor old man Horrocks closes his eyes every time I fail to call you m'lord, and then "m'lords" you at twice the normal rate for the rest of the day to make up for my impudence, I suppose. They like bowing and scraping here, and no mistake. "Yes, m'lord, no, m'lord, pray walk all over me, m'lord, do," he mimicked savagely. 'You'll need a new pair of boots when you reach York. These are on their last legs. And a new coat and shirt and stockings and hat, if you hope to impress the lady. There was money there, you know. An heiress, do you think?'

'No, I don't, and I'm not going to,' retorted Matt cryptically, leaving Jeb to work out what he meant and aiming a half-hearted blow at him at the same time, which Jeb dodged dextrously. 'And for your information, Miss Anna Berriman is most definitely not the purpose of my visit. I thought that I might ride over and take a last look at my childhood home.'

And that was another truth, and an unwelcome one. Whether it was the passing years or the sense of having lost something which he had not known he had treasured until it was gone, he had been experiencing a burning desire to see The Eyrie again. And what a terrible name that was for the beautiful Jacobean mansion which the first Earl Falconer had built after doing some dirty diplomatic business for James I, and which had been paid for by one of the few grants of money made by that miserly king to a deserving subject.

He could ride over from York to see it, if only from a distance. He had no intention of accepting the olive-branch which his father had offered to him. Too much water had flowed under too many bridges for him ever to set foot in The Eyrie again. It astonished him that he should experience such a sharp pang at the very thought of its loss.

A flash of memory showed him the room which he had occupied after he had graduated from the nursery and before he had been packed off to be a midshipman. He had been the third son, highly unlikely to inherit, but Frank, the second son, had died at a badly taken fence in the hunting field shortly after he had reached thirty—and a mercy for the estate that he had, since his career had been one long debauch. He had been drunk on the day of his death, unfit to ride, but had insisted on doing so.

And Rollo, the heir, who had looked as though he might live forever, had departed this life a year ago; how, Matt didn't know, nor did he want to know. Grimes had started to tell him something of it, but he had stopped him with a sharp, 'So far as I am concerned Rollo died for me twelve and more years ago; what happened to him since means nothing to me.'

But, astonishingly, The Eyrie did. He could see the plain of York from the turret window, he remembered, and sometimes, on a clear day, he could almost convince himself that he saw the Minster's towers rising from it.

So he told himself that it was neither Miss Anna Berriman nor his aunt's property in York and outside it which drew him there, but one last chance before he left England forever to see that window again. Even if it was only from a distance. Memory told him of the bookcase beneath its leaded panes, his treasures ranged along the top of it, and on the facing wall the old print which showed Charles II's ships firing on the Dutch fleet in one of that king's few naval victories. A Falconer had commanded a ship there, he remembered.

Only, when he reached York and discovered that his aunt had owned a house in the town, and a small manor house outside it, he decided to open the town house and stay there for the Christmas season—he might catch a glimpse of Miss Berriman. Each time that he walked the streets he looked for her—but had no luck at all. One might almost have supposed that he had imagined her, and the night that they had spent together.

He had casually asked the lawyer he had found in York, Hayes, someone jovial and rubicund, quite unlike Grimes, whether he had come across a Miss Berriman who had lately arrived in York, but that gentleman did not connect her with the Miss Anastasia Blanchard, the Bankeress, who had recently scandalised York, and had shaken his head.

'You might,' he had offered, when Matt had told him that he wished to find the lady, 'take the opportunity to visit the Assembly Rooms for the Christmas Ball. If, as you think, she is a person of consequence, she is almost certain to attend.'

Well, yes, he might attend the Christmas Ball at the Assembly Rooms, Matt told Hayes as well as himself, but not simply to meet Miss Berriman. Oh, no, that was not it at all—on the other hand he found it difficult to understand why exactly he *did* want to attend something which was the kind of event which he always avoided—the small beer of living! But how to attend, when he knew no one of consequence in York who might introduce him to the Master of Ceremonies who ruled the Assembly?

Fate was on his side, after all. By chance, walking along, admiring the Minster's east window, he met Jack Vernon, an acquaintance from his days in the Navy. Matt hailed him as though he had been his oldest and dearest friend, and Jack immediately invited him to join the party he was escorting to the Assembly Ball. Matt had remembered Jack as a man of the most undiscriminating goodwill, and his memory had not deceived him.

'I shall be escorting my wife and her sister to the dance—a classy little filly, my sister-in-law Phoebe—you not hitched yet? No? By Jove, she's just the girl for you, then, and a little fortune comes with her—not that you mind that it's little now, eh, seeing that that ne'er-do-well brother of yours has gone to meet his last rest?' And he gave Matt a poke in the ribs which left him bruised for days.

But he accepted the invitation all the same, had Jeb dress him to a turn, as he hadn't dressed himself for years, and found himself in the Assembly Rooms, part of Jack's party. He dutifully made a leg at Phoebe, who wasn't to his taste at all, thanked Jack, and was introduced all over again to Jack's cousin, Viscount Trotternish, whom Matt remembered as plain George Drummond before he had inherited.

'Matt Falconer! I do believe you haven't changed a bit since we fought together at Trafalgar!'

It was as though the scandal had never happened, or Jack and George were being tactful. Matt rather thought that they weren't. Neither of them had ever been tactful when they had been young, and they hadn't changed much with age, only grown fatter. He supposed that being a hard-working farmer himself had kept him in trim.

What Trot, as he insisted Matt call him, was interested in was heiresses.

Matt asked him impulsively, as though they were young naval lieutenants again, 'What the devil are you doing here, Trot? Not your sort of thing at all.'

'Might say the same to you, Matt. And where have you been all these years?

'Farming in Virginia.'

'Haw-haw, you always did like a joke! But I suppose you've come here for the same reason I have. Like to get your hand on the dibs even if you do have to take the great heiress as well! Now, I'd prefer little Phoebe, but she ain't got enough tin to keep the old home in lead for the roof, whereas this one——' and he raised his eyes prayerfully to heaven '——is rolling in it.'

'Now what great heiress is this, Trot? I'm not up to snuff about such matters these days.'

'Must be behindhand, then, Matt, eh, not to know the Bankeress, the Blanchard heiress? That's why there's so many unattached bachelors here tonight, and all sober. She's supposed to be coming with the Beauchamp party. Rumour says that they're all staying overnight at her place in York—and then she's off to Bramham with them tomorrow. You remember the Beauchamps, eh, Matt?'

Yes, Matt did remember the Beauchamps—just. He didn't, however, remember any rich Blanchard family in York, and twelve years out of England meant that he had little idea of what was what in the society line.

'The Blanchard heiress who is a bankeress, Trot? And what, pray, is a bankeress? You have me all agog. I don't remember any Blanchards around York.'

'Why, she owns Blanchard's Bank, Matt. You do remember Blanchard's, surely? She's old Louis' daughter. He died suddenly two years ago, left it all to her—to run! Imagine, a female owning Blanchard's! And run it she does. She arrived at the York branch three weeks ago, and came down on old Poxon the manager like a ton of bricks. Found out that he had been robbing the bank blind, and had her footman throw him into the street. Sacked half the clerks for helping him, and read the Riot Act to the rest in the bank parlour. They say she ran the bank herself for a week before she handed it over to the new man.'

Matt might have made the inevitable connection with Miss Anna Berriman immediately, before he had so much as seen her, if Trot hadn't grabbed him by the arm, exclaiming, 'Good God, yes! There she is, with the Beauchamps. Some might say she's a stunner, but she looks a cold fish to me. Still, the Blanchard millions would make up for that, eh?'

And, like Jack Vernon, he abused Matt's ribs all over again. Not that Matt noticed—he was far too busy staring at Miss Anna Berriman, who was Miss Anastasia Blanchard, and saying to himself grimly, of course, of course. The Bankeress. I might have guessed.

Stacy had had to admit that meeting her aunt Beauchamp again had revived memories and feelings which she had thought she had forgotten. Louis Blanchard had never cared for his wife's sister, but Stacy had always found her a loving aunt until the final quarrel with her father had occurred over his training Stacy to succeed him.

She had corresponded with Aunt Beauchamp, secretly and against her father's wishes, but she had not seen her aunt or her uncle again until two days ago when they had arrived at her York home and her aunt had thrown her arms around her, crying, 'At last, my love. Let me look at you. You are as lovely as I thought that you would turn out to be! But oh, my dear, what is this I hear of you? Running the bank in York? That might have pleased your poor, dear father but I cannot say that it pleases me! And you are still unmarried. I blame your father for that.'

'Dear Aunt,' Stacy had murmured tearfully, 'do not let us quarrel, rather let us agree to disagree. I have my life and you have yours. And from now until I leave Yorkshire I shall take a holiday from work. Mr Greaves has finally arrived, quite cured of the illness which overtook him on the way here, and will look after the Bank for me until I return home.'

With that her aunt had to be satisfied, and her uncle too, that amiable, jovial man, quite unlike Louis Blanchard—or Matt Falconer, for that matter. All the same, once her aunt was alone with Louisa Landen they had sadly agreed that poor Stacy had been done no favour by her father when he had trained her to succeed him in the Bank. 'But at least she is willing to attend the Ball,' Aunt Beauchamp had said, and had looked with pride at Stacy when she'd walked downstairs to join the party ready to leave for the Assembly Rooms.

Stacy's only regret was that Louisa was not coming with them. 'You do not need me now that you have your aunt,' she had told Stacy, 'and I am growing too old for such junketings.' She had never really recovered from her illness at Pontisford, and Stacy was beginning to realise, with a pang, that the safe world in which she had lived for so long, with Louisa always by her side, was beginning to disintegrate. Change was all about her.

To her surprise she found herself looking forward to the Ball. She had dressed herself for it with great care, and walked into the Assembly Rooms conscious that she was looking her best. She was wearing a dress of pale green silk with the slightly lower waistline that fashion now demanded, trimmed with seed-pearls on the bodice and skirt, and a splendid pearl collar around her long and swan-like neck. Her fan was large, decorated with arabesques of seed-pearls and tiny emeralds. The whole ensemble served to emphasise the glowing green eyes set in an ivory face of classical purity.

Her cousin Anthony Beauchamp, who was her escort for the evening, bowed over her hand, looked into her eyes and said, 'My dear Anastasia. If only you would allow us to introduce you to Society I am sure that you would become all the rage.'

'Oh, as to that, sir,' she replied, tapping his arm gently with her fan as though she had been coquetting with men all her life, instead of doing so for the first time, 'I have no time to be all the rage; my presence is required elsewhere.'

He bowed again, his eyes hard on her. 'You must allow me to suggest that you should reform your ways to accommodate Society's demands and allow us to enjoy your charming presence.'

Well, that was as may be, and Stacy was about to answer him as kindly as she could, for she had absolutely no intention of transforming herself into a copy of one of his sisters. Their conversation appeared to centre on balls, their latest *toilette*, and handsome young men——in that order. Shrugging a little, she glanced across the room—only to see, gazing at her with a face like thunder, Matthew Falconer, Lord Radley! And where had *he* sprung from? And why was he looking at her like that? It was he who had wronged her, not she him. Worse, he was advancing towards her with that empty idiot George Trotternish by his side.

Anthony Beauchamp, staring at his magnificent presence, said involuntarily, 'Who the devil's that?' to have his mother reply,

'Why, I do believe it's Matt Falconer—Matt Radley, I suppose we ought to call him now—and goodness, how he has changed. I'm not surprised that you didn't recognise him. But what is he doing here?'

'Matt Radley?' Anthony sounded as stunned as Stacy felt, and she could not be surprised at his astonishment. Beside Anthony's bland and civilised charm, Matt Falconer looked more than ever like some pirate out of a Minerva Press novel, come to life in all his barbaric glory.

His superb clothing only served to enhance his savage appearance: he was more leonine than ever. His coat and breeches were skin-tight, revealing the muscularity of a body which put that of every other man in the room to shame. His face was so stern and strong that ordinary canons of handsomeness seemed unnecessary—nay, even a drawback. And every woman's eye was on him.

Stacy could not tear hers from him either. Especially since his were fixed so determinedly on her that she had the unwelcome impression that she had lost every article of clothing which she was wearing. Worse still, she realised that she was looking at him and seeing his remarkable torso naked, as it had been that shameful night, in all its splendidly muscled glory, his clothing too having fallen away.

George Trotternish was, as usual, sublimely unaware, as was Jack Vernon behind him, of the sensation which their friend and guest was causing. To add to the hum of excitement which ran round the room, many of the older persons present remembered both Matt and the scandal, and were busy reminding one another of it.

Stacy saw with rising desperation that Matt neither knew nor cared about the brouhaha he was creating, only bowing impassively when Trot said eagerly, 'Dear

Lady Beauchamp, do allow me to present to you my old friend and fellow sailor, Lord Radley.'

Aunt Beauchamp said faintly, 'Oh, I have known Lord Radley since he was a child—but we have not met for many years. I am surprised to see you here, sir.' For some reason she felt unable to put down Trot or cut Matt. Possibly Matt's tremendous presence and his ignoring of the fact that he was officially *persona non grata* because of his disgraceful conduct so many years ago accounted for her consenting to receive him—which meant that everyone else at the Assembly Ball would.

Matt was taking Aunt Beauchamp's hand and bowing over it. 'I have inherited property in and near York, dear Lady Beauchamp,' he told her gravely. 'I have been in the United States since we last met. I remember, though, that you were kind to me when I was a boy and sailed kites with Anthony here.'

Aunt Beauchamp said feverishly, 'Oh, he was much younger than you, and I recall that it was you who was kind to him. I must introduce you to my party,' and she began the civilities which ruled the social world over which she presided.

Matt was behaving politely and modestly, quite unlike the savage Stacy remembered from Pontisford Hall. And now it was her turn to be presented to him, and he was bowing to her and saying, as smoothly as though he were meeting her for the first time, 'An honour, Miss Blanchard. I must admit that I have heard so much about you that I feel that I know you already.' And his eyes were defying her as he came out with this splendidly ambiguous statement.

'Oh, Lord Radley, there you have the advantage of me,' she threw back at him, for if he wanted to play games with her, then so would she respond to him, 'for I am sure that had we ever met before I could hardly have forgotten doing so.' Her eyes were sparkling at him, sending him a message that she was quite unaware of.

Aunt Beauchamp was saying, as the music began, 'My dear Matt, if you have no partner for this dance then I am sure that my dear niece would be willing to oblige you,' ignoring the black look with which her son was favouring her.

Indeed, as Matt led the unwilling Stacy on to the floor for the cotillion, for she was unable to refuse her aunt's wish, Anthony turned on his dominant mother.

'I do not understand you, madam. You know perfectly well that I wished to begin the evening by dancing with my cousin. Instead you have handed her over to a man of such ill fame that I am surprised that you even deigned to receive him, never mind commit an innocent young woman into his care!'

Aunt Beauchamp watched Stacy and Matt take their position in the set and begin to move through the dance's intricate pattern. She was a woman of great character, even if that character had no real depth, and she went her own way with little consideration for what others might think—even her own son.

'My dear Anthony——' she smiled at him over her fan '—I have no wish for you to marry your cousin. Cousins shouldn't marry—bad for horses and even worse for us—and you would never be able to stand up to Stacy. Not that I want her to marry Matt Falconer—but as to receiving him, that is a different matter. I thought that he was badly treated years ago, and it is time that story was forgotten. Both Rollo and Camilla Falconer are dead, and the scandal should die with them. Now, why don't you ask pretty little Phoebe Whatever-her-name-is, Jack Vernon's sister-in-law, to dance with you? She's the sort of child you ought to marry—pretty and biddable.'

* * *

So now he had madam almost in his arms again! But she was intent on keeping him at a distance. Her hand might be in his, but that was all. Matt tried to look her in the eye, make her acknowledge him, but she resolutely kept her own gaze modestly fixed on the floor as though she were a young girl at her first ball. The result was that he was prey to the most dreadful and conflicting emotions.

From the first moment that he had seen her, tall and graceful at the other end of the room, her long neck elegantly inclined towards the young popinjay to whom she was talking, he had been unable to stop looking at her.

Really, madam was superb. As always, she carried herself with such damnable unconscious pride, but, more than that, tonight there was a glow, a radiance about her which he could not remember her possessing at Pontisford.

She even laughed lightly once, and as he moved nearer to her in the dance he could not prevent himself from mentally stripping her beautiful gown from her so that he could once again visualise her splendid breasts. He could remember only too well that he had held and caressed them with both his hands and his mouth. And as she advanced and retreated towards him, head modestly inclined, Matt was suddenly agonisingly aware that his body, constrained as it was by his tight clothes, would, if he was not careful, betray to the whole world his rampant and aroused desire for her.

Lust! That must be what he felt for her, and why he should feel it for the Bankeress, a cold, calculating machine, according to York gossip, he couldn't imagine. Down, Fido, down, he told his treacherous body, for the mere sight of her was proving his undoing. He tried to turn his mind to other things, took his eyes away from her face, only to see that now she had raised hers and was studying him as though, he thought angrily, he were an insect laid out for her to dissect.

To no avail. The memory of the night when he had wronged her, and she had so enthusiastically helped him to do so, was as sharp and clear as though it had happened only a few hours before, instead of a few weeks. He must be going mad. Even when she turned away from him, and all he could see of her was the long and lovely line of her back, the thing which held him most was the smooth elegance of her graceful and rounded behind as it moved beneath her light clothing—and the memory of his hands stroking it!

He was turning into a satyr and it was all her doing. Desire, lust, whatever it was which held him in thrall, also demanded that he needed to speak to her, so that he might hear that enchanting if disdainful voice, provoke her into saying something, anything, even if it was only something to put him down.

'You are enjoying yourself, madam?' he asked her, his voice glacial.

'Indeed, sir. And why should I not?' Stacy was retreating away from him even as she spoke, only to meet him again, hand extended, and say, 'You appear uncomfortable, sir. Do I take it that you are not enjoying yourself?'

The bitch! She was mocking him, he was sure. Did she guess the pother that he was in? Surely not. She was a maiden lady of impeccable virtue, after all—or had been until Matt Falconer had seized hold of her and thrown her upon her bed!

He felt himself breaking into a sweat while she, the cold-blooded doxy, was raising her eyebrows at him as the music brought her back to him, so that he felt constrained to say, 'A gentleman's clothing, especially a cravat, seems especially designed *not* to dance in, which explains my discomfort a little.'

Only to have her remark when next they met, 'Oh, I

suppose that in the wilds of America you are more accustomed to perform clad simply in war-paint and feathers. This must make a most unwelcome change, I do agree—but you could hardly expect us to accommodate your more savage desires.'

'If I were to accommodate my more savage desires,' he told her between his teeth as he spun her around, 'you would be on the floor with me, and the company would retreat screaming.'

Well, I asked for that, was Stacy's inward response. She supposed that she ought to be shocked, but the picture which he had conjured up was such a wickedly amusing one that she was hard put to it not to laugh, especially when her next partner in the dance, her cousin Anthony, growled jealously between clenched teeth, 'If that fellow is annoying you, Cousin Stacy, do tell me, and I shall see that he ceases to do so.'

She shook her head at him and turned around, to meet Matt going the opposite way. She offered him her hand, wondering why, as he took it, a strange thrill always ran through her body when he touched her, or she him. Nothing like that had ever happened when Anthony Beauchamp took her hand in his.

Matt said, as they moved together, also through clenched teeth, she was amused to note, 'I see that you have a smile for that fribble who was entertaining you when I arrived. I suppose that you save your scowls and curses for me.'

'Of course,' she told him sweetly as the music stopped and they bowed at one another, 'for you deserve them, and he does not. After all, it was you who set upon me as though I were some lightskirt who prowls the Haymarket, while he has always behaved towards me with perfect rectitude.'

This goaded Matt into further unwise speech. 'Seeing that he is only half a man, I am sure that perfect manners are all he is left with.'

'True, and as you have no manners at all he must have inherited your share.'

'And who has inherited yours,' he asked her savagely as the music ended, 'seeing that we are an excellent match in the land where bad manners reign? My memory of your conduct at Pontisford is still fresh.'

'And I of yours, sir,' she said as they walked back to where her aunt's party was seated. 'But then, what can one expect of a savage who is accustomed to dancing clad only in paint and feathers?'

'The same as from a shrew who possesses a calculating-machine instead of a heart!' he ground back at her.

'Then we *are* well-matched,' Stacy informed him sweetly. She was astonished to find that, as before when she was with him, she had never felt so alive, every nerve in her body tingling and a strange excitement growing in the pit of her stomach. It was almost as though she wanted him to fall on her again. And, judging by his expression, if they had not been parading themselves in such a public place, fall on her he would have.

She could feel the tension in the strong body which walked so proudly beside her, and knew that it matched her own. When he looked at her the amber eyes grew ever more golden, the pupils enlarged—but she was unaware that as he betrayed the signs of sexual arousal, so did she.

He handed her into her chair, and, after the most polite fashion, as though he had not been insulting and assaulting her with every word, asked, 'You would care for a drink, madam? You look a trifle heated.' And she knew that he was tormenting her, was recognising what her body was telling her, and was taking a subtle delight in letting her know that he knew—and that he was breaching her defences.

Stacy could no longer bear to have him beside her.

She was in danger of saying and doing something which she would later regret.

'Indeed, sir, a cooling drink would be most welcome,' she replied, and she watched him leave her, moving through the company as though he were a panther prowling, and truly would be more at home wearing merely paint and feathers as she had mocked him.

After that the evening became a blur for both of them, but a blur against which each saw the other plain and clear. Even when Aunt Beauchamp engaged him in conversation, trapping him into agreeing to visit Bramham Castle to bring in the New Year, leaving Stacy to be surrounded by a crowd of admirers, all astonished that the Bankeress was such an unusual beauty, they remained completely aware of one another and no one else.

'I think, Matt,' Aunt Beauchamp admonished him as they watched Stacy performing in the quadrille with Anthony, Matt with something like murder in his heart at the sight, 'that it is time that you took my niece on the floor for the next dance. For you to ask her twice would not occasion comment. More would occur if you were not to dance at all. It is the waltz, but I think that her advanced years would save her from scandal.'

'Her advanced years!' burst from Matt involuntarily. 'Pray, madam, what years does she have? And why has no one yet claimed her in marriage? One would have thought that inheriting the Bank would be a great attraction.'

'Alas,' sighed Aunt Beauchamp, 'she insists on running the Bank, and few husbands would allow their wives to continue doing so after marriage—and she is naturally fearful of fortune-hunters. To be in her late twenties and have such gifts—I blame her odious father for encouraging her to follow a course more suited to a young man than a young woman.' And she rolled her eyes to heaven as Stacy, her hand on Anthony's arm, walked towards them.

Jealousy, pure and simple jealousy, roared through Matt at the sight. He could have strangled poor Anthony, whom years ago he had found a good friend and a kind and biddable child. Now he saw only a rival. But a rival to what? Bedding madam? Ravishing the Bankeress again? What in God's name was possessing him? And how could such a cold-hearted creature as Lady Beauchamp had just described arouse such passions in him? He felt sure that the strength of them was written on his face! He had not been in such a lather since he had first become aware in his early youth of why women had been placed on earth, and what delights a man could share with them.

Perhaps, however, nothing showed. For madam seemed coolness itself. Anthony Beauchamp, ever the gentleman, bowed unwillingly at Matt as Aunt Beauchamp announced officiously, 'I believe that Matt wishes to ask dear Stacy to waltz with him. Do you waltz, Stacy?'

Yes, she *was* matchmaking, thought her son angrily, whatever she said. And why should his mother think that his cousin ought to be handed over to such a savage disguised as a gentleman? For a moment he thought of objecting, of challenging the brute, but from long ago he remembered Matt Falconer's strength, his cold courage, and decided against it.

Which was just as well, for before Stacy could manage, Oh, dear Aunt, I am tired; I fear that waltzing is beyond me. Pray excuse me, Lord Radley, there was a sudden and excited stir around the ballroom as a party of late arrivals were bowed through the door by an obsequious Master of Ceremonies. Some great personage led them, no doubt.

Some great personage did. Quizzing-glasses were raised, ladies chattered excitedly behind uplifted fans, and by the time that the great personage had crossed the floor he and the object of his sudden interest were the only unmoved people in the room.

For once Stacy lost her own cool control a little as she saw first Aunt Beauchamp's face set in an agonised smile, and then felt Matt Falconer's whole body stiffen beside her. The newcomer, attired in the black silk court dress of the late eighteenth century and followed by a small group of splendidly turned out friends and relatives, seemed sublimely unaware of the stir he was causing.

He was making straight for them, Stacy realised, and as he did so, as he drew near, so that he was under the full blaze of the great main chandelier above them, Stacy saw him fully for the first time—and also saw something else.

Not only was he as tall as Matt Falconer, but, although a trifle stooped, he had also once possessed as splendid a body. Facially he informed her of what Matt would look like if he lived into his late sixties.

She turned querying eyes on both Matt and Aunt Beauchamp as the newcomer paused a little short of them and said involuntarily, for she could almost feel the pain radiating from the man beside her, 'Matt?'

It was the first time that she had used his name in other than despite, and he answered her distantly, not using her name as a weapon, his attention fully engaged by the man before him. 'No need to worry, Stacy. It's only my father. I present to you, Miss Anastasia Blanchard, the most noble the Earl Falconer, KG.'

CHAPTER NINE

'AND what, Radley,' asked the Earl Falconer of his son, after he had done the pretty with Stacy, Uncle Beauchamp, Aunt Beauchamp, the Honourable Anthony Beauchamp, Viscount Trotternish, Jack Vernon and wife, little Phoebe and the assembled nobility and gentry, and the music had started again, and Trot had carried Stacy off, Matt having been cornered by his parent, 'brings you here?'

'I would prefer, sir,' was Matt's stiff reply, 'not to be addressed by that name. I am plain Matthew Falconer.'

'But I, on the other hand, would prefer to use it,' was his father's reply to that. For a moment father and son, staring at one another, were as alike as two new-minted coins, showing heads with the profiles of eagles, or lions, or whatever animal or bird of prey you preferred.

'Come, Radley, you have not answered me. I asked you why you were here. Grimes distinctly informed me that you intended to leave England as soon as your business at Pontisford was over.'

'I changed my mind,' Matt returned coolly. He could hardly bear to look at his father. All his young life he had worshipped him, but nothing he had ever done had pleased. With the benefit of maturity he now saw that they were too much alike, not only in appearance but in character. Neither man brooked being controlled by others, or bending to another's will.

'But why York? And, seeing that you have chosen to visit York, could you not bring yourself to oblige me for once, and visit The Eyrie as I asked you?'

Matt's expression was a grim one. 'Now, sir, you of

all people should know why I never wish to see The Eyrie again. And have you forgotten that, on the last occasion I visited you, you ordered your footmen to beat me from the door if I tried to enter?'

The Earl's face twisted. 'If you must know, Radley, I regretted that order almost as soon as it was made. . .'

'I will beg leave, sir, to doubt that. I am coming to wish that I had left Pontisford only to take passage to Baltimore again. My home now is not The Eyrie but a plantation in Virginia, where a man is judged by what he does, and not what others think that he might have done, or by the bedroom he was born in.'

The old man before him, Matt saw with a savage pleasure, winced at this.

'Suppose I were to confess, Radley, that I have recently come to believe that I might have been mistaken in my beliefs about your conduct twelve years ago, that I might have been over-hasty?'

Matt, hardly able to credit what he was hearing, stared back at his father.

'Why, sir, I would be compelled to answer that such a re-examination of your prejudices is at least twelve years too late in coming. The Matt Falconer you knew then died long ago, and the new one does not need your belated forgiveness—should you feel inclined to offer it.'

His father bent his grey head in acknowledgement. 'Nevertheless, Radley. . .'

Matt could not bear to be addressed by that name; he said violently, 'Come, sir, I asked you not to call me Radley, and I meant it. I only knew one who bore the name, and I do not wish to be reminded of him. You say, or appear to say, that you are now prepared to question your long-established beliefs as to what happened between my brother, myself and my poor dead Camilla. That being so, I am astonished that you did not see fit to inform me earlier of your change of mind, in view of the speed with which you threw me off at my brother's lying behest.'

'Allow me to say that it is only since the circumstances of your brother's death that I began to question myself. The letter which I sent to you asking you to return to England so that we might discuss the possibilities of a *rapprochement* most probably arrived in Virginia after you had left for England. I am now in hopes that together we may review and reassess the past.'

Matt acknowledged this with a slight dip of the head, and said, 'Well, that being so, sir, I am happy to learn that you acknowledge that you *might* have been mistaken. And that, if you please, should cease correspondence between us. Twelve years ago you disowned me, and since then Matt Falconer has become an American farmer, and that is what he wishes to remain. I do not wish to discuss the dead past with you—ever. Let it remain dead.'

His cold impassivity contrasted with the pain on his father's face. That father remembered the days when this son had been famous for his youthful impetuosity, not for his cold self-control. The long years apart had brought great changes. The man before him possessed a strength of character which was beginning to convince the Earl that he might truly have wronged him. He tried again to reach beyond the cold mask which confronted him.

'Nevertheless, I must remind you, Radley, that you stand heir to a great name, and a great estate.'

Matt shook his head in wonder. 'Why, sir, as to that, I want neither. I almost changed my name from Falconer but, since that carries no burden of unwanted tradition or inheritance in my new country, it hardly seemed worth the trouble.'

The old man said grimly, seeing that the younger one refused to bend before him, 'Nevertheless, sir, like it or not, one day in the not too distant future you will be Earl Falconer.'

The music which had been playing as an accompaniment to their cold and painful conversation was coming to an end. Behind his father Matt could see Stacy in Trot's arms, being whirled into a series of spinning turns. He wondered why he could endure her being in Trot's company when the sight of her with Anthony Beauchamp filled him with jealous rage. He decided ruefully that it was because he thought that Trot was no real threat to him where the Bankeress was concerned, while Anthony Beauchamp was.

His father was saying painfully, 'You are not attending to me, sir.'

'I beg your pardon.' Matt was suddenly compelled to admit his gracelessness, if only because the desolation in the old face before him matched that which he had felt for so many years. 'But I was watching Miss Blanchard. Lord Trotternish is hardly the most suitable companion for her, I fear.'

The Earl turned to see Trot and Stacy exchanging final bows. 'Miss Blanchard? Do I understand that she is the young woman who now runs Blanchard's Bank? Are you acquainted with her, Radley?'

Was he acquainted with her? Of course he was. Had they not lain in one another's arms all night?

'Yes, sir,' he rejoined stiffly. 'I am acquainted with her.'

'Then I would wish to speak a little more with her. I knew her father—a most remarkable man. I am told that the daughter is equally so. You will do me the honour of presenting the young lady to me again. I was not fully aware of who she was when Lady Beauchamp introduced us.'

Why, the old goat, thought Matt derisively, he thinks that I may be interested in her, I do believe, and would not object to having Blanchard's Bank and Blanchard's money added to Falconer wealth! He wondered what his father would say to him if he told him the truth. That he had misjudged his son over the sad affair of his brother's wife, but if he assumed the worst in the relationship between the Honourable, the Baron Radley and Miss Anastasia Blanchard, spinster and ex-virgin, he would not be going far wrong!

'The whirligig of time brings in his revenges,' Shakespeare had once written, and Matt, reintroducing Stacy, most unwillingly, to his father, wanted to shout at him, You had better send for your footmen to attack me with their whips again, Father, for I have ravished a virgin—and the truth is I do not regret having done so. Far from that, I would have her in my bed again instantly if she would consent to come, for in it her sharp tongue and sharper mind are stilled, and she uses her intellect to promote our bodies' pleasure and not to make money!

But he said nothing at all, and watched with satiric amusement his father using all his undoubted charm on his son's late bed-mate.

'I knew your father,' the Earl was saying to Stacy, quite unconscious of the nature of his son's thoughts, thinking himself that Miss Blanchard was a fine-looking woman and that any man could do worse than marry her, seeing what a fortune she brought with her, 'and he and I were good friends. I always found his advice most useful.' He paused a moment, then added, 'I believe that I met you once, many years ago when you were quite small.'

Stacy bowed, murmured a trifle mischievously, 'I do not remember the occasion, sir, but I do have the honour of being well-acquainted with your account with us, if I may raise such a matter on the occasion of a Christmas ball!'

Clever as well as beautiful, a rare combination, and no wonder that his son was interested in her, was the

Earl's conclusion. He had seen a certain look in Matt's eye when Miss Blanchard had walked towards them, and he had read it aright. He was as aware as she was that the encounter between first Matt Falconer and the father from whom he was estranged, and now his obvious interest in the Bankeress, was causing universal comment and interest among the spectators which almost transcended common politeness. But like his son—and the woman before him—he never allowed such considerations as that to affect him.

'You know my son, Radley, I believe?' he asked her.

Now, how should she answer that? Suppose she gave him the correct answer—in the biblical sense of the word 'know', only too well! But that would never do. Some truths were best not uttered, so she remarked, a trifle undiplomatically perhaps, 'Well enough to know that he does not like to be called Radley.'

Far from antagonising the Earl, this amused him. He laughed a little. 'Yes, you do know him. I should have collected that Louis Blanchard's daughter would be blessed with judgement beyond the common run.'

Aye, thought Stacy wickedly, but what judgement did I display when I allowed your son to bed me so incontinently? She was unaware that such forbidden thoughts as these were beginning to melt the ice with which she had always surrounded herself, so that more than one man watching her wondered how anyone could ever have dubbed her cold.

They talked easily on neutral matters for a few more moments, until the Earl said, 'As a matter of interest, Miss Blanchard, although it is perhaps a question which I should not ask you, how did you come to meet Radley? On business, one supposes?'

Well, here was one truth Stacy could offer m'lord which could offend no one. 'Oh, you may certainly ask me, sir, and I shall equally certainly respond. On my way north to York, where I had some business at the

Bank and where I also intended to spend Christmas and the New Year with my aunt Beauchamp, my mother's sister, my coach broke down near Pontisford Hall during the recent great snow, and Lord Radley most graciously gave me and my entourage shelter for several nights until we were able to travel north again.'

Which was, when all was said and done, one way of telling a thundering lie so that it sounded like truth. The Earl took what she said at face value.

'You reassure me, madam. Most gratifying that my son has learned to conduct himself with such propriety. Gracious, indeed! Virginia must have had a civilising effect on him. I shall be delighted to observe it in action, for I am invited to Bramham for the New Year, and Lady Beauchamp informs me that she has also asked Radley to join us.'

The room swung about Stacy for a moment. How in the world was she going to be able to bear the constant presence of Matt Falconer in her life? She had never for one moment thought of having to dodge around him at Bramham. The effect that he had on her was so powerful, so disturbing, that she could hardly contemplate being able to endure it. The ice around her was melting with a vengeance.

More melted during the evening. She was relieved that Louisa was not there to watch and judge her. For some reason it seemed imperative that she show Matt that she made nothing of him at all, by making a great deal of such empty fools as poor Trot and the beaux from York who thought that they might have a chance of netting the Bankeress.

So light-hearted was she, so gay, that later on, after she had shared supper with Trot, Anthony Beauchamp, and a galaxy of young men who vied for her favour, Matt, who had spent most of the evening propped against the wall, looking morose and drinking overmuch weak-minded punch, growled at her as she arrived back after dancing the minuet, 'A word with you, madam.'

Breathless, rosy, her lips parted, strands of her dark hair curling loose around her face, so that she gave the impression of a woodland nymph who was only waiting to be caught by her satyr, Stacy nodded in his direction. 'Of course, sir.'

'What has happened to the cold-hearted mermaid who froze us all to death at Pontisford, madam? Are you intent on snaring every man in the room, married and unmarried? Oh, yes, I saw you cavorting with my sister's husband, Bibury.'

'For shame,' retorted Stacy spiritedly. 'I only dance where I am asked.'

Matt could not help himself. The man who had vowed never to commit himself to any woman was now in the thrall of the last woman on earth who he would have thought could move him.

'It is not your dancing I take objecton to, madam, but the way you conduct yourself before, during and after the dance.'

'Oh!' Stacy blazed at him. 'Who the devil are you to act as my chaperon? Recollect how you behaved yourself with me, and learn that all the men with whom I have stood up tonight have conducted themselves towards me with perfect propriety.'

He could not help himself; the words flew out before he could stop them. 'It is not their propriety which concerns me, madam, but yours.'

'Hypocrite!' she flung at him. 'Oh, base. Recollect your own lack of propriety where I am concerned before you animadvert on mine.'

'Animadvert?' he flung back, as thought it were a ball which they were tossing between them, his amber eyes glowing. 'Did you learn that at the Bank's desk? It might be better if you had remained in the Bank's parlour, and then we poor devils would all be safe from your lures.'

Had they not been in so public a place that they were compelled to exchange insults in so pleasantly polite a manner that they might have been exchanging words of the deepest love, Stacy would have cracked him across the face again. Instead, she lifted her fan and turned to Aunt Beauchamp, who, slightly alarmed by she knew not what, was coming towards them. 'I am a trifle warm, madam; perhaps we could take a turn in the ante-room where I understand it is cooler.' And she gave Matt another view of her magnificent back and bottom, which had him lusting after her all over again.

Decidedly the devil was taking a hand in matters at York's Christmas Assembly Ball, and there was still the New Year to get through. He would doubtless be ready to run mad before 1819 was well on its way if he was to be exposed to the constant temptation which Stacy Blanchard presented to him when they were thrown together at Bramham Castle!

Which was Stacy's conclusion as well as his.

After that, Christmas Day was something of an anti-climax for Stacy and Matt. Particularly as both of them desperately tried to avoid thinking of the other, but both, for quite different reasons, failed in their objective.

Stacy woke up on Boxing Day at Bramham Castle feeling strange and feverish. Polly, who was herself looking a trifle green, helped her to the small bathroom off her bedroom and held her head while she vomited into a porcelain washbowl decorated with flowers, before letting go of her mistress to be violently sick into the bowl herself.

Sweating gently, her skin feeling so sensitive that merely to have had Polly's hand on her forehead was distressing, Stacy sank back into a nursing armchair standing by the big tin bath which would shortly be filled with warm water so that she might wash herself all over in it, and wondered briefly whether any of the Christmas food which she had eaten had caused such an unwanted effect.

Oh, but she knew only too well that that was not it, not it at all. What was wrong with her was that she was missing her second set of courses. Not only was her skin sensitive, but her breasts were swollen and sore, and she was not so unversed in her knowledge of the world as to be unaware that one night of passionate love with Matt Falconer had resulted in the inevitable. She was pregnant.

Once Polly had finished, and had sunk into a chair opposite to her mistress, they looked at one another ruefully.

'Oh, Miss Stacy,' Polly began, 'I hates to 'ave to say it, but I am a fallen 'oman.' Like the clerk at Blanchard's, faced with a crisis, she had reverted to her normal manner of speech before she had been trained to be Stacy's personal maid by Louisa Landen herself.

She looked half slyly, half shyly at Stacy. 'And you, Miss Stacy?'

It was a direct question, and one which Stacy was compelled to answer truthfully. 'Alas, I fear that I am breeding too.'

Servant and mistress for once shared a common predicament, and Polly, her eyes big with wonder—for were they not now bound by more than the ties of domination and servitude?—asked, 'Oh, Miss Stacy, is it Mr Matt's child you are a-carrying of?'

Stacy answered this not with a reproof for insolence but with a wry nod, followed by, 'Seeing that it cannot possibly be anyone else's, the answer must be yes. And you, I suppose, are carrying Jeb's?'

Her maid's answer was a mute nod of the head, and

then a *cri de coeur* which Stacy shared with her. 'Oh, Miss Stacy, whatever are we a-goin' to do? We are both ruined—and on the same night, too!'

And that was undeniably true, and there was no answer which she, Stacy, could make to it. Instead she asked gently, 'And if Jeb Priestley asked you to marry him to make an honest woman of you, would you agree to do so?'

Polly nodded her pretty head vigorously. 'Oh, yes, indeed. I liked him famously. He made me laugh, and he treated me like a lady, which is more than any of the other servants who came a-courting ever did.'

Treated her like a lady, indeed—by giving her an unwanted present, no doubt. And how did Matt Falconer treat me? Like a servant, perhaps. And how did I behave with him? No, I cannot answer that.

Polly felt bold enough to ask, 'And you, miss. Would you marry Mr Matt?'

'Indeed not,' was her vigorous answer to that.

'Oh, but you must marry *someone*. Think of the scandal.'

Stacy thought of the scandal and closed her eyes. Yes, she must marry someone, she supposed—but not Matt Falconer. Never Matt Falconer. Why, she hated him, did she not? And not only because he had ruined her.

You did your share of that, her conscience reminded her.

She stifled its unwelcome voice by saying to Polly, 'If Mr Priestley does not wish to marry you, then I can arrange for you to go to some farm to have the baby, and I will see that it is loved and cared for.'

'Aye——' Polly was bolder than ever '—and what about yours, Miss Stacy? Who is going to love and care for him—or her?' she amended.

Him, thought Stacy. I know it's a him.

'I shall think of something,' she announced grandly.

'Then you'd better do so soon,' returned Polly practically. 'There's not much time left before we both start showing.'

Rising rapidly to her feet and beginning to feel much better, Stacy ordered briskly, 'For the meantime we say nothing,' taking it for granted that Polly would obey her. But the peasant shrewdness which Polly possessed in abundance was telling her quite another thing. For was not Mr Jeb Priestley a bigger catch than she could ever have hoped for? And she knew instinctively that Mr Matt Falconer would see her right—aye, and Miss Stacy too.

It wasn't like Miss Stacy to be so airy-fairy as to think that she could keep a love-child from the world's knowledge.

CHAPTER TEN

THERE was more than that which Miss Anastasia Blanchard could not keep from the world's knowledge, but that hammer-blow to her name and fame was yet to descend on her. For the present she contented herself with allowing Polly, once she had recovered, to help her to dress for the day. Afterwards, she went downstairs, pretending that all was well both in her private and public world.

Hardest of all to bear, she was to find, when the company arrived to celebrate the New Year, was not having Matt Falconer steadily watching her and steadily avoiding her, but the unwanted and admiring attentions of her cousin Anthony, who seemed determined to defy his mother and father's wishes by paying her the most insistent court.

The more he did, the more sardonic Matt's gaze grew. It was almost as though, across the room, she could read his mind. But what she didn't know was, could he read hers? Was he, could he be aware of the fact that she carried his child? Unaccustomed to being idle, to speaking only the nothings of polite conversation as carried on by gentlewomen, Stacy found life increasingly hard to bear. She most passionately wished that she could be back in London in the Bank's parlour, discussing policy with Ephraim, signing letters, and carrying out all the minutiae of the commercial life which had been her world since her father had first discovered her capacities when she was in her mid-teens.

Boredom rode on her shoulders. Matt found her, late one afternoon, in the gloaming hour, standing before a window which looked out over the gravel sweep which led to the front portico, watching the carriages which held his father and his father's party arrive.

'At last, madam,' he said softly in her ear, 'I have found you alone, without your cavaliers around you.' For not only Anthony Beauchamp, but Trot, who was also a fellow guest, and several other men, young and not so young, had been clustering around her like bees around honey.

Stacy did not turn to speak to him but addressed the window instead. 'I fear that I have little to say to you, Lord Radley, and you can have even less to say to me.'

He leaned forward, whispered into her ear, 'Ah, but we went beyond speech, did we not, madam?'

Her reply was a frozen one for, if she unbent at all, she could not trust herself to be able to hold him off. Even to know that he was behind her when they were not even touching was to have her shaking and quivering inside. 'I wonder you care to remind me of that, sir.'

'Unfortunately,' replied Matt a trifle bitterly, for he had never been so undone by a woman before, 'I cannot bring myself to forget what passed between us.'

'Nothing passed between us,' Stacy told the window as she watched Earl Falconer descend from his coach, Matt's sister Caroline, and her husband, Lord Bibury, following him and beginning to make their way into the house.

'I would not have thought the Bankeress's memory worse than mine,' was Matt's retort. 'Or is it reserved solely for the adding up of columns of figures or the examination of the balance sheets of failed businesses?'

Nettled, Stacy finally swung around to confront him. 'I wonder at you, sir. If I choose to forget what happened that night then the least that you can do is respect my wishes. What never happened cannot be regretted or remembered.'

This remarkable statement silenced Matt, if only for the moment. For cool pragmatism he felt that he had never met its match! Not only had the woman a mind like a knife, she also had the cunning deviousness of a politician.

He could not help himself; he finally came out with, 'By God, madam, with such deviousness at your command you should be a member of the Cabinet at the very least. More's the pity that a woman cannot sit in Parliament; you would grace the Treasury Bench itself. No ploy would be beyond you!'

Goaded, Stacy shot back, 'And is that supposed to be a compliment, sir?'

Equally goaded, Matt almost snarled, 'You may take it as you please.'

'What I please is to ask you to allow me to pass, sir. We have nothing to say to one another—let it rest at that.'

I shall never rest while I remember the night we spent together at Pontisford Hall, was Matt's secret thought. *She* may be able to forget it; I cannot. Thank God that the world has no knowledge of what happened there, else we were both ruined—and, whatever else, I do not want that for her, though, sure God, madam seems equipped to withstand anything—even that.

He took the thought downstairs with him to greet his sister and his brother-in-law; his father had already retired to his rooms. He thought Bibury, a rather dour man, if kind, looked a little sideways at him, but supposed that that was due to the reputation which had clung to him ever since Camilla's death.

Caroline kissed him warmly on the cheek and said, 'Dear Matt, how much better it is for us to meet affectionately in private, instead of having to be all formality in public. You look well. I cannot remember that you were so large and brown when we were last under the same roof together.'

Matt smiled, and kissed her back. 'Hard work, Caroline. I have been a farmer since we last met, and not a gentlemanly one, either. Hard labour is responsible for my increased size, not idleness and eating and drinking.'

Bibury, whose expression was still oddly quizzical, Matt thought—and why should that be?—drawled at him, 'You look strong enough to go several rounds with Gentleman Jackson himself, Radley.'

Well, it was useless to ask people not to call him that, Matt supposed, and when, a few moments later, Caroline took herself off to her room to change, Bibury drawled again, his hard advocate's face still quizzical, 'I should like a word in private with you, Radley, if you please,' Matt readily agreed. He did wonder, though, why his brother-in-law should be quite so formal with him. The fact that he had begun his early life as a lawyer, before his elder brother had been killed in the Peninsular War and he had inherited, was, he supposed, responsible for such a hanging-judge's manner.

They walked into the library, deserted at this hour, where Bibury sat himself down before a blazing fire and thrust his booted legs towards it, before drawing a paper from the pocket of his coat and handing it to Matt.

'I thought you ought to see that before anyone else at Bramham does,' he began without preamble. 'It will be all round London by now, and should reach York any day. Neither Caroline nor your father is aware of it yet—but they will be.'

Matt took the paper in his hand. It was a Radical news-sheet devoted to scandal and innuendo about the doings of the mighty, both in Government and out of it. Bibury had run an ink mark down the side of a couple of paragraphs on the front page, headed 'Doings at Pontisford Hall—the Bankeress and the Bear'. It was brief and brutally to the point.

> A country correspondent tells us that Lord R, fresh from the wilds of Virginia, while domiciled in his country home at Pontisford Hall entertained Miss A. B., commonly known as the Bankeress, to bed as well as board, when she was trapped there by the snow on her journey north. One supposes that the Snow Queen, as Miss B is also known, succumbed to the attractions of the Northern Bear and was thawed into submission. Are we to expect a baby Banker or Bankeress?

Matt stared numbly at the paper, aware of Bibury's cynical eye on him. How, he wondered, could anyone in London have learned of what had been done at Pontisford? And then he knew. He remembered the housekeeper, and her vow that he would regret turning her away. She must have gone straight to London and to the printers of the scandal sheet. She must have been told by the other servants his nickname, given to him because of his size, while he was still little more than a boy in the Navy.

He crumpled the paper in his fist and looked blindly across the library and through the windows at the wintry scene outside, avoiding Bibury's eye as he did so. 'Is this commonly known?' he asked.

Bibury shrugged. ''Fraid so. It was the talk of the Clubs.'

'And believed?'

'Oh, of course.'

'No use my denying it, then?'

'No, indeed. Silence is always the best weapon in these cases. One may hope that it will be a nine days' wonder, and then will die down.'

'But in the meantime. . .her reputation.'

'What reputation?' replied Bibury cuttingly and brutally. 'A female who pretends to be a man must always expect criticism. I suppose the scandal sheets have been waiting for such an opportunity to cut her up. Particularly since up to this time her reputation has been one of unbending virtue.'

He had not asked whether the rumour was true. Nor, he must have noticed, had Matt directly denied it.

He could only think of Stacy. Of his own reputation he thought nothing, for he had none. He waved the paper at Bibury. 'I may keep this?'

Bibury's face was wry. 'Oh, indeed, Matt, by all means.'

Matt was at the library door before Bibury spoke again. 'My dear fellow, you are by way of being my brother, so I feel compelled to warn you. Pray do not embark on anything rash—that can assist neither you or the lady.'

He made no answer to that, for there was none that he could make.

He found Jeb in his room, which overlooked the park at the back at the house. It was beginning to snow again. Jeb was folding his clothes. He had a shirt in his hand and an expression similar to that of Bibury's on his face. It seemed that everyone knew something which Matt Falconer didn't.

'You were saying?' he enquired politely of his unruly servant, although he felt far from polite.

'I wasn't saying anything.' Jeb was aggressive.

'No? Then you were thinking it. Out with it, man.'

'Oh, we are indeed Lord Radley today,' observed Jeb nastily.

The joke palled. Matt was too exercised by the paper in his hand to enjoy it. 'You will do me a favour by answering me.'

Matt might not be quite Lord Radley in manner yet, Jeb thought, but he was hovering near to being so.

'Very well, m'lord. It's Polly. She had some news for me this morning . . .' He paused.

'Had she, indeed? And is it something which should exercise me?'

'Both of us,' returned Jeb, his face one huge grin. He doubted whether m'lord would be quite so hoity-toity when he heard his news. On the other hand, he didn't feel quite so hoity-toity himself. It looked uncommonly as if Jeb Priestley might have to settle down at last.

'Polly tells me that she finds herself in the family way. We. . .uh. . .climbed into bed together the night that you and——'

Matt interrupted him. 'You are sure that it's yours?'

'Aye, and Polly's a lively lass. She'll make a good wife. I've a mind to make her Mrs Priestley—if that's all the same to you.'

'I agree with you.'

Matt found himself holding the scandal sheet as though it were contaminating him. He put it down on an armoire. Jeb picked up another shirt and began to fold it, saying, 'That's not all.'

'Not all?' Matt sank into an armchair in an attitude resembling that of Bibury—although without Bibury's obvious ease. 'What more can there be? You haven't given another wench a little packet, have you?'

Jeb snorted, rather as he had done at Pontisford when his betters amused him. 'Oh, not I, Matt. Polly's my lass, no one else. Haven't touched a wench since. No, begging your pardon, *Lord Radley*, it's you she was speaking of.'

'Me?' A dreadful suspicion struck Matt. He jumped to his feet, caught Jeb by the lapels of his coat, ground into his face, 'What the devil are you trying to tell me, man? For God's sake spit it out. I've had quite enough to try me today without you dancing me round too.'

Jeb pulled himself free, laughing, saying between splutterings, 'It's Miss Blanchard, Matt. Like master, like man, they say, and it seems that we both hit the target together—and on the same night too. Who'd have thought it?' And he continued to laugh uncontrollably, wishing that there were others with whom he could share such a splendid joke.

Matt's face was grey granite. 'You're quite sure? This isn't your idea of a joke?'

'No joke. Polly says that the Bankeress is even more overcome by her present than she is, but is carrying it off well. Of course, even the Bankeress can't carry it off forever. What suggestions do you have, *Lord Radley*, to help her out of her unfortunate situation?'

He would have to marry her to make matters right. He couldn't leave her to the tender mercies of a society which had already agreed to despise her, and would despise her the more when this news broke. He had thought that the existence of the scandal sheet was bad enough—but this. . . How could he have put her into such a compromising situation? What madness had overtaken them both that night at Pontisford?

He pulled himself together. Jeb was saying, 'I've already asked Polly to be my wife, and she's agreed. Says she doesn't mind going back to America with us—that is if *Lord Radley* still wants to return there.'

Lord Radley didn't know what he wanted. He bit back at Jeb, 'Lord Radley isn't likely to be as fortunate as you are. Somehow I doubt whether Miss Anastasia Blanchard will fall into my arms as quickly as Polly has fallen into yours. And as for returning to Virginia—what you have just told me is likely to alter everything.'

'Well, as to that,' remarked Jeb agreeably, 'I would be prepared to say that if she has any common sense at all Miss Blanchard had better make up her mind to be Lady Radley well before another month is out.'

Which was all very well, but Miss Anastasia Blanchard's version of common sense might not be the same as Mr Jeb Priestley's. Matthew Falconer, Baron Radley, didn't know whether he had any common sense left at all!

Stacy was taking tea with Caroline Bibury, whom she was finding an agreeable soul, ready to discuss matters other than dress and scandal, being happy to comment on Lord Byron's *Manfred* which she, like Stacy, had just finished reading. She had met him, Caroline told her, during his short and unhappy marriage to Annabella Milbanke, and he had struck her as a man of intemperate passions, exactly like those heroes of whom he wrote. 'The very model of *The Pirate*,' she finished laughingly. 'Just the kind of handsome and passionate reprobate whom we all ought to avoid, for who knows how we might behave if confronted by such a charming monster?'

Who knows better than I, indeed? thought Stacy ruefully, watching Matthew, Lord Radley, enter the drawing-room, remembering the passionate reprobate with whom she had shared a bed, and the consequence which had flowed from *that*. She also thought that Matt looked *distrait*, not at all like his usually damnably controlled self, and wondered what was troubling him. She knew only too well what was troubling her.

He came over to sit with them, and to drink tea as though it were wormwood which he was consuming, so that even Caroline noticed his strange manner and asked him whether he was ailing.

Matt shook his head. 'No, indeed. I find England strangely dark after the clear bright air of Virginia.'

Caroline questioned him about his life in the United States and he began to answer her with passionate enthusiasm. 'And you work, yourself, in the fields?' she exclaimed.

He nodded, and when he spoke his eye was on Stacy, not his sister. 'I would not have it otherwise. There is a cleanliness of spirit and a satisfaction about manual labour when it is performed for the love of it and not as a duty, enforced on one by others. I do what I choose, and what I please, and no one there thinks my labours odd. Imagine the brouhaha there would be if I toiled with my hands in the fields around the Eyrie!'

Stacy suddenly saw him, stripped to the waist, his tawny head blazing beneath a golden sun, his big body etched against a clear blue sky. The sensation this unexpected vision produced was so exquisite that she could almost have cried aloud. Ever since she had known that she was carrying his child the sensations of faint nausea which she occasionally felt were linked with a heightened sense of awareness of everything about her.

And the thing that she was most aware of was Matt Falconer. It was almost as though she were a part of him, so that for a moment she shared his memories of the life he had left behind him. She listened, also aware that Matt Falconer was talking to her, rather than to his sister, reminding her that he had a life of which she knew nothing, and to which he wished to return.

Or so he said.

Later, when Bibury and the rest came in, and Matt's father looking tired from his journey, Matt took the opportunity to ask her to examine some of the family portraits on the walls of the corridor which led to the drawing-room, a pretext so nakedly obvious that Stacy smiled at it.

'Come, sir,' she asked him as soon as they were alone before the portrait of an Elizabethan Beauchamp, gallant in huge ruff, pearl-sewn doublet, and trunks and hose of pale pink, 'what is it that you wish to say to me?'

Matt smiled ruefully—rueful seemed to be the only word which fitted his thoughts these days.

'I'm sorry if I appeared clumsy,' he began.

Stacy's exasperation showed. She was used to being spoken to directly, not to having men make pretty speeches to her on the way to being direct.

'I doubt whether anyone else noticed,' she returned, 'but I could not help being aware that you were becoming increasingly impatient at being constrained to speak to me before others—that you wished to speak to me privately. Something is troubling you, I collect.'

She did not say that where he was concerned she had acquired a sixth sense.

'Well, then, madam——' and Matt was suddenly savage, and as direct with her as she could possibly have wished '—allow me to tell you that I would have preferred that you had informed me that you were carrying my child, rather than have discovered it from the lips of Jeb Priestley. I'm not sure what etiquette governs these matters, but I cannot but believe that, as the child's father, I should have informed him, should I have so wished, rather than he me.'

'Oh!' Stacy was enraged, and could not help but show it. 'I particularly instructed Polly that she should keep that piece of news to herself, not go tattling it around Bramham.'

'Just so, madam. Did it not occur to you that you had a duty to inform me even before you informed Polly?'

'Etiquette, you said. What book of etiquette exists to assist an unmarried pregnant woman on the right line to take with the man who so incontinently made her so?'

'Oh, madam——' and Matt's smile was deadly '—the

same book which instructed you so well in how to fall incontinently into bed with the father!'

Now what could she say to that? Nothing but, 'Your being the father is an unfortunate accident. My child will be rich enough to be able to dispense with a father.'

'Would that matters were so easy, madam. I fear that any hope you might have entertained that you could somehow have your child and its origins remain anonymous have already been dashed. You had better read this.' And he handed to her the Radical broadsheet which Bibury had given to him.

If he had thought to overset her, he was mistaken. She took the paper from him and read it without so much as changing colour. She might as well have been casually examining something as innocuous as the latest *Book of Beauty*.

'So?' she remarked, handing it back to him.

'And is that all you have to say, madam?' His face was suddenly suffused, Stacy was fascinated to notice. He looked as he had done that night when he had fallen on her—and she on him.

'What is there to say?' she answered, her heart thumping, but determined to stay as cool as he was hot. 'It is the truth, is it not? Or are you prepared to dispute it?

She was prepared to drive him mad, that was it. Regardless of the fact that they might be interrupted at any moment, Matt seized her by the shoulders, ground out between his teeth, 'Are you determined to destroy yourself as well as me? That you care nothing of what is written there is one thing—but what of others who read it? That paper will reach Bramham in the next few days—and what reputation shall we have then? How shall we—you—face our fellow guests? If it were not for the fact that you are carrying the consequence of our madness, then we could deny what is written there, say it was concocted out of spite—as I believe it was. But nothing to that, madam, nothing to that. Our guilt will shortly be obvious to the whole world—unless you are prepared to say that the child is not mine—which would brand you a slut, as well as careless. Is that what you want?' And he began to shake her.

They were back at Pontisford, before they fell upon the bed. He had only to touch her and she was lost. Oh, she had dreamed of him in her arms night after night, as he had dreamed of her. Only the fact that a few yards away the assembled guests sat, innocent of the passions being released in the corridor outside, kept them from falling on to the floor to consummate those passions.

Both of them had been solitary beings so long, denying themselves, enduring passionless lives, telling themselves that fulfilment was not for them—each for their own different reasons—that they found it difficult to surrender, to admit what was burning so fiercely inside them.

Eye to eye, breast to breast, heart to heart again, wishing only to be united, but strongly denying the wish, they breathed and trembled together.

Finally, Matt released her, to lean against the wall shuddering with the force of passion rejected. He lifted his head, muttered hoarsely, 'There is nothing for it, madam. You must marry me and soon—before you grow big and all is lost.'

It was the most ungallant, unloverlike proposal a man could have made. But it was not that which enraged Stacy; it was his cold assumption that she had no choice.

Shuddering herself, burning, caught in passion's toils, Stacy murmured, her voice so low that Matt could hardly hear what she was saying, 'I suppose I should have expected that. You may keep your proposal, sir.

And what you say of that paper's news is yours to say. I shall say nothing.'

'Mad,' groaned Matt, 'you are mad. You cannot refuse me. Ruin lies before you, not me. I am already ruined—and you are a fallen woman. You will be a pariah.'

'I am already a pariah, so that is nothing new.' She came out with this splendidly, as though she were carrying a flag with the words emblazoned on it into battle. 'I am tolerated only for my fortune and the Bank. Men want to marry me only for my fortune and the Bank.'

'I want neither your fortune nor the damned Bank,' Matt growled at her. 'I want him—my child—to have a name, and his mother not to be called a whore. Is that so wrong?'

'Him?' And Stacy's voice was a reproach, even though her secret wish was that the child should be a boy—and look like him. 'Him? It might be a girl.'

'Boy, girl, whatever it is,' gritted Matt through clenched teeth. 'I won't have it farmed out.'

'I have not the slightest intention of farming my baby out. It will be brought up as a Blanchard—and, boy or girl, it will inherit the Bank.'

'It will be a pariah, too. You are a clever woman, Stacy. How can you be so stupid as to deny your child a name and an inheritance? Unless you marry me your child—our child—will have no name. Can you really want such a thing?'

Stacy. He had called her Stacy, not madam. And did she really want such a thing? If only he had shown her some affection, had put an arm around her, had said, I understand how you feel. Marry me and all shall be well. But he hadn't. He was worrying about the child, and her good name, not about Stacy Blanchard herself.

But what he had said about the child having no real

name had struck her hard. Was she being fair to this unborn creature which she carried beneath her heart?

Her expression changed, softened. Matt saw it, and pounced. 'You will consider my offer,' he said eagerly, and put a hand on her arm, showing her for the first time some small sign of affection. Afterwards he was to ask himself why he had been so hard with her, but somehow the passion which ruled him whenever they met so appalled him by its strength that he wished to deny it, and denying it he denied her.

A mute nod was Stacy's only answer. He followed up this small advantage. 'We need marry only for show,' he assured her, for he was certain that she could not love him, since she never unbent to him, only showed him her indomitable will. 'I shall apply for a special licence. We can remain married until after the child's birth, give it a name, and then we may part on agreed terms—you to the Bank and me to Virginia. There, I cannot say fairer than that.'

Before she could reply they heard the door open and footsteps come towards them. Matt seized her by the arm, half ran her along to examine another portrait, so that the advancing party, seeing them thus engaged, could have no idea of the passions which had ravaged them the moment before, and which were plainly written on both their faces.

Only, when he handed her towards the stairs, Matt whispered hoarsely in her ear, 'And you will give me an answer, madam, and soon, I hope.

To which Stacy answered, 'Yes,' which was saying anything—and nothing.

Nor would Stacy say anything more, merely mounted the stairs to talk to Louisa, who was still a semi-invalid, as though nothing in the world had happened to overset her. Matt must wait for an answer—but what answer she would give him was as unknown to her as to him.

CHAPTER ELEVEN

'AND Mr Anthony Beauchamp, who dances such attendance on you, Stacy, my dear— what would your answer be to him if he were to propose himself to you? He would be so much more suitable a husband for you than Lord Radley—as I suppose you realise. Such a charming and pleasant gentleman!'

Louisa and Stacy were seated together, each of them stitching away at a pair of tapestry cushions, before the blazing drawing-room fire at Bramham Castle. Caroline Bibury had been playing Haydn to them, a pleasing, tinkling piece, light and airy, not at all matching the dark and troubled thoughts which lay behind Stacy's apparently composed countenance.

Louisa had asked her question in a quiet voice, so that no one should overhear her, although she and Stacy were seated well away from the rest of the company, who had begun to play spillikins as though their life depended on it. The noise that they were making quite drowned out anything which Louisa might care to say—or Stacy, when she replied to her.

She jabbed her needle viciously into the likeness of a hen pheasant and murmured, almost below her breath, 'I have no mind to marry anyone, Louisa, as I have so frequently told you. I like my cousin Anthony, but not as a future husband.'

'I can see that there is no pleasing you,' sighed Louisa sadly.

No, indeed, thought Stacy. Sooner or later I must give Matt Falconer an answer, for sooner or later my condition will betray itself, and I still cannot make up my mind as to the best course of action to follow.

It had begun to snow again and a group of gentlemen who had been riding earlier came in, exclaiming at the cold, the hard ground, and the inclement nature of the weather, as though every January did not find them saying the same thing.

Matt, walking beside his father, was wearing his usual expression these days, Stacy noted clinically. He glowered. He was waiting for the unwelcome news in the scandal sheet to reach Bramham. So far it had not done so, but so far his Lady Disdain had refused to make up her mind to accept the inevitable and marry him.

Yesterday, catching her in the library, he had said, 'If you accept me, madam, before the scandal about us breaks here, then it cannot be scandal. You understand me, I'm sure. Cannot you give me an answer now? To do so would be to the advantage of both of us. Every time that the post arrives I live in a sweat of fear that all will be revealed.'

So did Stacy. So why was it that she could not say yes to him? He was so unloverlike, that was it! But why was that it? Had she not scorned all talk of love and romance these many years? So how was it that now she was like a green girl waiting for her beau to shower her with compliments, promising her moonlight and roses? Instead he showered her with practical, rational, logical advice, plainly, almost rudely offered, with no intent to deceive her by pretending that he loved her—the kind of behaviour which she had always told herself that she expected, and would welcome, from a man. But, alas, now that she *was* receiving it, she found that she didn't welcome it at all!

A coach was being driven along the sweep, passing the drawing-room windows on its way to Bramham's superb front door, with its noble flight of steps. Bramham, although still called a castle, had been rebuilt in the classical style in the 1770s. Matt watched a uniformed flunkey alight and begin to unload the boxes and sacks of mail which it was carrying in lieu of passengers. No, there was one passenger, a black-clad lawyer—Grimes. He of the rueful countenance and impudent disapproval of Matt Falconer and all his works. What the devil was he doing here?

No need to ask, Matt thought dismally, and no need to worry this time what the sacks of letters, newspapers and parcels might contain. He gave a short exclamation, rose from his seat and walked over to where Stacy sat, the picture of virginal and untouched innocence. A picture which only he knew was false. He was aware that Anthony Beauchamp was watching him sourly, and knew that, whatever Anthony hoped, Stacy would never accept him—least of all now that she was pregnant by another man.

Ignoring Louisa, after a brief polite nod to her, he murmured, almost below his breath, so that only Stacy could hear him, 'The time grows short, madam. It may be already too late for us to emerge from this with any credit. Give me your answer. Now.'

Had the man no manners? Stacy saw Louisa's head lift itself sharply from its concentration on her work, and said reprovingly, 'I have no idea of what you speak, Lord Radley. As to the answer I promised to give you—that will arrive in due course.'

He leaned forward to hiss into her ear so that no one else might overhear, 'At least before the child arrives, I hope!'

'We are watched,' Stacy told him severely on hearing this sally. 'You grow indiscreet.'

'*Our* indiscretion is about to be announced to the world. I am sure of that, madam. You have left us no way out.'

He watched Grimes being ushered into the room by a footman, watched the tea-board accompany his entry, to be set out for him on a low table, saw his father speak to him, saw Grimes bend his head deferentially to say—what?

Lifting the silver teapot to pour both himself and his powerful patron a cup of tea, Grimes was muttering quietly, 'It is of all things essential, sir, that I speak to you in private, and soon. You ought also to ask Lord Radley to be in attendance to be called in to consult with us when we have finished.'

'And what, pray, has Radley done this time?' queried the Earl, a look of extreme anger on his old face.

'That I cannot speak of here. Later.' And Grimes drank his tea and ate a ratafia biscuit with all the appearance of extreme enjoyment.

Matt Falconer felt no enjoyment. Instead he put out a large hand to grasp Stacy's small one, to prevent her from continuing with her stitchery. As usual her extreme composure was driving him rapidly, not slowly, mad. Added to his thwarted desire to bed madam again, her refusal to give him an inch was the most exquisite form of torture she could have devised for him.

'Attend to me, madam,' he whispered fiercely, aware of Louisa Landen's horrified eyes on him. 'We have but a few minutes left, and your refusal to face facts is becoming dangerous.'

'Unhand me, sir,' hissed Stacy.

'No, indeed,' he told her, his voice rising a little, 'not until you answer me plainly.'

'Here is your plain answer, sir,' she told him equally fiercely. Before he could stop her she used her left hand to pull her needle from her right hand and stabbed him with it in the back of the hand with which he was gripping her.

This was so unexpected that Matt, taken unawares, let out a roar of anger, mixed with surprise, and, yes, admiration for her spirit. She was looking him full in the face, and was smiling at him. Yes, dammit, the bitch was smiling at him! No, dammit, she was laughing at him! At the predicament he was in, and at his inability to retaliate against her for what she had so incontinently donc.

Every head in the room had swung towards them at the sound of Matt's bellow. Louisa, unbelieving, frozen with horror, watched Stacy throw down the offending needle and take Matt's damaged paw into her hand, to dab at it with her tiny lace handkerchief.

'Oh, sir!' she exclaimed, all innocence. 'Pray forgive me. I had not seen that your hand was in the way. Allow me to stanch your wound.'

The wound was light, and the pain was small. It was surprise which had wrenched the cry from Matt's lips. He saw his father's cold eye on him, and then Anthony Beauchamp was beside them, saying sharply, 'Cousin Stacy, is this fellow troubling you again?' and the look he gave Matt was a malignant one.

'No, not at all,' Stacy carolled, having discovered inside herself a fount of mischief which she had not known that she possessed. 'I wouldn't say that you were troubling me, would you, Lord Radley?'

Matt, holding her handkerchief over his damaged hand, looked up at Anthony, who was eyeing him as though he were some mad animal which ought to be shot on sight.

'No, not at all, Miss Blanchard, rather the contrary, I would say.' Which masterly and devious reply nearly overset Stacy, and had Anthony puzzling over its meaning. There was no doubt about one thing, was her inward judgement—Matt Falconer liked to sail close to the wind. She forgot that she was inclined to do the same.

Fortunately for decorum, for Anthony had just worked out the true meaning of Matt's reply and was squaring up to him again, the little lawyer came over to them, bowed, and said in his dry way, 'Miss

Blanchard, Mr Beauchamp, sir, you will forgive me for intruding, I trust, but the matter is urgent. Your father, Lord Radley, would like you to accompany us for a discussion in m'lord's private suite.'

He bowed so obsequiously that the company forgave him on the spot, particularly since he was rescuing them from a situation which was rapidly becoming embarrassing. Matt allowed himself to be led away, promising himself grimly that dear Lady Disdain would pay for her pin-prick if it was the last thing she did.

But she was already having payment exacted, first by Anthony Beauchamp and then by Louisa Landen.

'My dear cousin——' Anthony was all indignation '—I cannot understand what you see in that rude fellow. I collect that he works like a peasant in his fields in Virginia, and now he has come over to behave like a peasant in polite drawing-rooms. If he is really troublesome, pray let me know, and, as I offered once before, I will deal with him.'

'That is very noble of you.' Stacy was all sweetness and light, having put Matt in his place and now being determined on putting Anthony in his. 'But I am well able to deal with Lord Radley myself. Pray do not exercise yourself over the matter. Should I ever need assistance, I would ask for it. You may be sure of that.'

He was a little mollified, spoke to her for a moment about a variety of things in an effort to soothe her, though she needed no soothing, and then left her to Louisa.

Louisa, shocked to the marrow by the wild behaviour of both Stacy and Matt, moaned gently at her, 'Oh, my dear, however could you conduct yourself so outrageously? I own that Lord Radley spoke a trifle brusquely to you, but that was no reason to assault him with your needle. I am beginning to think that all the wildness which you should have worked through in your earlier years is being expressed in your maturity instead. Is it not enough that your conduct already attracts attention because of your running the Bank, without you behaving like a hoyden and thus attracting even more censure?'

'Oh, pooh to that, and to everything else.' Stacy was on her high ropes, and had no idea why that should be so. She had seen Matt's face immediately after she had stabbed him, and she knew that had they been alone he would have inflicted the most condign punishment on her. And oh, how her body ached and wished for it. Yes, she *was* going mad, and it was all much more exciting than being continually staid and proper as she had been for so many years.

At the same time she could not help wondering what Grimes and the Earl were saying to Matt—and then it struck her, so that her face paled, and she swayed a little. What a fool I am! They have seen the scandal sheet—and everything which Matt has repeatedly told me would happen will happen.

Louisa caught her arm, said feverishly, 'Stacy! You are not ill?'

'Oh, no,' she told her old companion. 'I can't afford to be ill now, Louisa. Most injudicious of me. But I should like a cup of tea, and would wish you to ring for one for me. That should set me up to be ready for anything.'

She was not wrong. Grimes, who for all his dried-up manner and appearance relished the more scandalous aspects of his work, had given the Earl the scandal sheet to read, and when m'lord threw it down, disgusted, said, 'I have spoken around London and it seems that they did spend a night alone together at Pontisford. I thought it might be my duty to inform you before anyone else did, remembering that Lord Radley has been involved in a similar brouhaha once before.'

'But I have been recently led to understand that we might have been mistaken over that.'

'Indeed.' Grimes was smooth. 'As there may be a mistake over this. I would advise you to discuss the matter with Lord Radley immediately. He may not be aware of this——' and he flicked a finger at the sheet '—and the talk which is going around London. There will be others who will find this in their post today.'

'No doubt.' The Earl rose and paced to the window to look out of it. The snow had stopped, but before it had done so had created a white world. The bridge over the lake, the little pavilion to which it led, the trees beside it were ornaments of silver filigree against a blank landscape. 'I had hoped that Radley and myself were coming to some kind of understanding—but this. . .' And he shook his head, began again, 'To destroy the honour of a young woman who has always possessed a reputation for extreme virtue. . . This is too much, and this time must be remedied.'

'There may, of course,' murmured Grimes smoothly, 'be a reasonable explanation. Might I advise that you speak to Lord Radley before reaching a final judgement?'

'Exactly so. You said that he was outside. Pray ask him to come in at once.'

Matt was in the ante-room. Restless, unable to sit quietly, he had been pacing the floor, examining cabinets containing rare china and curios from a dozen countries in the near and far east. He knew perfectly well what news Grimes had brought his father, and for the life of him he could think of nothing to say in extenuation of the conduct which the scandal sheet imputed to him.

If Stacy had already accepted him, then that would have been that. But she had not, and doubtless his father would put the worst interpretation on what he was supposed to have done.

Supposed? He had done it, and therein lay the rub. So, when Grimes beckoned him in, he squared his shoulders as he had done when a boy at Eton, waiting for old Keate, the headmaster, to beat him. And now, in his middle thirties, he was still in no better case!

Grimes withdrew with a bow and his father thrust the paper containing the record of his delinquency at him. 'I should like an explanation of this, Radley. I understood from you that you were not at your old disgraceful games again, but I see that I was wrong to believe you.'

This was easier to answer than Matt had thought possible. 'Hanged, drawn and quartered before I say a word in my defence, eh, Father? Still the same old story? Except that the old story was a lie, all of it, as I tried to tell you to no avail.'

'To the devil with the old story,' growled his father. 'It is this new one which exercises me now. Were you aware of this, sir?'

Matt said as coolly as he could, 'Aware that this sheet existed, yes. But I must tell you that I am not prepared to discuss with you, or with any man or woman, my relations with Miss Anastasia Blanchard.'

His father's face grew slowly red. 'You are not denying this vile libel, then, I see——'

Matt interrupted, 'Neither affirming it nor denying it. It is no affair of yours—or any man's.'

'This—this,' exclaimed the Earl violently, waving the paper about, 'makes it my affair! If a lie it impugns your honour, and the lady's. Hers most of all. If true then I have no words for you, sir. No words at all. Indeed, true or false, words fail me.'

Impudence was all that was left to Matt, and, dismally, he knew that it was the only weapon in his arsenal which he could use. Stacy's refusal to accept his proposal had deprived him of all others.

'Why, sir, that comforts me—to know that there are

to be no more words from you on the matter. In that case, I will leave you, unless there is anything further of moment which you *are* prepared to discuss with me?'

For one moment he thought that he had gone too far. Behind his outward bravado he could hear the inward bells of regret tolling. Since he had met his father again in York it had almost come to seem that they might become father and son once more, Camilla and Rollo's ghosts no longer coming between them. But now it was Stacy who had replaced them as a living and breathing barrier.

The Earl's hands curled into fists. He was a young man again. Had he a whip in his hand he would have struck his son with it. Lacking a weapon, he used the only one he had left to him: his tongue.

'You are no son of mine, sir, if your answer to this gross libel is silence, and a refusal to defend a lady's honour. How will she be able to withstand the inevitable shock of scandal when this. . .becomes known to the company?'

Matt couldn't defend himself. He couldn't answer his father's just anger as he might have wished by saying, The lady and I intend to marry. What is printed on that paper is neither here nor there. We both ask you for your blessing. Then and only then would gossip be silenced, and his father not be shamed by his son.

He bowed. 'I will leave you, sir.' He refrained from saying, Reflect that, as you were wrong about my behaviour towards my brother's wife, you might also be wrong about this, because the paper was telling the truth.

His father said heavily, 'Yes, you may leave, Radley. I have nothing more to say to you. Except that I am sorry for the lady. Her life is difficult enough, I understand, without this.'

He could have said, Her choice, Father. She has left

herself open to scandal by refusing my honourable offer of marriage. But no decent man could interpose a woman between himself and obloquy. In any case, the whole business had been his fault, and no one else's. The affair had been precipitated by his act of folly in pretending to be the butler, and had been further compounded by his falling upon her that night when they had been alone in her room. That thereafter she had co-operated with him most willingly and lustily did not lessen his own guilt—he was the older, the more experienced and the stronger. He should have stopped. . . He was suddenly aware that merely to think of being in her arms was to excite him. . .

He turned to let himself out, trying not to hear his father telling him that he was no son of his, that, after all, he had come back from America more unregenerate than when he had left, and that the best thing he could do would be to return there.

But none of that would help Stacy.

She knew. Oh, yes, she knew. The post had arrived and been distributed. There were letters for her, all dealing with business. Reports from Greaves at York, longer ones from Ephraim Blount in London, and a letter from Hamburg where the Bank had been doing business with some merchants of the old Hanseatic League, and her opinion was wanted on certain matters of importance.

But the letters of those around her were quite different. They were from friends and relatives, and their letters were chatty, gossipy, retailing the *on dits* which flew around London, or the great houses to which the nobility and great gentry—or, as it was sometimes known, the cousinry—retired during the winter months. And with the letters came newspapers, and among them, she knew, would be the sheet retailing the scandal about herself and Matt Falconer.

Even if the story had been a lie it would have stuck to them. But it wasn't a lie, and what Matt had forecast was coming true. More, the moment she walked into the drawing-room she knew that many there had already learned the delightful news: that Matthew Falconer, the renegade Lord Radley, already the leading player in one delightful scandal, was now the leading player in another. And, even more than that, the other player was the eccentric Bankeress, long known as an icy virgin, but who had been melted not by the summer rain but by the winter's frost!

Matt they had called the Bear. Quite wrong. He was her lion-man, and she was coming to understand that by refusing him she had been selfish, for it was he who stood to lose the most, just when the old scandal which had ruined him had finally died.

She sat on her own. None came near her. She had dressed in virginal white, as much to defy everyone as to proclaim to the world what was no longer the truth. She wore her collar of pearls again about her long and graceful neck, with one giant ruby, set about with seed-pearls, depending from it above her bosom. The dress itself was of the most elegant simplicity, with floating panels of gauze depending from the high waist above the smooth satin of her skirts. Her fan was white, her gloves and shoes equally so, and the small circlet in her hair was again of pearls.

Louisa came over to her, her face agitated. 'My love,' she began, her eyes brilliant with shock, 'I feel that you ought to know. . .'

Stacy leaned forward, put a gentle finger on Louisa's lips as though she were the old and wise one and Louisa her charge. 'Shush, my dear, I already do know, have known for some days. And so, I fear, does everyone else. We will not speak of it.'

'But. . .' began Louisa when the finger was removed.

'No buts, dear Louisa. You must be brave as I will be.'

How could she be so cool? was her companion's only thought. Caroline Bibury came in, moved straight to Stacy, took her hand and said, her eyes swimming, 'My dear, I am so sorry. I would have such creatures who write filth about us shot if I were in the Government. Bibury says that I must not exercise myself. He told me that you have known for some days. . . What can I say or do but offer you my most profound sympathy, and my admiration for your moral courage? We, by virtue of our rank and station, stand to be attacked, but this. . .this is the outside of enough. And poor Matt. . .'

Stacy's eyes filled with tears as the most extraordinary mixture of sentiments warred in her breast. For she knew that she was not innocent, and Caroline was assuming that she was, and she felt a cheat and a rogue for deceiving her. She was not sure how much Louisa knew or guessed, but kind Caroline was a different proposition altogether. She pressed the sympathetic hand which held hers. Looking about her, though, she noticed something odd. Only the senior men of the party were present. Earl Falconer, whose old face was so sad that she knew that he too had read the scandal sheet, was seated by the roaring fire. Beside him was Uncle Beauchamp, pulling his watch out to examine it as the normal hour for dinner had passed by and half the company were not yet present. The lawyer, Grimes, was sitting mumchance in a corner, watching, his eyes sardonic. And night was beginning to fall as the afternoon wore on.

She stood up, worried by she knew not what.

'What is happening, Caroline? Where is your husband and Anthony Beauchamp, Trot and the rest? Where are they? What is to do?'

Caroline, Lady Bibury, who had never run a great

bank, watched for signs of change in the money market, picked up hints and ideas from the movements of stocks and shares and the contents of speeches by members of the Government, had noticed nothing untoward. She looked puzzled, stared about her, said slowly, 'I only know that Bibury told me to go ahead. You are right. All of the younger men are absent. What can it mean?'

Stacy said, in the voice which she had often employed to dominate Ephraim Blount, Greaves, assorted bank clerks and the thieving manager at York, 'I don't know. But I intend to find out.' She picked up her fan. Louisa made to follow her, to have Stacy say, still in that cold, businesslike voice, 'No, stay where you are, I beg of you. I don't want anyone to follow me.' She waved down Caroline, who was beginning to rise, her face anxious.

Every female eye was on her as she crossed the room, straight-backed, head high, making for the door which led to the great entrance hall. Opening it, she saw at the bottom of the main stairway all the young men of the party. They had been lying in wait for Matt, who had just reached the last turn of the stairs before they opened on to the ground floor.

Anthony Beauchamp, his back to her, stood a little in front of the main group. He advanced on Matt, saying in a loud voice, 'Damn you, Matt Falconer. I want satisfaction from you for the slur you have brought on my poor cousin. I should have asked my father to have had you beaten from the door by the footmen before you ever set foot in Bramham. As it is, take this,' and before Bibury, who was plucking his sleeve and advising caution, could stop him, he struck Matt as hard as he could in the face, knocking him to the ground, and when Matt tried to rise was on him again.

Bibury and Trot pulled Anthony away. He was still

raving, his face purple. 'Satisfaction,' he roared at Matt. 'I want satisfaction from you, Falconer. You may choose what weapons you like. I shall take pleasure in killing you whatever the means I have to use.'

Matt had made no effort to defend himself. He was conscious of his guilt, of the misery which he had brought upon himself and Stacy by his own rash and ill-considered action. He rose slowly, said, his voice low but steady, 'I don't wish to fight you, Beauchamp, but I shall, and it will not be my own honour I shall be defending, but Miss Blanchard's.'

Which had Anthony raving again, shouting, 'You are not to name her. I will not have her named.'

Bibury said sharply to him, 'Be quiet, man. You heard what he said. Now let him choose his weapons, and we will decide the time and place for the action. Until then, all must be decorum. You must name your second, Radley—as must Beauchamp—and if you have no one here who will stand your second, then I shall do so, for form's sake.'

Stacy watched them, mute for once, and shaking inwardly, aware that her own delay had caused this. She decided to stop the folly being enacted before her. She might play a man's part when she ran the Bank, but she thoroughly disapproved of the whole code of honour which governed the lives of the men who belonged to the gentry and aristocracy. In the moment of silence which followed Bibury's statement she chose to speak.

'There will be no need for any action to take place. You, Cousin Anthony, are quite mistaken if you choose to provoke Lord Radley to a duel. He has already asked me to marry him, and I have agreed to accept his proposal. No one's honour is at stake here, least of all mine or Lord Radley's.'

All the men had turned and were staring at her, a different version of shock on each face, shock that not only should she have been present, but that she had chosen to speak so publicly before a party composed only of men. And of men engaged in an affair of honour—an occasion where women had no place.

Bibury released Anthony Beauchamp, who said hoarsely to Stacy, 'Cousin, you should not be here. It is neither fit nor proper. I am about to teach this fellow a lesson he will not live to remember.'

Stacy could see only one face, and that was Matt's. She had begun to shiver internally, but quelled the shivers, said in her best Bankeress voice, 'Oh, what nonsense, Anthony. Why should I not speak when I collect that the matter between you and Lord Radley is that of my honour, and that you are quite mistaken over the part he has played? Lord Radley and I have been grossly libelled, but it is no matter. We were waiting until we left Bramham before we announced our betrothal to the world but, seeing the misunderstandings that our natural desire for privacy has created, I release him from his vow of silence on the matter. We shall be married by special licence when we reach London, shall we not, my dear sir? No need for duellings and bravado; you may all wear wedding wreaths instead.'

She saw Matt walking towards her, the bruise on his face where Anthony had struck him slowly turning purple. He wore a small bandage on the hand which she had stabbed. He went down on one knee before her, said, 'Miss Blanchard, I honour you for your courage in speaking for me after such a public fashion. I respected your wish for silence, and respect the reason why you have now reversed it.'

A small hum of sound ran round the watching men. Anthony opened his mouth again, to protest, to reproach, no doubt. Bibury took him by the arm and said loudly, 'No need for bravado, indeed, Miss

Blanchard, nor any need for a duel. Let us all go into dinner. I, for one, am hungry.'

Anthony, his face white, hissed something in Bibury's ear as they all walked towards the drawing-room door, Matt and Stacy leading, her hand on his strong arm. Bibury shook his head and said mildly, 'You heard the lady, Beauchamp. There can be no grounds for reproaches, none at all. The first toast at dinner shall be to the prospective bride and groom.'

He threw open the door, and escorted Matt and Stacy through it. Matt had taken Stacy's arm, and led her to where Caroline, her face white, sat with Louisa Landen and Earl Falconer, all looking equally troubled.

'Caroline, my love,' Bibury told her gently, 'I think that your brother and Miss Blanchard have something important to tell you and your father.'

CHAPTER TWELVE

THE announcement that Matt Falconer, Lord Radley, was to marry the Bankeress, and soon, was exactly designed to set the Bramham house party alight. It would not be true to say that everyone was pleased by the news: Anthony Beauchamp, for one, was not, and it was to be supposed that Trot and the other young hopefuls were afflicted by the dismals once they realised that England's richest heiress outside the ranks of the nobility was denied to them.

Among those who were pleased was Matt's father, who was quite bemused by the news, coming as it did on the heels of the distressing interview with his son. Why in the world could Matt, once he had been challenged so ruthlessly, not have told him that he had proposed to, and been accepted by, the very lady whose virtue he had accused him of tampering with? He would never understand his wilful son, never.

It was perhaps as well that the exact truth was never revealed to him. Questioned by his father later that night, once they were alone and Stacy had retired, Matt offered no explanations, no extenuation for his strange behaviour. The fact that Anthony Beauchamp had secured the backing of the younger members of the party, before publicly challenging Matt over the insult offered to the woman to whom he was already secretly betrothed, could not be concealed from the rest of those at Bramham who were not in the know, and added to the Earl's confusion.

Anthony Beauchamp and Bibury were both reprimanded by Uncle Beauchamp, Anthony for his rash hot-headedness, Bibury for not having the sense to hold him in check. 'But by God, sir,' Anthony had exclaimed, exasperated, 'their betrothal having been secret, how could anyone be expected to know of it? As her nearest young relative it was my duty to defend her name. And, come to that,' he added, his blue eyes bright with suspicion, 'when *did* they become betrothed? They have hardly met since Pontisford, and what occurred there must be a matter for conjecture.'

'Then let it remain so,' his father instructed him. '"All's well that end's well", as the Bard once said, and for Radley to settle himself so well must be a source of congratulation to his father and all his relatives. As for the lady you and she are not suited to each other. She is older than you are, and doubtless a self-willed man like Radley will be better able to hold her in check than you would have been.'

'But I love her,' grumbled Anthony, half beneath his breath. 'And I doubt whether Matt Falconer does.'

'And that is no matter, either. There are plenty of pretty, biddable young girls who would be delighted for you to make them your wife.'

Again below his breath Anthony muttered, 'I don't want a pretty biddable young girl, I want Cousin Stacy.'

Cousin Stacy didn't know what she wanted. Somehow she had endured the polite uproar which had followed the announcement of her betrothal to Matt. His father had come over to her and said, 'Madam, I could hardly have expected my son to have made so worthy a choice. I understand that you both wish to be married as soon as possible. It is fortunate that Grimes is here. He may set all the legal formalities in train straight away. But it is not that which exercises my mind, it is my pleasure at welcoming you into my family. As I told you before, I knew and respected your father. I hope to love, as well as respect, his daughter.'

Whatever might be said in private, all that was said

in public was as proper as could be. Poor Trot, poor in every way, could only moan inwardly at the wretched luck that had handed the Blanchard wealth to a man who would be as rich as Croesus without it when he finally inherited the Falconer estates. But he, too, said all the right things on that interminable afternoon and evening which followed the revelation at the bottom of Bramham's stairs.

The only person to whom Stacy did not speak at any length was Matt himself. They were being watched so closely that they both, being a man and woman of some maturity of experience, in order to give nothing away, said as little as possible which was not light and innocuous. The private meat of their conversation, so to speak, would have to wait for the public hors d'oeuvres of it to be over.

Louisa, walking with Stacy to their suite of rooms, said timidly to her before they parted for the night, 'My dear, exactly how long is it since you accepted Lord Radley? I must say that I was as surprised by your news as the rest of the company.'

'I accepted him at exactly the moment at which it was proper for me to do so,' returned Stacy elliptically, and Louisa had to be content with that.

The servants were, as usual, wiser than their masters, knowing more of the truth than they did. Stacy and Matt's insistence on such a speedy wedding ceremony came as no surprise to them.

Matt, weary in body and soul, tired at having to behave in public with such circumspection, entered his bedroom to find Jeb there, laying his nightwear on the covers of the big four-poster bed which, he had been told, had once been slept in by the great Duke of Wellington himself.

Jeb, who would have had no more respect for the Duke than for Matt, said, 'So, you are to be turned off at last? Do I congratulate the Bankeress for capturing you? Or should my felicitations be more properly addressed to your good self? My own regret is that you didn't put a bullet into that pretty young fellow who calls himself her cousin.'

'My good self,' grated Matt, beginning to pull off the skin-tight clothing which was the current fashion, 'has only one wish at the moment, and that is for a good night's sleep. As for my future bride's cousin, however many bullets *he* had put in *me*, she would never have married him. Had she done so she would have eaten him in a week!'

'But you will eat her—or will the meal be mutual?' Jeb enquired suavely. 'At least your child will be legitimate now.' And he began to laugh. 'Is that why she accepted you?'

Matt, now naked, began to sponge himself down from the bowl of warm water which Jeb had poured out for him. He said, his voice muffled a little by the towel which he was using to dry himself, 'I don't think that she thought once about whether her child would be legitimate. It's my belief that she announced our engagement to stop an unseemly duel—for which I am grateful. I suspect I am more than a match for Anthony Beauchamp with either pistols, swords or fists, but honour alone would have prevented me from proving that I was.'

Jeb began to laugh uncontrollably. He threw Matt his nightshirt, spluttering, 'What a woman to win. By God, I'm reasonably happy to marry my Polly. She's a good girl, or was until I cozened her into bed, but she ain't a patch on the Bankeress for guts. I shall purely admire watching her tame you!'

A tawny head emerged from the ruffled neck of Matt's nightwear. He said gruffly, 'I shouldn't take any bets on that. I suspect a draw will be the result.'

* * *

Jeb wasn't the only man that night to discuss the outcome of such a bet. The comments of the women were more discreet, but followed roughly the same line. And, naturally, the question of whether the marriage was a forced one also exercised many minds.

The only response to gossip, Stacy felt, was to behave as normally as possible, to eat her breakfast, to talk briefly in the drawing-room to Caroline, and finally to retire to her own rooms—to sit by the fire, wondering what exactly she had done in handing herself over to Matt.

There was a knock on the door, not a timid knock, and of course it was Matt, looking larger and sterner than ever. He bowed to the rapidly departing Louisa—who was acknowledging that a betrothed couple might, ever under the strict etiquette then prevailing, safely be left alone together.

'I have come,' Matt told Stacy stiffly, 'not only to thank you for honouring me with your hand, but also to thank you for saving me from having to allow your cousin Anthony to put hole in me which might have proved fatal. I couldn't have put a bullet in him when he was in the right and I was in the wrong. I shall always remember, and treasure, your courage in speaking out.'

Stacy had never respected him more. She was suddenly aware that behind Matt's unconventional exterior was a man of impeccable honour—which made the details of the scandal which had destroyed his social position in youth even stranger. Stranger still was the manner in which he had behaved to her at Pontisford.

She murmured, 'It was the least I could do for you, sir, seeing that it was my dilatoriness in accepting your proposal which had brought you to such an unfortunate pass. I hope, also, that our betrothal has restored your credit with your father.'

None of this was what she wanted to say, it was all so stiff and stilted. And he was as stiff, too, running a hand under his carefully tied cravat and saying in a distant voice, 'Of course, the condition on which I offered our marriage still stands. One of convenience only, until our child is born—and after that we may honourably agree to go our separate ways. I have no particular wish to marry, as I am sure you have not——'

Oh, dear! Stacy's heart fell into her elegant kid slippers. She should have known. He didn't really want to marry that strange and eccentric creature the Bankeress. He must have had a syncope at Pontisford, and ravished her in the middle of it. He didn't, couldn't, care for her at all.

'I didn't want to marry in the first place,' she snapped at him, 'but, things being as they are, and seeing that for some reason which I cannot fathom we both ran mad at Pontisford, marriage is what we are doomed to. I must tell you that I have no intention of giving up my management of the Bank until my coming child compels me to do so. What you care to do with your life is of no consequence to me.'

And oh, what a damned lie that was! She cared most desperately, but if he was going to speak to her as bloodlessly as Ephraim Blount did, then she could not let him know that, whatever else he had done at Pontisford, he had caused Anastasia Blanchard to fall in love with him. She could no longer blind herself to that unwelcome piece of knowledge. And he, plainly, felt nothing for her—he cared only that their child might be legitimate.

'Nevertheless,' pursued Matt doggedly, wishing that his dear Lady Disdain would offer him something better than the cold face which she probably used when she was having thieving managers thrown into the street. He was a fool to think that she might care something for him—other than the moment of lust which had overcome them at Pontisford. 'Nevetheless, I have a duty to tell you what my plans will be once we *are* married.'

'Oh, that,' said Stacy as carelessly as she could, 'yes, that would be a piece of common courtesy, I agree.'

He wanted to jump on her, lift her out of the chair where she sat surveying him as coldly as if he were an insect—a stare he remembered from their earliest encounters—and shake her and kiss her until she lay panting against his heart.

And what a savage she would think him if he did any such thing. No, he must be as cold as she, and resign himself to having had her as his love, even if only for one night, only to lose her to the kind of marriage which he had always despised. A man and a woman tied together simply for the sake of two pieces of land and a son and heir to them. It was only too grimly appropriate that the busiest set of people involved in their marriage would be their lawyers, working out the details of the settlement of her estates and his. Grimes would be in his element.

'My plans,' he began, dragging his mind away from the cheerless prospect of an arranged and convenient marriage, the reason for which—an heir— had already been accomplished, 'are as follows. I regret that I shall have to leave England as soon as is decently possible to return to Virginia to settle the management of my estates in the United States. It is being borne upon me that my future, now that my brother has died, lies here. I shall be Earl Falconer one day, and the duties of a great estate will devolve upon me. I cannot neglect them, even though I might like to. I shall leave Jeb behind to be the overseer of my farm. I don't think that he wishes to stay here. His spiritual home is across the Atlantic.'

He did not say, As is mine, although he was thinking

it. He had not wanted Rollo to die, however much he had disliked his brother, because alive he would ultimately have become Earl Falconer and Matt would have remained a simple American planter. That dream was as dead as Rollo.

'I am sorry,' Stacy said truthfully. 'I know how much you love your adopted country.'

Matt waved a dismissive hand. 'No matter,' he told her. 'My one regret is having to leave you so soon after marriage, but I wish to be with you when our child is born, and to do that I must leave speedily, so that my early return is assured.'

He was speaking to her in the emotionless language of the world of banking and commerce—a language which Stacy had once thought was the only one which she would ever use. Pontisford had briefly introduced her to another, but that language seemed fated to be denied her in the future.

What would he say if she cast herself at his feet, crying, Damn everything, your and my duties, the Bank and the Falconer estates, and take me to Virginia with you, to stay there, for all I want is to be your true wife, and everything else can go hang?

Almost she did so, only unfortunately he continued, still emotionless, 'I know how much this marriage irks you, that you have no wish to surrender your independence. You may depend upon it that I shall make it as easy as possible for you to live as though it had never happened.'

His face was averted a little when he spoke, for he could not bear to look at her, knowing that they would be parted so soon and for so long. He remembered Camilla, thought bitterly, are all my loves to be doomed? But at least this love of mine is a strong woman, so I must be strong too.

Unknown to him, his strength was written on his face. Stacy, seeing it, stood up, began to move towards him, to say something of what was in her heart—and then, if he insisted on denying her, she would accept that denial, and learn to live with it.

She compelled him to look at her by the simple process of standing before him, her green eyes earnestly on his tawny ones. To be so near to him started her inward tremblings again, as though the child within her were already able to move, to tell her of his presence—something which she knew would not happen for another few months.

Unknown to her Matt begn to tremble too. Her scent, a compound of lemon and spices from the little bags of herbs which Polly had made up to store between the folds of her clothes, and from which the laundress at her London home had created the soft soap which she daily used, was temptation itself to him.

'Stacy,' he said hoarsely, putting out a hand to touch her chin, to lift it. His tawny eyes were suddenly glowing, the icy manner in which he had been speaking to her was suddenly gone. 'Oh, God, Stacy. . .'

He got no further. The magic moment which they were beginning to share, with Stacy turning longing eyes up towards him as he started to speak, was shattered. The door was flung open, to reveal Polly.

'Oh, Miss Stacy!' she exclaimed, taking in the scene before her as Matt stood back and the light which his impulsive action had lit in Stacy's eyes began to die. 'I'm so sorry. I thought that you were downstairs. I came. . .no matter. . .' And she shot out of the room as quickly as she had entered it.

Too late. Both Stacy and Matt had lost the impetus which was suddenly bringing them together. They were apart again, the spell broken.

Stacy put her hands behind her back and clenched them tightly. A lifetime of obeying her father, of suppressing her emotions, was preventing her from telling Matt what he would most have liked to hear.

As for Matt, he was so afraid of coercing her, a legacy of what had happened at Pontisford, that his usual forthright nature was strangely subdued.

He took up where he had left off, was busy outlining his—and her—future plans. 'We must, I fear, leave for London as soon as possible. My father will also be making plans to open Falconer House, off the Strand. I have spoken to Lord Beauchamp and I understand that he wishes to be present at the ceremony, and be responsible for you as your nearest living relative. I collect that you have no Blanchard relatives.'

Stacy was fascinated by this passionless and business-like recital, which seemed to be leaving so little to chance. 'Only a very aged great-aunt,' she told him, 'who has had nothing to do with either my father or me since I was a baby. She is now in her late eighties, lives at Bath, and has not left that city for these thirty years!'

'As Lord Beauchamp informed me. My father wishes us to be married at Falconer House, but I believe that your uncle and aunt Beauchamp would prefer the ceremony to be at their place in Bedford Square. I think that the decision should be yours.'

Stacy would have married Matt over the anvil at Gretna Green if she had believed that he loved her, but, seeing that he was all business, then so would she be.

'If Aunt and Uncle Beauchamp wish to extend such a kindness to me, then let it be Bedford Square.'

Matt nodded, still passionless, she noted sadly, the spark which had been so nearly lit between them quite extinguished. 'Most proper of you, madam, but no more than I would have expected of you.'

'You did not always think me proper,' Stacy offered a trifle dejectedly.

'You have my word,' he returned earnestly, 'that I

most truly regret my wretched behaviour to you at Pontisford and elsewhere!'

Which wasn't what she wanted to hear from him at all. She remembered the burning fire which had raged between them from the moment that she had mistaken him for the butler, and which had consumed them both on that fatal night. Whatever could have happened to it? Oh, it still raged in her heart, but it could find no outlet, no way in which it could light a similar fire in him.

The rest of their conversation was conducted in the same sad and emotionless tone. They would live at Stacy's home in London until Matt took ship for the States. Polly and Jeb were to be married quietly on the same day as Matt and Stacy, and would accompany him to Virginia. Stacy would work at the Bank until she grew too big for decorum and would then settle herself wherever she thought proper—in the country, he hoped, where she and the child could breathe the pure air, so unlike London's smoke and fumes.

At last they were finished. There was another knock on the door. This time it was a footman carrying a silver salver with coffee for them, and all that he interrupted was an icy exchange of courtesies.

Matt became a little more human, said, as Stacy poured coffee for them, 'I see, madam, that you are looking more in health than you were when you first arrived at Bramham. The child does not yet discommode you?'

The child, the child. He would never have offered her marriage if it had not been for the existence of the child, living proof of their scandalous behaviour which would, without marriage, effectively have ruined them both.

She replied, her throat closing as she did so, 'No, I am well now. I had some sickness when I first came to Bramham, but that has passed. If, once we are married,

I do experience distress, I shall be able to send for a doctor. At the moment common sense must be my guide, since no one must yet know that I am already pregnant!'

'Ah, yes.' Matt was almost satirical. 'Common sense! That has always been your guide, I believe.'

'Except once!' she could not help shooting back at him. 'Except once!'

And that, Stacy was dismally aware, was enough to stop any further conversation between them, other than on the most neutral matters such as the probable date of their departure from Bramham, the wedding, and her own plans to notify her lawyers to meet Grimes and his cohorts as soon as possible. The impossible marriage was to be put in train.

CHAPTER THIRTEEN

'So,' Matt remarked halfway through dinner on their wedding-day, 'it is accomplished. For good or ill you are Lady Radley now. I offer you a toast, madam. To you and our future.'

Stacy raised her glass to him and, as cool as he, offered him a toast in exchange. 'And to you, sir, and any child which may spring from our union.' Which was as plain as she dared be, surrounded as they were by servants who might suspect why they had married so precipitately but could not actually know.

He smiled a trifle ruefully at that, and later, when they had moved to the drawing-room, a stately place which owed everything to Louis Blanchard's taste and nothing to Stacy's, she said to him, looking around at its ornate splendours, 'Had you ever thought of visiting this room, I doubt that you could have anticipated the reason why you might find yourself in it!'

At last she had provoked his stern face into something resembling genuine amusement. 'Perhaps, madam, the speed with which I have arrived here after our first meeting is as remarkable as the reason for my being here at all.'

Stacy's response was a mute one, a nod of agreement. Indeed, long afterwards, looking back at her wedding-day and the events which led up to it, she always marvelled at how short a time it had taken to turn her life upside-down. There she was at the beginning of November, living the life which she had led since her late teens and then, in a few short weeks, all was changed, and changed forever.

She had thrown her reputation to the four winds,

been initiated into the delights of the bed, become pregnant and accepted marriage from a man whom in the terms of their world she had barely become acquainted with and wasn't sure she even liked—lust being a different thing. After that she had been united to him in the most hurried wedding-ceremony, although their union was merely a legal one, the body having nothing to do with it, and in consequence had seen the old Stacy Blanchard disappear to become Lady Radley—and who was she?

Always, when thinking of it, her thoughts became as breathless as that time itself, as though, the grammar of her life having been destroyed, the grammar of her expressing what had happened to her had disappeared as well!

Their wedding-day had been fine at first. Later, after the ceremony, a winter thunderstorm had followed, out of a clear sky, as though the gods were expressing their anger at the hollowness of what she and Matt had done. They were to spend their empty honeymoon at Stacy's London home, which Matt had visited for the first time twenty-four hours before the wedding. The cool nature of their first meal together as man and wife was to set the tone for their married life before Matt left for Virginia, taking a tearful Polly and a happy Jeb with him.

On that last late January day, when he came to see her before leaving London to take ship, Stacy was seated at her desk in what had been her father's study. She had cancelled her visit to the Bank, but was working on some proposition which Ephraim Blount had put before her. She was trying not to think of what Matt's departure meant to her.

He had been scrupulously kind and distant in manner to her from the moment that the Bishop had made them man and wife. No one could have been more considerate. Only afterwards, when he had gone, did she realise that since the ceremony he had not so much as touched her, indeed had scrupulously avoided all contact with her.

And so things had remained. In front of others they were charmingly polite, the very picture of a newly married pair. But once alone the politeness remained, and some of the charm, but the rapport which Stacy had hoped that they might somehow find was missing.

So now he was standing before her, dressed for travelling. She thought that he looked gaunt, that since their marriage he had lost weight, so that the cheekbones in his face were starker than ever, adding to its strength.

'Madam,' he began, and then fell silent. There was nothing of the semi-bantering, semi-mocking manner which he had adopted with her before they were married. All was deadly seriousness. Stacy thought that she preferred the lighter manner of their illicit relationship to the gravity of their legal one—but she could not say so.

Over the few weeks of their marriage she was coming to understand that, however much her father's tuition had made her ready to run the Bank, it had done nothing to enable her to express the feelings of her heart.

'Yes?' Stacy prompted, trying to help him, but in the doing she remained so calm that Matt, who had thought that before he left her he might fall on his knees before her and tell her how much he had come to love her, how little he wished to leave her, was quite daunted by such cold composure—the composure that Louis Blanchard had bred in his child, unaware that it might act like a killing frost quelling an unspoken but truly felt love.

Also, at the last, he didn't want to leave her—and miss how much she would change and blossom as the child grew in her. Some intuition, foreign to the hard man he usually was, told him that the coming child would change her, was already changing her, and this he would miss—although he fully intended to return well before their child was born. Would she always remain his dear Lady Disdain, so cold and controlled that his heart wept within him, that heart which he had once thought that he had left in the grave with his dear, lost love Camilla?

'I have to tell you, madam,' he said, as cold and controlled as she was, for he would not force himself on her, as that would be to behave as Rollo had behaved to Camilla—with such shocking results—'that all is ready for my journey to Virginia. Jeb, I need hardly inform you, can scarce wait to be gone. Polly, now, is a different matter. She wails that she does not like to leave her dear Miss Stacy to the ministrations of a half-trained girl, but she knows that her duty to Jeb, and to their child, demands that she make a new life for herself in Virginia.

And I, thought Stacy, screaming inside herself, could not I make a new life for myself in Virginia? For there is only the Bank to keep me here, but you have never once expressed the wish that we might settle there as Jeb and Polly are doing. But I suppose that true love lies between them, and it is plain that you regret what we did together at Pontisford, since now you can scarce bear to touch me.

She forgot that she was giving him no reason to believe that she felt for him anything other than mere tolerance for someone who thought that he owed her reparation for having forced himself on her and caused her to commit an act which she had subsequently bitterly regretted. The loneliness which had been the constant companion of both of them throughout their lives had only been endured by their proud rejection of any form of surrender in the way of asking anyone for love and pity. Even Louisa had never broken through the shell of pride which had hardened around Stacy's heart.

Matt, likewise, had taught himself to depend only himself—to love was, in the end, he discovered, to experience punishment and pain, and his heart shrank, as Stacy's did, from commitment to another. Worse, ever since he had married her he had feared to touch her, for he knew that to do so would result in rousing him to the degree where he might force himself upon her as he had done at Pontisford. And that he had vowed never to do again.

Stacy, still a prisoner of her upbringing, said, in that deadly polite fashion which had Matt hungering to smash it, but not knowing how to do so without injuring them both, 'I hope that you have fair winds on your journey, both to the Americas and back again. I shall write to you in the hope that some of my letters may reach you.' For she knew how untrustworthy communication was across 'the steep Atlantic stream', as the poet Milton had it.

'Indeed——' Matt bowed '—and I know that you will look after yourself, and our child, for the one thing which I most admire in you, madam, is your practicality—a trait few women share with you.'

Well, doubtless he meant that for a compliment, but Stacy would have traded it for any sign of true affection, however small. But, asking for nothing, she received nothing. She rose, accompanied him to the door, to the entrance hall where Jeb and Polly were waiting, and Louisa stood in the shadows.

Polly was tearful again, flung her arms around Stacy and sobbed her farewells. Jeb bowed before giving her his hand, as though she were a man, and then, suddenly, impulsively, as though they were equals, not mistress and almost-servant, he took her in a giant bear hug—of the kind she would have liked from Matt. He whispered in her ear before he released her, 'I will look after him for you, madam, and see that he returns in one piece, and by then I hope that you will have the wit to find one another, for you were meant to be the two halves of a broken coin brought together, or a split apple, if only you and he had the wit to see it!'

Matt, astonished, watched as, impulsively and warmly, Stacy kissed his friend on the cheek, thinking jealously, Why could she not favour me like that? But, like Stacy, asking for nothing, he received nothing, and she watched him follow Polly and Jeb out of the ornate front door and into the waiting chaise which was to take them on their journey north to Liverpool, where they would take ship for Baltimore.

The chaise was driven down the short avenue which led to the iron gates which separated them from the road to central London. Stacy's eyes followed it. Outwardly she stood calm and composed beside an anxious Louisa, who was worried for her charge. Inwardly she was shrieking, He is my love, and I have been cruel to him, and I have sent him away. If he could but have granted me one word of love, or had asked me properly, I would have gone with him to the ends of the world, shoeless and in rags, rather than live here in my meaningless wealth and comfort.

All the years of her father's instruction were being stripped away from her, and the final words which haunted her as, straight-backed, she walked into the house with Louisa were, Too late! Too late!

And Matt Falconer? Looking out of the chaise window as he was whirled away out of her life, he also was consumed with the most bitter regret, that he had left her without telling her of his love, and the same words echoed in his head, even to the moment when he boarded ship and watched England's shores slide away into the distance.

Too late!

* * *

Inexorably the world swung around the sun, and the seasons changed, and with those changes Stacy changed too, the child growing big within her. The day finally came when she left the Bank's office, not to return, she said, until the child was born. Nothing came from America, which was no surprise, until one day in late May a packet arrived containing letters from Matt, Jeb and Polly. They had docked safely at Baltimore, and were on their way to Virginia.

'I trust, Lady Radley,' Matt had written in a hand as big and bold as himself, 'that you and the child thrive, that my business here will soon be conducted, and that it will not be long before I see you again. I remain your most devoted husband and servant, Matthew Falconer.'

'Devoted husband and servant'. Well, they were hardly words of love, Stacy thought, but they were better than nothing. The rest of the letter was like himself, straightforward, telling of the sea journey—that Polly had been ill, so that her coming child had been feared for, but that she and the child had survived the crossing, and were now well and fit. Jeb and Polly's letters were like themselves too. Polly's was full of ill-spelt excitement, and her sadness that 'Miss Stacy'—and who was she now?—had not travelled with them. Jeb's entertained her by its impudent bluntness.

> Mad Matt is madder than ever, and I know that it is because he regrets that we are not all of us, including Mad Matt's wife, returning to settle permanently in Virginia. When I taxed him over his desire to return to the land of the unfree, his reply was as stiff as you might suppose it: that he had his duty to perform to all his vast estates in England now that he was the heir, and now that he himself was on the way to having an heir. I made so bold as to suggest that he might as well have put a deputy in charge of what he owned in England as easily as he

was putting me in charge in Virginia, and stayed in Virginia himself! I then had to endure a sermon on logic-chopping for my pains.

Almost as an afterthought, with a different pen and in different ink, he had written:

I pray you, madam, for the love and gratitude I bear him—he having saved my life—that when he returns to you you prove kind to him, or shall I advise him, that failing that, he must return to Virginia and I will make a burnt offering of myself by returning to run Falconer lands in England! You see what a sacrifice I am prepared to make for you both.

Tears gathered in Stacy's eyes as she put the letter down. She rose and walked to the window to see coming up the drive, towards the house, a coach with the Falconer arms on its side—a white shield with a black falcon, its wings outspread on it, a ring in its silver beak. She knew that Caroline Bibury was due in town, and had written that she would visit as soon after her arrival as was possible, but surely she would have come in her own carriage, not her father's?

She turned away from the window, but not before she had seen the footmen jump down from the box, one to throw the door open and the other to hand down the Right Honourable the Earl Falconer, Matt's father. Now, what was he doing, visiting his errant son's wife?

Stacy was soon to find out. The butler came to enquire whether she was receiving and, on being told yes, presently escorted my lord in, alone, no Caroline with him. She thought that he had aged since she had seen him at Christmas, was a little more stooped.

He bowed over her hand, and then Louisa's—Louisa being fully recovered from her Christmas malaise.

Once again Stacy saw the resemblance to Matt, and saw that in his youth he had been as vibrant a man as his absent son was.

'It is good of you to receive me,' he told her, before taking a seat. 'I arrived in town but two nights ago, and I do not intend to stay long. I am merely here to do some necessary business. I visited Blanchard's this morning to pay you my respects, only to be told that you will be away until after your child is born. I trust I see you well?'

Stacy smiled at him. 'Very well, sir. And you?'

'Tolerably, madam, tolerably. As well as one of my advanced years is ever well in London. I shall not be truly well until I am back in the Yorkshire countryside again. It is of that which I wished to speak to you. I cannot think that being in London during the summer is good either for you or for my coming heir, and since it has been the practice these many years for the Falconer heir to be born at The Eyrie—most fitting a name in the circumstances—I am here to ask you to remove to Yorkshire until the birth is over.

'My dear Caroline and her husband will be returning with me, and it would please an old man to look after his son's wife in his son's absence. It is commendable that not only does his duty demand that he give up his home in Virginia, to devote himself to his life as the Falconer heir, but that also his duty demands that he return to see that his affairs are wound up there in proper form.'

He had been speaking with great conviction and great formality, and then, suddenly dropping all formality, he said, almost as blunt as Jeb would have been, 'Oh, madam, my son and I have been at outs these many years, and it is now my one wish that we shall be at ins again, and what better thing can I do than care for his wife? I shall send for the best doctor from London for you, well before my grandchild is born, so have no fears on that score.'

What could she say? The old Stacy, if she had accepted his offer at all, would have made a cool and distant answer of acceptance, not letting her emotions show, but the months of carrying his grandchild and Matt's child had changed her, had softened her. Impulsively, her eyes filling with tears, she put out a warm young hand to take his cool old one which lay loosely on his black silk-clad knee.

'Oh, sir,' she told him, 'you do me a great honour. Of course I will come. I have never been part of a family, you know, have only ever had my dear Louisa to care for me. I am sure that Matt. . .Lord Radley. . . would be happy to learn that I shall be staying in his childhood home. He said before he left that he hoped that I would leave London to have our child in the healthy country air.'

This pleased the old man, she could tell, almost as much as her agreement to go to Yorkshire did. She would form part of his train when he travelled home again, he told her, 'And I have already sent word to The Eyrie that all must be made ready for you by the time we arrive.'

All the way north Stacy could not but think of the last journey she had made through the cold and the snow, and that the result of it was that she arrived at The Eyrie under the summer sun, a woman who was happy to live in idleness, so that her child might be born safely—even though both the Earl and Caroline protested a little when she insisted on walking out each day, as she had always been accustomed to.

Her rooms looked out over a lake with a folly in the shape of a miniature temple before it. It was there that she walked each day, sometimes with Louisa in attendance and sometimes Martha Williams, Polly's successor. There she sat in a large armchair, or reclined on a sofa fetched from the folly, watching the ducks paddle by, dozing a little, doing tapestry-work, reading, and altogether being as idle as a fine lady was expected to be, instead of being the Bankeress, that unfeminine model of diligence. It was as though she was making up for all the years of hard work which she had spent first with her father and then alone, after his death.

The only thing lacking was Matt himself, and, as if to remedy that lack, after many months' absence from them he suddenly began to walk in her dreams again. He was the lion-man, golden against the blue of the sky, tawny all over, skin and hair both. Sometimes he was walking and sometimes he was running on a parched and sun-baked plain, a dog, a large one, something like a wolfhound, following him. Sometimes he crouched by a cave at night, feeding a fire, the dog now lying beside him. Always the dog was present and always the dream ended in the same way. He would suddenly see her. His eyes would light up, she would run towards him, and he towards her, to take her in his arms, to. . .

And then she would wake up, to find herself alone, the ready tears about to fall, asking herself whether when. . .if. . .he returned she would still be able to be as frank and free with him in reality as she was in her dreams.

'Did Matt ever have a dog?' she asked the Earl one evening when they sat together talking after they had finished playing a rubber of whist.

The Earl answered her, looking a little puzzled by her question, 'Oh, I don't think so, no.'

Caroline, who was helping her husband to put away the impediments of the game, looked up to say, 'Oh, but he did, Father, don't you remember? He had a wolfhound, Prince; he was very fond of it, and Prince was very fond of him. When Prince was. . .killed Matt was broken-hearted, said that he would never have another dog. I would have thought that you would remember how he grieved over him.'

'Killed?' Stacy's voice was almost that of the Bankeress again, cold and hard, detecting a false note in something which she had been told. She saw the Earl change colour, saw that Caroline's own colour was high. 'How killed?'

Her voice was so peremptory, so commanding that Lord Bibury looked curiously at her, and Caroline answered her unthinkingly. 'It was an accident,' she said slowly. 'Rollo shot Prince by mistake. . . Matt took it very badly.'

So Rollo, the brother whom Matt never mentioned, whose wife he had supposedly run off with, had shot Matt's dog—and the Earl had chosen to forget that he had done so.

'How old was he?'

'Who, the dog?' Caroline appeared to be genuinely bewildered.

Stacy's sigh was impatience itself. She was the Bankeress again, questioning a prevaricating clerk, and the whole company, which included Caroline's other sister, Georgiana, and her husband, Dean George Tranter, were staring at her, good manners forgotten.

'No, Matt, I meant. How old was he? And Rollo—how old was he?' Stacy had thought it odd that no one ever spoke of Rollo, who had after all been their eldest brother and the heir, and had died comparatively recently.

'He was thirteen. Rollo was twenty-one. Matt was the youngest of us.'

Georgiana, a handsome woman, a little thrusting, determined one day to thrust her husband into a bishopric, exclaimed decisively, 'Oh, come, Caro, you were always too tender-hearted! You knew perfectly well, even if Papa didn't, that Rollo shot Prince because Matt loved him so. Matt and Frank could never have anything without Rollo wanting it. Rollo asked Matt to give him Prince and Matt refused. A week later Rollo shot Prince—accidentally, of course.' Her sneer as she said the last sentence was palpable.

An appalled silence followed. Stacy had got the answer she wanted and had, intuitively, half known was coming. Or was it the dream, where Matt roved a strange countryside, always with a dog beside him, which had told her? She had never seen him with a dog in real life.

She shivered involuntarily. The Earl saw her do so and said, 'Georgiana, I am surprised that you should make such an accusation about a brother who is dead, and cannot defend himself. If Rollo said it was an accident, done when we were all out shooting, as I now remember, then an accident it was.'

Georgiana sat down, picked up her canvaswork, abandoned for the game of whist, shrugged, and drawled, 'He never lacked a defender so long as you were there to defend him, Papa. Even now he's dead you can't acknowledge what a beast Rollo was. It's time you faced the truth. I heard him laughing about what he'd done with that groom of his. If he couldn't have Prince then he'd make sure Matt wouldn't, was the gist of it.'

The Earl's face was grey. He turned to Caroline, who was twisting her hands nervously together. 'Do you believe this to be true, Caroline?'

She nodded reluctantly. 'Yes, Papa. I was with Georgie when we heard him telling Yates—that was his groom's name, I remember—what he had done.'

Another silence fell as the Earl digested a bitter truth which he had long refused to recognise as a truth. Stacy was suddenly horrified at what she had uncovered, even if the sad story which she had just heard might make his father think a little differently about Matt. She avoided everyone's eye, cast off the mask of the Bankeress, picked up her own canvaswork and began to stitch as though her life depended on it. Silence fell again as each member of the party took refuge in some occupation, however trivial.

The Earl rose heavily, looking old. 'I should not be ungrateful to you, Caroline and Georgiana, for at long last telling me something which I should have known before. I think I will retire early, if you would all excuse me. I would like to reflect over what I have just learned when I am alone.'

Everyone, including Stacy, stood—to watch him walk slowly away, his years suddenly pressing heavily on him.

George Tranter began to reproach his wife, 'No need for that, my dear——' only for her to interrupt him spiritedly.

'Nonsense, my love. It's time he faced that, and even worse truths, about Rollo. Matt was always Rollo's victim, and it was not the worst thing which Rollo did to him, by any means——'

This time the Dean managed to silence her by thundering, 'My love, *no*. You have said enough. Matt's wife is here. You will distress her.'

Stacy shook her head, replied as steadily as she could, 'No, it was my own insistent questioning which provoked this. . .incident, and I apologise for it.'

Lord Bibury, who had had a soft spot for her ever since the night when she had publicly proclaimed her betrothal to Matt, came over to sit beside her and take her hand—she had laid her embroidery down. 'No, my dear. You must not reproach yourself. You naturally wished to learn about your husband's past. It was your bad luck that you hit upon something which had long been hidden.'

No, it had not been bad luck at all. She had, after some curious fashion, known what she was doing, even as she had badgered Caroline. She often knew when people were lying, or concealing the truth from her, as Caroline had been doing when she had spoken of Matt's dog. It was a talent which she had inherited from Louis Blanchard, and of which, when she had spoken to him of it, he had said, 'All the Blanchards have possessed it, my dear, and whether it is a blessing or a curse, who is to say?'

Later, in bed, she asked herself what the real truth was in the story of Matt's running off with his brother's wife, for there was a false note in that tale, she was sure, and one day, for Matt's sake she would try to find out what it was. Meantime, she must watch and wait for him.

Several days later Stacy was doing exactly that in front of the little temple. Martha had wandered off—doubtless to meet an off-duty footman, she was sure—and she was quite alone, a book of Lord Byron's earlier poems on her knee—all her reading was frivolous these days; she had no time for Blackstone now.

The afternoon was warm, she was reclining on the sofa which had been carried out for her, and she could see the ducks on the lake, and one small rail, who had left the water and was skittering about in front of her. The sun and the silence lulled her into the easy sleep of a woman who was now more than seven months gone. She realised with a sense of shock, just before consciousness left her, that Matt had come back into her dreams on the very day when she had felt his child stir within her.

So it was natural that he should come to her again, as she lay sleeping in the grounds of the home that he had loved, and that she should, in her dream, stretch her hand out to his dog, and call him Prince, and that Matt should smile at her as she did so. This time he didn't embrace her, but took her hand, the dog walking along behind them. And how had she known that Matt had once owned a dog and had loved him? She had never seen him with one, which was strange for a man who loved animals and the countryside.

This afternoon his embrace came at the end of their walk, and as he took her in his arms she awoke, as she always did—to see him standing there, tall and bronzed, an expression almost of awe on his face at the sight of her, big with his child. . .

CHAPTER FOURTEEN

BUSY though he had been during the short time he had spent in Virginia, Matt had found that he could not banish Stacy from either his daytime or his night-time thoughts. Camilla's death, and the manner of her dying, had made such a strong impression on him that he had told himself that he would never marry; any dealings he had with women would be both passing and superficial. He had never deceived his partners: he always made it plain from the beginning that any liaison he entered into would be temporary.

And now, in any pause in his work, when his mind began to wander, he found Stacy there with him. Always she was as she had been on that fatal night: wild-eyed, face aflame, her whole body vibrant and ready for him. Oh, he hungered for her as he had never hungered for anyone. With Camilla he had been her knight—protective, always ready to defend her, his love a gentle thing, as she had been gentle. He had been little more than a boy, after all, and chivalry as much as love had motivated him from the first moment he had ever seen her, shy and out of her depth at a grand ball, waiting for someone to rescue her—which he had done.

But Stacy! From the first she had been as fierce with him as he had been with her. She had traded him word for word, had stared him down, and when finally they had fallen into bed together it had been a contest of equals. As for shyness and needing to be rescued... He chuckled to himself a little wryly whenever he thought of the night when *she* had rescued *him* from the unwanted duel with Anthony Beauchamp. She had faced everyone down, had turned the whole business around, had been as bold in public as she was reputed to have been in private in York when dealing with her dishonest manager. She was quite the last kind of woman whom he could ever have imagined himself as finding attractive—but being absent from her told him that he loved her to distraction, that what he had felt for Camilla, although sweet and true, paled beside it.

He had concluded his business as quickly as he could, seen Jeb and Polly settled into the home which had been his, and had taken the first boat back to England on which there was a spare passage. All the way from Southampton to London he had had but one thought in his head and that was the hope that she was waiting for him. He had never thought of the child at all. It was as though once he had left Stacy behind in England she had turned back into the Amazon she had been at Pontisford, defying and mocking him every time they met.

By God, she was a woman in a thousand, and so he would tell her, and when he had done so they would celebrate his return in the most time-honoured way. He was burning as his coach turned into the drive of her home. . .

Only to discover that she was no longer there, had travelled to Yorkshire, to The Eyrie, of all places, to have her child. So there was nothing for it but to go and see Grimes, to discover that the improvements which he had asked to be made at Pontisford so that it would be habitable again had all been set in train, and then to race north to be reunited with her.

Impatience rode with him until The Eyrie came into view, and he was being welcomed into the entrance hall. Servants had gathered to strip his chaise of his luggage, to escort him to his room, except that that was not the thing which was most on his mind.

'Lady Radley,' he said eagerly, waving aside enquiries about his journey from Talbot, his father's secretary. 'Will someone please inform Lady Radley that I have returned?'

It was his father who, drawn by the noise of his arrival and coming to discover what was toward, told him that his wife was in the grounds by the lake, as was her wont on fine days.

Matt found himself so impatient that he was barely able to be civil to anyone, either his father or his sisters. Habit and long training rendered him apparently so. He allowed himself to be exclaimed over, congratulated by his brothers-in-law on his healthy colour—which his sisters deplored—and answered his father's questions on how he had fared in Virginia.

Finally he allowed himself to say, 'Pray send no messenger to Lady Radley. I will inform her myself of my return,' and was out of the door, still in the clothes in which he had travelled from London.

The Earl raised expressive eyebrows, but said nothing. If there were times when he had had doubts about the depth of his son's feelings for the remarkable woman whom he had married, then Radley's obvious desire to be with her again as soon as possible went a long way towards dispelling them. He had assumed that the marriage was that strange thing in their world, a love-match, by the unorthodox way in which it had come about, and Radley's conduct seemed to bear this out. What his son's wife felt for her husband was another matter.

Half running across the park to find Stacy again, Matt remembered himself and settled down into something resembling a determined stroll. With his good long sight he could see that she was alone, lying on a sofa, unmoving, a book upon her knee. Neither Louisa nor any other escort appeared to be with her.

His last few strides brought him before her. She was asleep, but it was not that which knocked the breath from his body, but the sudden sight of her, big with his child. He shook his head disbelievingly. How could he have thought that after all these months he would find her as he had first seen her, tall and virginally slender? Instead, lying before him was no airy nymph but his wife, a fulfilled woman. . .who opened her eyes to look at him at the very moment when the reality of her condition smote him hard.

Matt had thought often and often of how he would fall on his knees before her, to tell her of his love, of the passion which he felt for her, and would shortly hope to demonstrate. . . What a fool he had been, for here was a woman who carried his child, who was smiling at him, trying to sit up and finding it difficult because of her condition. How graceless of him it would be to babble of love and passion to a woman who was carrying the result of it—she would think him a heartless boor to try to force himself upon her in her present state. She deserved his care, his compassion, more than anything else.

'Matt!' she exclaimed as he bent over her solicitously to kiss her rosy cheek, his face tender.

'Oh, madam——' and his voice was thick with emotion '—do not discommode yourself, I beg of you. Lie still. There is no need for formal greetings between us, no need at all.'

Stacy smiled, but her answer to him was as forthright as anything which the Bankeress would have said before she had met and surrendered to the man in front of her. 'Oh, Matt. I am not ill. I am having a child, and that is a condition which most women endure, and I have no desire, no desire at all, to be carried about before it is necessary. And now let me tell you how well you look, and, in return, you must tell me all your news.'

He was drinking in the soft lines of her face as she settled herself back on the pillows. She had blossomed and matured since he had last seen her. Her beauty was no longer so sharp, so haughtily dominant; there was a touching quality about it; at least, it touched him. Was this what happened to a woman when she ceased to add up columns of figures, or was it the effect of the child within her?

But Stacy's outward appearance, he noted with amusement, had not changed the cutting edge of her mind. She was as keenly intelligent as she had ever been. She listened to him as he told her of his adventures, saying as he finished, 'You remind me of what Shakespeare said when he wrote of Othello telling Desdemona of *his* adventures at the beginning of their tragedy: "She lov'd me for the dangers I had pass'd, And I lov'd her that she did pity them." I hope our play has a better ending than theirs!' And her green eyes teased him.

'Loved, madam, loved?' he repeated softly, bending forward. 'You said "loved". Is that a current description of your feelings for me, or a forecast?'

Stacy trembled beneath the intensity of his tawny gaze. He was more leonine than ever. He had pulled his cravat loose and she could see the bright golden hairs at the base of the powerful brown column of his throat. For once she regretted the child—which leaped inside her to reproach her for her desire to be slim and graceful again so that she would be able to demonstrate her love for him without having to wait.

'Time will serve to reveal all. Of that I am sure,' she began, her eyes mischievous, but before she could continue the child kicked her again, so that she cried out.

Matt's eyes widened; all thoughts of love fled at once. 'You are in pain?' he exclaimed. 'You must tell me if it is too much for you to sit here talking to me.'

To his surprise, Stacy smiled gently, even as her mouth twisted a little at the end, as the child reminded her of its existence. 'Oh, no, the pain is light, but it comes unexpectedly, without warning, so that I cry out with it. Your son and heir wishes to remind me that I must not give all my attention to his father. See——' and, to his surprise and astonishment, as well as his pleasure, she took his large hand and placed it on the curve of her stomach so that he could feel the wave of movement which a tiny kicking foot was creating.

They sat thus for a moment, eye to eye, Matt's wide. He thought that her forthrightness was so admirable that he wished that there were some tangible way in which he could reward her, other than by a passionless kiss. The lack of passion was for his sake: he was still afraid to touch her for fear of what that touch might do to him, especially after so many months of abstinence.

To walk his mind into neutral ground he told her gravely, 'By the by, madam, I forgot to tell you that Mr Jeb Priestley asked me to give you his respects.'

Stacy blinked naughtily at him. 'Now *that* I do not believe. Jeb has never respected anyone.'

'Oh, but he respects you. He told me that had I not existed, and he had met you, he would have done his best to convince you that despite the difference in station between the pair of you a marriage with him would have been made in heaven.'

For a moment Stacy was silent, contemplating a world in which Matt did not exist and Jeb Priestley pursued her. What a strange might-have-been that conjured up!

'But he has Polly,' she offered gravely.

'So he has, and she is good for him. She ignores his flights of fancy, and her only care is to look after him.'

'Now that might be a text for me to follow with you, when once our little monster is born,' she told him, her eyes closing.

No matter what she had said, Matt thought, looking

at the delicate mauve shadows below her eyes and the white line around her mouth, carrying his child was tiring her, and he could suddenly understand why she had found refuge in The Eyrie.

To his astonishment he saw that she had fallen gently and sweetly to sleep again, even as they spoke, and when Martha returned he ordered her to look after her mistress while he walked back to the house to find the chair in which his mother had been pushed around the grounds when she was carrying him. He would push Lady Radley home, he said. 'And you must be sure to await my return,' he told Martha a little severely, 'for I know that your mistress will try to walk back: her will is stronger than her body at the moment.'

His head was awhirl, as Stacy's was when she awoke to find him and the wheeled chair waiting for her. There was such tenderness in his strong face that she wanted to cry gently at the sight. Tears had come easily to her during this last stage of her pregnancy, and the reality of Matt's presence was so much stronger than the image of him which walked her dreams that she was almost overwhelmed by it.

Matt was surprised by the transformation which the Bankeress had undergone. He had thought that she might resent her coming motherhood; he had not imagined that she would embrace it with such passion. But then he remembered how hard she had worked under difficulties at Pontisford... Yes, his heart told him, she puts *her* whole heart and mind into everything she does. And, knowing that, I also know that if she is to be a mother, then she will, no doubt, be the best of mothers.

Another thought struck him, an unpleasant one. And shall I see her after the birth, or will she insist on the strict letter of our agreement, that once the child is born and settled we part? In the joy of seeing her again he had quite forgotten the conditions to which they had agreed before he had gone to Virginia!

Unaware of all these seething emotions boiling about her, Martha trotted happily beside them, holding a parasol over Stacy's head to shield her from the sun. Together she and Matt helped her from the chair and into the house. Stacy had found walking troublesome these last few weeks for the child was large, and she had begun to worry that the birth might be difficult because of it.

Matt, however, seemed determined to save her from all discomfort, for once she was out of the chair he carried her into the house to the drawing-room, where, although dinner would shortly be served, Caroline Bibury had ordered tea for them as soon as their small procession had come into sight, and had had the big glass doors to the garden thrown open so that they might sit in the shade of the awning above it.

The warmth of early July enveloped them. Caroline had tactfully left them alone. Stacy gave a small sigh of pure contentment. Matt leaned forward, said softly, 'Did you miss me, Stacy? I missed you. How strange it is that I calculate that we have spent less than a month in one another's company, that in our early time together all we did was quarrel, and yet every day I turned to say something to you—and you were not there.'

Stacy's heart beat in time with her child's. Now it suddenly beat in time with his words. Surprisingly she found her throat thick with tears. She remembered words he had said then, and also Poxon's, flung at her in rage and contempt on his last day at the York bank. Was it possible that Matt could truly feel for her what she had come to feel for him?

She could not help herself; she muttered in a low tone so that Matt had to strain to hear her, 'You do not now consider me a high-nosed bitch, then? A woman lacking all the womanly arts which give my sex grace?'

As his own words, spoken early on that fateful night at Pontisford, came back to haunt him, Matt's face twisted in pain. 'God forgive me,' he told her, his own voice low and broken. 'It was my rage and temper speaking then. I could not forgive you for tempting me so, for calling to me, albeit unwittingly, in a way which no woman had ever done since. . .my first and only love died. No, whatever else you are, Lady Radley—— ' and he tried to speak lightly to lessen his pain and hers '—you are not lacking in womanly arts.'

His reward was a watery smile, and the words, 'Yes, I missed you,' but behind those simple words Stacy was registering 'my first and only love'. What, then, does he feel for me? And if it is only friendship, a meeting of minds, and, yes, of bodies, but not love, then I will accept it, and not bore him with my love.

Which was exactly what Matt was thinking as they moved away from the dangerous ground which lay between them—and which each was refusing to explore.

So, in the happy days which followed, when they laughed and talked together, and Matt pushed her around the grounds or drove them in Rollo's curricle, a magnificent thing, picked out in scarlet and gold, as far as the boundary wall, neither spoke openly of the love which might lie between them. They talked of everything—and nothing. Both of them usually silent souls, found in the other a partner whose tastes and attitudes matched their own.

Forthright himself, Matt began to love Stacy's forthrightness. A hater of shams and hypocrisy, Stacy found Matt's similar attitude towards them admirable. They liked the same books and the same music, which Caroline played for them in the evening.

So much were they at evens that they began to

wonder how they could ever have been so much at odds. Except that Stacy, laughing, raised the matter as they sat alone one evening in the dusk, before the candles were lit, by saying, 'I suppose the reason why we were so fierce with one another when we first met is because we are so much alike, both determined to have our own way, and in those days our ways differed,' and then, looking at him almost shyly, 'I wonder why they don't differ now?'

Matt drew a sharp breath, took her hand to kiss it, and answered her, with an admirable lack of sentimentality, 'That, madam, is because the coming child constrains you. When he has arrived, and you are bounding about, full of *joie de vivre*, you will be as harsh with me as you ever were, and I shall be compelled to point out once again where you are going astray!'

Was that true? Stacy wondered. Or, now that they were coming to know one another, were they both beginning to find in the other virtues that they were not previously aware they possessed? Could it be that they might come to love one another? Perhaps the coming child, which she had once resented a little because Matt had seemed to consider it more important then herself, was responsible for bringing them together? Or was it the long months of separation which had revealed to each of them that they had, as Jeb would have put it, lost their other half?

She was not to know that Matt was thinking the same thing! For strong-willed and determined people they were strangely diffident towards one another, even now, so far as their emotions were concerned, Matt because he was still afraid of commitment, and Stacy because she had not completely cast off the shackles which Louis Blanchard had bound around her. Neither could quite say to the other those magic words: I love you. To do so would be to surrender, and neither of them had ever willingly surrendered anything to anyone. But those about them saw more than they did, as onlookers often saw more of the game than the players did.

The Earl had summoned his son to his study soon after his return, to speak to him of the duties which he, as the heir, must take on, and of the way of life which Matt must then follow. As he had wryly said to Matt, 'The land owns us as much as we own the land.'

Afterwards, as Matt had prepared to leave, his father had said slowly, 'Stay a little longer, Radley; there is something which I must say to you.'

Matt, who had risen, sat down again, to hear his father continue, his face grave, 'I have learned a lot, during the year which has passed, of the true nature of my late son and heir, your elder brother, and what I have learned has not been pleasant. I know, for example, and I think that you ought to be aware of it, that he died a shameful death in a brothel, in a fight over a whore when he was drunk, and that he had squandered the fortune which came to him at your mother's death. I am ashamed to admit that I arranged that the cause of his death be hushed up.

'Because of what I have subsequently discovered about his mode of life, I fear that I may have misjudged you over the matter of Camilla, his wife; that what you said in defence of your behaviour at the time was most likely the truth.

'I have no proof of this, nor do I wish to seek any, for to set agents on your and Rollo's trail after so many years would be demeaning to you. I believe, from all that I have seen of you since living with you again, that you have a strong sense of honour, and your choice of a wife demonstrates that you possess common sense too. Shall we agree to put the past behind us—if you can forget my wilfulness in misjudging you—so that we may start again as father and son, living in harmony, if not always in agreement?'

This speech was so remarkable and so unexpected that Matt was almost stunned by it, and said so.

His father smiled sadly. 'Let us shake hands on it, sir, and then you may believe that I am sincere, and the past may no longer haunt us.'

Well, that was something which he had not expected. Time and chance had done their work, and now he might walk about The Eyrie with a sense of pride again. Matt no longer cared what the world thought of him, but his father's opinion was quite another matter.

From that day on one of the ghosts which had haunted Matthew Falconer, now Lord Radley, for so many years passed from his life. He would try to remember Rollo as he had been when Matt was a boy and Rollo was in his teens, before drink and dissipation had begun to destroy him. But the other ghost, that of Camilla, still walked with him. His father's forgiveness could neither exorcise her nor make him forget the manner in which she had died.

'I do believe, sir, that you are at last becoming civilised! The lion has ceased to roar, and the bear to rove the hills.' And Stacy moved her backgammon counter along the board to take her a little nearer to victory.

Matt muttered something rude beneath his breath about calculating women who could play chess and backgammon better than most men he knew, before he rattled the dice-box again.

'I should have known better than to play with you,' he told her ruefully a few minutes later, when victory became inevitably hers.

'But you lose so much more nicely now than you were wont to do when we first met.' And Stacy lay back against her pillows. She was now into her eighth month, and the doctor who was to supervise the birth was due to arrive at the Eyrie before the weekend. He was to take over from the one who rode twice-weekly from York to stare at her, and comment that 'Lady Radley is in great fettle, and by all appearances preparing to give birth to a fine boy'. He was to be the London man's assistant when he arrived.

'I can't recall that we played backgammon together when we first met,' retorted Matt, who was busy gathering up the counters and the dice. He thought that she looked particularly well that afternoon, with a fine colour on her—the pallor which had been hers before she had conceived seemed to have disappeared.

'No, indeed,' riposted Stacy, 'but we played other games, as you well know, and losing them appeared particularly galling to you.'

'But I can't recall losing any kind of game,' he replied, grinning at her as he carefully replaced the backgammon board in the ornate inlaid box which held it, the dice-box and the ivory counters. 'On the contrary, I distinctly remember winning.'

'Oh, yes, the last one.' Stacy's tone was careless, and the eyes she lifted to look at him as he towered over her were full of shameless mirth. 'I grant you that. For, behold, as a consequence of it you have reduced me to a condition in which I am fit for nothing but to be carried about and petted.'

'To make up for all the years in which you weren't,' he told her briskly, and bent down to kiss her warm and rosy cheek. Yes, madam looked particularly fine today, fine enough to drive a man mad, particularly a man who hadn't touched a woman since he had last taken the woman before him to bed.

The rapport between them was so strong now that Stacy leaned forward to take his hand and kiss it, being unable to lift herself up to kiss his cheek. 'I do believe,' she had said that morning, 'that I am about to give birth to a veritable giant. It must be a boy; I could not wish a girl to be so large.'

'You wish to renege on our bargain?' he asked her now quietly, so that Caroline and Georgiana, sitting on the other side of the room and chatting about a ball which they were due to attend at York, could not hear them.

'Bargain?' Stacy repeated dubiously, as though she had never heard the word before—and when had she learned to be so teasingly naughty, so that she was provoking him with every word she uttered? 'I can't remember a bargain, sir. On what piece of paper was it written? Remind me, so that I may refresh my memory as to the details of it.'

Matt had dragged up a chair, to sit on it facing her. He leaned forward and took her happy face in both his hands. 'You witch, to tease me so! You know perfectly well to what bargain I refer. The one to which we agreed before our wedding—that our marriage would be in name only, and that we would part after a suitable interval, once our child was born.'

He was still holding her face and gazing into her eyes, regardless of what his sisters might think, when she answered him. 'Oh, that bargain! I believe it was one which you proposed. I cannot remember any countersigning on my part.'

Matt drew in his breath sharply, and took his hands from her face. He leaned back, said hoarsely, 'Have you no idea, madam, of the effect which your words have on me? And that I am helpless before you in your present condition. Stop playing the Bankeress with me and remember that you are my wife, and that you promised to love, honour and obey me! Did none of those words mean anything to you, madam?'

Stacy decided not to taunt him further. There was a look almost of agony on his strong face. The lion seemed to be wounded. She murmured softly, 'As much as you wish them to mean, Matt. As much as you wish. . .'

The air between them vibrated, was full of a strange magnetism. It was as though they were completely on their own, out of space, out of time. The room they were in, the people near them, had gone. Everything but the other disappeared.

'Are you saying, madam, what I think you are saying?' Matt finally ventured, only to have Stacy return,

'Now who is playing with words, sir?'

'You taught me,' he answered her, all brevity.

'Then you are an apt pupil, sir, who does credit to his teacher.'

'And if the pupil told his teacher, and the client told the Bankeress, that he wished to renege on the agreement, and wondered what strange maggot had invaded his brain that he could have ever conceived of such a thing, what then?'

'Why, then the teacher, as well as the Bankeress, would answer that the same maggot must have invaded her brain to cause her to agree to such a proposition, and furthermore that an agreement entered into by two persons whose sanity was in doubt at the time could hardly hold—so let us agree to forget it.'

It was, Stacy afterwards thought, typical of them both that they could declare the love they had come to feel for one another in such a roundabout and oblique fashion—the magic words were still unsaid.

But Matt's response to her invitation was not oblique. He gave a sudden shout of laughter so that Caroline, being timorous, started and dropped her needle, and Georgiana, being fiery, glared at him. ''Pon rep, Matt,' she exclaimed, 'think of your poor wife! You will overset her with your noisy ways.'

'Overset her?' choked Matt, taking Stacy's hand and covering it with kisses. 'By no means, never. My dear wife is never overset—least of all by her husband. No, she makes a practice of oversetting him! And now, to celebrate her latest feat, I will, like the magician in the fairy-tale, tell her that I will grant her any wish she cares to make, seeing that she has granted me my dearest one. Come, madam, wish!'

He was transformed. Usually stern, and a little forbidding in his bearing, like his father—as that father was coming to recognise—he was suddenly all playfulness. Georgiana was to say afterwards to her sister and her father that marrying Miss Blanchard was the strangest thing that Matt could have done, but was quite the best. 'She is turning him back into the man he was before he lost Camilla, and for that we should all be grateful.'

'I have no wishes left,' Stacy told him, 'since my one wish has been granted.'

'Come, there must be something. A diamond necklace, perhaps?'

Stacy shook her head. There was one thing which she *had* come to wish for in the last few days as they had driven about the park, and perhaps, if she asked him nicely, he would agree to grant it, even if it was only a small thing.

'No, Matt, I have enough jewellery to make the Tsarina of all the Russias envious. What I would really like is to leave the grounds, for you to drive me, not around the park, but into the open country. Pleasant though it is here, I have begun to feel a little imprisoned.'

Matt said, laughing, 'Is that all? A most frugal request for the Bankeress to make. But are you sure that you are fit to undertake such a drive? You would not be overset?'

'No, indeed. I would like a breath of the wide world. and so, I think, would you.'

'When I think what you might have demanded of me! A fortune perhaps—and all you wish is an extended drive. So be it. Tomorrow, then, if it be fine, and, if not, the first fine day. We must celebrate, must we not?'

Georgiana overheard this last. 'Celebrate, Matt? What's to celebrate?'

He could hardly tell her that they had just agreed to be truly man and wife, seeing that they were already married! Instead, he answered her airily, 'Why sister, we have just decided that if the child is to be a boy, then he will be Henry, after our grandfather, I believe, Adolphus after my father, and Louis, after Lady Radley's. Is not that a splendid thing?'

'Well, I think so,' agreed Stacy, to whom Matt's fertile invention had come as a surprise, almost as big a surprise as to learn that he had been thinking of what to call his future son, if son it was. 'Especially since he has left to me the choice of names if it is to be a girl—but I have not yet made up my mind what they are to be. He is before me there.'

'Bravely said,' replied Matt, thinking that once again Stacy had trumped his ace so to speak; after having had a boy's name sprung on her she had counter-attacked by claiming the right to decide on a daughter's name. Oh, he could see that life with madam was going to be lively, full of surprises. He wished with all his heart that their child would soon honour them with his or her presence so that they could start living that life as soon as possible.

And if she wished to go on being the Bankeress, then so be it. Somehow he would arrange to let her have her wish—if that was what she truly wanted.

That night they were more loving than they had ever been, and Matt came to Stacy's room after she had retired, and sat by her on the bed, holding her in his arms, enjoying the sweet torment which that provoked in him, and thinking of all the sweeter ecstasies which were to come. . .

CHAPTER FIFTEEN

'YOU are quite sure that you are well enough to undertake such a long ride in the country?' Matt asked anxiously. 'After all, so far we have stayed inside the park on easy roads and pleasant ways. You will not find the motion too distressing?'

He had already lifted Stacy into her seat in his curricle; grooms were holding the horses' heads to prevent any chance that they might rear before he was fully in control of them and cause her discomfort—he did not think that she would be frightened, for nothing seemed to frighten her.

She shook her head as he sat beside her, taking up his whip. 'No, indeed. I ailed a little in the first few months, but of late I have felt most amazingly well. Today I feel that, if it were not for the burden which I carry, I could move mountains. Truly, I have never felt so well in my life.'

She gave him an enchanting sideways glance, which had him trembling again, before adding, 'Why, I do believe that you are going back on your word.' Stacy was still revelling in her new-found powers of mischief and of teasing gaiety, which she had been unaware she possessed until she had met Matt. It was as though he was getting the benefit of all the flirting which she had never done, but now felt able and willing to do.

'Never,' he told her, with a grin, as the grooms released the horses and they started off. 'But if you *do* feel any discomfort you must tell me so immediately and we shall return home at once.'

Home. Matt had spent many years denying that the Eyrie had ever been, or could ever be, his home. As for Stacy, it was odd to think that she could call somewhere home which she had only known for a few months, but she had already come to love The Eyrie, which would one day be truly hers and Matt's.

It felt strange to reach the big gates and turn out of them on to the York road, and then to make not for York itself but for the open plain. The Eyrie was situated between York and Selby, in open country criss-crossed by small lanes and ditches which were even more primitive than the road on which they were travelling, the one which the mail-coaches took.

They had taken no groom or tiger with them—not that Matt possessed a tiger—something which he was later to regret—but he did not intend to be out for long, and he had become accustomed to living informally during his years in Virginia. It had taken him some time to grow used again to the press of servants who were needed to make The Eyrie run smoothly. Once he had taken them for granted, but after Virginia he would never do so again.

'He's a good man to serve, the new lord,' the staff at The Eyrie had agreed, 'not like the bastard, his older brother.' There were those who remembered Matt as a boy, and thought that he had grown into someone who commanded affection as well as respect.

'Oh, do let us go along there!' Stacy suddenly exclaimed as they came to a side-road which led gently down to a small valley through which a stream, a tributary of the Derwent, ran beneath over-arching trees. 'I would love to be able to paint it.' Then she added wistfully, 'There are times when I wish I had not given up painting, but Father said that, like music, it was a waste of time best occupied by more serious matters.'

It was unguarded disclosures like these which told Matt something of the rigorous life which Louis Blanchard had inflicted on his daughter. If it had made her a strong woman, it had also deprived her of many of the small pleasures of living. He had already made a private resolution that once their child was born he would encourage her to enjoy herself by indulging in all those innocent amusements which one by one her father had vetoed in favour of the stern regime which had come to dominate her life.

Matt shook his head, murmured, 'I am sorry to disappoint you, my darling, but we have already come quite a long way from The Eyrie. I think that we ought to turn for home. The plain of York is a lonely place.'

'But peaceful,' said Stacy, and then, 'It also seems a long way from the Bank. Please, Matt, let us go just a little further before we turn back.'

She accompanied this plea with such a charmingly wilful expression that he felt compelled to give way. 'Very well, my naughty minx, just a little further. I see that having our child is making you lose all your high-minded caution.' And he touched the horses lightly with his whip and they turned into the narrow lane. Any narrower and he would have refused to go down it at all.

Here, among the scents and smells of the open country, Stacy found it hard to believe that the Bank existed, that it had been the centre of her life for so long. Her father had become a distant figure, no longer the demi-god who had dominated her, and he was fast receding into the past. It was not that she no longer loved him, or his memory, but she was at last freeing herself from the prison of lovelessness into which he had unintentionally thrust her. Ephraim was sending her regular reports, and she dutifully commented on them and wrote back suggestions, but it was like posting letters to Mars, or the outer planets, she sometimes thought.

She turned to share this odd notion with Matt after he had negotiated a bend in the lane and was turning for home again—he had already told her that the road, such as it was, was growing too poor for them to go much further—when disaster struck.

They were bowling happily along when they disturbed a large nye of pheasants, which, the cock-bird leading, exploded out of the bushes which lined the lane, straight into the path of the horses.

Neighing and snorting, both horses reared and stumbled. That alone might not have caused an accident, but the nearside horse, despite all Matt's efforts, lost his footing, tried to recover it, lost it again, and, as he did so, took his companion down into the ditch with him, the curricle and its occupants following. The nearside horse broke his neck immediately, his fellow his leg. Matt, half stunned, landed among the ruins of his carriage, with Stacy beside him. She lay there unmoving. One moment she had been enjoying the afternoon sun, the next she had been flung sideways, and now was hardly aware of where she was.

After a little time, through the almost pleasant haze she was lying in, she heard someone say hoarsely, 'Stacy, oh, my darling Stacy. I have killed you in my folly. Dear God, not twice. I could not bear this to happen again.'

In her dazed condition she thought that she was lying in the wreck of her coach in the November snow, and she could not imagine why Hal should be saying such strange things to her. A horse was making a dreadful noise, as though it was in great pain.

She tried to sit up, but found that she could not, and then someone was freeing her, lifting her and carrying her some little distance to lay her down on the ground—in the snow? What a strange thing to do. Someone—could it possibly be Hal?—had his arms around her, and was holding her tenderly. She looked up to find out who it was, but at first all that she could see was the sunlight shining through the trees—and then she saw Matt's agonised face—and remembered everything. . .

It was not November, it was July. And she was no longer Anastasia Blanchard, but Anastasia, Lady Radley, expecting her first child, and it was her husband who was holding her, and begging her to speak to him, if she could. Yes, they had gone for a drive, they had driven down to a stream, and then away from it, but after that. . .nothing. . .

Her head began to clear. She said, weakly at first, then more strongly, 'Matt, what happened?' And now she could see him properly. His face was white. There was a great bruise on his cheek, his coat was torn, but otherwise he didn't seem to be hurt.

'Pheasants flew at us,' he told her, 'frightened the horses. I couldn't control them—I doubt whether anyone could have done. . .which is no excuse. . .' He held her tightly to him. 'Oh, God, Stacy, what have I done to you?'

Her voice muffled, because he was holding her so tightly against him, she answered him, 'Nothing; I don't think I've taken an injury. . .' She paused, then continued doubtfully as he released her a little, 'I must have caught my head on something, for it feels very odd, but it is growing better now. And I have a pain in my back. I think I must have twisted it when we fell. But what about you?'

'Oh, me,' he answered her dismissively. 'I think I might have damaged my ankle—we're both lucky to be alive. Fortunately neither of the horses fell on us, or kicked us. Unfortunately one is dead, the other badly injured, and the curricle is done for.'

That must have been the horse which had been making a noise and was now silent. She was to learn later that while she was still semi-conscious Matt shot it with one of the horse pistols which he always carried when not riding in the park.

'God forgive me for not bringing a groom with us, but I have grown out of the habit of having servants trailing around after me. Forget that,' he said anxiously. 'I can see a cottage not far away. If I can get you there you can shelter in it, and we can send someone to The Eyrie for help. Do you think that you could manage to walk?'

Her head was still misbehaving, but Stacy said, as bravely as she could, 'If you will help me up I shall try.'

It was almost a question of the blind leading the blind, for Matt was limping badly—his ankle was more sprained and swollen than he had admitted—and the pain in Stacy's back was so severe that she found difficulty in walking.

She could tell that he was in pain, so she tried not to lean on him too much, but as they made their way up the track, to where a cottage stood on a small rise in the ground, she felt such a sharp pain in her back that she gave a little cry, and sat down abruptly on the ground.

Matt was squatting beside her immediately, his face more drawn than ever through pain and worry. 'Stacy! What is it?'

She looked up at him, trying to control herself. 'Oh, Matt, I'm sorry to make a fuss, but the pain was so strong and came so suddenly, without warning. . .' She gave another small gasp. 'It's not continuous, it's coming and going, which makes it hard for me to bear it.'

Stacy had not thought that Matt could grow any paler than he already was, but he did, and she felt the arm which he had put about her shoulders tighten, but he said only, 'Try to walk, my darling, but if the pain grows too bad, then I will carry you.'

But she didn't want that, and somehow, half leaning against one another, they drew near to the cottage.

Matt, who was not suffering as Stacy was from the

after-effects of a blow to the head, saw before she did that something was wrong. The cottage looked neglected; it had once possessed a garden, but it had been allowed to run wild. A dirty child in ragged clothes played in it, casting feral looks at them as they approached, before running through an open door. No, not a door, but an opening where one had been.

His heart sank. He helped Stacy into the garden and laid her down on a small patch of rank grass beside some bedraggled fruit bushes which had run wild. The child reappeared—it was difficult to tell whether it was a boy or a girl. He asked, trying to keep his voice gentle and steady, 'My dear, is either your mother or your father at home?'

Matt thought wryly that he might have been speaking Greek for all the impression he made on the wild creature before him. He started for the doorway in order to enter the cottage, to see if anyone was there, but the child ran before him, darting in, to come out again dragging with him a woman, as ragged and dirty as he was. The woman stared at him. She was as feral as the child. For the first time he saw that a tinker's cart stood near to the cottage, but there was no sign of the tinker.

The woman said slowly, in an accent so wild and strange that he could barely understand her, 'What's up, maister?'

Nothing in Matt's life had prepared him for such indifference as she was showing him. Even as he spoke to her her eyes ranged away from him to stare into the distance while he tried to explain what had happened, that he was Lord Radley, and that he would like someone to go to The Eyrie to fetch help, for he did not wish to leave his wife on her own. To his dismay she didn't answer him, but shouted unintelligibly at the boy, who stared at him again and then began to run away from the cottage, towards the lane from which they had so painfully walked.

He saw that Stacy was sitting up, and was holding her back. The woman walked over to her, said something which Stacy could not understand, and then she put her hands into Stacy's armpits, pulled her erect, and began to walk her into the cottage. She said to Matt as she passed him, 'Coom in, then. Thy missis is having thy child.'

'Having thy child!' The world spun around Matt. he cried hoarsely, 'No!' Time turned in on itself. He was in an inn, and a woman was saying fiercely to him, 'Couldn't you see that the girl you have brought here is about to give birth? Shame on you for dragging her around the countryside in such a state. . .'

He was back on the plain of York again, walking into a small, dark room. There was a table, a bench, a rude fireplace without a fire in it, and something which passed for a bed in a corner. His brain told him that the tenant farmer who had lived here was long gone, and that a tinker's family had taken over the derelict cottage. Where the tinker was God only knew. All he knew was that he had brought Stacy to this terrible place, and history was about to repeat itself. . .

The woman sat Stacy down on the bench and fetched a clean blanket from a wicker basket which lay on the dirt floor before the empty hearth. Matt joined Stacy on the bench. She turned a white face towards him, exclaimed feverishly, 'Oh, Matt, she says that I am about to birth the baby! Do you think that she can possibly be right?' Even as she spoke her face contracted again, as the pain in her back struck harder than ever this time, and she said numbly, once it had subsided, 'Oh, I do believe she is, but surely the pain is in the wrong place?'

All that Matt knew about the birth of babies was that Camilla had died trying to deliver one—something of which even now he could barely think. He pushed the thought away. The woman came over and put the blanket on the bed, saying to Stacy as she passed her, 'Coom on, then, gal. On to the bed wi' ye. Stay there while I fetch old Grandam Outhwaite to help yer. He——'and she jerked her thumb at Matt '—will 'ave to look after ye until she cooms.'

Stacy looked wildly round the room. The bed did not appear to be particularly dirty but, apart from the blanket which the woman had just laid down, wasn't particularly clean either. Whenever she had imagined having her baby she had never foreseen anything like this! She had seen herself on the large bed in her room back at The Eyrie, servants coming and going, perhaps faithful Louisa sitting in a corner, Matt striding along the corridor outside as Georgiana had told her her husband had done when her first child had been born. One of England's most famous doctors would have been in attendance; the best doctor in York was to have been his faithful aide.

But the only person attending her was Matt, and all that she was being promised was some peasant midwife, who was probably having to be fetched from the nearest village—wherever that might be. This was certainly not how she had visualised giving birth to the heir to all the Falconers!

For once even her brave spirit faltered. Matt saw her face change and came to sit beside her on the makeshift bed, to lift her up a little, to hold her against his chest, to say anxiously, 'Oh Stacy, my darling, what a time to tell you. I should have told you before, but for some odd reason I never found the courage to do so. . . I love you so dearly that I can hardly bear to see you suffer. I think that I have loved you ever since I opened the door at Pontisford and saw you standing there, so brave and defiant, and look at you now, at what I have done to you. . . How can you love me after this?' His voice broke on the last words and she could feel his poor heart beating furiously as he held her against him.

They were the words which Stacy had always wanted to hear him say, and what a time to choose to tell her! Even through her pain and rising fear she felt that she had to reward him by saying, her voice hoarse and broken as she fought the all-consuming pain, 'Oh, Matt, you must surely know that I have loved you since Pontisford, and what we did there was done together—together we made our child, and I was as willing and eager as you were. . .'

And then the pain took her, and this time it was he who held and comforted her, not she him, and he felt with her the pain which was tearing her apart. After it had passed they rested in one another's arms, until Matt said tenderly, trying to control his own rising fear that he was in danger of losing his wife and child just as they had found each other, 'Is there anything I can do for you? Have you any idea how soon it is likely to be before the baby arrives?'

Before she could answer him another pain—they were coming thick and fast now—tore through Stacy with such force that she could not prevent herself from writhing and crying out, putting her fist into her mouth to stop herself from screaming. This time the pain was in the front, and when it had passed she told Matt what she thought the woman had said: 'It won't be long, me duck.'

'Won't be long!' Matt muttered something blasphemous under his breath, and then, 'And how long before she returns with this old wise-woman, and how useful will she be?'

Stacy didn't answer him; she was too busy trying to cope with other things—one a great gush of water which she knew, from questions which she had compelled the York doctor to answer, was the breaking of the waters which preceded birth.

'Oh, really, Lady Radley, I do not think it my place to discuss such matters with you, nor would it be proper for you to know of them,' he had twittered at her.

To which she had replied in a voice of steel, 'Well, it is I who am having this child, sir, so kindly do as I ask. I have no wish to die as the result of ignorance like the late lamented Princess Charlotte.'

He had also told her that the pains she would feel would come more and more rapidly as the time for the birth neared, and there was no doubt that this was beginning to happen. Once the latest pain had subsided a little she told Matt so, adding, 'You are going to have to help me if you wish your son and heir to be born alive, for there is no one else here to do so.'

She could not have anticipated his reaction to this news. She had felt him shaking when he had taken her into his arms, and now she felt him begin to shudder violently. She twisted her head a little to find that he was not grey, but yellow, and looked as though *he* was about to faint.

'For God's sake, Stacy,' he muttered, 'do not say so. It is not half an hour since the accident, and I always understood from what I heard of my sisters' talk, and from the women on the plantation, that birthing a baby usually takes a day at least.'

One thing was certain, he learned immediately, and that was that Stacy's fiery spirit had not been quenched by what was happening to her.

'Well,' she told him bluntly, 'you had better pray that the baby does come soon, for one thing is certain—a day of pains such as these would be the death of me——' and then she was writhing again in such agony that he gently laid her down on her back again, thinking that that might ease her.

He remembered being present after Camilla's agony, and after the birth of one of the black servants on his

Virginia farm, and that on both occasions there had been blood everywhere—although the black servant's child had lived and Camilla's had not. Stacy would need some clean linen, and water. She had begun to sweat heavily, and he used his fine cambric handkerchief to wipe her face tenderly—but she would need more than his handkerchief if the child was coming.

'Listen,' he murmured urgently, during the interval between her pains, 'if the baby is coming soon, which God forbid, then I must try to find some water—there will almost certainly be a well at the back of the cottage, or a running brook nearby. Do you think that you could hold on for a moment or two while I reconnoitre?'

It was the last thing Stacy wanted, to be left alone, but there was no help for it. She offered him a twisted smile and a murmured, 'Yes,' while she concentrated on preparing to withstand the next pain.

When it came she closed her eyes, gripped the corner of the blanket and thrust it between her teeth to stop herself from screaming at its force, so that on Matt's return some little time later, carrying a bucket of water and a battered pewter cup, she was able to offer him a brave face.

'There *was* a well,' he told her, 'and the water looks and tastes sweet. Would you like to drink some?' For he thought that she was now beginning to show the effects of severe pain added to the shock of the accident.

Stacy took the offered water, drank it greedily, and then watched with some astonishment as Matt took off his jacket, untied his cravt and pulled off his fine linen shirt, which he began to rip apart, creating from its back one large piece, and tearing off long strips from its sleeves and front. He put his jacket back on again, and offered her one of the strips. 'To bite on,' he told her, 'when the pain become too great to bear. That's what the surgeons did on board ship after a naval battle when they were looking after the men. The others will do for later, when the child comes.'

Taking the linen strip, and doing as she was bid, Stacy didn't inform him that she had already used the blanket for that purpose. He looked so ill and worried that one might almost have thought that he was about to have the baby himself! Surprisingly, even through her pain, the thought made her want to giggle.

For a time nothing changed, the pain came and went, but after about an hour, by which time the pains were coming continuously and she could no longer suppress her screams at their strength, Stacy's body began to tell her that the baby's birth was imminent. She was now half sitting up again, Matt was holding her, and when she turned to say to him, 'Oh, Matt, I think that the baby is about to come,' it was at this point that he broke.

He laid her down on the bed, put his head in his hands, and groaned, 'I can't, Stacy, I can't bear this, not again, not twice. Oh, God, I don't think that I shall be able to help you!' He had, unknown to her, gone back more than ten years. He was in another room, the bedroom of an inn, and he was looking down at poor, dead Camilla, at her child who had been born dead, and the ghastly evidence of a painful, mismanaged birth all about them. It had unmanned him then, and he had tried to suppress the memory of it, but, faced with Stacy in a similar situation, he was unmanned again. Was he to lose another, and stronger love in the same painful way as the first?

Stacy, overcome by surprise as much as by shock when Matt buried his face in the blanket on her bed, stared at him, even through her agony. She was sweating, her hair had come down and hung in wet tendrils around her face, and the man whose strength and courage she had always admired, the man who had saved Jeb's life, rescuing him against fearful odds when his farm has been attacked by roving brigands, was telling her that he was unable to help her to bear their child. Whatever could be the matter with him?

'Matt,' she almost shouted over the pain which was destroying her, 'you must help me. Look at me, Matt, look at me! Of course you can help me. How many mares have you helped to bring their foals into the world?'

He lifted his head to show her a face nearly as agonised as hers. 'But you are not a mare, Stacy, you are my wife, and——'

'And bosh,' she roard at him rudely, the Bankeress *in Excelsis Gloria*, as an irreverent wit had once named her. 'What am I now but a two-legged mare, about to let her foal slip into your hands? Would you do more for your horse than you would do for me?'

Slowly, unwillingly, as the memory of Camilla's deathbed faded from his mind, driven away by the strength of his wife's words, he gave a slow and reluctant grin at her unquenchable spirit.

'By God, madam,' he told her softly, 'you rightly rebuke me. Yes, we will birth our foal together.'

'Then see to it at once, Radley, do you hear me? For I shall shortly have little more reason left than your mare, and it is you who will have the greater burden——Ah, God, Matt——' and she gave a shrill scream '—I believe he is nearly here.'

This time he was ready for her, his courage restored, and for the next few hectic minutes, as Stacy panted and pushed their child into the world, Matt was helping her and encouraging her, as though she were the mare she had claimed to be. And when at last the baby emerged into the cruel world, crying its protests at being born at all, it was Matt who caught him in his large hands, who wrapped him gently in the remains of his father's linen shirt—for yes, he was the boy whom

Stacy had always claimed that she was carrying. And it was Matt who showed him to his mother and let her hold him for a moment, saying, 'Hal, my boy, you must meet your mama at last. Stacy, my darling, here is your foal.'

To which she replied weakly, but with a smile, 'Oh, no, Matt, he is my lion-cub. See, when his hair dries it will be as tawny as yours!'

Matt thought that he had never seen anything so beautiful in his life as his wife as she lay there, cuddling their child, never mind that she bore about her all the stigmata of a difficult, if rapid birth. And so he told her, the pair of them sharing broken endearments over the head of their child.

And finally it was Matt who carried the protesting Hal over to place him in the wicker basket from which the blanket on the bed had earlier come.

As he bent down there were shadows and noise at the door, and the woman who had earlier gone for the wise-woman entered. Behind her came an older woman, bent and wrinkled, who took in the scene before her—the large man holding the howling baby, the exhausted woman on the makeshift bed.

Grandam Outhwaite said in a cracked voice, 'Why, I believes as 'ow yer didn't need me arter all,' before she went over to Stacy to finish the business of birthing, finally washing both her and the baby down with an infusion of herbs which she had brought with her in a little blue bottle.

The heir to all the Falconers had been successfully born, on a blanket in a deserted cottage in which a family of tinkers had been squatting, with only his father and mother to help him!

'I am sure that something must be dreadfully wrong!' Caroline Bibury was wringing her hands. It was late afternoon and Matt and Stacy had been gone for some hours. They had been expected back long before. 'Matt would surely not have taken Stacy on a jaunt as extended as this in her condition.' And she looked helplessly around at the assembled company.

Earlier that afternoon the Beauchamps had driven over from Bramham, and Anthony, still smarting from losing Stacy to 'that fellow', muttered ungraciously, half beneath his breath, that, 'Nothing that Radley did would surprise me.'

His father cast warning glances at him, so he subsided, but if he didn't speak again he thought a great deal. The Earl ordered the grooms and stable-hands to ride out in the direction which Radley had gone, but so far no one had returned with any news. Aunt Beauchamp persuaded Uncle Beauchamp to stay longer than they ought to do before returning home, in the hope that they might see Stacy safe before they left, but even so they finally had to make ready to take their leave.

The Earl and his family, by now seriously worried, walked to the stable-yard to see the coach for the Beauchamp parents driven out; Anthony had ridden over on his horse. The Earl did them the honour of coming out himself. He was leaning on his stick, his mind in turmoil as a result of Radley's non-return, when a ragged child who had been lurking about the yard suddenly sprang at him, howling something incomprehensible.

Thwaites, the head groom, who was busy supervising operations, leaped forward to remove the child bodily. 'Danged little tyke bin a botheration to us all arternoon,' he grunted. 'Shouting and roaring his nonsense at us. You mind your manners, lad. 'Tis the Earl you're saucing.'

At the mention of the Earl the child howled again, trying to escape Thwaites' strong arms. This time the Earl thought he heard something familiar.

'You heard that,' he said to Anthony Beauchamp who was making ready to mount. 'He distinctly said Radley. Now how would he know that? Let him down, Thwaites. Let him come and speak to me, since that is what he wants.'

Thwaites, muttering, put the child down. He immediately ran to the Earl, fell on his knees before him, and began to speak. The name Radley was now distinctly heard by all of them in the yard.

'He's trying to tell us something about Radley,' the Earl announced incredulously. 'Slowly, lad, slowly.'

The child nodded his shaggy head, mouthed at the Earl so that he could make out that Radley had had an accident and, ' 'E's at whoam, 'e is. At whoam.'

'And where's home?' the Earl asked him gently.

The child pointed towards where Selby lay, took the Earl roughly by the sleeve and began to pull him in that direction. There was no doubt that he was trying to tell him that he knew where Lord Radley was, and that he was to go with him to find him.

'Is Lord Radley injured? Hurt?' he added, when he saw that the child had not at first understood him.

The child shook his head, said something incomprehensible, and repeated it when he saw that the Earl had not understood him. This time, 'Nay, the ooman,' came out quite plainly.

Anthony Beauchamp said feverishly, 'My God, it is Stacy who is hurt. We must go to her at once. Cannot the child show us the way? If necessary I will go alone.'

The Earl shook his head. 'No,' he said, 'I will ride there, and you may accompany me if you wish.'

And so it was that they came at last to the lane below the cottage, the child riding with Thwaites and pointing out the way, the Earl and Anthony Beauchamp following. They passed the ruined curricle and the dead horses lying in the ditch. Anthony swore blackly below his breath and the Earl's heart sank within him. But when the boy slid off his horse and began to run up the track to the cottage, he dismounted and set off after him, fearful of what he might find.

He and Anthony had not reached the cottage before Matt came out to meet them, after hearing the sound of men and horses. He had been helping Grandam Outhwaite to undress Stacy and put her into a coarse but clean nightgown, after giving her a draught from yet another blue bottle—'Poppy,' she had told him briefly. ''Er 'll sleep soon.'

He had such an expression of joy on his face as his father had never seen. The grim, rather dour man had gone: he had the manner of the happy boy he had once been. 'Father!' he exclaimed, and there was joy in his voice as well. 'I knew that you would come to find me if the lad could only find the way.'

'Your wife?' panted the Earl, sinking on to a bench beside the door.

'Stacy—what have you done to her? We saw the ruins of the curricle on our way here,' burst from Anthony, who was privately vowing to kill Matt Falconer if any harm had come to Stacy.

Matt was still wearing that queer look of triumph. 'She's as well as can be expected,' he said. 'Come.' And he waved them into the cottage.

To their astonishment they saw Stacy lying propped against a pillow, covered by another coarse blanket. She was half asleep, already under the poppy's influence, and gave them only a distant smile, while Matt bent down to a basket by the hearth, to lift from it his son, who, roused from peaceful sleep by his father, gave a howling welcome to his grandfather.

'Your grandson greets you, sir. Allow me to introduce Hal Falconer, not yet an hour born. He came so rapidly into the world that his mother and father were hard put to see him into it properly.'

Anthony looked aghast. 'Here!' he almost moaned. 'The poor child had her baby here—with only you present!'

'Aye,' said Grandam Outhwaite, bobbing an indifferent curtsy to the gentry, more as a mere token of respect than anything else, 'an' what better place to have it, wi'out a pack o' useless noddies dancin' around her, but wi' her own true love helping her, and me to see her right when 'twas all over? Sleep now, me duck,' she told Stacy firmly. 'Tek no notice of 'em. The maister and I will look after ye until ye are fit to travel 'ome agin.'

Stacy's last sight before she fell into a black pit of healing sleep was of the Earl's half-amused face and Anthony's outraged one as the old woman ordered them about. The last sound she heard was that of her protesting son, whom Matt was still holding as though he never intended to lay him down again. He was to ask himself afterwards whether the fierce pride he had felt for the boy-child in his arms was because he had assisted at his birth, not been fetched in when all was over and shown a spotless baby lying in a spotless cradle covered in lace, as though he had been dropped from heaven clean and washed and clothed in the finest garments!

Instead little Hal Falconer wore nothing but the remains of his father's shirt, and was to do so until Thwaites rode back to The Eyrie with the news of his birth. He carried with him a request that many of the baby-clothes wrapped around bags of lavender and lying in the drawers of the waiting nursery should be brought to the poor cottage where the latest Falconer had been born, along with his mother's nightrail and enough bedlinen, towels, soap, perfume and other etceteras to make the cottage a more suitable place for the Falconer heir until he and his mother were fit to be carried back to The Eyrie.

The small, dark room seemed smaller and darker still, filled as it was with more people than it had known for many a day. The Earl looked round it and said, 'I believe that a yeoman used to live here, but he died some years ago, unmarried, leaving no children behind. The land being marginal and hard to farm, I never let it out again. I take it that this poor woman and her child are squatting here, for want of anywhere else to go?'

'Then, whoever you are, you takes it wrong,' a harsh voice told him as the owner of it stepped into the room. 'And who the devil are all of ye to be in my whoam? And who the devil's she?' And he was pointing at Stacy, happily asleep, all her problems solved, dreaming that she was roving across a great plain, Hal in her arms, Matt by her side, and a large dog following them. . .

CHAPTER SIXTEEN

'WELL, one could hardly blame the poor man for being surprised. To step into such a galaxy of great men, all sitting in his one small room, and me asleep on the only bed in it, must have been a great shock for him!' Stacy was responding to Matt's tale of what had happened while she had been happily unconscious after Hal's birth. 'I hope you were all suitably kind to him for the shelter his wife gave us. Otherwise Hal might have been born in the open!'

'Oh, Father is arranging that,' responded Matt, who had been on his highest ropes ever since Hal had been born and Stacy had survived his birth, 'and if he hadn't done so I would. After all, you were given bed and board there for several days until the York doctor allowed that you might safely be moved.'

Stacy laughed again as she remembered the great man's shock on hearing how Hal had come into the world, and a letter had been sent to the even greater man in London telling him that his services were no longer needed.

She had been back at The Eyrie for some days, in her own bed again, and was waiting to feed Hal, reluctant to disturb him while he was sleeping peacefully. Louisa was distressed by Stacy's insistence that she feed Hal herself, and was constantly worrying her over it, 'Are you sure that you would not be better with a wet-nurse, my dear?' being her usual refrain.

'Perhaps I should,' Stacy had told her robustly, 'but seeing that master Hal arrived so incontinently into the world that there is none available, nor will be, I am told, for another few weeks, he is going to have to be content with his mama.'

Whether it was Matt's ministrations during the birth, or Grandam Outhwaite's herbs, potions and care after it that did the trick, as Matt was fond of saying, Stacy recovered amazingly quickly from what Anthony Beauchamp, Caroline and others persisted in calling her 'ordeal'. Far more rapidly, Georgiana said acidly, than *she* had ever done with her more conventional *accouchements*.

It had seemed like an ordeal at the time, Stacy thought, but afterwards, well, that was quite a different thing. Like Matt she thought that she loved young Hal the more because they, and only they, were responsible for his presence. Not simply in creating him, but in seeing that he was safely born.

'So brave, Stacy,' everyone said, but Stacy always maintained that Matt had been the brave one. Anthony and others had tried to blame him for taking her to such an out-of-the-way place when she was so near to her time, but she wouldn't have that either.

'Why, I was the wilful one,' she always said, 'not Matt, seeing that it was I who insisted on going down that final lane where the accident happened, when Matt had wished to turn for home earlier. So, there's no more to be said.'

But there *was* one more thing to say, and when Matt came into her room to see how she and Hal were faring she patted the bed and asked Matt to come and sit by her. 'For,' she told him, 'there is a question I must ask you, sir.'

'Oh,' said Matt, gazing at her fondly, 'and what question is that?' He thought that since Hal's birth she looked more beautiful than ever. Motherhood had softened her, put a faint blush in once pale cheeks, had rounded her even more delightfully in every direction. Only her sharp intelligence remained unchanged, which was all to the good, he thought, for he was coming to treasure it, and could not imagine why so many men wished to have fools for their wives.

'I am curious,' she said, speaking slowly, 'as to why a man whom I know to be brave out of the common run—no, do not contradict me, sir, Jeb Priestley told me of your exploits in America—should behave so strangely when his wife was having their child. I thought at one point that you were about to faint. Most unlike you. I would have imagined, beforehand, that you would have taken all in your stride.'

To her surprise he changed colour, and then rose to walk to the window and look out of it at the golden afternoon, before he turned to speak to her.

'If I said that most men of any sensitivity would be distressed at the sight of their wife giving birth then I should not be speaking the entire truth. There was more to it than that. . .' He paused.

After a time Stacy said, 'Yes, I thought so. You said something odd at the time. "Not twice," you said. "I can't bear this, not again, not twice."' And then swiftly and tenderly she added, 'Oh, my dear, if it distresses you to speak of it, then pardon me for having raised a matter which might hurt you.'

He came back to the bed to sit by her again and take her hand before saying quietly, 'No, it doesn't hurt me now. Not like it did. Indeed, I think it might be better if I told you why I was so distressed.' He paused again. Stacy pressed his hand, and he pressed hers back. Since their child's birth they had been more tender and loving with each other than she could have believed possible. One day, soon, when the pains of the birth were behind her, they would celebrate their love as it deserved to be celebrated, wildly and fiercely, no doubt, as it had been that night at Pontisford, but for the present simply to be together, and Hal not far away, was enough.

'I was a happy child,' he began slowly. 'I was the youngest and a little spoiled. I never knew my mother; she died when I was only four years old—she had never been strong, they said. And while I was very young Rollo seemed not to resent me. I realise now that when they grew up he resented both his brothers, as though we were somehow his rivals. So when I grew older he changed towards me. I was given a dog, a wolfhound. Prince, I called him. Rollo wanted Prince, simply because he was mine, I now think. He asked me to give him Prince. I said no, Prince was mine. I loved him and Prince loved me. He said nothing when I refused, only softly, "You'll be sorry."

'I didn't really understand what he meant by that. I did about a week later. We were out on the moors shooting, the dogs were with us, and Rollo shot Prince dead. He always claimed it was an accident. Only he and I knew it wasn't, that it was quite deliberate. After that I was careful never to show that I cared much for anything when he was about, for I knew that if I did he would do something like that again, or would take it away from me.

'And then I met Camilla. It was at a ball at York Assembly Rooms. She was not at all like you. She was a little thing, with silky blonde hair, eyes like cornflowers and a tender, delicate face. She was shy, and was seated quite alone, with an old aunt by her side, while the young men fought over her three elder sisters. I fell head over heels in love with her. I wanted to protect her, to make her smile. I asked her to dance, and, seeing that I couldn't dance with her more than twice or cause gossip, I sat by her and talked to her. She seemed to like talking to me.

'She was the youngest daughter of a family of gentry who had lost their money through unwise speculation in the late wars. They lived in a tumbledown manor house near York. All the older sisters married early and, if not well, quite decently. Her parents were naturally overjoyed when I began to show that I was serious in my intentions towards her. After all, I was Earl Falconer's son, even if only a younger one, and he would see that we had a decent living one way or another.

'My way was to go into the Navy, and before I left for my first service in it it was agreed that when I came home on leave the arrangements would be made for us to marry. Both our parents thought that we were a little too young to rush into marriage straight away. I suspect that for some reason my father delayed it—her parents were much more eager.

'At first she wrote to me quite regularly, although as was the way at sea I often got a whole budget of letters at one go, after receiving nothing for months. Suddenly the letters stopped altogether, until one day I received one from her. . .' He stopped, turned his face towards Stacy, and she could see that he was not with her; he was reliving the pain of that day again.

'It said, quite simply, that she no longer wished to marry me, that what we had shared was a boy-and-girl love—that Rollo had proposed to her and she was going to marry him! It was the story of Prince, and a score of other hurts, all over again. She wasn't the sort of girl whom Rollo had ever shown any interest in before. He liked them big and showy. It was just that she was mine, and he was taking her away from me. I learned afterwards that her parents brought enormous pressure on her to throw me over. After all, if they had thought Earl Falconer's younger son was a great catch, imagine what they made of it when his heir offered for her, a virtually dowerless girl. Perhaps she was a little dazzled by him, too; he was considered to be very handsome. Although now I think not. I don't think that she ever cared for him, but she dared not defy her parents.

'I'm not sure what my father thought. Probably that all she and I had shared was puppy-love, as they say, and Rollo at that time was the apple of his eye; he could do no wrong. Later was a different matter, but by then it was too late.

'They were married when I was at sea. I didn't come back to The Eyrie for a long time after that, not until I was wounded at Trafalgar and they sent me home. I was put on half-pay, so I lost even my navy career, the thought of which had been something of a consolation to me after losing Camilla. Father wanted me to go into the *Corps Diplomatique*. He had a lot of influence then, but what subsequently happened put an end to that.

'When I went home all that I could think of was that I would see Camilla again. What I never thought of was how much she might have changed. She had always been delicately pretty, pink and white, with a charming manner and what I had thought was an enchanting laugh. Nothing of that was left. She was sallow and haunted-looking. When I met her again she turned her face away and could hardly look at me.

'Rollo's manner to her in public was always correct and loving. He claimed to be puzzled as to why she was so constantly ill. She was breeding, he told me carelessly, and that was probably why she looked such a fright.

'"I hope to God she looks a little more *comme il faut* when she has had the heir," he drawled at me. "I can't stand all this weeping and wailing; she's forever having the vapours, and never seems fit enough to perform her wifely duties." I think that he talked like that about her to taunt me.

'I wasn't feeling very well when I first got back to Yorkshire, but as I recovered my strength Camilla's condition worried me more and more. Seeing her again had revived all my old love and compassion for her.

Oh, I know now that it was quite a different sort of love from that which I feel for you—there was no passion in it, and what would have happened if we had married sometimes worries me. But then, I was ablaze with anger at what I clearly saw was Rollo's mistreatment of her. And my father couldn't seem to see it.

'Matters came to a head one day when I came across her in the gardens; we had been avoiding one another. She was sitting in the small gazebo, looking away from the house, not the folly you used to sit in before Hal was born. She had been crying. I remember that it was a warm day and she was wearing quite a heavy shawl. She was so different from the little fairy that I had fallen in love with that I could hardly believe that she was the same person.

'I remember that I asked her if there was anything I could do for her, since she was so plainly unhappy. She shook her head and said no, nobody could help her. She couldn't help herself. She had made a mistake in marrying Rollo, and that was that. I couldn't help myself; I put an arm around her. God knows, I meant nothing by it; she was big with my brother's child and I was only trying to comfort her.

'She gave a great cry and pulled herself away from me, and half-shrieked, "No, don't touch me, don't." I don't know why I did it, but as gently as I could I pulled the shawl away, and then I saw. All the great bruises down her arms, and even on her neck. I knew then why she wore long sleeves in the height of summer, and dresses with high collars.

'I remember sitting there trembling, saying to her one word—"Rollo"—because her condition explained so much. She put her thumb in her mouth and whispered through it, "He mustn't know you know. He'd kill me." I asked her why she hadn't told my father, and she said that she was afraid of him. Not that he had done or said anything unpleasant; he was always kind to her, but he thought the world of Rollo. . . I could see that it was hopeless; Rollo had broken her spirit.

'I didn't know what to do. I was still little more than a boy, only twenty-one, and despite my hard life in the Navy, and all I had seen and done there, I was still inexperienced in the ways of the great world. For several days I debated what to do to save my lost love, and then events took their own course. My father went away to London—he had a minor post in the Cabinet—which gave Rollo the freedom to practise even more cruelties. That last afternoon he drank too much at dinner, snarled at me, snarled at Camilla—I remember how she shrank away from him—until finally he took her by the hand and dragged her off to their rooms. He shouted at me as he left that he was tired of seeing my hanging-judge's face, and couldn't wait for me to leave.

'I went to my own rooms. About an hour later I heard noises, running feet, Camilla's voice raised. She was outside, in the stable-yard—my room overlooked it—talking to one of the grooms, a boy who was always ready to do things for her.

'He was doing something for her, something he should not have been doing. He was readying one of the small chaises for use. I saw that Camilla had a bag in her hand; she was calling feverishly to him to hurry. Finally she climbed into the chaise, the groom was on the box and they were off, clattering out of the yard. There was no sign of Rollo.

'I picked up my coat and ran downstairs. I ran into the yard and roared at Beckett—he was Thwaites' predecessor—Where is Stephen taking Lady Radley?

'He looked at me as though I were witless. "He's not taking her anywhere, Mr Matt."

'I said something like, Don't treat me like a fool, Beckett, and then Sim Farrell came running up. "He's taking her down to London to her folks, Mr Matt, and about time too. We all know what m'lord's been a-doing to her!"

'Beckett was as nonplussed as I was, and roared at Sim, "You fool, Sim, that's your job gone!"

'I stood there, my head whirling. She was very near her time, and setting off for London with only an ignorant boy with her was the last thing that she ought to have been doing—and where was Rollo?

'Beckett was so shocked he was almost witless himself. As well he might have been—he was turned off for not having the gumption to stop Stephen—even though he had no idea what Stephen was doing.

'I had only one thought in my head; to go after her and help her. Saddle my horse, I flung at Sim. I'll ride after them, try to get her back.

'That ride passed in a dream, a nightmare. I finally caught up with them after changing horses at Selby. I nearly rode past the inn where they had stopped to change horses again, but fortunately, or unfortunately, I recognised the chaise as I rode past the inn-yard.

'Camilla was sitting in the parlour. She looked worse than ever. I ran over to her, said something wild about whatever did she think that she was doing.'

He was suddenly not with Stacy any more. He had gone back in time. He was in the parlour, holding Camilla's hands.

'You must come back with me, Camilla. You're not fit to travel to London when you're so near your time.'

She looked up at him, the once cornflower-blue eyes dark with suffering. 'I won't go back, Matt. I will kill myself rather. You have no notion of how dreadfully he treated me. This afternoon he started to beat me so cruelly I began to fear for my baby's life. I fought him. He was so drunk he found it difficult to overmaster me. I hit him over the head with one of the bronze statuettes from Pompeii. He fell down and didn't get up again. I know that I didn't kill him, for he was still breathing. He was only stunned. I can't stay with him, Matt. Don't make me go back. I want to go home to my father and mother. I know that they're in London.'

She said all this in a tired, matter-of-fact voice which had Matt trembling. 'You must go back to The Eyrie,' he told her desperately, for he knew that her father and mother would not stand by her. They had sold her to Rollo, and that was that. 'I shall go to my father and tell him the truth.'

She began to shiver and shake, her hands writhing together, her face ghastly. 'I won't go back. I would rather die in a ditch than go back. I have an aunt in Chelsea; perhaps she will take me in.' Then she added almost inconsequentially, 'You know, Rollo often told me that he only married me to take me away from you. He said that you wouldn't want me when you saw what I had turned into.'

Matt took her into his arms as gently as he could and told her the truth. 'I shall always love you, Camilla, and I shall always try to help you.' But he had never felt so helpless. In the face of her determination and her suffering he could no longer argue that they should return to The Eyrie.

Stephen came in. Matt said wearily, 'I suppose you know that you'll be turned away for this?'

'So?' Stephen shot back at him. 'A fine sort of man I should be to stand by and see what I have seen without doing something. I'm surprised at you, Mr Matt. Want her to go back for him to beat her again, do you?'

'No,' he said, and made up his mind. 'I'll take her to her aunt at Chelsea, if that's what she wants.'

He told Stacy, whose face was now as white as his as she listened to his long and painful tale, 'But, of course, we never got to Chelsea. Twenty miles further on her pains started. I had left my horse at the last stop and was travelling with her. The postilion was driving, Stephen beside him on the box. I stopped the coach at the next inn and carried her in, as I carried you into the cottage where Hal was born.

'But Camilla's baby was born dead. It had been dead for some little time. And Rollo had probably killed it, if what Camilla said to me in her delirium after his birth was true. I cannot tell you how much she suffered while her child was being born, and how long it took.

'I was not with her. But I sat on the inn stairs and could hear all her agony. The landlady thought that we were eloping; she was certain something discreditable was happening and she raved and shouted at me for making a woman in such a condition travel at all.

'They let me in to see her when it was all over, and even now I can hardly bear to think of it. I had seen what a war-ship looked like after a battle, but what I saw in that bedroom beggared description. And my poor Camilla lay there dying, killed by my brother as surely as though he had run a sword through her heart. . . So now you know why I was not brave when Hal started to arrive, and why I thought that I was going to lose you. That I would have two loves and would lose both of them in the same cruel fashion.'

'But you were brave in the end,' riposted Stacy, squeezing his hand lovingly. 'Without you Hal might not have survived. And, now that you have shared your story with me, I understand why you felt and behaved as you did. The only thing that I don't understand is why everyone blamed you, why you had to leave home and were given such a bad name. After all, you only went after Camilla to save her.'

Matt's smile was a twisted one. 'Oh, when Rollo came to, and found out what had happened and started after us, he arranged everything so that the blame fell on me. Stephen and Sim were turned away and told that if they betrayed what had actually happened he would make sure that they would never work again, which was enough to silence them. Beckett, too, was bought off. By the time my father was informed and arrived on the scene, several days later, it was fully established that Camilla and I were running away, that we were guilty lovers. Rollo couldn't pretend that Camilla's child was mine, but everything else which could blacken me was thrown at me.

'The landlady at the inn didn't help; she blamed me for making Camilla travel when her time was so near. Nobody helped me, or would listen to anything I said in my defence. My father believed every word Rollo said. Camilla's parents accused me of killing her. If I hadn't persuaded her to run away with me, they said, then the child would have been born alive at The Eyrie and Camilla wouldn't have died.

'No one thought to ask themselves where in the world I could have been taking Camilla to, without a penny in my pocket, and no home of my own. I didn't help myself much. I was incoherent with grief and anger. When I tried to tell anyone—even my father—the truth of the matter concerning Rollo and Camilla I was called even worse names for attempting to blacken the character of the grieving widower. One of the reasons I was so harsh to you at first, at Pontisford, was because you reminded me of all the fine ladies who had torn my poor Camilla to pieces after her death.

'She was given a hole-and-corner funeral, which I was not allowed to attend, and when I said that I wanted to leave the Navy—the Navy didn't want me anyway—and go to the small estate which my mother had left me in Virginia everyone was only too happy to see the back of me.

'So there you have it. Until I met my dear Lady Disdain, organising and managing everyone's affairs, driving me mad because I could see that beneath her icy exterior there were fires of passion blazing in which I wished to immolate myself, I never felt true affection or love for a woman again. I think that I was afraid to. . .' There were tears in his eyes as he finished.

For a moment there was silence in the peaceful room. Stacy gently stroked the hand which held hers. 'Oh, Matt, what a terrible story. Poor Camilla, and poor you. I can quite understand that when I began to give birth so incontinently, and in such an isolated situation, it revived all your most painful memories and fears. I am astounded that you found yourself able to help me at all.'

She stopped, and for a moment they were silent again, Matt remembering his lost first love and Stacy seeing a young Matt, quite alone, desolate, and his life lying in ruins about him. It explained so much that had puzzled her. She told him so, adding, 'And will it be too painful for you to stay in England, my love? I know how much you loved your American home.'

Matt shook his head vigorously. 'If I were still the younger son, with no ties, then I would take you back there, but I am not. I am the heir and I have my duty to do, and will do it cheerfully, I hope, with you by my side.'

He leaned over to kiss her cheek. 'And now I'm not afraid to give my heart to you, to risk you having another child, thanks to your bravery while you were bearing Hal. And to some extent I think that I have my father's affection back again. He may never know the whole story of Rollo's treatment of Camilla, but I could not wish him to. Let us leave him with some of his illusions. As to the future—well, I only hope that for our next child there will be a warm, comfortable bedroom, a doctor and nurses standing by, and that I may be allowed to pace outside in the corridor with my shirt safely on!'

Stacy kissed him back with interest. 'Well, I hope

that you may have your wish, sir, and that we may soon set about fulfilling it. But, I warn you, I shall also expect Grandam Outhwaite to be present, with both of her blue bottles, for, although you and I birthed the baby, she made sure that we all recovered from it afterwards.'

At that moment there was a series of loud squawks from the nursery next door. Stacy laughed up at her husband, whose face had lightened appreciably since he had at last rid himself of some of the burden which he had carried for so many years.

She said mischievously, 'One day I shall tell you why I call Hal our little lion-cub, but in the meantime you must fetch him to me so that I may feed him, and while I do so we shall discuss buying a wolfhound for you, to replace Prince, for life is about renewal as well as death, my dear.'

Her husband did as he was bid, and sat and watched her feed their 'little cub', as she called him, and thought that on the day on which he had opened the door to the Bankeress he had opened the door to a new life for them both as well.

AN ANGEL'S TOUCH

by

Elizabeth Bailey

Dear Reader

My own early introduction to Georgette Heyer gave me so much pleasure that it is always a tremendous thrill to me to write historical romance for others to enjoy. This imagined world becomes all too real to me, and yes – sometimes the characters do take over! Writing is akin to directing a play: one creates the whole image, and controls everything living within it – rhythms, emotions, motivations, the very stuff of human endeavour. Both disciplines demand a sense of the dramatic – and, let's face it, an addiction to fantasy and fairytale: one tends to live, eat and breathe the story during the creative process. I have in recent years become both a playwright and director, often directing my own plays – both adaptations of classics, and original material. This has been an exciting development, and in future I will be concentrating on these pursuits – alongside writing novels. I could never abandon the delight of creating romantic fiction. I am definitely one of the 'incurables'. If, as I suspect, you are too, then this story is written for you.

With best wishes.

Elizabeth Bailey

Elizabeth Bailey grew up in Malawi, returning to England to plunge into the theatre. After many happy years 'tatting around the reps', she finally turned from 'dabbling' to serious writing. She finds it more satisfying for she is in control of everything; scripts, design, direction, and the portrayal of every character! Elizabeth lives in Surrey.

Other titles by the same author:

SWEET SACRIFICE
JUST DESERTS
HIDDEN FLAME
SEVENTH HEAVEN
FRIDAY DREAMING
ADORING ISADORA
A FRAGILE MASK

CHAPTER ONE

THROUGH the window of the slow-moving coach, a patch of bright colour in the valley below caught at the traveller's idle, wandering gaze. Leaning forward in her seat, Miss Verity Lambourn discerned a clutch of gaily painted wagons grouped about a neat clearing, from the centre of which emanated a plume of smoke.

Since this sunny afternoon in mid-July was fine and warm, it was to be inferred that the fire was lit for the purpose of cooking the gypsies' dinner, rather than the provision of illumination for a night of wild revelry to the strains of a fiddle and the beat of a rhythmic drum.

But the young lady whose clear hazel eyes were devouring the peaceful serenity of the scene was of an imaginative turn of mind. Already she had conjured up a mental image of a dusky, raven-haired beauty, of voluptuous mien, improbably attired in a flouncing petticoat of violent hue, dancing with wicked abandon about the flickering flames, while her handsome counterpart looked on with a brooding, sullen passion that boded ill to his erring inamorata.

For in such manner was Miss Lambourn prone to enliven the tedium of her days, and in particular the hours of enforced inertia on the present journey to Tunbridge Wells. The heavy old-fashioned coach made but ponderous progress from one stage to the next, even though drawn by six horses. They had of necessity had to traverse a cross-country route from their home village of Tetheridge in the county of Hampshire, and the roads, being less well-kept than the main pike thoroughfares, were not conducive to speed. Then, too, Lady Crossens had declared that she would not rattle her old bones more than she need, and the journey had occupied five days at a snail's pace when two might well have sufficed.

They had joined the main road from London to Tunbridge Wells at Sevenoaks, however, on this last leg of the journey, and the smoother ride had encouraged her ladyship to sink into slumber, her chin resting on her chest, leaving Miss Lambourn free to the indulgence of her visions.

So Verity leaned from the window to people the gypsy camp with the creations of her vivid imagination. Her ideas were perhaps ill-informed, culled as they had been from the products of the pens of more experienced observers than herself, and she had the wit to realise it.

But perhaps they were not so far removed from the truth, she thought with an inward smile, as her glance found the nearer figure of a man very much like the sultry figment of her mind, and, by his rough clothes and the spotted handkerchief about his neck, clearly a member of the gypsy clan from the encampment in the valley below. And those two children there, below the big tree by the roadside—a small boy, not much older than her little brother at home, who guarded with both hands an infant as yet unbreeched, who might be of either sex. Were they not gypsy urchins? Her hero's bairns perhaps? she wondered amusedly as she saw the gypsy man halt in his way and turn to look at the two.

Then, as Verity gazed on the scene from the window of the passing coach, it was as if a curtain lifted, dissolving the dream and presenting her with several incontrovertible signs of stark reality. She took them in all at once, her thoughts racing to a swift conclusion.

The children's attire bore the unmistakable stamp of gentility. Sporting a well cut frock-coat and breeches, a neat neckcloth and boots, the boy was every inch the miniature replica of a country gentleman. And no gypsy child would be swathed in that baby bonnet or the plain white round gown, embroidered and laced. The infant was whimpering, little hands clutching at the other small body whose protective arms now gathered it to him, in his face a look of fear as he stared at the gypsy not twenty yards away.

Almost without conscious decision, Verity was up, grabbing at the little window above the forward seat by means of which the passengers might converse with the coachman and the groom by his side, and pushing it open.

'Stop! Oh, please, Brading, stop *at once*!'

It took a moment or two for her anxious voice to penetrate the ears of the coachman on the box above, and by the time the vehicle came to a standstill the little drama being enacted was several yards behind it.

But Verity did not wait for the wheels to become completely motionless. She thrust open the door, gathered up her skirts, and sprang somewhat hazardously down into the road. She stumbled a little, for the coach doorway was some few feet off the ground. But in her anxiety for the children she made nothing of it, righting herself swiftly, and not even hearing the sleepy but exclamatory tones of Lady Crossens from behind her. 'What. . .what. . .? What is amiss?'

Then she was running back and in seconds saw that her surmise was correct. The gypsy had started towards the children, and the boy was backing away, having inexpertly lifted the infant in his arms, hampered by the added burden of its weight from taking to his heels.

Verity, calling out, came hurtling towards them, and she saw all eyes turned on her in amazement. The gypsy halted, staring, and the boy looked as if he feared equally an attack from this new quarter.

'Gracious, where have you been?' gasped Verity in mock exasperation as she arrived out of breath at his side. 'We have been hunting for you all over!' Then, leaning down to him a little, she dropped her voice. 'Are you in trouble? May I be of service to you?'

The boy blinked at her and clutched closer to his inadequate bosom the infant, who now began to cry in earnest. Under cover of this fresh noise, Verity added, 'Don't be afraid! I will help you if I may. Let me first get rid of this man.'

Then she turned to the gypsy and called out. 'So foolish of my little friends! They lost their way. But they will be safe now with me.'

The gypsy's face darkened with a flush, whether in anger or shame Verity could not tell. He stared hard at the little group for a moment or two, and then his eyes went past them just as Verity heard a footfall behind her. She turned to see that the groom, who had come down from his perch on the box of Lady Crossens' coach and followed her, had taken a step or two forward as if to offer his protection.

'Pray don't!' she said to him softly. 'There is no need for alarm, I am persuaded.'

'Maybe not, miss,' muttered the groom gruffly, 'but I'll be keepng me place beside you all the same.'

It was impossible to tell whether the gypsy overheard this exchange, but he shrugged slightly and turned away, walking unhurriedly off in the direction of his camp. Within a short time, he disappeared from sight as he descended into the valley.

Miss Lambourn, satisfied and not a little relieved, turned back to her protégés. She was forestalled, however.

'Her ladyship says as how you're to come back at once, miss,' the groom told her apologetically.

'Yes, yes, I shall do so directly,' Verity said impatiently. 'I must first see how we can assist these poor young things.' Then without further ado, she began to speak to the boy.

'Tell me, if you please, how I may help you. You are

lost, perhaps? I know you cannot be out here all by yourselves on purpose.'

The boy shook his head, his initial fear fading. Whether it was her friendly manner or the presence of the burly groom, he was visibly relaxing, though Verity noted that his thin shoulders were still shaking.

'It was Peggy,' he said in a grudging tone, as if the explanation were forced from him, indicating with a dip of his chin the small child he still clutched to his meagre chest.

Peggy was wailing so loudly that Verity felt impelled to do what she might to stem the flood before she could expect to converse with any degree of coherence. She crouched down, therefore, and addressed soothing blandishments to the little girl.

'There now, little one, don't cry so! You will be home directly, darling, I promise you. Come, now, come. All will be well, you'll see.'

Surprise arrested the child's sobs, and she stared at the stranger out of big blue eyes, luminous still with her tears. But when Verity held out her hands and would have taken the infant into her arms, Peggy pulled back and turned her face into the boy's chest.

'Tittoo,' she uttered plaintively. 'Tittoo! Tittoo! Peddy want Tittoo.'

'She means her nurse,' the boy translated, seeing Verity's puzzled look. His young arms were tiring and he set the little girl down. Though she clung to his slim torso, Peggy made no protest, but eyed the strange lady with interest, whimpering for 'Tittoo' now and then.

Had she had any knowledge of such things, Peggy would have noted that Miss Lambourn was far from fashionable. She was neatly turned out in the forest-green greatcoat dress of linen that had been made for her for travelling, and a pretty tall-crowned beaver hat embellished with ribbon. The feather tippet and muff for extra warmth against draughts had been discarded in the coach, but the ensemble lacked that touch of elegance that would have taken from it a countrified air.

Miss Lambourn was no beauty, either, though regular features in a fresh complexion, taken together with her candid direct gaze and the dark curls rioting under the hat, had an attraction all their own. That was, for those ready to overlook the defects of a plump bosom, and height a little below the average. She had, however, an uncommon degree of animation and a very friendly smile, which no doubt encouraged the waifs she had encountered to extend to her their trust.

'Peggy is your sister?' Verity guessed.

The boy nodded again. 'Yes. She was in the garden with Kittle—that's her nurse—and I saw her run off towards the woods.'

'Didn't—er—Kittle see her?'

'She weren't watching. Gossiping with one of the gardingers, she was,' the boy said, with an austerity that sat uneasily on his small person.

'How very shocking!' Verity commented primly, suppressing a smile. 'But could you not have called out to her?'

'I *did* call out,' protested the boy, tossing his head indignantly so that the straight fair locks that rested on his shoulders flicked about his cheeks. 'I called *plenty* times. Only I was quite far off, you know. And Peggy can go ever so fast when she wants, though she is not much above two years old. I had to run myself, but she was into the woods before I could catch her. And she would not stop when I shouted, not she!'

'But you did catch her, after all,' Verity said admiringly. 'You *did* do well.'

'Course I caught her!' scoffed the child. 'I am near seven myself, you know. And I *am* a boy.'

'Of course you are. How silly of me! I beg your

pardon,' apologised Verity hastily. 'But then why did you not take Peggy back at once?'

The boy flushed and looked away. 'I—I *should've*, I know. But—but I thought p'raps it would teach her a lesson. Kittle, I mean. If—if she thought she had lost Peggy for a bit.'

'Ah, I see,' Verity nodded understandingly. 'I dare say you were right. She must have had a severe fright.'

'Yes,' agreed the boy dubiously, looking shame-faced. 'Only I—I don't know the woods well. I'm not allowed in them mostly. 'Cause of poachers, you know.'

'But you do manage to spend some time in them, for all that,' she suggested with a twinkle.

He reddened again. 'Well, yes. But not enough to—to know them as I'd like, and—and. . .'

'And the long and the short of it is that you missed your bearings and became lost. And who shall blame you for that? Gracious, what a misadventure! I think, though, we should get Peggy back home as fast as we are able, don't you?'

'Yes, but they'll come for us soon, I think,' the boy announced, with an unconcern that, together with his self-possessed air and his very grown-up manner, spoke more eloquently than his clothes of a privileged background. 'That's why I made for the road. They are bound to come looking this way, for this is all *our* land. We are out of the 'state grounds here, though.'

Even as he spoke there came the sound of many hoofs, and Verity turned in time to see several horsemen approaching from behind the coach. She noticed as well old Lady Crossens' gaunt features peering out at her, and urged the groom to run back and reassure her that she would rejoin her in a moment. But the groom was mindful of her ladyship's orders. 'For heaven's sake, Dogget,' she had uttered distractedly, 'get after her and fetch her back! And mind she comes to no harm, for she is in my care, and if I must face dear Grace and the Vicar with the tale of a vanished daughter, I shall likely go off in an apoplexy!' He chose therefore to remain stalwart by Miss Lambourn's side until it should please his mistress's oddly behaved young guest to recover her sanity and get back into the coach.

There was no time for Verity to persuade the groom to do as she asked, or herself to call out a reassurance to the old lady, for the horsemen were upon them, reining in and dismounting in a flurry of exclamatory comment.

'Good God, my lord, what a dance you have led us!' called a slim, youthful individual with a gentlemanly air.

'You have her safe, me lord!' came from a thick-set man in fine livery. 'God be praised!'

'Your lordship had best come quick. Fat's in the fire now, and no mistake!'

The last words, muttered by a lad with the look of a stablehand, who had flung off his horse the first and was closest to the boy, were accompanied by a significant jerk of the head.

Verity, following the direction of his gaze, saw that a phaeton had drawn up a few yards away. It was driven by a slight young man who turned a lean countenance set in lines of severity upon the errant children, and handed his reins to the middle-aged groom who sat beside him.

The group about her fell silent, and Verity watched with interest as the man descended, slowly and with apparent difficulty, from the phaeton into the road. The groom handed him a cane and as he advanced towards them, a pair of dark angry eyes fixed intimidatingly on the boy, it was to be seen that he walked with a pronounced limp, seeming to drag his hip over a stiff right leg.

No one spoke as he came up, and the boy met that menacing eye with a look of sullen apprehension in his own.

'Well, Braxted?' the young man demanded in a quietly controlled tone. 'Have you anything to say for yourself?'

The boy's eyes, big and blue like his sister's, flashed momentarily, and then sank. He compressed his lips firmly together and steadfastly regarded the ground. But Verity saw his small hands tighten on the shoulders of his little sister, whose arms still clung about him.

Peggy let out a squealing protest which drew all eyes. The young man looked at the gentlemanlike member of the entourage of three.

'Inskip,' he said quietly. The man addressed immediately leaned down and prised the infant's hands from about her brother's person. The boy instantly let her go and stepped back a pace. The little girl was swung up as the man in authority added, 'Take her to the phaeton. Hoff may hold her. I will not be above a moment.'

The other nodded briefly, and went off with Peggy. The other men took the opportunity to retreat a step or two. Verity could not blame them. There was such a heavy charge of held-in fury emanating from the authoritative young man that it was almost tangible. She found it uncomfortable, and oddly inapposite. For he looked so insignificant a man.

He was quietly, if respectably dressed in a green frock-coat over buckskin breeches and top-boots, cravat neatly though unimaginatively knotted, and a plain, round-brimmed beaver over a quantity of rich brown locks drawn back and tied in the nape of his neck. His features were good, though marked, young as he was, with lines of suffering that ran down to a well-shaped mouth, tight-lipped at this moment, and a resolute chin. It was his eyes, so dark as to be almost black, that were his most striking attribute, attractive even as they burned with the anger that he turned back on the boy.

'Well, Braxted?' he repeated, in a voice that was not the less threatening for its quiet control. 'Your pranks are one thing, and to be discussed between us at some more convenient time. But to be involving your little sister in them goes beyond the line of what may be tolerated.'

He paused, but the boy, though he raised his blue orbs to stare defiantly up into that smouldering gaze, had nothing to say.

'I trust,' continued the man softly, 'I make myself plain?'

'Yes, sir,' the boy asserted gruffly.

'Upon my word!' ejaculated Verity, suddenly entering the lists, as the implications of this speech burst in upon her. 'And I trust, sir,' she said, rounding on the young man in righteous indignation, 'that you will take the trouble to enquire more particularly into this affair before you inflict the dreadful punishment that I suspect to be in your mind!'

Taken aback, the young man jerked round to face her. He almost tripped up in his clumsy haste and had to support himself with his cane. The liveried servant behind him sprang forward to his assistance, but he waved him away without a backward glance. It was evident that he had not even noticed Verity standing there, but the look of surprise was swiftly succeeded by one of scarcely veiled annoyance.

'And what, ma'am,' he demanded icily, 'has this affair in any way to do with you?'

'I will tell you!' Verity declared at once, not in the least deterred by his manner. 'I happen to be in possession of the true facts of the matter, having come upon the scene a few moments before yourself. I would have supposed, sir, that anyone with the least degree of common sense must perceive at once that the boy is far too protective of his sister to be likely to implicate her in any pranks he might play. And in this instance, as you would have known had you troubled yourself to *ask* the child before *flinging* accusations at his head in that—that *brutish* fashion, there was no *prank* in the case!'

Then, without giving her astonished auditor an opportunity to open his mouth, Miss Lambourn dropped to her knees before the boy and grasped him urgently by the shoulders.

'My dear young friend, do, I beg of you, *think* for a moment. I dare say it is all very brave and *manly* for you to take the blame for something which is in no way your fault, but you cannot have thought the question through. Only consider! Another time you may not be at hand to see the danger, and what if the nurse should be so careless when you are not by to dash so gallantly to the rescue? Then you would have cause to blame yourself indeed! For by your keeping silent, you know, the nurse will *never* be corrected, for I cannot think that she will confess her fault.'

The boy Braxted looked much struck by this, and, grasping his hands and smiling coaxingly at him, Verity added, 'What good can it possibly do for you meekly to accept a punishment which you have done nothing to deserve? Indeed, only misery can come from such a gross injustice. To you, perhaps to your sister and the nurse. And indeed——' with a fleeting glance up at the stern countenance above her ' – to your mentor himself. I wish, *dear* friend, you will think better of it and tell him *everything*!'

Braxted now also cast a quick look up at the young man standing silently by. He noted that the features had relaxed, and the dark eyes had lost their fire. His stiffness melted and he grinned suddenly.

'Well, I will, then. I like to have a friend like you.'

Verity smiled and pressed his hands before releasing them. 'I am glad. I hope we may meet again.'

She rose to her feet and turned to look again at the young man. Like Braxted, she saw that the anger had vanished from his eyes, to be replaced by a gleam which she strongly suspected to be of amusement. An amusement she deprecated, for his conduct had been disgraceful! Then he spoke, and his words disarmed her.

'It is apparent that I owe you both apology and thanks,' he said, adding with an ironic little bow, 'I have certainly been put very firmly in my place.'

Verity bit her lip on a laugh, her outrage dissipating fast. The implication was not lost on her. There was no doubt she had been extremely uncivil. 'I have to beg your pardon, sir.'

'Pray don't,' he pleaded, and Verity thought there was a lurking twinkle in the black depths of his eyes. 'You have done me a signal service—albeit unwittingly, for I do not flatter myself that such was your intention!—and I am only sorry that I cannot stay to express my thanks more suitably. You see, I must get Margaret home.'

'Margaret?' repeated Verity, vexed to feel herself blushing at the implied rebuke. How unhandsome of him when she had already apologised!

'Peggy, he means,' chimed in Braxted.

'Oh, yes, of course. Do go at once!' Verity begged, thankful for the excuse that would afford instant relief from her embarrassment, and feeling rather guilty for forgetting the infant's needs while championing the boy Braxted.

But when she looked up at the phaeton she saw that Peggy seemed quite contented in the competent arms of the middle-aged groom who managed both to nurse her and hold the horses without apparent difficulty. It crossed Verity's mind that perhaps the child was more often to be found in the arms of servants than in those of her own mother. She had certainly called in her distress for 'Tittoo', her nurse Kittle, rather than for 'Mamma'.

There was no time for further speculation, however, for the young man, having muttered some words of farewell that she scarcely heard, was already climbing laboriously into the phaeton, while Braxted hopped nimbly up to take his own place, squeezing in between the groom and his father.

His *father*? Verity supposed he must have that identity. Though he did not behave in the least like a father should. Admittedly, he had owned himself at fault, but his attitude to the children had been far from loving! And then, too, though everyone had addressed Braxted as 'my lord', none had offered a similar courtesy to the young man. Perhaps he was merely Braxted's tutor. He certainly acted more in the manner of a schoolmaster than of a father! she thought with severe disapprobation.

'You may tell me your tale on the way, Braxted,' she heard him say to the boy as the phaeton started forward, in a tone that lent credibility to her last theory. Especially as the childish treble did not pipe up in response as it ought to have done at a parent's bidding. At least not to Verity's ears. Or perhaps it had been drowned by the clatter of the horses' hoofs, she thought, trying to be charitable.

To the obvious relief of Lady Crossens' groom, who had been hovering on the fringes of the group all this while, she began to walk back to where the old coach stood waiting. The groom hurried ahead of her to let down the steps and hold open the door.

The phaeton and its accompanying horses were already lost to sight as Miss Lambourn, apologising to the groom for keeping him waiting all this time, climbed into the coach. She was greeted by the querulous voice of her patroness.

'And now, miss, if I might trespass upon your valuable time, perhaps you would be so obliging as to tell me the meaning of this extraordinary conduct?'

It took some time to persuade Lady Crossens of the justice of her actions. But although Miss Lambourn patiently explained the circumstances, she could by no means subscribe to her ladyship's freely expressed view that she ought to learn to mind her own business.

'You would not have had me drive on and leave those poor little mites to their fate?' she exclaimed, shocked.

'If this is not precisely of what your dear mama warned me,' complained Lady Crossens, ignoring this home question. 'Impulsive, that's what she said of you. Impetuous and impulsive!'

'I dare say I am, ma'am,' Verity admitted, in her honest way, 'but even Mama would not, I am persuaded, denounce my having interfered in the matter. And Papa——'

'Oh, you need not tell me what *Papa* would say!' uttered her ladyship crossly. 'I am well able to imagine it for myself. If he had his way, he would doubtless clutter up the vicarage with a score of waifs and strays. As if there were not enough of you as it is!'

This was undeniable. The Reverend Harry Lambourn might count himself blessed in the possession of his seven surviving daughters, and in particular of his last-born and most treasured only son, but his adored and adoring wife was at her wit's end to know how to dispose suitably of this bevy of maidens.

Faith at twenty-eight was a matron with children of her own, having snaffled the most eligible of the local gentlemen to become the village doctor's wife. Prudence, already on the shelf at twenty-four, had been sent to Kingsclere to stay with her mother's brother, in the hope of contracting a suitable alliance. For Patience, just a year younger, had achieved a respectable engagement on a visit to her more prominent Lambourn cousins in Winchester. Lady Lambourn, however, with two daughters of her own to be suitably established, was hardly likely to saddle herself with any more of the sisters at present.

Mrs Lambourn had greeted with heartfelt thanks, therefore, Lady Crossens' kind suggestion that Verity, now eighteen, should accompany her to Tunbridge Wells when she went, as had long been her custom, to take the waters during that no longer fashionable six-week season in the summer. True, when both Prudence and Patience, in their turn, had gone there with her ladyship a few years earlier, Mrs Lambourn's high hopes had not been rewarded. But with three more girls already in their adolescence, a needy parson's wife ought never to look a gift horse in the mouth. So she had argued with her spouse when the reverend gentleman had demurred.

'You would not have it thought, Mr Lambourn, that we are ungrateful for her ladyship's kind offices on our daughter's behalf.'

'My dear,' protested the gentleman, 'we are already so much beholden to Lady Crossens for so many kindnesses that I hesitate, I do indeed, to add to the burden of indebtedness.'

'Good gracious me, Mr Lambourn, there will be nothing of that sort, I do assure you! Why, how in the world do you suppose poor Lady Crossens could manage without some young attendant to run her little errands, and perform those offices so very arduous to a woman in her declining years?'

Mr Lambourn suggested that Lady Crossens' servants, her maid in particular, might be employed upon such work. But this foolish idea was summarily disposed of.

'As to that, her ladyship's woman is always permitted to take a holiday at this season. And well does she deserve it! I never knew a female so cantankersome as our kind patroness.'

'I hope you are not suggesting that Verity should go to Tunbridge Wells in the capacity of lady's maid!' objected her husband in accents of disgust.

His fond helpmeet cast him a look of scorn. 'Nothing of the sort. Lady Crossens will employ a local girl, of course. But apart from her coachman and groom, she will have none of her own people about her. Verity's assistance will therefore be invaluable to her and in such a cause I should not care to refuse to allow our daughter to go. Prudence and Patience did so well by her that it is not to be wondered at that she should be anxious to secure Verity's company. Indeed, I do not know how she will go on otherwise! I may add, you made no objection to *their* going.'

'If that is your recollection, my dear, I can only say that it is not mine,' said her spouse with an ironic look. 'Be that as it may, and indeed taking the case of Prudence and Patience into consideration, I am doubly reluctant——'

But Mrs Lambourn had all her ammunition at her fingertips and loosed a shaft that silenced the enemy once and for all. 'Do you tell me that you would put a bar in the way of your daughter's pleasure? Why should not poor Verity also see something of the world? And that she deserves this treat, you will scarcely deny!'

Mr Lambourn was far from denying anything of the kind. He was well aware that to Verity's lot had fallen the care and entertainment, and to some extent the education, of her three younger sisters for the last few years, for Mrs Lambourn's attention had been almost entirely taken up with anxious solicitude over her one and only son in his infant days. For it was in these early years that she had lost several of those seemingly endless baby girls, as they succumbed to various ailments that proved beyond the power to mend even of the zealous practitioner who had at length become her son-in-law.

That she was assisted in this delicate task by every one of her daughters, all of whom adored their baby brother, in no way mitigated the good lady's conviction that young Master Lambourn was the child most in need of maternal devotion.

The reverend could not acquit himself of an almost equal devotion to his only son, and consequently went through periodic torments of remorse at the neglect from which he imagined his girls to be suffering. If he suspected his wife's chief motive in packing her fourth daughter off to Tunbridge Wells, he said nothing of it, merely agreeing that Verity deserved her good fortune and taking care to thank Lady Crossens in suitable style.

Her ladyship's manner of receiving these thanks, however, left him in no doubt that the whole scheme had been concerted between the two ladies for one purpose only.

'I'll do my best to get her off your hands, Harry, but, as I told Grace to her face, I don't hold out much hope. Tunbridge ain't what it was, but if any eligibles under sixty come within hailing distance I'll spread my net, never fear!'

It was on the tip of Harry Lambourn's tongue to withdraw his consent, his sense of what was fitting revolting against the idea of any of his daughters being given in matrimony to a man his own age or older. But he knew her ladyship to affect an exaggerated form of speech and so held his peace.

In truth, for all her crochets and complaints of Harry

Lambourn's boundless and reckless charity, for he could ill afford it, Lady Crossens was very fond of the vicar of Tetheridge parish, which came largely under her patronage as the major landowner of the area. She had early become an ally of poor Grace Lambourn in the formidable task confronting her with so many female offspring, and had often enough lamented to her that she had no son or grandson who might take one of them to wife and so provide for the rest. Whether in fact she would have permitted such an unequal alliance had such been the case, Mrs Lambourn privately doubted. But in fact Lady Crossens had ever been childless and had no suitable nephews or near connections whom she might have offered up on the altar of matrimony to succour one of the Lambourn sisters. And her husband's heir was already a family man. Nor, since she had been invalidish for many years, was she part of the fashionable social whirl, and could not therefore take a stray Lambourn under her wing for the season in London.

What she could do, however, she did with a good heart, and, if some little return for her generosity was to be made out by services in kind, who could cavil at it? So Prudence and Patience had both had their chance in the admittedly limited opportunities of Tunbridge Wells.

And now there was Verity, who had most fortunately reached an appropriate age just when Lady Crossens should feel well enough once more to attempt the journey after some four years' absence from that favourite haunt of her golden youth.

For to Lady Crossens, as to others of her generation, Tunbridge Wells was steeped in nostalgia, and she could derive almost as much pleasure in the early nineties in talking with her cronies of the dear old days as she had enjoyed in the reality of its heyday in the forties and fifties when Beau Nash reigned supreme.

By the time the coach rumbled into the town, and fetched up outside the coach office, the questionable behaviour of Lady Crossens' protégée had given way to an argument over the identity of the man who had incurred Verity's wrath.

'From what you have said,' offered her ladyship, 'I should guess this boy Braxted has come into his inheritance a minor, and this person is his guardian.'

'Yes, that is quite possible,' Verity agreed. 'I suppose he is an uncle or cousin. He certainly exhibited the sort of breeding that would suggest a genteel background.'

'But that would not preclude his taking a post of tutor or secretary,' argued Lady Crossens. 'Indeed, one would employ none but a gentleman born on such work.'

Verity thought about this. 'I must say I should be glad to know him for something insignificant of that sort, for his conduct towards those poor children was quite abominable, and I am still very much out of charity with him! But I must confess that the other men treated him with a deference that argued against it. I am inclined to think you are right, Lady Crossens. Let us suppose him a guardian—and a remarkably bad one at that!'

'Pish! What should he do? Fawn all over them and indulge them to death like another I could——' Her ladyship broke off, belatedly recognising the infelicity of this retort.

But Verity was not in the least offended and she knew very well what the old lady had intended to say. 'Like Papa, you mean. Yes, I know he indulges us. He is the best and kindest of fathers!'

And the most sentimental, her ladyship might have added. But she did not. There was a degree of intimacy in the Lambourn family that in truth she envied a little, in spite of her strictures, and she could readily appreciate Verity's disgust at the quite different circumstances that apparently prevailed in this boy Braxted's household.

But Miss Lambourn, having settled to her satisfaction the probable station in life of her late antagonist, had moved on to indulge her ready imagination in a fantastic flight of fancy. In her mind's eye she was turning the limping, angry young man into a hideously deformed and ravening monster, who coveted his young ward's title and lands and was even now plotting to eliminate him and bury his bones in the dried-up moat surrounding his sinister castle.

Lady Crossens' voice recalled her from a scene of terror in the young lord's bedchamber, where the grotesque figure of the murdering guardian leaned over the angelic sleeping child, dagger raised ready to strike.

'Here we are!' trilled the old lady excitedly. 'Oh, do but look about you, child! Isn't it heaven? I can hardly believe it. I am back at last. Back at the Wells!'

CHAPTER TWO

'MAY I say what an inestimable pleasure it is to welcome your ladyship back among us? You have been sorely missed these last years.'

The speaker, a dapper, middle-aged gentleman with a manner that nicely blended respect with an air of self-importance, nevertheless spoke in all sincerity. Mr Richard Tyson, the present master of ceremonies for Tunbridge Wells, had a healthy fondness for any and all of the wealthy and high-ranking patrons who still chose to grace his domain in the summer. Especially those like Lady Crossens who, although holding fast to old customs, still cared to dress with the times and so keep the Wells a little in fashion.

Her ladyship had put off her travelling dress and arrayed herself for the evening in an open robe of figured French lawn over a muslin petticoat with a large cross-over handkerchief that effectively concealed her scanty bosom, and was sporting a dashing feathered turban over powdered hair which was suspiciously lush for her years.

It was not perhaps a costume that would have made fashionable London stare, but it was quite good enough for this watering place and had evoked lavish compliments from Mr Tyson. For he, and many like him, depended on this custom for their livelihood, although the increasing number of new residents was beginning to boost the hitherto meagre pickings during the rest of the year.

'You will find us very little changed,' Mr Tyson said comfortably, 'though we have done what we may to improve the amenities. The Walks have been repaved this year, you know.' He coughed and, with a sly sideways glance at Lady Crossens, corrected himself. 'The *Parade*, I should say, for so it has now been decided to designate it.'

'Parade? Parade?' echoed her ladyship in disbelieving tones. 'Bless me, Mr Tyson, whatever next?'

The master of ceremonies shrugged and spread his hands, uttering in a self-deprecatory tone belied by the smirk about his mouth, 'Wiser heads than mine, Lady Crossens, wiser heads than mine!'

'Pish and tush! "Parade" indeed! They shall never hear such a nonsense on *my* lips, I promise you.'

'Are you speaking of the Pantiles?' asked Verity, rather at a loss.

'The *Walks*, ma'am,' explained Mr Tyson, 'was used to be the official title.'

'Pho!' ejaculated the old lady. 'The Pantiles it has ever been, and will so continue, mark my words! All these new-fangled ideas. I dare say I may find every pleasant custom overset, never mind that poor old Nash may be turning in his grave!'

'By no means, I assure you, dear lady,' said Mr Tyson reassuringly. 'You will find everything just as it used to be. We still have our little pleasures in the Rooms—our concerts and balls, and *cards*, as I know you will be glad to hear.'

'Ah!' sighed Lady Crossens with satisfaction. 'Yes, I have missed my whist. Of balls you may speak to my companion. I am not going to make a figure of myself in the minuet at my age!'

The master of ceremonies turned obligingly to where Verity was seated, by the windows of the little parlour from where she was enjoying a view of the main thoroughfare of Tunbridge Wells. For the lodgings that Lady Crossens had taken, as she always did, were only a couple of doors down from the coach office, in a suite of first-floor rooms situated directly over the paved walkway affectionately known as the Pantiles.

The effect in the still light summer evening was very pretty. On the pavings below a number of persons, in pairs and groups, were strolling gently. Across the way ran an avenue of graceful trees concealing to some degree the buildings on the other side. A theatre was visible, though clearly just now uninhabited, and a species of large hall from which plentiful light streamed. There was a small musicians' gallery, with trellis barrier and pretty columns and, looking down the Pantiles, there could just be seen the end of the colonnade that Verity had been told ran the length of the street under the low roofs below her. There was a sound of music and an occasional trill of laughter floated up to the open window.

A rising thrill of pleasure fluttered in Verity's breast as she accepted with a word of thanks a copy of the master of ceremonies' rules and regulations as Mr Tyson enumerated the entertainments on offer.

These appeared to be considerable to one accustomed to the quiet backwater that constituted Tetheridge village. Verity hoped her modest wardrobe would be adequate to meet the demand likely to be placed upon it. Unlike her patroness, she had donned a simple chemise undress gown of sprigged cotton and threaded a bandeau through her dark curls.

But it looked as if she must soon delve into her supply of more formal attire. The programme promised two balls a week with minuets, a cotillion and country dances, as well as recitals and theatrical entertainments. All this besides chatting with the company in the coffee-rooms and meeting at the spring to drink the waters of a morning.

'Not that I should suppose, with so charming a complexion, you have any need to do that,' said Mr Tyson gallantly.

Verity laughed. 'No indeed! I am in excellent health. Though I shall be surprised if it does not break down in all this gaiety. Upon my word, I had not looked for such a round of dissipation!'

'Well, well,' the gentleman uttered, visibly gratified. 'I believe we are not quite in a decline.'

'Decline! I dare say I shall be obliged to leave you all to your revels and take to my bed with a good book within the week!'

Laughing heartily at this pleasantry, Richard Tyson assured her that in that case she might surely find some suitable tale on the shelves of one of the two circulating libraries.

'I recall your sister—Miss *Prudence*, I think?—partaking very lavishly of such delights some years ago.'

'Oh, yes, Prue told me how happy she was to find all the latest published novels immediately to hand. I shall certainly follow her example.'

It did not take many days for Verity to become familiar with all there was to do and see in the social centre of Tunbridge Wells. She very quickly became acquainted with everyone, residents and visitors alike, and so was instantly able to pick out an alien face as she hurried from the Assembly Rooms to execute a commission for Lady Crossens.

A light drizzle was falling and, clutching her pelisse about her, she ran quickly across the Walks towards the shelter of the colonnade on the other side. She stood for a moment, shaking off the drops and pushing her hood back off her dark curls. She caught sight as she did so of someone standing before one of the shop windows, looking at the wares displayed there.

At once she knew he was a stranger, and choked back the automatic greeting with which everyone saluted one another as they met in the street. The place was all but deserted on this inclement morning, and she hesitated a moment or two, uncertain whether to proceed. Then the man turned his head at some slight sound she made and shock rippled through her chest.

It was he! That same pale face under the plain beaver hat. She could not mistake! And as her eyes dropped down as if to verify the fact, she noted the cane, which had been slightly hidden by the folds of his greatcoat, on which he leaned a little.

She saw the startled recognition leap into his eyes and knew a moment of sheer panic. Should she greet him? What could she say? That awkward meeting at which she had not hesitated to lash out at him! And the brief, sardonic comment he had made that showed how mannerless he had thought her conduct!

The whole, almost forgotten scene flashed back to her in vivid detail and she felt her cheeks grow hot with embarrassment. Heavens, she must get away!

Her errand was to Mr Sprange's place and her way unfortunately led past the shop where the gentleman stood. Lowering her gaze to the paving, she began to move. But, in spite of herself, she could not resist a peep up at him as she passed. It was a mistake.

Her eyes looked straight into those black ones and her feet stopped of their own volition. It was only for a brief moment she hovered thus, but he lifted a hand to his beaver and doffed it, bowing slightly.

Verity's cheeks flamed anew. She gave the tiniest of nods in response and hurried on, her heart thudding so hard that she felt breathless.

Absurd! What in the world was the matter with her? The man was a monster! Had she not intervened, he would undoubtedly have beaten that poor little boy Braxted. She had no reason to feel discomfited. It was, on the contrary, he who should feel mortified, meeting once more the stranger who had been obliged to take him to task!

It occurred to her suddenly that there had not been any sign of discomfiture, either in this brief glimpse she had just had of those black eyes, or at the time. Had he been chagrined? Abashed? He had not! Instead he had had the temerity to laugh at her!

Arrived in Mr Sprange's shop, it was with the words and smiles of an automaton that she responded to the lad who served her, requesting the playbill for Mrs Baker's next theatrical presentation with scarcely a thought to what she was about. Fortunately there was little chance of the assistant mistaking her needs, for there was only the one theatre in Tunbridge Wells and Mrs Sarah Baker had a monopoly on the productions that were staged there.

She dawdled over the various prints and bills of coming events, hoping desperately that the young stranger would go away. There was no sign of him when she eventually came out of the shop, but as she made her way back to the Assembly Rooms she was conscious of a slight feeling of disappointment.

The capacious building she entered was the central meeting place and the venue for most of the season's events. The rooms were large and airy, with huge columns and marbled ornamentation after the fashion of those in Bath. But they contrived, perhaps because of the many knots of people seated in the alcoves made by settees and well-placed screens, to appear remarkably cosy. Yet when the main room was cleared for dancing, its size showed to advantage.

In one of the corners near to the adjoining card-room, the lady's favourite haunt, Verity found Lady Crossens deep in conversation with an elderly widow, Mrs Polegate, whom Verity had already come to know well. For this crony of her patroness was an almost constant companion, and it had been obvious to the young lady when Mrs Polegate visited them on their first evening that her two elders were ripe for a high old time.

A greater contrast to Lady Crossens could not have been found than this lifelong friend. She was a dewy-eyed sentimental dame, with the mind of a butterfly, who took the world as it presented itself to her eyes, never troubling to look beneath the surface. She had none of the shrewdness that characterised her friend, but equally none of her acerbity. Inveterately though she gossiped, she had not a particle of malice in her nature, and this trait endeared her to her friends even while the more discerning among them dubbed her a fool—including Lady Crossens, who did not scruple to call her so to her face.

'Dear Emilia, I was quite overcome with happiness when you wrote you was coming at last,' she had fluttered that night, her plump countenance wreathed in smiles that crumpled the remnants of an erstwhile prettiness into a multitude of wrinkles. 'I declare, it has been a desert here without you! And last year in particular, when we had such frolics and jaunterings about—so delightful!'

'If it was so delightful, my presence can have only been superfluous,' said Lady Crossens drily, unimpressed by the worth of her friend's protestations.

'Oh, yes, but your being there would have added so much to our pleasure,' uttered the other lady sincerely.

Biting back a laugh, Verity wondered if Mrs Polegate was merely impervious to irony or quite incapable of recognising her own inconsistencies. Lady Crossens had no such doubts.

'Your wit has not improved in my absence, at any rate, Maria.'

'Oh, but I am not at all clever, Emilia. You know I am not.' She looked across at Verity. 'I never was, you know. Poor Emilia has had much ado to put up with my silliness all these years.'

'Pish!' scoffed her ladyship, adding gruffly, 'You're a good-hearted girl, Maria. And that, believe me, counts for a deal more than a sharp tongue.'

To hear her patroness address a lady quite her own age as a *girl* almost overset Verity, but she contrived to keep her countenance, smiling kindly at the visitor.

'Very true, ma'am. But I wish you will tell me, Mrs Polegate, how you became acquainted.'

'Oh, I know what you mean! So unlikely a friendship, don't you feel?' said the lady, displaying so unexpectedly accurate an understanding of Verity's thought that she felt herself redden a little. But Mrs Polegate did not appear to notice. 'You may say we are *Wellsian* friends, I suppose, for we met here, both in our very first season. What days they were! Dancing on the green! Do you not remember, Emilia?'

'Do I not! I ruined my best satin shoes and lost a diamond buckle!'

'How your mama did scold!'

Like all the elderly habituées of Tunbridge Wells, the two ladies were forever to be heard reminiscing about the 'dear old days'. Today was no exception, and while they rattled on Verity had time to recover her poise, which had been very much overset by the unexpected encounter with the angry young man of her adventure.

She therefore greeted the sight of the widow's plump, unsuitably clothed figure with relief now. For in spite of Lady Crossens' freely expressed criticisms, Mrs Polegate arrayed herself always in the chemise gowns she loved, exposing a good deal of bosom and demonstrating the girth of her thickened waistline all too clearly with the gathered-in style, and the sash that all but vanished between the rolls of flesh above and below. She was addicted, moreover, to large mob-caps which most unflatteringly framed her round pink face and only added to the unfortunate impression of mutton dressed as lamb.

'And of course you recall that dreadful Mrs Montagu and her blue-stocking set,' she was saying to her friend. 'So clever! I never could understand the half of her discourse.'

'That woman!' Lady Crossens snorted. 'She was not near so clever as she would have us believe. Setting herself up for a queen to all the men of letters! I was never so happy as when her coach overturned.'

'Oh, no, ma'am, how uncharitable!' exclaimed Verity, startled out of her preoccupation.

'Oh, yes, Emilia,' echoed Mrs Polegate. '*Poor* Mrs Montagu! Not but what the coach did not in fact overturn. But she was very much shaken.'

'Poor Mrs Montagu indeed!' said her ladyship impenitently. 'You had as well say poor Miss Chudleigh!'

'If I had not forgotten her!' shrieked Mrs Polegate. 'Scandalous, shameless woman!'

'Why, what did she do?' asked Verity, glad of something sufficiently diverting to keep at bay the intrusive memories of a certain gentleman.

'What did she not do?' countered Lady Crossens.

'Well, my dear,' began Mrs Polegate, with an air of unfolding a great mystery, 'Elizabeth Chudleigh was an extremely beautiful lady and the gentlemen were mad for her, but in the end she married the Duke of Kingston. And *then* it transpired that she was already married!'

'And so it all came out,' put in Lady Crossens. 'She was tried for bigamy by the House of Lords.'

'And convicted?' asked Verity, quite shocked.

'Oh, yes,' said Mrs Polegate. 'But they could do nothing about it, for she *was* a peeress! She was ruined, naturally. But she went abroad——'

'Taking, so it was said, the Duke's money with her.'

'Yes, but, Emilia, he *was* dead.'

Verity was betrayed into a choke of laughter. 'Gracious! I had no idea Tunbridge Wells was such a den of vice!'

'Oh, but all *that* occurred in London, you know,' said Mrs Polegate excusingly. 'She behaved *quite* respectably here. And she was very beautiful.'

'Does that make it any better?'

'Beauty and wit may generally excuse a good deal,' said Lady Crossens shrewdly. 'Not that there has been much of the latter in evidence at the Wells.'

'But, Emilia, only think of the Water Poets!' protested the widow. 'Some of the verses were very witty. And so elegant and pretty.'

'Who in the world are the Water Poets?' demanded Verity.

'Anyone who could turn a verse. Or, indeed, who *thought* they could,' her ladyship explained.

'They were used to write verses in a book kept at the bookseller's on the Walks. We—I mean the ladies, for they were nearly always written in compliment to one of us—were used to go daily to read them.'

'Yes, and afterwards scratch out the eyes of those so honoured, or, if one should be oneself chosen, peacock about the place well set up in one's own conceit.'

Verity smiled. 'Now I understand why you return here year after year, dear ma'am. Tell me, did Lord Crossens address such verses to you?'

Her ladyship's lips twitched, for anyone less romantic than her bucolic lord would be hard to imagine. 'Oh, I was no subject for such fripperies. Too tall, too skinny. Always was. But Maria had many an admirer pen his ardour thus.'

'Oh, Emilia!' protested the good lady, blushing.

'Well, you were an uncommonly pretty girl, Maria, I will say that for you. But Mr Polegate—God rest his soul!—who was *not* the handsomest of men, nevertheless carried her off in the teeth of them all.'

'Oh, yes,' sighed Mrs Polegate. 'Dear William! What days they were!' Her smiling face reached Verity's and fell suddenly. 'But how dull it must be for you, poor Miss Lambourn! Alas, we have no water poets now!' She shook her head sadly so that the frill of her ridiculous mob-cap rippled. 'Scarcely any young persons at all, let alone eligible gentlemen of rank and fortune. I am afraid you must find it sadly flat.'

'Oh, no,' Verity disclaimed at once. 'Though I must say it seems sadly expensive. Why, there is a fee and a gratuity to be dropped at every hand!'

'Very true. They are shocking robbers!' agreed Mrs Polegate in a hushed voice, casting glances about as if she expected to be set upon there and then.

'Don't be ridiculous, Maria!' scolded Lady Crossens in a lowered tone. 'You know very well all the servitors depend upon gratuities for their livelihood.'

'So they do!' Mrs Polegate said, apparently struck, although in fact she regularly tipped lavishly without giving the matter a thought.

'And you need not concern yourself with such matters, Verity,' added her ladyship. 'I will take care of all that.'

Miss Lambourn could only be thankful. The Vicar was not a poor man, but his small personal fortune and the stipend of his profession had been very much dissipated by the exigencies of keeping a large family, and all the girls had been bred in habits of the strictest economy. To have been obliged to defray the innumerable little impositions of such persons as water-dippers, waiters, sweepers and even the minister who attended the King Charles Chapel, not to mention the master of ceremonies himself, would have seriously embarrassed her slender purse.

It seemed, a day later, that she might do so in quite

another matter. She was idling in one of the toy shops that abounded under the colonnade. These places provided all the little knick-knacks, both useful and merely decorative, that anyone might require: snuffboxes, ivory notecases, thimble-holders or pincushions; metal buckles or brooches, candlesnuffers and scissors, corkscrews, needle and bodkin cases; and little pieces of gilt jewellery. Any sort of oddment, in fact, that might be fashioned in a pretty way to delight or amuse. But they also sold the wooden goods that had come to be known as Tunbridge Ware, and which Verity so much liked that she had already whiled away a good many moments examining them.

Having been greeted by the friendly proprietor, she spent some time looking with great interest at a number of writing-cases and boxes of one sort and another, all beautifully made with designs of inlaid wood in a variety of colours.

She had just picked up a large box and, on opening it, had found it to contain another, smaller version, when the shop door opened. Turning her head, Verity saw first a cane, and then the neatly garbed figure of a young man limping through the doorway.

It was *he* again!

She gasped with shock, and the box fell from her agitated fingers, breaking open on the floor and scattering its inner secrets in every direction. To Verity's horrified eyes, it appeared as if there were broken boxes everywhere she looked in the confined space of the shop, although in fact the nest was composed only of four.

'Oh, gracious heaven!' she uttered distractedly, bounding forward and stooping to retrieve them.

The proprietor, tutting distressfully, came out from behind his little counter to assist.

'No, no, madam. Allow me!'

'So stupid!' Verity muttered, aware of burning cheeks. 'I am so very sorry!'

'No matter, no matter.'

The unwitting cause of the commotion stood quite still, one hand resting on the doorknob, the other grasping his cane as he watched the two of them scramble for the boxes. As they began to fit them back together, he let go the handle of the door and gently reached out to touch Verity's arm. Her clear gaze came up to meet his in an enquiring look, though her heightened colour demonstrated her intense embarrassment.

'I beg your pardon,' he said quietly, 'but this last little errant knave appears to have escaped your notice.'

So saying, he poked with his cane at a very small box which had stayed intact and had come to rest by the door. Easing it into the room, he added, 'I regret that I am unable to perform the correctly gallant action and pick it up for you.'

But the proprietor was already seizing the box from the floor as the spontaneous smile sprang to Verity's lips.

'Oh, pray don't trouble yourself on that account! Indeed, it was shockingly careless of me.'

'I had rather have said it was careless of me—to have so unkindly startled you, I mean.'

'You didn't—it wasn't——' Verity stammered, flushing again.

She was rescued by the proprietor, requesting her to hand him the remaining box she still held.

'I hope they are not damaged,' she said anxiously. 'Such a beautiful piece of workmanship!'

The shopkeeper was examining the boxes with a sharp eye for any scratches, but at length he somewhat grudgingly professed himself satisfied that no harm had been done.

'Thank goodness!' Verity said, with a sigh of relief.

She could not but have offered to buy the boxes had they been spoiled, and she knew the price of them to be well beyond her means, and was thankful to be spared the necessity of making such an offer.

But it was plain from the proprietor's expression that he thought she should have done so in any event. Before he could say anything, however, the young stranger intervened.

'I have no doubt that the boxes are as good as ever,' he said in the quiet well-bred tone that seemed to be habitual to him. 'Wood, you know, can stand a great deal of wear and tear.'

It crossed Verity's mind fleetingly that he looked rather meaningfully at the proprietor as he spoke, but as she was only too anxious to encourage this point of view, the thought quickly passed away.

'That is very true. Though perhaps, as it is inlay work, it might be a trifle more delicate?'

'Not at all,' said the gentleman instantly, responding to the note of appeal in her voice. 'I have known whole tables and armoires of inlay that have lasted a good century and more. The wood is no less durable for being put together in small pieces, you know.'

'I devoutly hope you are right,' Verity said frankly.

'Unlike the other day,' he returned smoothly, 'when you very definitely felt me to be wrong!'

The betraying colour rushed into Verity's cheeks and she stared up at him in mingled dismay and indignation. How could he bring that up now? Just when she was beginning to warm to him! And there was that gleam again in the depths of his black eyes. He was laughing at her! She drew herself up.

'You must excuse me,' she said stiffly. 'I have an errand to perform.'

'No, pray——' he began, putting out a hand.

But Verity had already stepped past him to the door. She wrenched it open and saw his hand drop. Next instant, she had left the shop and was hurrying away down the colonnade.

Until this moment, she had thought of her actions that day as perfectly justified. Now, suddenly she saw them as they must appear in the eyes of this man. A strange young woman, escorted only by a groom, accosting him in the middle of his legitimate business and taking him to task in front of a number of servants. By rights he should have been either angry or ashamed. Or both. But it was evident that the episode was to him merely amusing. He must take her for a very odd sort of a female, she supposed. Indeed, considered from his point of view, she imagined her conduct must have seemed positively eccentric! How mortifying it was to reflect that the man she had been busy despising had been enjoying a laugh at her expense all this while! Had she righted a wrong about which the perpetrator remained quite undisturbed?

These worrying thoughts occupied her, all that day and into the next morning, almost to the exclusion of all else, so that it was perhaps fortunate that she was obliged dutifully to escort Lady Crossens from one place to the next. It seemed in her preoccupation that the same conversations took place over and over again, only with different persons. There were few young people about, those in evidence mostly, like herself, in attendance on their elders unless, as with a few, a slow carriage or wan features dictated an obvious reason for their presence.

But Verity had not lacked company, for although she could not believe that Lady Crossens' acquaintance were particularly anxious to meet her—for she was no beauty!—the master of ceremonies took his duties seriously, and made it his business to perform introductions.

On this particular morning, after they had gravitated to the Assembly Rooms, she had just seen her ladyship settled and was moving away, when she was accosted by a gentleman whom her patroness always stigmatised an old bore, for all that he had been presented as the resident Wellsian playwright. It appeared that he had seen her reading the playbill for Mrs Baker's forthcoming productions.

'Are you a lover of the theatre, Miss Lambourn?' demanded Richard Cumberland.

'I regret that I have had no opportunity to find out,' Verity answered candidly. 'I have never been farther afield than Winchester before, you see.'

'Do you mean to say that you have never witnessed a theatrical production?' asked the gentleman, shocked.

'I believe I did so once as a child,' Verity said, feeling as if she ought to be apologising for this lack in her education.

But Mr Cumberland beamed. 'Then it will be our privilege to introduce you to the greatest pleasure a man may enjoy.'

'The greatest? What of reading?'

'Pshaw! Mere books, Miss Lambourn, are nothing compared to the live rendition of words! It shall be my happiness, ma'am, to prove this to you. Yes, yes, I shall read you one of my own plays.'

'God help you!' murmured a voice close to Verity's ear.

She turned her head to find standing rather too close to her an old gentleman who was another of the local residents. For all his age, Sir John Frinton was something of an exquisite. Although he refrained from adopting the extravagant costume of a dandy, he was always elegant, as today, in suits all of a piece with the exception of his waistcoats, which were flowered or striped. But he adhered both to his wig and his powder, and was always rouged with a provocative patch, in spite of fashion's decree against such an outdated adornment.

'Really, Cumberland,' he went on, addressing the playwright, but with a wink at Verity, 'enough to put the poor girl off for life!'

'Sir!' uttered the playwright, outraged, his cheeks reddening. 'You are offensive!'

'I am sure Sir John is funning,' Verity put in quickly. She found Sir John's nearness cloying and edged away a fraction. 'For my part, I should be happy to hear one of your plays, Mr Cumberland, though I would be loath to trespass upon your time.'

'I should not grudge a moment of it,' responded the other, gratified.

Verity bestowed her friendly smile on him. 'You are very kind, sir.'

'There now, Cumberland, you are amply rewarded,' said Sir John, thrusting his tall person rudely between them. 'You may take yourself off now and leave Miss Lambourn's entertainment to me.'

Mr Cumberland, his features darkening, compressed his lips, bowed to the lady and moved away, leaving Verity wondering whether this acceptance of defeat sprang from a dislike of quarrelling before a lady or the fact that Sir John was his social superior, not to mention the undeniable advantage of his slim, tall figure as against the playwright's portly frame. Sir John, meanwhile, smiling at her in triumph, was calmly possessing himself of her hand.

'His plays are tedious in the extreme, Miss Lambourn, and so I warn you! You will find my company far more amusing.'

'Will I indeed?' said Verity politely, removing her fingers from his clutch. 'How is that?'

A pair of thin lips curved in a smile that must once have been ravishing, and which still had some power to attract. 'Long practice, my dear.'

Verity had to laugh. But she said severely, 'And do you always practise on ladies who might well be your grandchildren?'

'Naturally,' said Sir John suavely, not in the least abashed. 'Or at least, whenever possible.'

'I take it that is not very often in Tunbridge Wells.'

'Alas, no. And there is always a duenna to spoil sport.'

He sighed as he spoke, looking over to where Lady Crossens sat, glaring across at him. He turned back to Verity, ruefully grinning.

'She knows I am not a marrying man, you see. Otherwise, I dare say I should receive all kinds of encouragement.'

'My dear sir, I assure you I am not on the catch for a husband,' Verity said indignantly. 'And if I were——'

'Emilia would scarce consider me an eligible parti for you,' he finished, laughing. 'But she would, you know. There are so few of us bachelors at the Wells.'

'Well, even if *she* did, I would not!' declared Verity frankly.

'Ah, so you *are* on the catch for a husband!' teased the old man.

'I am nothing of the sort!' Verity said, rather flustered, as she tried to banish from her mind the picture of a pale-featured face that had unaccountably jumped into it. 'I have quite other plans, as it happens.'

He looked intrigued and would have enquired further into the matter, but that Lady Crossens was making unmistakable signs for Miss Lambourn to go over and join her.

'Your guardian is growing anxious,' he said with a twinkle, 'so I must let you go. I shall look forward to another such exchange.'

Verity only smiled and left him, but her eyes followed the old man as he wandered about the room in search of other prey. Her imagination was afire: the attractive smile on his thin lips spreading rapidly into a wolfish grin as he towered over the shrinking form of the young and lovely heroine, manoeuvring her into a corner while the flickering candlelight played tantalisingly over the white swell of her bosom where his lascivious eyes rested.

Her thoughts were interrupted by her patroness's voice. She turned to find that Lady Crossens was on the fidgets.

'Bless me, if I had not forgot to warn you about John!' she was saying in an urgent undervoice. 'It was most remiss of me! Now you must be on your guard, Verity.'

'Against what, ma'am? Surely you cannot think me so foolish as to fall in love with a man who must be old enough to have sired my own father.'

'There is no saying what young girls will do,' said her ladyship acidly. 'Do not be taken in by his amusing ways, child. He is a confirmed rake and has been so from a boy!'

'Have no fear, ma'am! If I was to be taken in, it would be by—by someone far other than Sir John Frinton!'

Lady Crossens' attention was claimed then by one of her friends, so that she did not notice the telltale colour that had crept into her protégée's cheeks.

Murmuring an excuse of having forgotten something at their lodging, Miss Lambourn sneaked quietly out of the Assembly Rooms and wandered under the shade of the trees beside the Pantiles where the market women sold fruit and vegetables. Her thoughts were very far from the vendors crying out their wares as she passed.

That man! How dared he force his way into her mind, cutting up her peace? Just because a gentleman had a pair of black eyes that seemed to pierce a path into a person's very soul, was that any reason for him to come barging in where he was least wanted? As if there was any danger of her being 'taken in' by such a man! How idiotic it was of her even to think of him in such a connection!

Her aimless feet had taken her to the end of the tiled walkway, and as she turned to retrace her steps, a familiar sound broke her absorption. Just as she identified the dot and carry tapping of a cane on the pavings, she saw the limping leg from the corner of her eye.

Turning, she looked up just as the young man stepped forward to intercept her.

'Oh, no!' she uttered faintly.

'I do beg your pardon,' he said a little diffidently, 'but I must beg the favour of a word.'

Confronted so suddenly with the subject of her thoughts, confusion engulfed Verity, and she responded so curtly as to be almost rude. 'Well, what is it?'

A frown came into his eyes. 'I will not keep you long, ma'am. Though I came here today expressly to find you.'

'To find me? Gracious heaven! But why?'

'For a sufficient purpose, which you will learn if you will give me a moment of your time.'

Nettled by his manner, Verity snapped, 'Well, sir?'

His tone became much less cordial. 'It is nothing very much. Merely that I thought you might care to take possession of these.' He held out a package towards her.

Verity's eyes widened, for the size and shape was all too familiar. 'Is that——? I hope that is not——' She broke off, staring at him in rising indignation. 'Are you offering me that nest of boxes I dropped yesterday?'

'Well, yes, ma'am. I really have no use for them and——'

'Upon my word!' Verity burst out. 'After all you

said about wood and—and inlay lasting so well! You have actually gone and purchased the wretched things!'

'It is usual in such circumstances,' he said coldly. 'But I could see very well that——'

'That I was reluctant to purchase them myself!' Verity finished furiously. 'And so you have shown me up to be either mean or poor in the eyes of that man, and I shall never be able to enter his shop again!'

The gentleman's face fell ludicrously. 'Good God, ma'am! I never intended anything of the kind!'

'No! Just as you never intended to make a mistake in the matter of poor Braxted. Never have I come upon a more high-handed, arrogant manner of conduct!'

The black eyes sparked sudden fire, but the calm voice was like ice. 'Indeed, ma'am? Then it ill becomes me to force it upon you further. I will wish you a very good day.'

Turning on his heel, the gentleman limped off across the Pantiles, the cane echoing his uneven step as it sounded an overloud tattoo on the pavings.

Verity stood watching him go, fighting an irrational urge to chase after him with a mouthful of apologies.

CHAPTER THREE

PULLING herself together, Miss Lambourn straightened her shoulders and walked quickly back to the Assembly Rooms, her mind in disorder.

Why should she apologise? she thought crossly. Was it not he who was guilty of an unpardonable liberty? Without so much as a by your leave, he had taken it upon himself to compensate the proprietor of the toy shop—and now she thought of it, remembering the look he had bestowed upon the man, he had planned it at the outset!—for a piece of negligence that had nothing whatever to do with him. It was *her* responsibility, and, if she saw no need to buy the boxes, what right had he to interfere? And then to offer them to her, positively rubbing her nose in her own blunder!

Here, however, Miss Lambourn's innate honesty intervened. No such malice had been intended, she knew. It might have been more tactful to have kept his charitable act to himself, but at least the man had meant nothing but kindness. He had evidently perceived—how she could not begin to guess—that she was unable to recompense the owner of the shop herself, and had stepped in to relieve her of the necessity. For if he had thought her merely tight-fisted he would not have tried to bestow the boxes upon her. And now, she reflected, a trifle conscience-stricken, the poor man was stuck with a set of perfectly useless items!

As she decided, rather reprehensibly, that it served him right, a giggle escaped her.

'What an age you have been, child!' came the voice of Lady Crossens, startling her back into awareness.

As Verity's gaze focused on the old lady's face, she saw that she was being sharply scrutinised.

'You look positively impish, girl! What mischief are you brewing?'

'None, upon my honour, ma'am,' Verity said earnestly, but there was a telltale colour in her cheeks.

'Don't tell me! *Something* has occurred to bring that look to your face. And you were chortling as you came in. I heard you.'

To her confusion, Verity found herself the cynosure of several pairs of eyes, Lady Crossens' remarks having been clearly audible to the friends she had about her. She noted with dismay that not only was Mrs Polegate looking at her with avid interest, but the teasing eyes of Sir John Frinton were also fixed upon her. Miss Lambourn, unused to society, and brought up imbued with her reverend father's conviction of the efficacy of the virtues of truth and honesty, was quite unable to prevaricate.

'If you must have it, ma'am,' she said as if the words were forced from her, 'I have had another encounter with that man we met on the road.'

For a moment Lady Crossens looked blank. 'What man?'

'With the children, ma'am. On our way here, remember?'

'Oh, him! Bless me, you have not quarrelled with the wretched fellow again, I hope!'

'Well, yes, ma'am, I am afraid I have,' Verity confessed. 'It was all rather unfortunate. But quite an accident and very much my own fault.'

'But what in the world. . .?'

'Dear ma'am, do not ask me!' Verity begged in a low tone, with a significant glance cast at the people about them. 'I will tell you the whole presently.'

'Heavens, yes!' uttered her ladyship, recollecting

herself. 'What am I about? Here, John, don't you go asking any awkward questions! Nor you, Maria.'

'Oh, Emilia, as if I would!'

'Well, mind you don't!' conjured Lady Crossens, unimpressed. 'I know you, Maria. Gossip mad, you are!'

She turned to Sir John, but he met the challenge in her eyes with a bland smile. 'I am silent as the tomb, dear Emilia. I would not for the world embarrass Miss Lambourn.' He gave his arm to Mrs Polegate. 'Come, Maria. Let us take ourselves off and leave the ladies to converse in private.'

'I don't know how he conceives the Assembly Rooms to be private,' said Lady Crossens as they strolled away. 'You had better tell me everything over dinner.'

But when in due course Verity told the story, she had had sufficient time in which to calm down and the fluent account she gave of the brief meetings that had occurred was so prosaic that the elder lady had nothing to say, beyond a wry comment that she could not see what Miss Lambourn had found to amuse her.

Mrs Polegate, however, proved less reticent than her old friend had hoped. The next day being Sunday, Verity was up betimes to take herself to early morning service while Lady Crossens joined the daily routine of drinking the waters.

The Tunbridge Wells social scene being entirely encompassed in the area of the Pantiles, it was impossible for Verity, walking to and from the King Charles Chapel at the far end of it beyond the well itself, where the water-dippers dispensed their glasses of health-giving liquid, to miss the early morning ceremony of taking the waters.

It was amusing to see all the valetudinarians wandering about in their dishabille. The ladies were in undress gowns, chemise robes closed from bosom to hem with buttons or ribbon ties, worn with or without a sash, their hair tucked into mob-caps or turbans. The gentlemen sported brocaded dressing-gowns of virulent hue, full length and tied with a girdle, or, in the case of Indian banyans, falling to the knee and magnificently frogged. Their shaven heads were covered by velvet nightcaps, except for those modern-minded gentlemen, who had fallen into the coming fashion of wearing their own hair, some of whom saw fit to twist their greying locks into rag curlers which stuck out all over their heads.

The company seemed quite unconcerned at the extraordinary picture they presented, and it was, to Verity, a question whether they came there to partake of the health-giving chalybeate spring, or to meet their acquaintance. For the chatter and laughter quite outdid the groans at their aches and ailments and complaints of the bitter taste of the waters. Lady Crossens was in her element, her scrawny figure almost darting about as she greeted some newly arrived old friends with enthusiasm and traced in exhaustive detail their several meanderings in the intervening years since her last visit.

After a hearty breakfast, once Lady Crossens was more comformably dressed, they went over to the ladies' coffee-room for another bout of gossip, and again, when that palled, passed across the Pantiles to the Lower Assembly Rooms for yet more of the same, for there were no dances and no card playing on the Sabbath. Verity found a chair a little way behind that of her patroness, and here she was very soon joined by the plump form of Mrs Polegate.

'Poor Miss Lambourn! Are you dreadfully bored?' began that lady, innocently enough.

Verity turned to find the widow had seated herself with a rustle of her wide taffeta petticoats, and was regarding her with a kind of wistful pity.

'Not at all, ma'am,' she said smiling. 'There is no occasion for you to worry yourself on my account. I am doing very well.'

'Oh, I do hope so,' said the lady mournfully. 'It is so melancholy to see young people moped quite to death.'

'Gracious me, ma'am, I promise you I am nothing of the kind!' She saw that the lady looked unconvinced and added cheerfully, 'One must of necessity be quiet on a Sunday, you know.'

'That is true. I abominate Sundays for that very reason, do not you?'

'Being a clergyman's daughter, ma'am, I cannot say that I do,' Verity replied, twinkling.

'Of course, yes. How silly!' laughed the widow merrily. 'I suppose you would not look for excitement and adventure at all.'

'Oh, I am not the less anxious for them on that account, believe me!'

'No, of course you are not! How should you be, so young and full of life as you are?' Her expression changed as she leaned closer and said on an enquiring note, 'And as to adventure, you rather hinted at some such thing yesterday, I think.'

'Oh, that!' Verity said offhandedly. 'Well, you could call it that. Really, it was nothing.'

'Do not say so! A *man*! And children, was it?' asked Mrs Polegate, her eyes avid with anticipation in their frame of white lace. 'Did it happen on your way here?'

'Well, yes,' confessed Miss Lambourn, sure that her patroness would disapprove. But she was incapable of deception and knew not how to parry the other lady's probing without discourtesy. Moreover, she was by now quite anxious to know the identity of the man who would persist in crossing her path, and she thought perhaps Mrs Polegate might be able to enlighten her.

She told the tale as briefly as she could, and, although the widow did not listen without a good deal of exclamatory comment, she no sooner heard the name Braxted than she identified it at once.

'Mercy! They must have been Salmesbury's children!'

'Salmesbury, ma'am?'

'From Braxted Park,' announced the lady, as if this must explain all. 'The Marquis, you know.'

'*Marquis*! But the boy——'

'Oh, the boy is the Earl of Braxted. An honorary title, of course.'

'Oh.' Verity blinked. 'We quite thought he must have come into his inheritance a minor.'

'Oh, no, indeed. The Marquis is still a young man, I believe. Not that I know him. I doubt if anyone here does, for no one of that sort comes to the Wells any more,' she said regretfully.

'But then, the man who took charge of him.' An appalling thought came into her mind. But no! No, it was not possible! 'Mrs Polegate, he *surely* cannot have been the Marquis?'

'I should not think so at all. I dare say the Marquis is at Brighton. These great men, you know, are rarely at home. No, no. Some minion, no doubt, entrusted with the care of the estate.'

Which summarily disposed of that dreadful suspicion! thought Verity thankfully. She must otherwise have died of mortification! Of course he could not have been the Marquis! These men of high estate had better things to do with their time than to chase after errant children, had they not? Why, he and the Marchioness must of course be *far* too occupied with—with balls and—and routs and the like, to bother their august heads with poor Braxted and his sister Peggy! No, indeed. That sort of mundane consideration fell into the far from amiable hands of this steward, or secretary, or whatever he might be.

Here Verity's conscience intervened. She was unjust.

He had shown himself to be both thoughtful and amiable, to *her* at least. Indeed, she could almost find herself liking him, were it not for that wickedly quizzing gleam in his eye! It would give her a great deal of satisfaction to tell him what she thought of his misplaced amusement! Not that she supposed he would ever speak to her again, she acknowledged wryly, after the manner of their last parting.

This thought was so unpalatable that she tried to shake the whole memory of the black-eyed young man from her mind and force her thoughts into other channels.

A day or so later, having dismally failed in this object, sheer exasperation drove her to *take steps*. Accordingly, she left Lady Crossens to indulge in a lie-in, for the old lady's chancy constitution was beginning to wilt a little under the dissipations she was enjoying.

'Shall I fetch a physician to you, ma'am?' Verity had asked her worriedly.

'Don't dare! I won't have any of those old fossils fussing about me. I have enough to bear of that at home!'

'But if you are ill, ma'am——'

'Pho! I am nothing of the kind. Merely a little tired. Don't fidget me, girl! I shall rest a little longer today, and get up only in time to catch up with Maria at the Rooms.'

Verity looked doubtful, but as her ladyship was insistent, ordering her from the room at last, she gave up and took herself to Baldock's library which was situated towards that end of the colonnade nearest to the chalybeate spring.

She spent an agreeable hour browsing amongst the books on offer there, hesitating between the latest Gothic novel, a form of literature of which she was inordinately fond, and one of Dr Smollett's tales which had not previously come in her way. Remembering how much she had enjoyed the adventures of Roderick Random, she at length decided in favour of Smollett's story about Peregrine Pickle, feeling that with such a name it was probable that the hero's activities would be calculated to amuse. The idea of the Necromancer might attract her, but she knew from past experience that it would only set her imagination working, and there were far too many daily engagements here at the Wells for her to have time to spare for her little hobby. No, Peregrine Pickle let it be!

Taking the volumes, she gave her name to the librarian, who had a word to say about her choice as he always did to all who came there. Verity stayed chatting a moment or two until she noticed by the clock on the mantelpiece that she had overstayed her time.

'Gracious, I must fly! Lady Crossens may need me to help her dress for the Assembly Rooms.'

She sped to the door and dashed out, only to collide on the threshold with someone who was about to enter. The impact was severe, knocking the breath from her body and causing her to drop her books and grab at the door-jamb to prevent herself from falling.

The other party was less fortunate. He staggered back, shoved a leg behind him to save himself, and threw out a hand to clutch at air. The cane flew from his grasp and clattered to the pavings, and his bad leg, unable to take the unbalanced weight, crumpled under him. He crashed to the floor in an ungainly heap, losing his hat in the process.

'Oh, no!' gasped Verity as, with a sudden lurch of the stomach, she recognised the pale features. 'Not *you*!'

A servant in livery, who happened to be passing at that moment, started forward to the gentleman's aid. At the same time, the librarian, who had witnessed the accident, came running out. But Verity was before them both, crouching down and seizing the gentleman's arm.

'Oh, I am so very sorry,' she uttered contritely. 'Have I hurt you very badly?'

It was evident from the way the poor man was gripping his underlip between his teeth that he was in a good deal of pain, but he managed a faint laugh.

'You are determined—to see me—humbled, are you not? I trust this may be—lowly enough for you!'

'Oh, pray do not! I did not mean it!' Verity cried, distressed. 'Let me help you, sir.'

But it was in fact the two men who lifted him to his feet, while Verity scurried to catch up his cane and hat. He took them from her with a word of thanks, but visibly winced as he put his weight on the injured leg.

'You *are* hurt!' Verity said anxiously. 'You must sit down at once.'

Without hesitation, she moved to his side and slipped an arm about him. 'Lean on me, sir. We will go back into the library.'

'No, no,' he said at once, reddening and trying to shake her off. 'I will be perfectly well in a moment.'

'You will be nothing of the sort,' argued Verity firmly. 'Why, you are looking absolutely white!'

He grinned slightly, and his tone was faintly apologetic. 'I always do, you know.'

'You are *much* paler than usual,' Verity assured him, and looked at the other two men who were hovering about them. 'Please help the gentleman into a chair.'

She stood back to allow them access. In their zeal to be of service, they crowded either side and half carried him, protesting, into the library, where they placed him tenderly in an easy-chair. Verity, belatedly recalling the volumes she had dropped, collected them and dusted them off, relieved that they also were undamaged. Ever helpful, once in the library she took away the gentleman's cane and hat and laid them aside, and then directed the servant to go in search of a doctor. An easy task in this town where physicians were two a penny.

'Good God, no!' ejaculated the poor young man with some vehemence. 'I assure you I do not need a doctor! If I may just rest here a moment, I shall be quite well presently.'

'Are you certain?' Verity asked worriedly. 'You may have damaged something, and I could never forgive myself if you were to be disabled all through my fault!'

'My dear girl,' he said, in a tone somewhere between amusement and exasperation, 'my *disability* is entirely my own doing. I am quite used to it, you know. Have no fear. I would feel it if anything had gone seriously amiss. But if it will make you happy, let me assure you that I will have my own physician examine the limb thoroughly when I return home. Will that content you?'

'I suppose it must,' Verity said reluctantly. She smiled at the servant. 'Thank you so much for your trouble. We will not detain you any longer.'

'No trouble, madam,' said the man. 'I only hopes as the gentleman takes no lasting hurt.'

'Indeed, so do I!' Verity said devoutly.

The man went off and the librarian asked if there was anything more he could do.

'No, I thank you,' said the gentleman with a smile. 'Don't let me keep you from your work.'

The librarian bowed, and, bringing forward a straight-backed chair, he set it for Verity. 'Pray call me, ma'am, if I may be of any further assistance.'

'Thank you, you are very good,' she said warmly, sinking on to the chair and placing the books on her lap.

'He is indeed,' echoed the gentleman, low-voiced. 'If he had not brought that chair, I should have felt impelled to offer you this one.'

'Oh, stuff! As though I should care for punctilio at such a moment!'

A faint smile curved his lips. 'No, I fancy a too-rigid adherence to the rules of etiquette is not your besetting sin!'

Verity's own lips quivered, though the ready colour tinged her cheeks. 'I—I have been impolite, I know,' she faltered. 'I—I have wanted to—to beg your pardon for——'

'Pray do nothing of the kind!' the gentleman interrupted instantly. 'You have nothing for which to beg my pardon, I assure you.'

'But I have!' she protested. 'I said *such* things and——'

'*No*!' he snapped, quite roughly. 'I will hear no apologies from you! Believe me when I say that I require none!'

Verity bit her lip on a sharp retort, for a frown creased his brow on the words and he closed his eyes briefly as if a spasm of pain had attacked him. Instead she gazed anxiously into his face, and spoke with unwonted diffidence.

'Are you sure you do not need anything? You are dreadfully pale still! A glass of water, perhaps?'

A grin lightened his sudden severity. 'From the chalybeate spring, I suppose? No, I thank you. I am not yet in such straits.'

She gave a choke of laughter. 'Oh, dear, I hope not! Though I dare say the waters would do you all the good in the world. I don't blame you for refusing them, however. My patroness—the lady I am with, I mean—says they taste excessively nasty.'

'So I am led to believe,' he agreed.

There was a pause. Constraint returned. There was so much to unsay, so much awkwardness in this encounter. Every word that rose to Verity's lips seemed inappropriate, and she felt unusually tongue-tied. The more so because this was the first time she had seen the man without his hat, and she was struck both by the luxuriance of his long hair which was a trifle dishevelled—rather endearingly so—from the late clash, and by the pale countenance now exposed to her sight. In spite of the lines of suffering, his features were pleasing, she realised with a sense of shock. And she had thought him a monster!

She was glad suddenly that she had chosen to wear the pink gingham gown and the flower-trimmed hat of chipstraw, for she knew them to be becoming. The thought made her blush as she glanced at him and found his black eyes were upon her, roving, it seemed, over her features.

He smiled. 'Are you enjoying your visit here?'

'Very much,' Verity said warmly, seizing thankfully on the neutral topic. 'There is so much to do, and the company is very amusing.'

He stared at her. 'Amusing? Good God!'

She smiled. 'Oh, I know they are mostly advanced in years, but to tell you the truth I have been so much in the company of children of late that I am enjoying the change.'

'It seemed to me,' said the gentleman, his black eyes showing that suspiciously reprehensible gleam, 'that you like children.'

'Yes, I do,' Verity replied slowly, eyeing him warily. Was he mocking her? 'But constant association with them can be very wearing.'

'So I should imagine.'

She frowned. How oddly he spoke! Though perhaps these words bore out her suspicion that he spent little or no time with young Lord Braxted and his sister Peggy. Before she could formulate any of her thoughts into a question, however, he spoke again, on quite a different subject.

'What book have you there? The latest romance?'

'Certainly not! I hate romances.'

His eyebrows lifted. 'Indeed? I know you to be quite unlike the normal run of young ladies, but you cannot be as different from them as that!'

'Can I not?' Verity said indignantly, by no means pleased by this fresh reference to the unconventional way she had behaved towards him. She ignored the gambit, however, and pounced on another point. 'Pray why should you suppose that just because one is a female one should care only for such nonsense as that?'

'I beg your pardon,' he said with a suspiciously demure lowering of his black eyes. 'I see I have gauged the situation quite wrongly. Do tell me, then, what is the *serious* matter of the book you have chosen. A history, perhaps?'

'No such thing——' Verity began, and stopped. He was looking at her again and the glint was more pronounced than ever. In spite of herself, she felt a rueful smile curve her own lips, and she held out one of the volumes for him to see. 'As a matter of fact, it is by Tobias Smollett. One of his humorous adventure books. But before you say a word, let me tell you that I *almost* picked one of those Gothic horror things, to which I will confess I am positively addicted. Now tell me how like all my sex I am in enjoying such arrant nonsense!'

The gentleman grinned. 'I should not dare! Particularly as I have a predilection for such novels myself. In my defence, let me say that most females of my acquaintance are more inclined to sigh over Sir Charles Grandison and Lord Orville than young Master Peregrine Pickle.'

'What, those dead bores!' cried Verity, making him laugh out. 'It is shocking of me to say so, of course, because my father is a clergyman, you must know, but I have always found these romantic heroes quite tediously virtuous.'

'And the heroines quite tediously lachrymose. Yes, I agree with you. How much more exciting to read of villainous monks and terrifying castles with their evil inmates ready to trap the unwary!'

Verity, remembering all at once the way she had woven just such a plot in her head about him, found herself stricken to silence. Fortunately, the gentleman himself saved her from the necessity of continuing the discussion.

'Tell me! Do you think our several rather unfortunate contretemps justify an exchange of names?'

'Oh, of course,' Verity gasped thankfully. 'How very rude of me! I am Verity Lambourn.'

He inclined his head. 'My name is Haverigg. My family name, that is, Miss Lambourn.'

'Oh, I am not *Miss* Lambourn,' Verity explained. 'There are two sisters still unwed before me, you know. Although I suppose as I am alone here, there is less need for such accuracy.'

'There are three of you?' he asked politely.

'Three! We are seven sisters, sir.'

'Good God!'

'You may well exclaim. My mother is in despair! For how in the world is she to establish us all suitably?' Her friendly smile dawned and she added merrily, 'Now, if real life were anything like a novel, you, Mr Haverigg, instead of being a sober married man with two children, would turn out to be the prince in disguise!'

Mr Haverigg gazed at her blankly. 'But I am not——'

'Oh, gracious!' Verity ejaculated suddenly. 'I was forgetting. Of course, you are not those children's father at all!' She smiled confidingly at him. 'I quite thought you were at first, you know. But then you spoke to poor Braxted in *such* a way, and paid scarcely any attention to little Peggy, that I knew you *couldn't* be their papa. Naturally, it is not your business to be *fawning* over them, as I am assured by Lady Crossens—oh, she is the lady who so very kindly invited me to come here with her, by the way—is the case with *my* papa. Have you children of your own?'

Mr Haverigg appeared to be struck dumb. His face was paler than ever, and the black eyes held a sombre expression that gave Verity pause.

'I—I beg your p-pardon,' she stammered. 'I am speaking quite out of turn.'

'Not at all,' he said quickly, still with that strange look. 'I am—I am afraid I cannot—I can't——'

Verity suddenly thought she understood, and the colour flooded her cheeks. The poor man was a cripple! He was probably not even married, never mind having any children. She started to speak again, hardly aware of what she said, concerned only to cover up the dreadful *faux pas* she had made.

'Are the children well? I do hope so. And none the worse for their adventure, I trust.'

'I—I hardly know,' responded Mr Haverigg. He seemed dazed. 'I have not seen them.'

'Not seen them!' echoed Verity, astonished out of her confusion. 'But how is this? You are not Braxted's tutor, I take it. But surely if the Marquis is away, it is your responsibility to——' She broke off in consternation. 'Have I been mistaken? I quite thought you were the great man's steward, or secretary, or some such thing.'

There was an inflexion of a question in her voice, but Mr Haverigg still hesitated, looking away. Good God, what could he say?

'I am not his secretary, nor his steward,' he said slowly. 'The fact is. . .you see, Miss Lambourn, I——'

He glanced at her again and found her cheeks aflame. Another attack of conscience? he wondered.

'I'm sorry,' she said contritely. 'I did not mean to be vulgarly inquisitive.'

'Not at all,' he murmured politely, feeling the words to be hopelessly inadequate.

He tried to think of something appropriate, some way to rescue her from her obvious embarrassment. But Miss Lambourn was rising from her seat and putting out her hand.

'I must leave you now, Mr Haverigg. I hope you will suffer no ill effects.'

He took her hand and began to push himself forward.

'No, please don't get up!' she begged quickly. 'Pray remember me to Lord Braxted, if—if you should see him. I don't suppose Peggy will remember me. They are delightful children. So pretty. Their parents must be so proud of them! Goodbye!'

She turned on the words and walked quickly out of the library, leaving him gazing after her, ashen-faced and dumb.

Thank God she had not waited! For he could think of nothing to say. Not a word! How could he answer? What could he possibly say? She had entirely misread the situation, but good God, how could she not do so? And yet it was not her misconception that had almost annihilated him. In a few simple sentences she had stripped him bare, exposed his every failure, rent the protective skin he had grown and left him prey to the promptings of the still, small voice within.

Sighing deeply, he reached for his cane and hat, placed the latter on his head, and rose painfully to his feet. The librarian rushed to his assistance, but he politely and firmly fended him off, and made his way out into the street, down past the springs and across to the edge of the common where his phaeton waited in the charge of Hoff, the middle-aged groom.

This worthy took one look at his face and began

tutting and scolding with the freedom of an old retainer.

'There now, if it ain't just as I said it would be! You've knocked yourself up, me lord, and no wonder!'

'Don't fuss, Hoff!' said the gentleman wearily. 'I have taken a fall, but it is nothing.'

'A fall!' exclaimed the groom, shocked. 'And you've called no doctor to you, I'll be bound!'

'Of course I have not. But I shall send for Claughton to look me over.'

'Aye, that you will, me lord, if I've to fetch him to you meself!' promised his henchman grimly. 'Now just you wait while I find a boy to hold the horses and I'll help you up, me lord.'

'Don't be a fool, man!' snapped his lordship. 'I can manage very well.'

But he winced as he hoisted himself into the phaeton, a sign of pain that was not missed by his anxiously watching attendant, who lost no time in deprecating this foolish independence in a spate of heavy sarcasm.

'Aye, that's right, me lord. You go for to make everything worse for yourself with your obstinate ways! Don't you pay no mind to them as has nursed you through all those tricksy times when your lordship never thought to walk on your legs again!'

'Damn you, Hoff, be silent!' begged his master, closing his eyes tight shut against the memories that these words brought crowding in.

The groom, seeing the reins held in his master's competent hands and the horses quietly standing, ventured to let go their heads and leap nimbly up to take his place in the phaeton. The gentleman was leaning one elbow on his good leg and had shaded his eyes with his hand. The groom's gruff tone entirely failed to conceal his anxious concern.

'Do you pass over them reins, me lord, afore you falls out of this here rig!'

His lordship brought his hand down, rapping out, 'I am quite capable of driving this vehicle to Braxted Park, and I'll thank you to mind your place and your tongue!'

The curt tone was alien both to him and to his faithful attendant.

'As your lordship pleases,' said Hoff stiffly, drawing himself up into the erect posture of the perfect servant.

His master turned to look at him. Hoff had been with him since his own childhood, and was devoted to him as he well knew. He realised that this unaccustomed and undeserved harshness had deeply hurt the man.

His hand went out to briefly touch the groom's arm and, when the servant looked round, he gave him a rather wan smile.

'Forgive me, Hoff. I am not myself. But I *must* drive. I need—I need occupation.'

'Well, o'course, me lord, I understand,' said the groom, unbending at once. 'Just you let me have the reins whenever you feel yourself tiring.'

All the same, he kept a sharp watch and held himself in readiness to intervene at need. He knew his master, and if something had not happened to bring back that dark period—those days when the whole household feared at times for his lordship's reason, let alone his life!—then his name was not Samuel Hoff!

The groom was perfectly right. The Marquis of Salmesbury, struggling with his own particular demon, was indeed remembering the appalling events of two years ago, when his careless haste had cost his children their mother's life and had left him a cripple.

CHAPTER FOUR

Miss Lambourn, hurrying away to her lodging, with her mind all chaos, was shocked, but secretly relieved, to hear from the maid hired for the season by her patroness that her ladyship had got up from her bed and gone with Mrs Polegate to the ladies' coffee-room.

'She said as she would see you in the Assembly Rooms later, miss,' added the girl.

Verity thanked her and escaped to her little bed-chamber, glad of a few minutes of solitude to collect her disordered thoughts.

How much more discomfiture must she bear on account of this wretched Mr Haverigg? She could scarce open her mouth in his presence without letting fall some incautious word that resulted in her own confusion. Was she so tactless? Or was he merely touchy?

No, that was unfair. After all, who would not be a trifle out of temper after being knocked so violently to the ground? Poor Mr Haverigg had taken it remarkably well, she was forced to admit. It had not been *that* which had caused him to clam up and look so—so—yes, *bleak*, poor man! If ever anyone looked to be in the grip of care, it was this pale-faced young gentleman just before she had left him. All had been well until *she* had mentioned marriage and children, reminding him no doubt of his infirmity and how it had destroyed his chances of connubial happiness.

Come to think of it, she was obliged to admit that on the whole the difficulties that had arisen between them had been all of her making. *She* had attacked him on the first occasion. *She* had dropped the boxes, precipitating the next unfortunate encounter——

Here her thoughts suffered a check. But no! He had come specifically to Tunbridge Wells to find her. He had said so! Just to give her that nest of boxes. She frowned at her own reflection in the glass where she had been absently looking, prinking her dark curls back into order and straightening her bonnet.

Was that all you wanted of me, Mr Haverigg? she wondered. A pulse leaped suddenly in her throat, and she felt her heartbeat quicken. How odd! The idea that he had deliberately sought her out gave her an obscure kind of pleasure. As if she had not positively taken him in dislike at their first meeting! And he had returned today. But—but she did not dislike him! How could she, when he had shown himself to be both pleasant and forbearing?

Verity gave herself a mental shake. What was she thinking of? Of course he had come, just as she had, to find a book at the library. The recollection left her feeling curiously flat. However, the likelihood was she would not see him again, she decided, turning away from the mirror. It was pointless to think about the man. If there was a nagging suspicion at the back of her mind that his absence would make the Wells seem sadly empty, she resolutely declined to acknowledge it.

It was with a determined air of cheerfulness, therefore, that she went down to the Assembly Rooms in search of her patroness, still concerned about her health. But she found her happily engaged in her favourite pastime, indulging in a rubber of whist with the old nabob Martin Yorke, another lady and Sir John Frinton. Lady Crossens brushed her anxious solicitude aside with scant words, her eyes on the cards in her hand. Verity abandoned her questions. All four players were so deeply engrossed that even Sir John, whose love of cards was seen to surpass his propensity for dalliance, merely called a greeting before turning back to the game.

But Mrs Polegate, no card player, was fidgeting from group to group, clearly at a loss. She no sooner saw Verity than she made a beeline for her.

'Miss Lambourn, I have been on the look-out for you.' She grasped Verity's arm and lowered her voice, her eyes fairly dancing with excitement. 'I have *such* news!'

'Why, what, ma'am?' asked Verity, startled.

But the widow had first to drag her away to sit in a quiet corner. 'For if we look to be absorbed in our conversation, no one will venture to disturb us.'

'I bow to your worldly-wise knowledge, Mrs Polegate,' Verity laughed. 'But what in the world is this about?'

'It is the *Marquis*,' whispered Mrs Polegate in thrilling accents. 'So dreadful! I knew you must be interested after meeting his children so opportunely.'

'Do you mean this Lord Salmesbury? What of him, ma'am? What has occurred?'

'Oh, nothing *now*. It is just what Sir John told me. I happened to mention his name, you know,' she said airily, making a business of arranging the ruffles about her neck, for she had on a tippet lavishly trimmed with ruches of ribbon.

Did you indeed? Verity thought to herself grimly. Aloud, she said, 'And did Sir John know him?'

'Oh, yes, he knew all about it. And so should I have done, only that it was the year I did not come here, and so I knew nothing at all of the matter.'

Verity blinked in bewilderment. 'Mrs Polegate, I have not the remotest understanding of what you are saying!'

'Of course, yes, how silly!' fluttered the lady, opening her fan and plying it with energy. 'I declare, I am so much overset, I scarce know myself what I am saying!

The thing is, when dear Emilia did not come here, I missed her so dreadfully that I vowed I should not set foot in the place the next year. Nor I did. But that was just when it happened and so of course I heard not a word about it, for by the following year it had been forgotten. As everything is, you know, for old events must give place to new!'

'But what *was* it?' Verity demanded.

'I am coming to that,' said the widow, and her face crumpled into sorrowful lines. 'Such a tragedy! The poor poor Marquis!'

'What, ma'am? *What*?'

'His *wife*, my dear,' uttered Mrs Polegate in accents as stricken as if she had herself suffered the loss. 'The Marchioness. She was *killed.* A carriage accident, they say. So young, too. Barely three and twenty years of age she was, it seems.'

'How—how *terrible*!' Verity said faintly. 'Those poor children!'

'Yes indeed. The little girl was but a babe—a few months old.'

Miss Lambourn was looking quite appalled. No wonder Peggy had only wailed for 'Tittoo', as she called her nurse! She had no mama. Had been motherless almost from birth. And Braxted! Her heart ached for the child. She knew what it was to lose one close to her, for her sister Constance, but a year her senior, had been taken from them at the age of twelve. It had been painful even when the infant girls had died. How much more so must it have been for that lonely boy, who had not even the comfort of siblings to assuage his grief. For Peggy could not have offered the easing that her own sisters had done in their shared loss. And from what she had been privileged to observe it did not appear that his father was of much help. Unless. . .?

'Mrs Polegate, what of the Marquis himself? Was he——?'

'Oh, my dear, that is the worst aspect of the whole business!' declared the widow. 'The poor man was so devastated that he shut himself up in Braxted Place and has not been seen since!'

'He did *what*?' Verity demanded in accents of strong indignation. 'How abominably selfish!'

'Oh, no, dear Miss Lambourn, how can you say so? Such a romantic devotion!'

'Romantic fiddlesticks! How should his shutting himself up serve anyone at all? Pray did *you* find it necessary to make such a ridiculous charade out of your grief?'

'Oh, no, indeed no!' said Mrs Polegate, somewhat flustered by this severity. 'But then, you know, dear William had enjoyed *many* years of a very good life. And he was so ill at the end that one could not but feel it a *mercy* when he did leave us.'

'Yes, I dare say, ma'am,' Verity said, brushing this aside, 'but my sisters enjoyed scarcely *any* life, and yet we continued about our business. It—it was hard, it is true,' she conceded, tears standing in her eyes, 'but I cannot think we could have made it easier by moping in solitude! And what of those poor little children? They are surrounded only by servants, and must bend to the will of that heartless Mr Haverigg, who I suppose is busy about the Marquis's affairs, while the great man indulges himself in this foolish fashion in his ridiculous ivory tower!'

The same conclusion had been reached by the Marquis himself as he drove back to Braxted Park. The dreadful truth had been laid out for him by that slip of a girl who had shoved herself and her opinions into his life. Her low—*deservedly* low, God help him!—opinion of his role as a father had thrust on him the realisation that he was as bad as no father at all! Buried in his own sorrow, his own guilt, he had deprived his children of himself as well as of their dead mother.

Miss Lambourn. . .what had she said her name was? Verity? Yes, Verity for truth. How apt! Miss Verity Lambourn had begun by showing him how much at fault he was in jumping to conclusions about Braxted's supposed prank. And scarcely had he stopped smarting from that rebuke when she had all unwittingly delivered another. A blow more violent than she had any idea of! She had realised that he could not be their father because, if you please, he had 'spoken to poor Braxted in such a way, and paid scarcely any attention to little Peggy'. Good God, she must have supposed him utterly indifferent to his children! *Indifferent*! God help him, if only he were!

But Miss Lambourn could not know how closely Braxted resembled his mother, how so exactly his small features caught her every expression, so that he could scarcely bear to be in the child's presence for the constant reproach that his countenance made to the Marquis's sorely troubled conscience. And then there was Peggy, equally the image of the mother she had hardly known and whose name she bore. How could he have endured to hold that innocent little body in his arms, knowing that he had as good as slain her natural protector?

Such had been the cause of his distancing himself from his blameless offspring. Only now did he see how selfish and inhuman an act this had been. Remorse gnawed at him, more painful than any of the bodily hurts he had sustained this day.

Small wonder he had been unable to correct the false impression Miss Lambourn had acquired of him! She knew, evidently, or had found out, that Braxted was the son of the Marquis of Salmesbury. How could he tell her that he was the same Marquis, after the strictures she had uttered? Already so much had been said, so much had occurred to produce misunderstanding between them. If he now told her his true identity, he did not know which of them must be the more embarrassed!

No. Better he should remain 'Mr Haverigg', as she had mistakenly called him. After all, it was unlikely that they would meet again. He had only to keep away from Tunbridge Wells. That should not be difficult. He was already something of a recluse. Let him become more so. But not, he decided suddenly, as he turned his horses into the gates of Braxted Park, to his children!

Accordingly, he accosted his butler as that worthy opened the big double front doors to his master.

'Cradoc, where shall I find Lord Braxted at his hour?'

The servitor, far too well-trained to betray his stupefaction, nevertheless opened his eyes a little. 'Lord Braxted, my lord?'

'Yes—my son!' said the Marquis impatiently.

The butler eyed him uncertainly.

'Well? Have you gone deaf, Cradoc?'

'I beg your lordship's pardon, but has Lord Braxted incurred your lordship's displeasure?' ventured the butler.

'Good God!' ejaculated the Marquis. 'Have you run mad?'

Cradoc prudently held his peace, but Salmesbury was shocked. Was he so formidable a father, then, that he had hitherto only sought out his only son—his heir, damn it all!—to scold him for some fault? He had not thought himself so harsh a parent. But perhaps it was true. Contrary to all appearances, he had rarely had occasion to chastise the child, but until now he had not realised that virtually the only contact he had had with the boy had been when there was a homily to be delivered. So much so that apparently even his butler felt it necessary to protect the child against him.

'The boy has done nothing, Cradoc,' he said quietly. 'I would like to see him, that is all. Now where may I find him, if you please?'

The butler bowed, evidently satisfied. 'I believe he will be in the schoolroom with Mr Eastleigh, my lord.'

Thanking him briefly, the Marquis limped away towards the grand staircase that dominated the huge open hall of Braxted Place. It was typical of the ornate building which had been erected by the present Marquis's grandsire after the Italian fashion. A vast baroque structure, with high domed ceilings and spacious rooms, decorated throughout with a profusion of carved plaster cornices, with angels and demons peering from odd corners, and marble statues nestling in every niche.

The Marquis, inured to the splendours that had surrounded him from birth, traversed the long gallery above without once glancing at the paintings that hung there, and made his way to the corridor that led to the upper floors where the children and servants dwelled out of sight.

As he opened the door into the schoolroom where he had himself been tutored, he did not fail to notice the look of apprehension that came into his son's face when he glanced up to see who had entered. Clearly, Braxted shared the butler's fears.

Mr Eastleigh, a gentleman in orders of late middle age, who was chaplain to the Haverigg family as well as tutor to the hope of the house, looked almost as surprised as the boy himself.

'My lord!' he uttered faintly.

'Good morning, Eastleigh,' said the Marquis quietly, but his eyes were on the boy's face. God, how like Margaret he was! With an effort, he dragged a smile on to his lips. 'Good morning, Braxted.'

'Sir!' uttered the boy, springing to his feet, the wary look more pronounced than ever.

What have I done? What have I done? thought Salmesbury in silent anguish. Aloud he said, 'What are you studying today?'

Braxted blinked. 'G-Greek, sir.'

'*Greek*?' The Marquis frowned, looking at the tutor. 'Isn't he a little young for Greek?'

'Oh, no, my lord,' Eastleigh said earnestly. 'If a boy has the aptitude, it is never too early to begin. Master Wystan—my lord Braxted, I should say—has a most superior understanding. Most superior! He is quite a scholar, my lord.'

'Is he indeed?' said Salmesbury, looking at the child with a new interest. How little he knew of the boy! 'I am—delighted to hear it. But I wonder if I may be permitted to—to interrupt his scholarly activities for a short while.'

'But of course, my lord. You are the boy's father, after all. Naturally, you may order his studies as you see fit.'

Yes, I am his father, thought the Marquis. Yet he seems a stranger to me. As I must to him, poor child!

'Thank you,' he said quietly. 'Braxted. . . Wystan. . . Would you care to—to walk with me a little?'

Braxted's jaw fell open and he stared at his father as if he could not believe his ears.

The Marquis gave him a wry smile. 'Come, is it *so* odd a request?'

'*Yes*, sir,' said the boy frankly before he could stop himself. 'I—I mean——'

He broke off and Salmesbury looked at the chaplain. 'By your leave, Eastleigh. Perhaps you would be so good as to give us the room to ourselves a moment. There is—something I wish to—to discuss with—with my son.'

'Of course, my lord, of course,' said the cleric hastily,

and, concealing his astonishment, he bowed himself out of the room.

When he had gone, the Marquis hesitated for a moment, hardly knowing how to begin. The child remained by the desk, his big eyes, still registering suspicion and doubt, never leaving his father's face. Salmesbury could not meet that blue gaze, so reminiscent of poor Meg's innocent sweetness. He felt as if he were on the rack, and longed to leave the room so that he need not look upon it. Instead, he moved to the window and gazed down at the view of the ornamental garden some way below.

'I have met a friend of yours, Wystan,' he said.

The boy eyed him, fresh doubts entering his mind. *What* friend? Was his secret blown?

'Yes, sir?' he said, the doubt in his voice.

The Marquis turned. 'Yes. A lady.'

Relief blanked the boy's mind a moment. Then he realised some response was required of him.

'L-lady, sir?' he stammered.

Salmesbury smiled at his obvious amazement, real amusement making him far more natural. 'You think I am mad, I dare say.'

'Oh, no, sir,' the boy said automatically, but his frank eyes belied him. He took courage. 'What lady, sir?'

'The lady who saved you from the scaffold! Or rather, from a very unjust punishment.'

The boy's eyes widened. 'Oh, *her*.'

'Yes. Her name is Miss Lambourn and she is staying at Tunbridge Wells.'

Braxted came away from the desk at last and ventured to approach a step or two. 'Did you see her there?'

'I did,' replied the Marquis. 'She asked to be remembered to you.'

The boy grinned suddenly. 'I 'member her very well. She was kind.'

'Very. She—she asked after you, also. Unfortunately, Wystan——' Salmesbury looked away briefly and then forced his dark gaze back to the child's ' – unfortunately, I could not tell her how you were, for I had not seen you from that day to this.'

Braxted did not speak, but his lip trembled a little, though his gaze remained steady on the sombre one above him.

'I—had not realised,' continued the Marquis with difficulty, 'how ill-acquainted we have become.' He threw up a hand as the boy winced. 'Oh, it is not your fault, Wystan. The blame is entirely mine. But I—I would like, if you will let me, to remedy this.'

He paused, but the child did not speak. He was flushing, and he swallowed once or twice. With a pain at his heart, Salmesbury realised that he was desperately trying to stop himself from bursting into sobs. He put out his hand, and his voice was gentle.

'Will you help me, Braxted?'

The boy nodded, biting his lip, and, as the tears spilled from his eyes, he reached out to take his father's hand.

'It is part of the war effort, ma'am,' Mr Tyson earnestly informed Lady Crossens. The master of ceremonies was fervently seeking support amongst the well-to-do patrons for a day of diversions to be held on Tunbridge Wells Common on the coming Saturday.

'We have had these troops quartered in Waterdown Forest, waiting to be sent off to France, and they have eaten the locals out of house and home.'

'Indeed? And do you imagine we are able to make good these depredations?' demanded her ladyship, raising her brows.

'No indeed, ma'am. It is rather for morale, you understand, that the people may see that their sacrifices have not gone unrecognised, and that the officers and men are engaged in a worthy cause against a common enemy.'

'Yes, yes, there is no need to lecture *us*, Tyson,' said Lady Crossens testily.

Richard Tyson bowed, and said with the utmost urbanity, 'Naturally you are quite conversant with these matters, ma'am, and will understand that we are also anxious to promote the interests of those few *émigrés* who have come among us.'

This her ladyship could appreciate, for the steady trickle of those unfortunates escaping from the Terror over the last few years was known to all the world.

'Poor benighted wretches!' she said, shaking her head. 'They arrive destitute and are thrown wholly upon our charity.'

'Quite so, ma'am. It is hoped that we may be able to alleviate their lot a little.'

'Very well. How are we to assist?'

The expected aid was, of course, pecuniary, for it was necessary to supply a number of prizes that might be won in the various races and raffles, the proceeds of which would be used for the fund to help the French refugees. But the master of ceremonies thought it would be a graceful gesture if some of the gentry would condescend to lend the occasion the cachet of their presence.

'You may count upon me, Mr Tyson,' said Verity at once. 'It sounds a delightfully entertaining manner of spending the day.'

'Most enjoyable, Miss Lambourn.' He glanced doubtfully at Lady Crossens. 'If, that is, her ladyship permits?'

'Oh, you will consent, dear ma'am, will you not?'

Lady Crossens frowned. 'You will not go unescorted, child!'

'Oh, stuff, ma'am! I dare say Dogget will be pleased

to escort me, if you must have it. I am sure he will want to attend.'

Her ladyship could not like the idea of her protégée wandering among a gathering of common people accompanied only by a groom, but once she was assured that several of the gentlemen residents would be present she did not withhold her consent.

Verity, learning from Mr Tyson—who took care to inform her of it only when her patroness was out of earshot—that there were additionally expected to be in evidence stalls of various kinds, together with jugglers and acrobats and all the usual adjuncts of a fair, found herself looking forward to the treat in anticipation of no common degree of enjoyment. It would serve admirably, she decided, to turn her thoughts from the Marquis, and his ubiquitous assistant, Mr Haverigg.

Not that the latter's conspicuous absence from the Wells was of any interest to her. Oh, no. But it was odd that he had not been near the place since that unfortunate accident at the library almost a week ago. She could not help wondering whether he had been hurt more severely than he had thought. It would be comforting to see him again. Only to be certain, of course, that he was quite well. How could she forgive herself if he had been injured all through her carelessness? Useless, she supposed, to think that he might attend these diversions. Not even to accompany the Marquis's children. Gracious, no! There was no hope of that.

'Shall we go out into the garden today? It is close in here.'

Young Lord Braxted nodded. This was the third morning during the past week on which his father had taken time out from the business that occupied his secretary and himself for the better part of his time, and sought out his son, and Wystan was beginning to relax a little. So far there was not much pleasure to be gained in the rather stilted conversation between them, but the look he had hitherto dreaded, that bleak, white-faced look that had scorched him out of those vivid black eyes, had been absent from the man's face. The boy was still wary, for, although he did not remember his father ever being this way before, there was no saying how long such an unprecedented mood would last.

For the Marquis, the sessions were nothing short of torture. All the time he was with the boy, he was unable to forget the vision of Margaret's face, unable to drive out the haunting memories. He could only hope that familiarity would lessen the sensation. He had not yet subjected himself to the added torment of approaching little Margaret, though he promised himself to do so as soon as he could meet his son on comfortable terms.

They left the schoolroom, and Salmesbury very quickly found a fresh source of discomfiture as Braxted had to make an obvious effort to adapt his youthful bounding energy to his father's halting pace. Everything, it seemed, conspired against the closeness he was trying to establish. His limping progress was a fresh arrow that soon became so deep an irritant that he must express it.

As they slowly traversed the long gallery towards the grand staircase, he muttered fretfully, 'I am a poor hand at this! Perhaps we should have stayed in the schoolroom!'

Braxted was silent, looking at the injured leg. At last he ventured a glance up at his father's face.

'Does it hurt you?'

A short laugh was surprised out of Salmesbury. He looked down and recognised in the boy's face only the academic interest of childhood. There was no sympathy there. It was oddly comforting.

'Like the devil sometimes!' he answered with a rather twisted smile.

In fact the accident had smashed the bone of his thigh and thrown it slightly out of kilter with his hip. Although the surgeons had saved the leg, the bone had knit unevenly and he could no longer move his leg forward without an awkward manipulation of the hip. He was therefore unbalanced on his feet and any undue exertion or move put a strain on both the limb and the hip above it.

Braxted was examining the leg and the cane that aided his father as he walked, with the detached look of one who merely desires information.

'Will it get better?'

'I don't know,' Salmesbury answered truthfully. 'Probably not in the long term, the doctors tell me.'

'If it gets worse, will they cut it off?'

'My God, I hope not!'

'They would if it got gangrene in it,' said the child prosaically.

'It is more likely to lead to gout.'

'Mr Eastleigh calls that the drinking man's disease.'

'Very true,' agreed the Marquis solemnly. 'I had better not overindulge in the port, had I?'

'I never heard that you drunked,' Braxted announced unconcernedly. 'So I dare say it will be gangrene, after all.'

'I thank you,' said his father wryly. 'Perhaps you would care to prophesy a few more disasters for me!'

The child looked up, grinning suddenly. 'Oh, no, I think one leg is enough for any man!'

There was an answering twinkle in Salmesbury's eye. 'I cannot agree with you. I had by far rather keep the two!'

The boy burst into laughter, and for the first time in many months a little of the pressure lifted from about Salmesbury's heart.

When they eventually reached the gardens, however, talking together with much less constraint, the Marquis was brought up short by a very odd sight indeed.

'What in the world——?' he uttered, staring.

Braxted followed the direction of his gaze across to the outskirts of the park where the first few trees broke up the smooth lawns that rolled before them. Strung between two trees some yards apart was a long rope. Attached to this by a pair of leading strings was the Lady Margaret Haverigg, chasing between the two trees at her stumbling run, while some distance off her nursemaid stood, unconcernedly chatting to a gardener who was leaning on his rake, puffing at a clay pipe.

'That's how Kittle keeps her now,' explained Braxted. 'Ever since Peggy ran off into the woods that day.'

'Does she indeed?' demanded the Marquis wrathfully. 'We'll soon see about this!'

He set off at once, limping as fast as he was able, oblivious to the dull ache that was at once set up in his hip.

'Peggy don't mind it,' the boy said, keeping pace beside him.

'Well, I do! Do you think I will have my daughter tied up as one would a dog? Outrageous!'

'Kittle says she may guard her better this way.'

'Oh indeed? Pray, is *that* how she guards the child, ignoring her while she gossips with a fellow servant? The woman is not even looking at her!'

In fact the nurse was now looking in their direction with, as they were able to observe as they came nearer, a not unnatural trepidation. Before they could reach the place, the gardener had gone off about his business and Kittle was rapidly closing the distance between herself and her charge. Peggy, however, having caught sight of her brother, had set up a delighted squeaking.

'Wissen! Wissen!' she shrilled, straining against her leash.

Braxted abruptly broke into a run. Just as the nurse came up, he reached the little girl, whose arms were stretched out ready to clutch him as he bent over her, laughing.

'Are you a dog, Peggy?' he cried gaily. 'Woof! Woof!'

'Oof! Oof!' she echoed.

'Peggy's a do-og! Peggy's a do-og!' chanted her brother.

'Peddy a do-yod! Peddy a do-yod!' mimicked the infant, without the smallest understanding of what he meant.

At any other time, Kittle would have scolded such impertinence in Master Wystan in no uncertain terms. But her attention was all on the approaching Marquis, and she scarcely heard the squeals and giggles as Braxted threw himself to the ground and began to play with his sister, tickling her and teasing her with his new chant.

Kittle was a motherly-looking woman of some thirty years of age, whose eyes dilated nervously as she watched the approach of her employer.

'What, may I ask, is the meaning of this—this *bestial* usage of her ladyship?' demanded the Marquis in a voice of ominous quiet.

'M-my l-lord?' faltered the woman.

'And do not try to foist your feeble excuses of *guarding* the child on to me. You may have fooled Braxted, but you do not pull the wool over my eyes.'

'Oh, your lordship does not understand,' began Kittle in a whining tone. 'I only——'

'I understand well enough,' interrupted Salmesbury coldly. 'Your desire is to escape an irksome duty because Lady Margaret is now old enough to use her legs, though I doubt she will run you off your feet!'

'My lord, I did it for the child's good, I swear it!'

'Be silent!' ordered the Marquis, his black eyes snapping. 'Do you take me for a fool? Even if I did not already know that Braxted was obliged to perform your part because you were too busy gossiping that other time, I should not now doubt the evidence of my own eyes. Go to the house at once!'

Dissolving into tears, the nurse hesitated. She glanced over to where Peggy was bouncing on her brother's chest, although Braxted, even as he cheerfully endured this indignity, had half an ear cocked to what was going on between the two adults.

'But—but Miss Peggy. . .' ventured the nurse. 'I mean, Lady Margaret—shan't I——?'

'You may leave her to me,' Salmesbury said, his face softening as he too looked over to see the children so merry together. Then he recalled his injury. He could never manage Peggy alone. He called after the nurse who had started disconsolately off.

'Send Hoff to me, if you please. Then go and see Inskip and await me there.'

Braxted, meanwhile, had risen and untied the leading strings to release his sister, and he now took her by the hand and led her over to their father.

'Do you mean to turn her off, sir?' he asked.

'Certainly,' Salmesbury said, but his eyes were on Peggy's pretty baby face with the yellow curls escaping from under her lace cap, and the big blue eyes looking up at him in open curiosity. He doubted very much whether the infant was aware of his identity.

'Hello, Peggy,' he said gently.

The little girl stuck a finger in her mouth and edged closer to her brother, but her eyes never left the face so far above her.

'Wissen,' she muttered, and, when her brother did not respond, she pushed at him, quite violently, saying crossly. '*Wissen*! Peddy want to pay!'

Wystan had been looking thoughtfully after the retreating nurse, but another little fist hitting at his chest brought the boy's head round.

'Stop it, Peggy!'

'Peddy want to pay!'

'Not now,' said the boy, his eyes going to his father's face where he discovered an amused smile.

'An insistent young lady, your sister,' said the Marquis, as another demanding 'Wissen', accompanied by a buffet, escaped the child's lips.

Braxted grinned. 'She's shockingly stubborn.' Then he frowned, casting another quick glance at the disappearing figure of Kittle. 'And that's why——'

A puzzled look appeared in Salmesbury's eyes as he broke off. 'What is it, Wystan?'

The boy looked at him doubtfully.

'Come, I shan't bite! What is it you wish to tell me?'

'Well, sir, it's Kittle. Turning her off, I mean,' he said in a burst of candour. 'I think you'll catch cold at it, that's all!'

'How so?'

'It's Peggy, see. She's all right now 'cause I'm here,' explained the child. 'But if Kittle don't come back, or—or she's not there when Peggy goes back to the nursery. . .'

He left the sentence unfinished, but the implication was clear enough. The Marquis cast his now frowning eyes over to where the infant had left off plaguing her brother in favour of investigating a butterfly which had fluttered down on to a nearby patch of wild flowers.

'She is so fond of Kittle?' he asked, still watching the little girl.

'There's no one else, see,' Braxted said.

Though he spoke in a matter-of-fact way, the words sent a sliver of pain into Salmesbury's chest. Here was yet another instance of his neglect! If he could not give his daughter a mother, he should at least have ensured that the substitute was worthy. He sighed heavily. There was no end to his self-inflicted punishment!

He noticed Braxted watching him curiously and forced a smile to his lips. 'Come, do you collect Peggy and we will start for the house. I will have to think this over.'

The butterfly having flown out of reach, Lady Margaret made no objection to being removed from its vicinity, but trotted happily at her brother's side, able, even with her unsteady gait, to keep pace with their much slower father.

By this time the unaccustomed exertion had begun to tell on the Marquis, and he was obliged, after crossing the lawn, to sink down on the low stone wall that ran up to the ornate double stairway which marked the entrance to the house.

'I am sorry, children, but I must rest awhile,' he said faintly, and immediately came under the scrutiny of his son's intelligent gaze.

'Are you very bad? Shall I fetch Inskip to you?'

'No, no. Hoff will be here presently,' Salmesbury said, and managed a self-deprecatory smile. 'I had meant him to carry Peggy, you know, but perhaps he will after all have to play nursemaid to me!'

'Oh, I can carry Peggy piggy-back,' Braxted said offhandedly. 'Hoff may help you, by all means.'

'Let us hope he is not obliged to carry *me* piggy-back!'

Braxted found this idea so exquisitely humorous that it was some time before he could speak. His laughter was infectious and Peggy soon joined in, shrieking with mirth.

But even while the Marquis smiled in sympathy, images crossed his mind of the many occasions when his faithful groom had in fact borne his weight, after he had collapsed in exhaustion in those early attempts to get back upon his feet that Hoff had himself bullied him into making. But for Hoff, he would probably be bedridden to this day, for he had been able to find no incentive in himself at that time for resuming his life, and no representations by his doctors or certain members of his family had served to induce him to throw off the invalid. Only Hoff, who had guided his first steps when, as an infant not much older than Peggy was now, he had tottered into the stables to look at the horses, had been able to persuade him to learn to walk all over again. Hoff, who was, he knew, as successful at pacifying the daughter as he had been the father. His eyes were on the little girl.

'Do you think she will come to me?' he asked Braxted suddenly.

The boy was still chuckling, and in his present mood he did not hesitate, but lifted his sister and handed her up to the man sitting on the wall.

Peggy's own squeals were instantly quenched as she gazed uncertainly at the face of the man who held her on his knee.

'Peggy, do you know who I am?' the Marquis asked quietly.

Watching with interest, the young boy poked at his father's arm. 'Who's this, Peggy? Who is it? Who?'

The infant looked from one to the other, a little pink tongue travelling uncertainly about her lips. One tiny finger pointed at the man and she looked to her brother for guidance.

'Oo dis?'

Braxted poked again. 'It's Papa, Peggy. *Papa*.'

The word on his lips warmed Salmesbury's heart, and he cradled the infant a little closer. She was looking at him again, savouring this new identity, as if she was not quite sure of its significance.

'Oo dis?' she asked, pointing again.

'I told you,' her brother said impatiently. 'This is Papa. *Papa*, Peggy.'

The lesson had gone home. Her little finger jerked forward and prodded the Marquis in the chest. She said it with confidence.

'Papa. Papa.'

Salmesbury could not speak.

CHAPTER FIVE

'IT WILL not do, Inskip!'

The gentleman addressed, who had served as secretary to the most unexacting master anyone could wish for since the Marquis came into his inheritance just after the birth of his son, nodded his head.

'I agree, my lord. But it is difficult.'

Salmesbury frowned up at him from the huge desk that dominated one end of the saloon that served as his office. His secretary had a smaller desk on the other side of the room, but in practice he rarely used it. For since the accident, it was he who generally attended to the administrative details of the business of the estate. His master, once he had recovered enough to be capable of participating, preferred to spend long hours driving around, ostensibly visiting tenants and examining areas which were in need of repair or had been complained of. Although Inskip suspected—not without some justification—that Salmesbury could the more readily brood in isolation aboard his phaeton without incurring criticism from his long-suffering well-wishers, Hoff in particular.

Thus Inskip was invariably to be found on the other side of the Marquis's desk where all the accoutrements of the job were conveniently to hand. He had long fallen into the way of making decisions without referring them, so that his master's access of sudden interest in the children, and more particularly in the vagaries of Lady Margaret's nurse, had taken him by surprise. His faculties were for the moment dulled.

'It is difficult to know what to do, I mean,' he added apologetically, noting his employer's frown.

'Well, I know what to do,' the Marquis informed him with decision. 'She must be got rid of.'

'Yes, I see that, my lord,' agreed Inskip. 'But as you are no doubt aware, her ladyship will not tolerate the nurse's absence. Already, I am informed, she has—er—made it known that Kittle was missed when she returned to the nursery.'

The Marquis smiled. 'My dear Inskip, don't be shy! You may as well say she kicked up the devil of a dust and be done with it!'

The secretary grinned. 'Quite so, sir.'

'My hand may have been forced temporarily, for obviously I had to let her remain for the present. Nevertheless, after what I saw yesterday, she will have to go. Good God, I could not reconcile it with my conscience to leave Peggy in the charge of such a woman!'

He saw an odd look in his secretary's face, and had no difficulty in interpreting it. 'Yes, yes, I know, Inskip. I should have done something before this. And so I would have, had I known of it! But that is in the past, and I do not mean to allow myself to become ignorant of these things again.'

Inskip met his eyes. 'I am glad of it, my lord. We have missed you sorely.'

'Thank you,' Salmesbury said simply, and there was no need for more words between them on the subject.

The secretary paced a moment or two while his employer drew absently on a sheet of paper, his mind busy.

'I wonder, my lord,' Inskip said suddenly, 'if we could try a little subterfuge.'

'By all means, if you think it will answer.'

'Say that we employ a *second* nursemaid—at least so we shall inform the world at large—and allow Lady Margaret time to become used to her.'

Salmesbury sat up eagerly. 'The very thing! Once

Peggy accepts her, we may give Kittle notice and the change will be less drastic. An excellent idea!'

'It may not work,' cautioned the secretary. 'Children take odd fancies to people, and it may be——'

'Odd fancies indeed!' scoffed his lordship. 'Nonsense, Inskip! One nurse is much like another. It is all a matter of whom one is used to.' He saw that Inskip was eyeing him uncertainly and a bitter smile twisted his lips. 'You would wish to tell me that Kittle stands to Peggy in place of her mother, I dare say. But I cannot agree. Recollect, Inskip, that persons of our order are in general in the company of servants. Why, I scarce saw my own mother above a half dozen times in a month, I dare say.'

'But she was *there*, sir,' said the secretary with meaning.

The black eyes gazed at him, pain in their depths. Salmesbury's voice was very quiet. 'I can do nothing about that, Inskip.'

The secretary disagreed, but he did not say so. If the Marquis would only go out into the world, he felt, it would not be long before some young lady captured his interest. But he sighed inwardly, thinking how unlikely it was that his employer would expose himself as a cripple before the public eye. He was destined to be surprised.

After a moment the Marquis spoke again, his tone determinedly cheerful. 'Now we have that settled, I must have your help on another matter. It is Wystan's birthday in a couple of days and I would like, if possible, to think of something to do. Something different, unusual.' He looked hopefully at his secretary. 'Come now, Inskip, you are such a clever fellow. I am sure you can think of some suitable entertainment.'

Inskip smiled. 'Well, sir, an idea does spring to mind. Lord Braxted himself mentioned it to me, though where he had his information I am at a loss to imagine.'

'Good God, don't sound so mysterious, man! Out with it!'

'It seems there is to be one of these—er—diversions on Saturday.'

The Marquis covered his eyes with one hand and groaned. 'God help me! You don't mean one of those appalling occasions where old men puff tobacco for a quart of gin and young women engage in a donkey race?'

'Exactly so, my lord,' confirmed Inskip, grinning. 'It is to be held on Tunbridge Wells Common in honour of the soldiers who have gone off to France.'

'Tunbridge Wells!' echoed his lordship, and experienced an abrupt jolt in his chest as the image of bright hazel eyes and a friendly smile surrounded by black curls leap into his mind.

'Master Wystan—I mean, his lordship—did speak rather wistfully of a desire to attend the event,' offered Inskip in an apologetic tone. 'It seems there is expected to be quite the atmosphere of a fair. Lord Braxted expressed a strong wish to see a—a bearded lady who is to appear, and——'

'A bearded lady! Good God!'

'Yes, sir. And an enormously fat pig is promised. However,' he added, as a look of horror passed over his employer's face, 'I did venture to point out to his lordship that it was unlikely that——'

'No, no,' interrupted the Marquis. 'If he has set his heart on it, how cruel it would be to fob him off with some other amusement that he would not like half as well, I dare say. Besides, it will serve admirably for a birthday treat. We may celebrate here on Friday, the day itself, and then make an expedition of it to these diversions.' He nodded, briskly determined. 'Yes, we shall go. We shall take Peggy and Kittle, too. And you and Eastleigh may accompany us.'

'Well, if your lordship does not mind,' Inskip said hastily, 'I have a great deal of business on hand.'

The Marquis smiled. 'But I do mind, Inskip. And if you imagine that I will attend this dreadful event without your support, you were never more mistaken. Moreover, it was your idea, my friend. On your own head be it!'

Saturday dawned fair and bright, much to the Marquis's chagrin. He had half hoped for rain, which would have afforded a legitimate excuse to cry off the promised treat. But no such fortune occurred, and the whole party set off just after ten so as to be there in good time for the asses' race which was scheduled to begin at twelve. Inskip having provided himself with a programme of events, they were able to plan the day to encompass all those that Braxted particularly wished to witness.

The Marquis groaned in spirit when they arrived at the Common to find an enormous crowd of persons wandering about in their holiday best.

'For the Lord's sake, let us keep together,' he said in a tone that already sounded harassed.

'I think, my lord, it will be as well to appoint a place of rendezvous at which we might seek each other out should we become separated,' suggested Inskip.

'Yes, indeed,' agreed Mr Eastleigh. 'At my advanced years, you know, one cannot be racing about hunting for persons in a crowd. And I dare say you, my lord, would not wish. . .'

He left the sentence delicately unfinished, but the Marquis laughed. 'Very true, Eastleigh. But Hoff will stick with me to succour me if I should be overcome by fatigue.'

'That I will, me lord,' said the groom grimly, who had joined the party on his own insistence for no other purpose.

A meeting place was appointed, and it was agreed

that anyone who became lost should proceed to that point on the hour and wait there to be rescued.

'The pig, sir!' Braxted piped up, impatient of the delay, and becoming excited by the clamour and bright cloth awnings and ribbon-decked poles he could see dotted about. 'You said I might see the fat pig!'

'So I did.' The Marquis looked about rather hopelessly, daunted by the press of persons. 'Now, where in the world is the wretched creature to be found?'

Mr Eastleigh tutted, equally at a loss, and Inskip fell to studying his programme, hopeful that the celebrated pig's whereabouts might be mentioned therein. It was Hoff who saved the day.

'Never you fret yourself, me lord. Nor you neither, Master Wystan!'

With that, he let out an ear-piercing whistle and an urchin materialised out of the crowd.

'It's me sister's boy, me lord. Here, Tommy!' he called, pulling forward the lad, who came shyly, twisting his cap in his hands. 'Lives here, he does. I've arst him to find out where everything is so he might lead us there, me lord.'

'What admirable foresight, Hoff! And thank God! Well, then, young Tommy, lead on!'

It was therefore with surprising ease that the Marquis's party made their way through the throng, although their progress, hampered by the necessity of shouldering a pathway through the crowds—a task taken on by Hoff and Inskip—was necessarily slow. This was to his lordship's advantage, and Salmesbury and his children, with Peggy carried in the nurse's arms, were able to move in a fairly leisurely way.

The little group attracted some attention as they passed through, for the quality of the Marquis's garb and that of his son was marked, although both wore countrified frock-coats and breeches of quiet hue. Added to that were Mr Eastleigh's clerical black,

Inskip's neatness and Hoff's livery. Such an array could hardly fail to draw interest. But such was the festive mood of the party that none of them even noticed.

They caught a glimpse of the course on which the races were to take place, which had been marked out by the beribboned poles Braxted had seen, and there was plenty to look at on the way: stalls with sweetmeats and toys for sale, vendors with trays wandering through the crowd, and several tents in which were advertised other freakish objects to be gawped at.

But very soon they found themselves in the presence of the fat pig, which was indeed a revolting creature, so large as to have difficulty shunting about its make-shift sty. This did not prevent it, much to Braxted's delight, from rustling up to push its eager snout over the poles in search of further sustenance.

'It's so *fat*!' Wystan uttered in unaffected glee, and began to chant. 'Greedy greedy pi-ig! Greedy greedy pi-ig!'

Up piped the echo almost immediately.

'Geedy geedy pi-id! Geedy geedy pi-id!' sang Lady Margaret, making the assembled company laugh.

'Quite so, Peggy,' the Marquis said, grinning. He looked with revulsion upon the grotesque animal and added, 'That is quite the most disgusting sight I ever remember to have seen!'

'For once, sir,' said a new voice at his elbow, 'I find myself in entire agreement with you!'

Turning his head quickly, Salmesbury found himself looking straight into the clear hazel eyes of Miss Verity Lambourn.

'Good God!' he ejaculated. 'I had not thought to run into you as easily as this!'

He had spoken without thinking, surprised by her sudden appearance into forgetting his company. As a twinkle appeared in the bright gaze before him, his heart gave the oddest leap, and a sensation of warmth struck him at the sound of her voice.

'You will at least do me the justice to own that I refrained from *running into* you on this occasion!'

He smiled, conscious for the moment only of her presence. 'I do, ma'am, and must profess myself astonished at your forbearance!'

'Oh, that is easily explained,' Verity laughed, 'for you have brought my little friends with you.'

She turned to hold out her hand to Wystan, whose attention had been diverted from the pig as he recognised her voice. She was, coincidentally, attired in the same forest-green greatcoat dress she had been wearing when they met before, and she was thus more familiar to him than she might otherwise have been.

'Lord Braxted, how do you do? Do you remember me?'

Wystan grasped her hand eagerly. ''Course I do! You saved me from hi——' He broke off with a guilty look up at Salmesbury, and added adroitly, 'From the gypsies. This is a capital pig, I think. Don't you like it?'

'It is perfectly horrid, Lord Braxted,' Verity said frankly, prudently ignoring his slip, 'but I can see you like it extremely.'

'I should say I do! But you mustn't call me Lord Braxted, you know. I'm Wystan.'

'Now that is very friendly of you, Wystan. My name is Verity, you must know. Verity Lambourn.'

Braxted's quick glance went this time to his tutor Eastleigh, by whose precepts he was wont to conduct himself, and he said uncertainly, 'Yes, but I can't call you that. It—it wouldn't be polite.'

'Oh, stuff! If I do not care for that, I am sure you need not.' She smiled mischievously at Salmesbury, having missed the look at the clerical tutor. 'And your mentor will bear with us, I believe. After all he has undergone at my hands, I am sure it is only what he would expect!'

The Marquis had by now not only recollected the presence of other people, but was stricken all at once with the fear that someone in his retinue might inadvertently betray him. But he responded to her rallying tone with admirable sang-froid.

'One becomes inured to unconventionality in your society, certainly, ma'am.'

Verity chuckled. 'How unhandsome!'

The gleam appeared in his eye. 'I have never aspired to be an Adonis, ma'am, but it is hardly kind in you to tell me so.'

'I did not mean that at all, you wretch!'

'Unkinder still.'

He smiled as she bubbled over, but, catching a grin on his secretary's face out of the corner of his eye, he was again brought back to the danger attendant upon this meeting. It naturally did not occur to him to make known the members of his entourage to Miss Lambourn, but the remembrance of their presence made him suddenly aware of her solitary state and he frowned as he glanced about her.

'I trust, Miss Lambourn, that this odd streak of eccentricity of yours has not led you to visit this place alone.'

Verity's laughter was quenched. A trifle frostily, she answered, 'Not at all.' She indicated a burly man a few paces behind her whose face was vaguely familiar to the Marquis. 'Dogget is looking after me. He is Lady Crossens' groom, you must know.'

The lessening of warmth in her voice was not lost on Salmesbury. The black eyes looked an apology, though the suspect gleam was back in them. He moved a pace closer and spoke in a lowered tone meant for her ears alone.

'I do seem to have an unhappy knack of touching on

precisely those matters which you justly believe to be no concern of mine, do I not?'

At once the colour stole into her cheeks. 'Oh, n-no! You are v-very right. My patroness was most insistent that I have an escort.'

Then before he could say any more, she quickly turned her eyes on the infant, still held in her nurse's arms. 'And here is little Peggy. Do *you* like the fat pig, too, Peggy?'

Lady Margaret eyed her a moment. Then her finger shot out, pointing at the animal. 'Pid.'

'Yes, it is a pig,' agreed Verity. 'A very fat one, too. Do you like it?'

'Peddy no like Pid. Pid geedy!' the little girl confided. 'Wissen no like pid.'

'Yes, I do!' argued her brother hotly. 'Wissen like pig very much!'

'No!' shouted Peggy. 'No like pid.'

'That will do!' intervened the Marquis as Braxted opened his mouth to retort.

'I should think so!' Verity put in with a merry laugh, as the two children glared at each other. 'I hope you do not mean to quarrel over the bearded lady, too.'

'Have you seen her?' demanded Braxted, diverted at once.

'Oh, yes, and I am sorry to say she is sadly disappointing. I was much more taken with the sword swallower.'

'Sword swallower!' echoed Braxted, eyes sparkling. 'Where is he? Oh, may I see him?'

'I am sure you may,' Verity said, smiling at his enthusiasm. 'There is a fire eater as well. Would you like me to show you?'

'Oh, yes, if you please!'

Miss Lambourn looked to Salmesbury for permission. 'May Wystan come with me? I will take every care of him, I promise.'

'I have no doubt of that, and I have only to thank you,' said the Marquis at once, almost glad of the excuse to get rid of her, for every moment the peril of discovery loomed large.

Not that he wanted Miss Lambourn to remain in ignorance of his identity, but he would choose to make the disclosure in private so that he might have an opportunity to explain himself. He hardly recalled his decision to keep away from Tunbridge Wells in order to avoid her company and so spare them both embarrassment. He only knew now that he must tell her the truth at the first opportunity, for it had become, in some inexplicable fashion, intolerable to him that she should hold a false impression of him.

Advising Miss Lambourn quickly of the rendezvous they had all agreed, and appointing a time for a reunion, he said he would himself repair to the racecourse to watch the coming events, and the party separated.

It was some time before Verity was able to drag young Lord Braxted away from the performances of the man who swallowed swords and his colleague who put out burning torches in his mouth. He was in such spirits that he seemed almost a different boy from the child she had met on the road. Then he had seemed too serious for his age, behaving in a manner worthy of an adult. Today he was far more juvenile, and consequently much more approachable and friendly.

He was finally induced to come away by a timely reminder from Dogget to Miss Lambourn that they would miss the donkey race if they did not hurry.

'Oh, no! I wanted *partickerly* to see that!' groaned Wystan.

'Then let us make haste,' Verity advised.

The boy took her at her word, and, grabbing her hand, rushed her through the crowd as he made for one of the beribboned poles, so that she arrived flushed and out of breath by the edge of the makeshift racecourse.

'Gracious, Wystan! Do you wish me to expire on the spot?' she protested, laughing.

'Pooh!' scoffed the boy. '*You* have not a game leg!'

She knew not how to reply to this oblique reference to poor Mr Haverigg's disability, for, while she felt the callous remark deserved rebuke, she was loath to jeopardise the good relationship she had established with Braxted. Fortunately, he was far too interested in what was going forward to notice the lack of response.

It was not so for Verity, who, reminded of the man once more, found it hard to shake him out of her thoughts. She had seen him with the children quite by chance as she was passing the booth, and at sight of the slight figure with its supporting cane, her pulses had quickened—with shock, naturally!—and she had moved to speak to him almost without volition. He had answered her in so friendly a way that she had found herself relaxing at once. She was delighted to see the children, too, but she was conscious of a wish that she might find a further opportunity to converse with Mr Haverigg.

There was the usual delay to the start of the asses' race, and a good deal to provoke hilarity among the onlookers. They greeted with gleeful jeers and catcalls the attempts of the would-be jockeys—not in fact females but lusty young teenage village lads—to mount, and the recalcitrance of the beasts, who proved either stubbornly static or so precipitate that their riders were unable to get them neatly arranged at the starting line.

Verity, deriving more amusement from Wystan's unaffected delight than from the antics of the entrants, noticed his hand go up in a surreptitious wave. A little surprised, she followed the direction of his gaze and noticed a small boy, dressed in near rags, grinning and signalling.

'Who is that?' she asked, nudging Braxted.

He looked up and away again, shrugging. 'No one. At least, no one I know.'

Verity saw him glance across at the boy, who had obviously taken in the situation and had averted his eyes.

'Wystan,' she said seriously, 'it is not becoming to disown one's friends. Particularly if they are of humbler station than yourself. That is to appear insufferably high in the instep!'

Braxted reddened and shuffled his feet, looking at the ground.

'Who is he, Wystan?' she asked again.

'Jed,' the boy answered in a low tone. 'He's—he's a climbing boy.'

'Well, that is not his fault. How did you meet him?'

'Fell down the chimbley in my chamber one day,' explained Wystan, gaining the courage to look up at her. The blue eyes pleaded. 'You—you won't split on me, will you?'

'Do you take me for a talebearer?' Verity demanded indignantly. 'Of course I shall not. But I wish you will call Jed over. Only think how badly he must feel if he thinks you are ashamed to speak to him in public!'

'I thought if they knew of it, they would forbid him to come to the Park,' Wystan confessed frankly, 'and then I should have no friends at all!'

'He comes there to see you?'

Braxted nodded with enthusiasm. 'They think he is cleaning the chimbleys. And 'course he *is*,' he added hastily, '*some* of the time. But we go birds'-nesting in the woods and—and such things as that.'

'How splendid!' Verity said encouragingly, thinking hard thoughts meanwhile of that horrid Marquis who was so busy mourning that he neglected to provide his son with suitable companions for his age.

But no one was more surprised than Jed when his friend signalled to him to join them. He looked furtively about him as if seeking the custodians of his friend's person, and Braxted had to beckon furiously before he would cross the race track to join them. Verity welcomed him with a friendly smile and Wystan performed the introductions.

'Didn't think as how you'd make 'em bring you, Wys,' whispered the urchin in some surprise. 'How'd you manage it?'

Braxted grinned. 'I telled Inskip and he fixed it. It's my birthday treat, see. Mind, I never thought *he* would let me!'

'Nor me,' said his friend, awed. 'Ain't you glad I tipped you the wink?'

'Of course I am. It's a capital go!'

Verity overheard this exchange with a swelling of indignation. If she could but have an opportunity to confront this *he* herself! For she had no doubt Wystan meant the Marquis.

She was diverted then by the beginning of the race. Both boys became so excited, jumping up and down and shrieking imprecations at their chosen donkeys, that Jed completely lost his initial shyness of his exalted company in heated debate with his friend over the outcome when both their favoured mounts lost.

Verity bought them both toffee apples from a passing vendor, and was just congratulating herself on the success of her tactics when a remark of Jed's caught her attention.

'Ain't that your sister Peggy, Wys?'

'Where?' demanded Wystan, fright taking hold of him. In spite of Verity's wisdom, he still had doubts of his various mentors' possible reactions to this unsuitable friendship.

Jed pointed. 'There. With that there Kittle. Don't go up in the air,' he advised sapiently. 'Them nobs o'yourn ain't with her.'

'Is that the same nurse?' Verity asked in disapproval as she saw that the infant was drooping in the woman's arms. 'I cannot think she is very good at her job.'

Jed let out a crack of rude laughter. 'That she ain't! More like a kennel-keeper.'

Seeing Miss Lambourn's frown, Braxted explained about Kittle tying the little girl up. 'There was talk of turning her off,' he added, 'but Peggy screamed the place down when she wasn't there and they had to let her back.'

'Oh, dear.' Verity watched the child, dark thoughts again occupying her mind against the Marquis. The poor infant was exhausted! She was toying with the notion of going over and inviting the nurse to bring the little girl to rest at her lodgings, when Jed again drew her attention.

'Beats me why Kittle should be jawing with that there Sam Shottle.'

'Who is Sam Shottle?' demanded Braxted, noting for the first time the thickset man in rough country clothes, who appeared to be arguing with the nurse.

'He's a bad 'un, is Sam Shottle,' Jed told them, his tone disparaging.

'A bad 'un!' echoed Wystan, round-eyed. 'Why, what has he done?'

'Ah! What ain't he done, more like. Why, he beginned by thievin' and poachin' when he was no more'n a lad like me. Now he says as how he got grander plans nor that. Reckons to make his fortune, he says. Huh! Me, I reckons he'll end in Botany Bay, if he ain't put to bed with a shovel!'

'Do you mean he could die?'

'By the rope, the road he's goin',' confirmed Jed.

'How in the world does Kittle come to be acquainted with such a man?' Verity asked, quite appalled.

'Ah!' nodded Jed. 'That's what I'm arstin' meself.' He grinned suddenly. 'And I reckons as how they be sweethearts, Wys.'

'Surely not!' Verity protested, shocked.

'How come he goes for to fondle her rump, then?' demanded Jed with a complete lack of self-consciousness.

Verity was obliged to control a reprehensible desire to giggle, and, as she saw that Braxted was interestedly studying the nurse and her companion, she devoutly hoped that he did not understand the significance that was clear to his more worldly-wise friend.

'Wystan, I think you should call to Kittle, and then we must go and find the meeting place. I am sure we are late.'

At this, Jed circumspectly withdrew, having even less dependence on the magnanimity of the 'nobs' surrounding his friend than even Wystan himself.

'Kittle! Kittle, I say!' called out Braxted.

The nurse turned her head and Verity was hardly surprised to see the look of consternation that spread across it. No doubt she had thought herself unobserved. What did surprise her was that the man Shottle, instead of effacing himself, seemed rather to relish this sight of the boy.

He had an unprepossessing face, with heavy jowls and a nose that looked to have once suffered a breakage. A pair of keen eyes passed over Braxted, dwelling on his face until his companion said something to him in a low tone. He nodded and, as it seemed to Verity, reluctantly removed his gaze from the boy. A word to the nurse, and he had turned and made off through the crowd.

Kittle came towards them, an anxious look on her

face. Whatever she had been about to say was forestalled by Braxted, however.

'Miss Lambourn thinks you should come with us now.' Then he turned to Dogget, who had been behind them the whole time. 'Do you know where the coach office is? We are to meet there.'

The groom nodded, and his relief was visible, at least to Verity. 'This way, sir.'

As they wended a path through the crowd, which was beginning to thin as a number of people made for the alehouses, Verity found her mind dwelling on all the things she wished to say to Mr Haverigg about his precious Marquis, and she had only half an ear to spare for Wystan's chatter. But, when the boy stopped in his tracks and urgently grasped her arm, she jerked into full awareness.

'What is it?'

'That man!' whispered the boy urgently, and there was fear in his voice. 'It's that gypsy!'

CHAPTER SIX

'WHAT? Where?'

But even as she asked, Verity's darting eyes found the figure of the man whose appearance had precipitated her into her adventure and acquaintance with the inhabitants of Braxted Park.

'Gracious heaven, I believe you are right!' she uttered, her voice pitched low.

The handsome gypsy was standing by a stall, idly glancing at the wares set out there: a collection of scarves, together with cheap rings, fans and necklaces. At once Verity thought of the gypsy dancing girl she had visualised, and saw in her mind's eye this man fastening a gold chain about her bare neck and placing his lips to the back of it. Involuntarily she shivered, as if she were the recipient of that intimate caress, and, as in her imagination the lady turned to look at her lover, she knew that his face was not that of the gypsy.

'They are camped on our land, you know,' Braxted told her as they moved on.

'Indeed?' she said absently, still shaken by the strange vision that had entered her mind. Whose face was it? Her eyes were still on the gypsy and, as if he felt her gaze, he suddenly turned, looking straight at the boy. She felt Braxted close into her, and groped for his hand.

'Don't be afraid!' she whispered.

'Oh, no!' he whispered back, but his hand clung tightly to hers. When they were safely past, he added, 'I wonder if I should ask my father to turn them off.'

'Turn them off!' repeated Verity in a shocked tone.

'No, no, Wystan. That would be shockingly cruel! Why, they have done nothing.'

'Gypsies are dangerous,' Wystan said obstinately.

'Stuff! I am sure they would not think of harming you.'

'Why did you stop that day, then? For you thinked he meant us harm. You know you did!'

'Yes, that is true. But it was because, like you, I reacted to an unnatural prejudice,' Verity explained. 'It was wrong of me. Very wrong. But that is just the difficulty, you see. Gypsies have such a shocking reputation that we are all stupidly afraid of them, when I dare say all they wish is to be left in peace to enjoy their lives just as you or I.'

Wystan digested this in silence for a moment or two. 'Very well, then, I shall say nothing—yet. But I 'spect they're poaching our woods. Jed says there are any number of them here at the fair, picking pockets, I'd wager!'

Verity was about to deny this assertion with some heat when they were interrupted by Salmesbury's voice.

'There you are at last! I had begun to imagine you had all been spirited away by the gypsies.'

This was so apposite that both Miss Lambourn and Braxted burst into laughter.

'I am glad you are so merry,' said the Marquis, smiling, 'but I must ask you, Wystan, to go with Eastleigh. You, too, Kittle. Inskip has procured a nuncheon and it is awaiting you.'

'What about you?' asked the boy, poised to run to where he perceived his tutor waiting a few yards off.

'I have eaten. Go on. I want to talk to Miss Lambourn.' He saw a suspicious frown come into his son's eyes and added gently, 'To thank her, you know.'

Braxted flushed. 'Oh, yes, of course. Thank you,

Miss—I mean, Verity. It was capital! Will I see you again?'

'I hope you may——' Verity began, but was cut off.

'Certainly you will see Miss Lambourn again. Now be off with you!'

'Well, really, Mr Haverigg!' protested Verity as the boy scampered off.

But 'Mr Haverigg' was not attending. He was addressing her groom. 'You need not fear to leave Miss Lambourn to my escort. I promise I shall return here with her within the hour.'

Dogget, looking extremely worried, turned to Verity for guidance. As she had a strong wish to talk to Mr Haverigg privately, she endorsed this view.

'Oh, yes, Dogget. I am sure you need refreshment. Do you go and find some and meet me here in a little while.'

Thus adjured, there was nothing for the groom to do but take himself off. The Marquis turned to Verity.

'Let us remove from here, Miss Lambourn. There is something I particularly wish to say to you.'

'Oh, yes, and I wish particularly to talk to you, Mr Haverigg,' Verity said eagerly, turning to stroll beside him.

He had met them across the road from the coach office and now began to lead her away from the centre of things to the outer areas where the Common stretched away, and where those pleasure-seekers who did not come for the alehouses were sparsely dotted about, seated on the grass, enjoying their own impromptu picnics. So anxious was Verity to talk to him that she did not see Sir John Frinton wave to her, and so did not notice the old man's eyes following them as they walked away together.

'Miss Lambourn,' began the Marquis, about to tell her that he was not in fact Mr Haverigg, 'I hardly know how to say this, but——'

'Oh, Mr Haverigg, I beg you will not trouble yourself!' chimed in Verity at once. 'You are going to disclose to me the shocking tidings about the Marquis, are you not? But there is no need. I have heard the terrible story of the accident that killed his wife and I am heartily sorry for it! Indeed, that is why I wanted to talk to you, for I am sure you, in your situation, must have some influence.'

'Miss Lambourn, you mistake my situation,' he said desperately. 'I am not——'

'No, no, do not say it!' she interrupted. 'If you are not a relative of some sort, you must be in his employ. But I am not blind, sir! You are treated with a deference accorded to no servant and even Wystan answers to you. You cannot tell me you have no power to change things.'

'I have indeed,' agreed poor Salmesbury, trying to stem the flow, 'but the fact is I——'

'Then, Mr Haverigg, you *must* do something to persuade that dreadful man that his attitude is grossly mistaken!'

Utterly confounded, Salmesbury could say nothing for a moment. Good God, he must speak now! Tell her that he was 'that dreadful man'. But his tongue refused to obey his command, and after the briefest of pauses Miss Lambourn had resumed speaking.

'You see, Mr Haverigg,' she was saying in a tone both persuasive and passionate, 'I *know* how it must have been for him, indeed I do! I, too, have suffered such a loss. More than one. And I do understand. But to become a hermit, to forswear the world, and leave those poor little children to the indifferent care of *servants*! Oh, it is too bad of him!'

It was too much. Salmesbury stopped walking and turned to her, his face pale and set. 'Forgive me, Miss Lambourn, but you do *not* understand. Oh, yes, it is just as you say. Shockingly self-indulgent! And believe me I—that is, the—the Marquis—is only too well aware of it. But what you do not know—how should you, indeed?—is that the accident was caused by the Marquis himself. It was *his fault*!'

He stopped and the distress in his black eyes pierced Verity to the heart. Her own eyes filled.

'Oh, poor man!' she uttered brokenly. 'Poor, tormented man!'

They gazed into each other's eyes for a long moment, in an empathy too deep for words. Until a raucous voice shattered the intimacy.

'Cross the gypsy's palm wi' silver?'

Verity blinked, stepped back hurriedly and turned to see an old crone, swathed in shawls of bright patterns with large hoops in her ears, standing close beside her and grinning toothlessly up at her out of a wizened face.

'Cross the gypsy's palm wi' silver?' she offered again in a cracked voice thick with a west-country accent. She reached up to take Verity's mittened hand. 'Tell yer fortune, dearie?'

'Oh, no!' Miss Lambourn said, trying to retrieve her hand. 'No, thank you.'

The gypsy kept hold of her hand and looked closer into her face. Her own features lost their smile. 'Tears, dearie? Let old Mairenni seek out reason in yer hand.'

The Marquis, jerked out of the mood he had himself evoked, was about to order the gypsy to leave them alone when he changed his mind. Here was an opportunity to dispel the tension, and perhaps amuse Miss Lambourn and so bring the smile back into her eyes. At this moment, revealing his identity was quite impossible.

'Why not, Miss Lambourn?' he said encouragingly, digging a hand into his pocket.

'Oh, I could not,' Verity protested, but the gypsy

was already turning her hand, looking at its shape, and she began to be intrigued.

'It is a holiday, Miss Lambourn,' Salmesbury said, slipping a silver coin into the old woman's ready palm. 'To partake of such amusements is positively *de rigueur*!'

'Off with the glove, dearie,' ordered Mairenni, tugging herself at the mitten and exposing Verity's hand.

She studied the palm in silence for a moment and Verity waited, succumbing to the age-old curiosity of every young lady to know what was to befall her. But when the old crone glanced up at her, she saw trouble in the woman's face.

'What is it?' she asked, seized by an apprehensive chill.

'No wonder ye weep!' said old Mairenni. 'Many a sorrow have ye weathered, dearie, only to encounter more.'

'Gracious, don't say so!' exclaimed Verity.

'Worry not, child, worry not!' chided Mairenni, clicking her tongue. 'For though, t'be sure, there be many tears to shed, there be smiles to come hereafter.'

'I am glad,' put in the Marquis with an attempt at lightness. 'I had begun to think I had done you an ill turn!'

Verity chuckled, but Mairenni's sharp old eyes sought and held Salmesbury's black ones.

'So ye have, sir, so ye have,' she cackled. 'But not fer crossing my palm!'

'What in the world do you mean?' demanded Verity, looking from one to the other.

'Gentleman know,' said Mairenni, and winked at the Marquis.

'Do you?'

He smiled, but with an effort. 'Possibly. We will talk of it later.'

'Very well, then, is that all you have to tell me?' Verity asked.

'And what d'ye want more?' asked the old woman, eyes glinting. 'Shall I see fer ye a handsome stranger to wed ye and a quiverful o' brats, eh?'

'No, but——'

'Aye, but ye shall have 'em. Ye shall have 'em all! And beyond that, dearie, ye shall have you'm heart's desire, fer that ain't it. Only it happens you'm mistaken, and one fine day that wild imagination o'yourn that fires yer mind with visions shall find a home. But by then ye'll have found it out, for the heart be its own mistress, dearie, and, looking fer you'm heart's desire, ye'll find ye have it in yer hands.'

Verity stared at her, quite dumbfounded. But Salmesbury laughed out loud.

'You speak in riddles, old woman! Miss Lambourn, if you are able to make head or tail of all that, I wish you joy of it!'

The crone cackled and gave him a knowing grin. 'She'll have joy, sir. . .at the last.' Then she handed Verity her mitten and went off in search of further custom.

Verity looked at Salmesbury. 'That was uncanny.'

'Did she hit on a truth, then?' asked the Marquis with a faint smile.

'What she spoke of as my heart's desire,' Verity said slowly. 'She certainly seems to have known how I use my leisure time. And I *do* dream of——' She broke off. 'Oh, well, it must all be nonsense, I suppose.'

'My dear Miss Lambourn, how could you possibly tell? She said nothing to the purpose, and what she did say could be applied to any set of circumstances you care to name. I beg you will not take it seriously.'

'Of course not. Upon my word, if I did, I should be in a fever of anxiety about these sorrows which she says are gathering about my head!'

'Let us hope she is mistaken. Indeed, I am sure she is. I cannot suppose, Miss Lambourn, that anyone of sensibility would wittingly give you any cause for sorrow.'

Something in his voice arrested her, and as she looked at him there was more than a smile in the back of his eyes and her pulse did a little dance.

'Oh, Mr Haverigg!' she sighed unvoluntarily.

His face changed and the smile left it. His voice sharpened. 'They might, however, give you cause for anger.'

She flushed a little and drew back. 'You mean I am quick-tempered, I dare say. Alas, I know it!'

He shook his head. 'I did not mean that. Miss Lambourn, it is quite time that I——'

'*Salmesbury*!'

The shout came from his left. In instinctive reaction he turned his head, and realised that she did, too. A dapper young gentleman with a pleasant face, all smiles, was waving a beaver hat in the air.

'Salmesbury, you sly dog!' he called as he approached. 'Went to visit you at Braxted, like the good cousin I am, only to be told you'd slipped your leash and gone off raking! Here's a new come-out, old fellow. What do you mean by it, eh?'

There was an ominous silence. Seeming to become aware of tension, and catching the Marquis's glance, the new arrival saw that the young lady was staring at his cousin with dilating eyes, her colour fluctuating.

'How *could* you?' she got out in a barely audible voice. 'Oh, how could you deceive me so?'

'Have I,' asked the unfortunate newcomer, 'said anything in any way out of place?'

'No, of course not,' answered the Marquis automatically. 'Miss Lambourn——'

Verity, her lip trembling, and tears pricking at her eyes, shook her head.

'The gypsy was right, *my lord*!' she threw at him huskily, and, turning, she fled from him to seek refuge in her lodgings, her happy day in ruins.

Salmesbury stood where she had left him, his pale features quite ghostlike.

His cousin touched his arm. 'I'm so sorry, old fellow, I seem to have blundered. Though I've not a notion what is going on!'

The Marquis clasped the hand on his arm and gripped it, dredging up a weak smile. 'Quainton, it is not your fault. It is I who have blundered. I meant to tell her the truth, but I allowed myself to be distracted and. . .however, it can't be helped. I dare say it would have provoked the same reaction if I had told her myself.'

Mr Leonard Quainton tutted sympathetically. 'Poor fellow! You never seem to have any luck!'

Salmesbury managed a laugh. 'Oh, it is not as bad as that! Besides I do have luck. Meeting Miss Lambourn has been the greatest piece of good fortune to befall me in many a long day. Thanks to her, I have begun to make some very necessary and long overdue alterations in my way of life.'

'I can see that!' agreed his cousin bracingly. 'To see you at a fair of all things! You could have knocked me down with a feather when Cradoc told me where to find you. Didn't believe it, in fact. Said I'd come and see for myself. And here you are, large as life!' He pressed his cousin's shoulder. 'I'm devilish glad to see you out like this, old fellow.'

The Marquis smiled, in genuine amusement this time. 'I should think you might be! After all, you have been plaguing me to come out of hiding for months.'

'Yes, and a fat lot you did about it!' retorted Quainton. 'Who is this Miss Lambourn, that she succeeds where we have all failed?'

A shadow clouded the Marquis's smile. 'She is

heaven's messenger, and I cannot *bear* it if she is to harbour this ill opinion of me!' He turned to his cousin and grasped his hand. 'You must help me, Leo!'

'Anything in my power, old fellow. My mistake. Only too happy to help to set it to rights.'

Mr Haverigg—the Marquis! Oh, it was too mortifying!

Pacing the carpet in the small parlour of Lady Crossens' lodgings, Verity clasped and unclasped her mittened hands. The tears she had been obliged to keep back as she hurried across the green had given place to justifiable anger. Her thoughts had been so much occupied that she had passed by Dogget, anxiously awaiting her return, without even seeing him.

'Miss! Miss!' he called out, and then had to chase after her and forcibly put himself in her way. 'Are you all right, miss?' he asked in quick concern, noting her distress. 'Shall I fetch you to her ladyship?'

'No, no, Dogget, I am perfectly well,' she lied hastily. 'I am—I am a little fatigued and so I will go home. Thank you for your escort.'

But Dogget, knowing his mistress would expect it of him, insisted on seeing her to the door of her lodgings. He determined to wait outside also, for with miss in one of her odd moods there was no saying but she might not dash out again at any moment and run off the Lord alone knew where!

Miss Lambourn's mood was decidedly odd. While she raged at the deceit that had been practised upon her, she was haunted by the memory of that tragic look in the black eyes when he told her that it was his fault that his wife was dead.

His wife. *His* children! Everything began to fall into place at once. She had *told* him that she did not think he could be the father. She had expressly stated her opinion of him—as the Marquis. How could the poor man have revealed himself after that? What a wretch she was! To say such wounding things! Though to be sure she had no notion then that she could hurt him.

Fool that she was! Papa would say that she merely quibbled. Could she not have found out, made certain? Remembering now the way he had behaved, the reaction of his servants, she thought how blind she had been not to guess at once. But no! She was shackled to her prejudice of what a Marquis *should* be! And so she refused to believe that so insignificant, so mild a man could occupy such a place.

The image of him came into her mind and she realised at once that of course he was not insignificant at all. He had a power, a presence that made one notice him. It was not merely his title that commanded the respect of his people. Nor was he mild. She smiled at her own simplicity. What an epithet for a man of such inner fire! He was far from mild, in spite of that quiet manner of speech, that pale face and the limp he carried with becoming dignity.

'Oh, dear God!' muttered Verity aloud suddenly. 'He was injured in the accident! Oh, Mr Haverigg!'

Tears rose to her eyes again and she dashed them away as she realised what she had said.

'Fool. He is *not* Mr Haverigg. He is the Marquis of Salmesbury,' she told herself savagely, 'and the sooner you realise that Miss Verity Lambourn and the Marquis of Salmesbury are poles apart, the better it will be for you!'

After which, she collected the second volume of *The Adventures of Peregrine Pickle* and retired to a comfortable armchair, where she sat with the book open in front of her, her eyes gazing unseeingly into the middle distance, and thought about the Marquis without cessation until the return of Lady Crossens obliged her to assume a cheerful aspect she was far from feeling.

'There you are, child!' said her ladyship, walking

into the parlour. 'Dogget tells me you left the diversions somewhat precipitately. Are you unwell?'

'Oh, no,' Verity said at once, blushing a little. 'It was—I—oh, I was overcome by the press of people, ma'am, that is all.'

'I am not surprised. We have been positively deafened by the appalling din!' Lady Crossens complained. She animadverted somewhat bitterly for a moment or two against the unwisdom of persons who saw fit to ruin the peace of visitors by allowing the mob to cause a riot and rumpus at their very doors.

Miss Lambourn could not allow this to pass. 'Dear ma'am, you surely cannot begrudge them one day of rational enjoyment! Besides, it *was* extremely pleasant until——'

She broke off, flushing, and Lady Crossens looked at her rather hard. She had noticed of late a tendency in her young charge to go off into daydreams when she thought no one was observing her. Indeed, Grace Lambourn had warned her to expect this. But her ladyship was not a fool, and she was certain there was something behind Verity's odd silences. If she had not been upset today, Lady Crossens was no judge of the matter! Even if her faithful groom had not reported the threatening tears he had observed.

'What ails you, child?' she asked with unwonted gentleness.

At once there was a pricking in Verity's eyes and she averted her face. 'If you please, ma'am, I—I would rather not talk of it.'

There was a moment of silence, and then her ladyship said with sudden energy, 'I declare, I am famished! Where is that woman with the dinner?' She crossed to the bell and tugged at it. 'Tell her to serve as soon as she can, Verity. I will be in my room. Do not forget there is the special ball tonight. After all, if the villagers may disport themselves on the Common, I am sure we may do likewise at the Assembly Rooms!'

Miss Lambourn had little heart for the event, but she could not refuse to attend. Since it was a special occasion, she arrayed herself in her best evening gown of primrose silk, open from the waist over a petticoat of pale yellow gauze worked with gold thread. From the lace tucker about her low *décolletage*, the swell of her bosom peeped, and her dark curls had been coaxed into ringlets and tamed into a chignon at the back. Not surprisingly, this charming picture drew a great many jaded male eyes.

In keeping with the mood of the day, Mr Tyson had decided that all formality would be dispensed with, the company taking their partners for a succession of country dances without any preliminary arrangement or introduction. Since everyone in Tunbridge Wells was already acquainted, this relaxing of the rules might have been thought superfluous. But it did, as Verity soon found out, mean that gentlemen might mingle freely to solicit the ladies of their choice rather than politely standing up with the members of their immediate circle.

Miss Lambourn consequently found herself going down the dance with a variety of elderly gentlemen, who had until now been content to leave a clear field to Sir John Frinton. She was in the middle of a particularly trying ordeal, involving the energetic gyrations of the old nabob, Martin Yorke, who was wheezing a tale of his dancing prowess in the old days in India, and treading on his partner's toes the while, when she became aware that a good deal of attention was being directed towards the entrance, where Richard Tyson was bowing deeply and ushering in some new arrivals.

As he moved aside and her view cleared, Verity missed her step and almost stumbled. Two gentlemen stood revealed, in whom, in spite of the unexpected elegance of their attire, she had no difficulty in recognising the Marquis of Salmesbury and the young man whose revelation had plunged her into gloom.

It quickly became obvious that 'Mr Haverigg' had abandoned any attempt to maintain that identity. In the fans raised to cover mouths, and the cupping of hands against ears, Verity recognised the passing on of a juicy titbit of gossip. For as each fan lifted, two pairs of eyes cast significant glances over to the slowly moving procession as Mr Tyson performed those introductions he considered essential. But Sir John Frinton walked up to the Marquis unannounced and greeted him as an old acquaintance.

With a sinking heart, Verity realised that the erstwhile 'insignificant' man had leapt into the role of guest of honour merely by virtue of his rank. She shrank into herself, cravenly hoping that he would not attempt to single her out. For that must give rise to the sort of tattling that would embarrass not only herself, but also her kind patroness.

Judging by his previous form, however, Verity could place no dependence on the gentleman's discretion. Even as she thought this, keeping a surreptitious eye upon the pair the while, she saw the second man glance over in her direction and nudge his companion.

Quickly looking away, Verity was glad to find the dance ending, hoping that she might disappear into the crowd as the dancers left the floor. She was deposited at Lady Crossens' side, and pounced upon immediately by Mrs Polegate.

'My dear, do you know who has just come in? I declare, I am all of a twitter! Salmesbury, of all people! He is exciting no little attention, I can tell you. What in the world should bring him here?'

Miss Lambourn did not enlighten her, but she could not prevent a faint flush from creeping into her cheek and was aware of Lady Crossens' penetrating eyes upon her. Her ladyship, however, merely scoffed.

'Pish, Maria! Why should he not come here? If he has decided to show his face in society again, what better than a gathering such as this to give him a little confidence?'

'Oh, yes, poor man!' sighed the widow at once. 'I dare say he is quite unused to be stared at.'

'Well, he is certainly getting a deal of practice in enduring that!' Verity said tartly, pointedly placing herself so that she presented her back in case those black eyes should be seeking her out. Heavens, nothing could be worse than to have him attempt to speak to her in this assembly! Though she had to make a valiant effort to suppress a growing feeling of pleasure that he had come at all. The thought flitted across her mind that she had not realised how very attractive he was. Whether it was the silvered blue brocaded coat with the buff satin breeches, or the powdered hair, that enhanced his appearance, she could not have said. But he seemed so much less pale that the black eyes were more dominating than ever.

Mrs Polegate's speculation and exclamations continued unabated and Verity was glad when the musicians struck up, for she was sure to be solicited for a dance. Indeed, she could see Richard Cumberland bearing down on her, but, before he could reach her, a voice spoke at her side.

'Miss Lambourn, may I have the pleasure?'

Even as she turned, Verity recognised the voice, but a ripple of shock went through her just the same. Salmesbury's companion stood bowing before her, his dark coat and breeches lending him an elegance belied by a cheery, chubby-cheeked countenance.

'Oh!' she uttered foolishly, all coherent thought suspended.

By the time she was able to think again, she found

that her hand was tucked into the gentleman's arm and he was leading her into one of the sets then forming.

'May I make myself known to you, Miss Lambourn? Leonard Quainton. Salmesbury's cousin, you know.'

'Have you a title?' Verity asked abruptly, and her voice shook. 'I mean, I should not l-like to make another s-stupid blunder!'

Mr Quainton reddened. 'Must beg you to forgive me, ma'am. Stupid sort of thing to do. Had no idea, you see. That you didn't know him, I mean. But no. No title. I'm not a Haverigg, you understand. Cousin on his mother's side.'

'Oh, I see,' Verity managed, though she was hard put to it to speak at all sensibly. 'But please don't apologise. It—it was not your fault, Mr Quainton.'

'So Salmesbury says,' uttered Mr Quainton gloomily. 'But I set the cat among the pigeons, nevertheless.'

'Please, don't let us speak of it,' begged Verity.

'Must speak of it!' protested the gentleman. 'Pledged my word, you understand.'

They were separated at this moment by the movement of the dance, and Verity went with her head in a whirl, and a rush of gratification in her bosom. He *had* come for her! He had braved the world again, exposed himself to the minefield of Wellsian gossip, just so that he might mend the breach. At least, so she must suppose. Surely this Mr Quainton had come to her in the guise of peacemaker, had he not?

So it proved. 'Miss Lambourn,' he began at once, as soon as they were together again, 'Salmesbury begs only the favour of a word, that he might explain himself.'

'Oh, no, there is nothing he need explain,' Verity assured him quickly.

'Good God, yes, he must, ma'am! Even I can see that.'

Verity gazed at him and her cheeks burned. 'Has he—has he told you *everything*?'

'Pretty well, I think,' Quainton said earnestly, anxious to convey his understanding.

'Oh, gracious heaven!' Verity uttered, appalled. 'About—about the library, and—and the boxes?'

'Ha! Ha! Yes, indeed, ma'am. And didn't I roast him heartily! Never thought to see the old fellow caught up in such a chapter of accidents!'

His bright laughter was not shared by his partner, and under that wide, clear gaze he coloured a little, and coughed in embarrassment.

'Tell me,' Verity said coolly, 'does his lordship find it as amusing as you do?'

'Good God, no! Poor fellow is quite cut up. Vows he will set all to rights with you before he comes down to Brighton.'

A cold hand seemed to grip Verity's heart. 'He is going to Brighton?'

'Well, hasn't exactly agreed to it. But I'm hoping to persuade him. Best thing for him, you understand. And while he has a mind to venture out of his hidey-hole, seems to me I'd best strike while the iron's hot. Get him used to it again, you understand.'

'Yes, I dare say you are right,' Verity said automatically, struggling with an inexplicable desire to burst into tears.

'I am,' agreed Quainton confidently. 'Don't want him bolting for cover again the minute you go off. Tells me it's all due to you he's come out of his shell at all.'

'I fear he flatters me, Mr Quainton,' Verity said, with an attempt at lightness.

'No, no. Sticks to it buckle and thong—if it hadn't been for you——'

'Then I am happy to have been of service,' Verity interrupted, unable to bear any more. 'I beg you will tell his lordship that I understand everything and that no explanation is due to me of any kind.'

'But he wants to talk to you himself,' protested Quainton, dismayed.

'Believe me, it is quite unnecessary that he should do so, sir. I think you should certainly put forth your best endeavours to persuade him to accompany you to Brighton.'

There was time for no more, for the dance was coming to an end and they were obliged to abandon conversation as the dancers began the *grande ronde* that completed it.

Afterwards Verity hurried across the floor with her mind all chaos, lending only half an ear to Mr Quainton's continued protests. The news that the Marquis was to be spirited away to Brighton—having first made 'all right' with her, so he had said!—had dealt her an unaccountably heavy blow. She had never known him as the Marquis. To meet him now in this guise, as if they were strangers, before all these avid Wellsian eyes, must be unendurable. Better she should remember him only as the 'Mr Haverigg' with whom she had enjoyed a brief acquaintance through the adventures of a pair of adorable children. Better never to see any of them again!

Yet here was Mr Quainton asking of her, as if it were a small favour, to face that fearsome ordeal! She *could* not do it.

'I say, Miss Lambourn, won't you at least speak to Salmesbury?'

'Pray say no more, sir,' Verity begged, and turning at her patroness' side, she resolutely held out her hand. 'Thank you for the dance, Mr Quainton. Goodnight.'

The discomfited intermediary had nothing to do but to make his farewells and return disconsolate to relay the ineffectual result of his mission to his principal. Miss Lambourn, who would have liked to run away to her lodgings to indulge in a hearty bout of tears, was denied this solace. For Mr Cumberland had waited for her return, jealously determined not to be ousted a second time.

As she took to the floor again on this gentleman's arm, she had the doubtful satisfaction of seeing my lord of Salmesbury limp out of the room set aside for dancing and into the cardroom where, apparently, he remained for the rest of the evening. Although Mr Quainton was to be seen dancing several times with other ladies, he did not again approach Miss Lambourn.

A restless night brought Sunday, and the opportunity to pray for help in a matter that was fast becoming an obsession. Dear Lord, if I am never to see him again, please help me to bear it! But she was no nearer to a reconciliation to this dismal prospect on the following morning when she was wakened early by the maid.

'What is it, Dawson?' she asked sleepily.

'Begging your pardon, miss, but her ladyship sent me to fetch you at once.' The maid simpered knowingly. 'There's a caller in the parlour, Miss. A *gennelman*.'

CHAPTER SEVEN

VERITY let out a small shriek and leapt from the bed. 'Oh, gracious heaven! Oh, no! Oh, Dawson, what shall I do?'

'Seems to me you'd best get dressed, miss,' said the maid practically. 'I've brought your hot water.'

Crossing to the table, she proceeded to pour water from the jug into the basin. Then, as Verity began hastily to wash, she chose from the meagre wardrobe, with great presence of mind, a chemise gown of floral chintz which she laid out on the bed.

Ten minutes later, her heart hammering and her legs like jelly, Verity entered the parlour. The gentleman rose from his chair by the window and moved into the centre of the room. It was Mr Leonard Quainton.

'How do, Miss Lambourn?' he said pleasantly.

Verity was so much disappointed that it was a moment or two before she could say a word. Fortunately Lady Crossens saved her the trouble.

'There you are at last, child! Bless me, how long it has taken you! Here is Mr Quainton left with only an old lady's chatter, when all the time he was hoping to speak to you.'

'H-how do you do, sir?' Verity managed, holding out a hand that trembled still. 'What a surprise!'

'Ah, well, you see, had to come early so as to catch you before you got lost in the dissipations of Tunbridge Wells! Ha! Ha!'

'Pray be seated again, sir,' Verity said politely, herself taking a chair by Lady Crossens. 'What is it that you want of me?'

'Ah, yes. Come to ask if you'd care to join a—a

party of pleasure, ma'am. Going to High Rocks, you understand.'

'High Rocks?' she repeated stupidly, as if she had never heard of that famed place about which the Tunbridge Wells crowd were wont to rave. Her heart, which had lain like lead in her chest, suddenly came to life again, making speech difficult. She pulled herself together. 'Oh, yes, High Rocks. It is a—a notable site, I collect.'

'Then you've not seen it yet? Capital. Come with us, ma'am. Make a day of it.'

'Well. . .' Verity began, with a glance at her patroness.

'If you are looking to me,' said the lady at once, who had no notion of putting a bar in the way of her young friend becoming further acquainted with the first eligible male to come in her way, 'you may take it that you have my full permission.'

'But——'

'If you are thinking of a chaperon, my dear,' went on the old lady, 'I am sure you will find that Mr Quainton has provided for all that. How many are in your party, sir?'

'Oh—er—quite a number,' the gentlemen said, a little red about the gills. 'Several very respectable females, of course. I suppose there must be seven or eight of us.'

Verity was at a loss to know what to do. To accept, she knew, must put her in the position of deceiving Lady Crossens, who would not, she was sure, give her consent did she know the likely composition of this *party*. Mr Quainton's acquaintance at the Wells was next to non-existent, she knew, and as for the Marquis of Salmesbury—— Well, unless they had made friends on Saturday night, she had little doubt that the party would be found to contain one small boy and his entourage, and that the 'respectable females' would number among them a toddler in leading strings!

To refuse, however, would mean that she truly would never see the Marquis again. For surely, if she rejected his olive branch a second time, he would abandon any further attempt to make contact with her. She *should* so reject it. It was the only sensible course to pursue. But Verity was not feeling very sensible.

'Well, Miss Lambourn,' Quainton said, a trifle anxiously, 'can we count upon your joining us? Wish you would! I mean, very much hope you can see your way to——'

'Tush, sir!' broke in Lady Crossens irritably. 'Of course she will go with you. Come now, Verity. Go and get your breakfast—for allow you to go off with nothing inside you I will not!—and then fetch your pelisse and bonnet and be off with the pair of you!'

It was a relief to have the decision taken out of her hands, but as Verity moved to the little dining parlour she vowed secretly to confess all to her patroness at the earliest opportunity. When she sat to her meal, however, she found herself unable to swallow more than a few mouthfuls of coffee. Her nerves, already in shreds, were not improved when, as Quainton handed her up into the Marquis's phaeton, he spoke in a low tone so that the attendant groom should not hear.

'I dare say you have guessed that Salmesbury sent me. Said I made wretched work of it at the dance. Quite true. I bungled it shockingly. Must thank you, though. He would have had my head if I'd come back without you this morning!'

His words did much to lighten Verity's heart, but the presence of the groom prevented any further conversation on the subject. Verity put an oblique question. 'Where is the rest of your *party*, Mr Quainton?'

'Meeting them at High Rocks, ma'am.' He glanced

at her, the picture of guilt. 'Not exactly a party, mind. Had to hoax the old lady, though.'

'I am aware of it,' Verity said repressively.

He looked relieved, and added, 'Set out early myself, so they should all be there by this time. Only a couple of miles, you understand.'

'Yes, so I believe.'

Apparently cheered by her mild response to his deception, Quainton kept up a steady flow of small talk on the short journey, the sort of thing that came easily to *habitués* of fashionable society. Miss Lambourn, though she bore little part in it herself, was grateful for it, for the stream of inanities kept her imagination from winging ahead to the forthcoming meeting, the thought of which was causing a profusion of butterflies to dance around her stomach.

But when the phaeton reached High Rocks and pulled up next to a carriage with a crest on the panel, such a commotion greeted their arrival that the first moments of meeting passed almost unnoticed.

Braxted, seeing the approach of the carriage, set up a shout. 'Here's Verity, sir! Verity! Verity!'

He began to run towards them, while behind him, a little voice echoed, 'Vetty! Vetty!'

Then little Lady Margaret, too, started forward, but, catching her foot on a protruding rock on the uneven surface, she fell headlong and began at once to wail.

Two females sprang to the rescue, scolding as nurses did, and Braxted dashed back to add his voice to the cacophony, explaining heatedly to his father, who had limped on to the scene, and Mr Eastleigh, tutting ineffectually, that he was not to blame.

'Can I help it if she follows me all over?' he demanded. 'Kittle had ought much better to keep her on a lead!'

'That will do!' said the Marquis. 'No one is blaming you.'

'No indeed,' corroborated the tutor. 'But, you know, Master Wystan, it is your part to have a little foresight where your sister is concerned.'

'But I wanted to greet Verity,' protested Wystan, causing the Marquis to turn at once towards the phaeton.

By this time Verity had already been handed down by Mr Quainton, and was walking towards the agitated group. For a moment there was pandemonium, as several voices greeted her at once, calling loudly over Peggy's wailing.

'Gracious, what a to-do!' she exclaimed, laughing, her nervousness forgotten. 'And here is Mr Quainton inviting me on a party of *pleasure*!'

Salmesbury grinned. 'Indeed, you might well be pardoned for climbing straight back into the carriage and demanding to be driven home!'

'Pooh!' chimed in Braxted. 'She ain't so poor-spirited, are you, Verity?'

'I trust not,' smiled Miss Lambourn, and moved forward to address the grizzling Lady Margaret, who was nestling in Kittle's arms. 'What happened, Peggy? Did you fall?'

Peggy, seeing a new face, ceased her lamentations to stare at it. Apparently she remembered it, for she pointed to the ground. 'Peddy faw down.'

'Oh, that was too bad!' Verity said sympathetically. 'But you're such a brave girl, I know. You won't cry any more, will you?'

Peggy considered this for a moment. Then a bright smile creased her face. 'Peddy no cwy. Peddy bave.'

'And so you are!' agreed Verity admiringly. 'And will you show me High Rocks? I have come to see them, you know.'

This was going too far, however, and Lady Margaret frowned. 'No sow. Peddy pay.'

'Very well, then, I shall ask Wystan to show me,' Verity said equably.

But Peggy would have none of this either. 'No! Wissen no sow you! Wissen sow Peddy.'

'He won't!' began Braxted loudly. 'Wissen no——'

'Come along,' intervened the Marquis quickly. 'We will all go. After all, there they are.'

He turned and pointed to the high cliff-like rocks that stood towering above them some distance away. It was enough for Braxted, who set off at once, calling to the rest to follow. The two nurses hurried along with Peggy, who was pointing after her brother and shrieking his name, and the rest of the adults followed more slowly.

Quite how it happened, Verity did not know, but, long before they reached the Rocks, she found herself strolling beside the Marquis, whose progress was necessarily slow, while the rest of the company had gone some way ahead.

When he judged them to be out of earshot of the rest of the party, Salmesbury left off discussing the merits of the Rocks they could see ahead, and abruptly stopped and turned to his companion.

'Miss Lambourn, now that we have a moment to ourselves, please allow me——'

'Oh, no, pray!' Verity begged quickly, stopping in her turn and showing him a face lit with such warmth that his breath caught. 'You must not say anything, sir! If I seemed to you—if I said anything to—oh, gracious heaven! What *can* I say? I have said *too much* too many times already!'

'Nonsense!' broke in the Marquis. 'It is I who——'

'No, no, no! I will not have you blame yourself! All the conclusions I drew—so *false*!—were of my own doing. I had no right, no business saying *any* of the unutterably cruel things I did say. Believe me, sir, if I have a fault, it is a too over-active imagination which is apt to lead me into——'

'If you have a fault, Miss Lambourn,' interrupted Salmesbury firmly, 'it is that you will never permit a fellow to edge in a word!'

Verity stared at him open-mouthed, taking in the teasing gleam in his black eye and the twitch at the corner of his mouth. Her own lips quivered irrepressibly and she began to laugh.

'That is better!' he said, smiling. 'Now, if you will allow me to speak?'

'You have the floor, sir,' Verity gurgled. 'Indeed, you are very right. I am all too ready to——'

'*Miss Lambourn*!'

'I beg your pardon!' Verity said contritely, and resolutely closed her lips, though her eyes danced.

'Miss Lambourn,' the Marquis repeated, in a much gentler tone, 'let us by all means agree that there have been faults on both sides. How could it be otherwise? But your outspokenness—if it *is* a fault!—has been of immense service to me, and I am far from subscribing to your own critical view of it. But there can be no excuse for my failing to enlighten you as to my real identity at those accursed diversions, as I promise you I had the intention of doing.'

'Had I only allowed you to edge in a word!' Verity put in.

'Quite so!' he agreed, grinning. 'Or if you had only deigned to notice me that night when you looked so lovely and so—so *unnervingly* unapproachable in all your finery.'

'*My* finery!' gasped Verity. 'Upon my word, sir, I can scarcely believe my ears! There *you* were, so very much the Marquis, so *elegant*! Gracious heaven, how could I possibly have borne you to approach me after all the dreadful things I had said about you?'

'Don't, *don't*! You make me feel so badly.' The

black eyes had grown serious again. He reached out to take one of her hands. 'I owe you so much, Miss Lambourn! Forgive me!'

Tears sprang to Verity's eyes as he bent his head and kissed her mittened fingers.

'There is nothing to forgive, sir,' she said huskily, and felt his fingers tighten briefly on hers before releasing them.

There was a brief pause. As Verity struggled to regain command over her voice, the black eyes looked into hers. He must perceive the tears there, she thought, but he remained tactfully silent. She became conscious then of what he had said and spoke suddenly.

'What do you mean by saying you owe me so much? You owe me nothing.'

He smiled and shook his head. 'You must allow me to be the judge of that.'

'I don't understand,' Verity said frowningly.

'I will explain it to you presently, but not today.'

Verity thrilled to the implication that they must meet again. Then perhaps he meant to stay at Braxted Park!

The Marquis gestured towards the Rocks with his cane. 'Shall we go on?' he suggested, and they turned together and began to stroll towards the others.

'Your cousin told me you are thinking of going to Brighton,' Verity ventured, hardly aware that she held her breath as she waited for his reply.

'Perhaps,' he said, his tone offhand. 'It depends. At present Brighton holds little attraction for me.'

Her heart leapt at his words and it was with difficulty that she refrained from asking on *what* his decision depended.

'I dare say,' she said carefully, 'that it would do you good to go among people of your own kind once more.'

'I don't know that,' he responded lightly. 'I was never very much a social animal, you know, even before——'

He broke off and Verity, conscious of awkwardness in this reminder of the dreadful past, rushed into the breach.

'No, I suppose merely because one is—is born to it, there is no guarantee that one will enjoy the social advantages of one's rank.'

'Precisely. In fact, although I would be the last to deny that it is very comfortable to enjoy these privileges, there are certain disadvantages.'

'Gracious, I should think so!' Verity agreed at once. 'I can think of nothing worse than to be obliged to keep up vast estates and employ hordes of servants. Had I my choice, I should like a quiet cottage, with perhaps a maid and a cat, where I might shut myself up for hours with my pen, and indulge in——'

It was her turn to break off, putting a hand to her mouth as if to force the words back in, and glancing up at her companion in consternation. He was looking puzzled.

'You intrigue me greatly, Miss Lambourn. Am I to understand that you *write*?'

'Oh, pray do not ask me!' she begged. 'I should not have said so much. I did not mean to do so.'

The Marquis had halted again and was staring at her. 'But Miss Lambourn, what is there to be ashamed of in that? Good God, you must be very clever!'

'Oh, I am not!' protested Verity, blushing. 'And as for being ashamed, it is no such thing! Only I am obliged to prevaricate a little, you see, because my parents would be quite shocked if they knew of my plans.'

'Nonsense! They must be proud and pleased,' argued his lordship.

'Oh, pray hush, sir! You do not know! My father is a clergyman, and, although he is the best and kindest of men, I cannot think he would regard with anything but horror the knowledge that one of his daughters plans to live by the writing of Gothic tales of adventure!'

'Live by it?' echoed the Marquis. 'I should think not indeed!'

Verity's eyes flashed. 'And pray why should I not? Because I am a female?'

'Well, partly, but——'

'Let me tell you, sir, that, if I had the good fortune to succeed in having a novel published, I would certainly consider myself entitled to live on the proceeds, in preference to depending on *marriage*, which I take it you imply to be my lot in life!'

'Miss Lambourn, I meant nothing of the sort. I assure you, this wrath is misplaced,' said poor Salmesbury. 'I had no idea of incurring your displeasure.'

'I beg your pardon,' Verity said stiffly, turning away from him. She breathed deeply once or twice to recover her temper, and turned back, speaking with an apologetic air. 'You see, sir, the case is that my mother has a positive bee in her bonnet on the subject of matrimony. I suppose it is because there are so many of us and she has always believed it her duty to see us all off. That is why I was sent here, of course. Though why she should suppose anything could come of it when both Prudence and Patience failed so dismally to procure husbands when they came here, I am at a loss to imagine!'

'Are you all named for the virtues?' asked Salmesbury, seizing on a change of subject that might divert her.

'Oh, yes, it is the greatest trial to all of us!' Verity said instantly. 'You see, Mama is called Grace, so I suppose that is why they thought of it. They began with Faith, Hope and Charity and continued from there.'

'Good God!' exclaimed the Marquis, amused. 'How

in the world did they find such names for—was it six sisters you said you had?'

'Oh, they managed far more than that. We lost so many of my sisters, you know, and they could never bring themselves to use a name of one of the dear ones who had died. So by the time I was born—and I was the seventh—they were hard put to it to find anything acceptable.'

'I think Verity a charming name,' commented his lordship with a smile.

'Oh, I do not mind it. It is my younger sisters who suffered most. Poor Mercy and little Peace are in despair! And when it came to *Temperance* and *Obedience*, who were the last, it was the outside of enough!'

The Marquis could not help laughing, 'I should say so!'

'Yes, but *most fortunately* both of them died, poor little dears.'

'Very understandable,' murmured Salmesbury, the gleam in his black eyes pronounced.

'Ah, but that was before either knew anything of the matter, so I don't feel they can have done so by *design*,' Verity said seriously.

The Marquis's lips twitched, but he managed to preserve his countenance. 'And have you no brothers at all?'

'Only the one,' Verity answered. 'He is the baby, and naturally everyone's favourite. He is spoilt to death and will doubtless grow up to be quite unbearable!'

'Do tell me! I am agog to know. Does his name accord with family tradition?'

'No, it does not!' Verity said with unexpected heat. 'Would you believe it? After saddling us girls with all those terrible names, what did Mama and Papa do but come up with something quite ordinary. After my sisters and I had raided the Bible, too, and discovered several quite unexceptionable *virtuous* names. But all they could think of was "Henry". The most common-place name in the world!'

There was a silence. Then Salmesbury said, a little diffidently, 'Do you—er—dislike the name "Henry"?'

'Not precisely. For my father is Harry, which is why——' She stopped and stared at him, struck with a sudden thought. 'Oh, no! Don't say *you* are called Henry?'

The Marquis nodded, ruefully grinning. 'I am desolated to be obliged to confess it, but yes.' He bowed. 'Henry Wystan Haverigg, ma'am. Very much at your service.'

'Oh, *no*!' cried Verity, and went off into a peal of laughter, in which Henry Haverigg readily joined her.

Then they both became aware that someone was calling to them.

'Sir! Sir! Verity!' Braxted came running up. 'Don't you mean to come and see the Rocks? What are you laughing at?'

'We have been discussing Christian names,' Verity explained. She looked at the Marquis. 'And this, no doubt, is Wystan Henry Haverigg?'

'That's right!' Braxted shouted, surprised. 'How did you know?'

'Pure deduction, Wystan,' Salmesbury said. 'Miss Lambourn is an extremely clever lady, you must know.'

The comfortable privacy was shattered for the day. There was no rational conversation to be had with every other sentence punctuated by Braxted's chatter or Peggy's terse comments, delivered at the level of a shriek. It warmed Verity's heart, however, to see the children so joyous, their pleasure unalloyed by any suppression of high spirits. For the Marquis forbore to scold, rather smiling at their exuberance, and the rest of his entourage took their tone from him.

Miss Lambourn had been interested to note the

presence of a second nurse, and found an opportunity to make the woman's acquaintance. She chose a moment when the gentlemen were engaged with Braxted, who was pointing out the scars made by previous visitors cutting into the stone of the great rocks.

'How do you do?' she said in friendly fashion, smiling at the woman. 'Kittle I have met, but you are new, I believe?'

The nurse dropped a curtsy. 'Yes, ma'am, I'm the junior. Bradshaw is the name.'

'And how do you like the position, Bradshaw?'

'Early days, ma'am,' said Bradshaw frankly.

She was a rather gaunt woman, a year or so younger than her senior nurse, but there was intelligence and kindness in her gaze, and Verity suspected that a warm heart beat under the gruff exterior.

'I envy you the charge of little Peggy,' Verity said. 'She is a delightful child.'

Bradshaw's face softened. 'Yes, poor little mite! But she's a handful, ma'am—except when her brother is by. Adores the lad, she does.'

Verity nodded. 'And he her.'

'Small wonder, ma'am!' commented the nurse, a trifle grimly.

The eyes of the two women met and a look of understanding passed between them. Verity made no reference to it, however. She could not be seen to gossip with Henry Haverigg's servants. She smiled warmly instead.

'I am glad you have come, Bradshaw. Take good care of the little one.'

There was time for no more, for Kittle came up with Peggy, her eyes going from one to the other in quick suspicion. It was evident, Verity thought, that there was some rivalry here.

She had also managed to acquaint herself with the

cleric, Mr Eastleigh, and discovered him to be so sensible a man, and so warm in his praise of young Lord Braxted's potential, that she found herself thinking of both children with an easier mind. As if it was any of her business! she chided herself. But the conviction that it *was* her business—that *Henry* was her business!—could not be shaken off.

She thought Mr Eastleigh cast puzzled glances at his employer now and again as he exchanged laughing banter with his cousin, his children and herself, and guessed that the picture Henry was presenting of carefree domesticity was something new, and her heart swelled.

It seemed no time at all before the picnic, served by liveried attendants, had been disposed of, and the Lady Margaret's drooping eyelids signified the end of an enjoyable day. As the disposition of persons in the carriages was being discussed, it became apparent that Salmesbury had the intention of driving Miss Lambourn back to Tunbridge Wells. All at once, the difficulties of her position came home to Verity and she contrived to draw the Marquis a little aside.

'Pray, sir,' she begged in an undervoice, 'do not you trouble to escort me. I can very well go with the groom.'

'You will do nothing of the kind!' argued Salmesbury in a somewhat peremptory tone. 'Good God, how could you think I would treat you so shabbily?'

'No, no, you mistake me,' Verity told him urgently. 'I don't think that. It is only—oh, can you not see how such a course must give rise to gossip?'

The black eyes flashed in sudden anger. 'Are you afraid to be seen with me, ma'am?'

'Well, of course I am!' Verity responded frankly. 'Gracious heaven, what do you suppose people will say of me if it is reported that I left town with one gentleman and returned with quite another?'

'Oh!' said the Marquis blankly.

'Exactly.'

'Hell and the devil!' he swore, and then, recollecting himself, stiffly begged her pardon.

Verity brushed this aside with an impatient gesture. 'You must also realise that it would be quite ineligible for me to be seen with you, in any event, now that you are known in Tunbridge Wells.'

'Oh, indeed?' he returned ominously. 'May I ask why?'

'Well, what a stupid question! Because I am only a clergyman's daughter, and you are a Marquis, of course.'

'What in heaven's name has that to say to anything?'

'Everything! You must know what a hotbed of gossip is the Wells. It may be very well for you to ignore such whisperings, but I, let me tell you, am obliged to be more circumspect.'

Tight-lipped, he stared at her, the black eyes snapping. When he spoke, that intimidating ice was back in his voice. 'Does this mean that I am barred even from calling upon you?'

Verity met his challenging gaze bravely, but her own eyes were bleak. 'I think perhaps it does, yes,' she said, in a sad little voice that spoke volumes.

The anger vanished from his eyes and he caught her hand. 'Forgive me! I thought——' He lowered his voice to a murmur. 'I thought you were attempting to warn me off.'

'Oh, no!' Verity said quickly. 'It is only——'

'Say no more! I comprehend prefectly and I would not for the world embarrass you.' He smiled and pressed the hand he still held. 'Quainton shall take you home.' Abruptly his hand tightened on hers. 'My God, if I had not forgot!'

'What is it?' she asked, made a little anxious by his manner.

'Wait one moment!'

He limped quickly to his coach and leaned inside. As he came back towards her again, Verity saw that he held a package in his free hand.

'What in the world. . .?' she began.

'You cannot now refuse it,' he said, a gleam in his black eyes as he pressed the package into her hands. 'A memento, Miss Lambourn. Until we meet again.'

Verity looked up at him, a smile of mischief hovering on her lips. 'Not those wretched boxes?'

'The very same,' he said softly. 'And God bless them, say I, for they brought us closer!'

'Th-thank you,' Verity managed, her fingers around the package trembling while her eyes spoke her feelings more clearly than any words.

Henry read them, and grasped both her wrists. 'Verity! I can't speak my mind here, but I hope—I believe—— Oh, God, Miss Lambourn, I shall see you again very soon! I *must* see you. Somehow I shall contrive it.'

Then, before she had a chance to speak further, he released her, turned and was calling to his cousin. There was hardly time for a conventional farewell before the phaeton was bowling back along the road to the spa town, but, although Mr Quainton kept up his usual stream of small talk, Verity answered him quite at random. She was not even listening. Her thoughts were wholly occupied with that last disjointed speech from Henry Haverigg, which argued much more than a simple desire to see her again. Breathless against the hammering of her heart, she heard his voice over and over again. '*I can't speak my mind here. . . I must see you.*' There had been a wealth of meaning in those words. Might it be—did she dare to hope that he, too——?

Afraid to put her thoughts into words, she found instead as she turned the package over and over in her hands that his name kept revolving in her mind. Henry, Henry, Henry. But it was as Henry Haverigg she thought of him, she realised with a start. Not as the Marquis of Salmesbury. It had been Henry Haverigg who had intruded into her life. That he was also a Marquis, *the* Marquis, was almost incidental. Except, of course, that he *was* the Marquis. That he lived in some huge house, among who knew how many servants, in a vast estate, no doubt peopled by such minions as her father was to Lady Crossens in the village of Tetheridge.

An impossible vision of herself in such a milieu presented itself to her mind, and was at once superimposed by a creature with a shadowed face who haunted the heart and memory of the Marquis of Salmesbury.

But not Henry Haverigg! No, not Henry! she begged silently. Only it was Henry Haverigg who was scarred and lacerated by that vision. How could she, ordinary Verity Lambourn, hope to oust it?

A profound depression settled on her spirits, and it was with an effort that she roused herself to bid farewell to Mr Leonard Quainton at the door of her lodging. She found Lady Crossens chatting to Mrs Polegate as both ladies partook of tea and cakes, and was glad that she had had the forethought to dart into her bedroom to take off her bonnet before entering the parlour. She did not want to be obliged to explain away the nest of boxes reposing in the package on her dressing-table.

'Oh, you are back,' remarked the latter unnecessarily, her eyes darting past Verity to the door as if she sought her escort there. 'Mr Quainton did not come up with you? What a pity! Not extremely wealthy, of course, but *most* eligible, as I have been at pains to assure dear Emilia.'

'Maria, be quiet!' snapped Lady Crossens, quite

exasperated. 'Sit down, child, and have some tea. I will ring for another cup.'

'Oh, no, thank you, ma'am,' Verity said, sinking into a chair beside her. 'But what are you doing at home, ma'am?'

'Oh, she has not been out all day!' exclaimed the widow. 'Poor dear Emilia is not feeling at all the thing! I have been trying to persuade her to have the doctor, but——'

'Maria!' said Lady Crossens warningly.

But Verity turned horrified eyes on her patroness. 'Oh, ma'am! Why did you not tell me? I should not have left you alone!'

'Pho, child! What could you have done? Besides, Maria has been with me, the good creature.'

'Oh, yes, and we have enjoyed *such* a delightful cose,' chimed in Mrs Polegate.

'I am so glad you stayed with her, dear ma'am,' Verity said warmly. 'And how do *you* do?'

'Never mind me,' said the irrepressible widow impatiently. 'How was your day? Did you like High Rocks? Who was of the party?'

'She can only answer one question at a time, Maria,' said her ladyship drily.

'Oh, I know, but I am *so* eager to hear it all,' fluttered her friend, fixing Verity with an eye alight with anticipation.

'It—it was a very pleasant day, ma'am,' Verity managed, though her cheeks were tinged with colour as she thought of all that had passed.

'And was the Marquis there?'

'Maria!'

'Yes, he was,' Verity admitted, wondering how she was to avoid revealing the actual composition of the party.

Fortunately, Mrs Polegate appeared to be quite satisfied with the presence of Salmesbury himself, confining her flood of questions to his appearance and demeanour, and his conversation.

'He—he is a very amiable man,' Verity said lamely. 'Quite unlike what I had been led to expect.'

The widow was disappointed. 'Was there no air of melancholy about him, then?'

'None that I could see,' said Verity truthfully.

'Pish! Would you have him wear his heart upon his sleeve, Maria? You may depend upon it that his breeding would preclude such a display of emotion. More to the point, did you find Mr Quainton agreeable, child?'

'Oh, yes, quite,' Verity said, with a marked lack of enthusiasm.

Lady Crossens looked at her rather hard, while Mrs Polegate broke into a sentimental diatribe about young persons falling in love on just such an outing as dear Miss Lambourn had enjoyed.

At length Verity managed to turn the subject back to her patroness's health, and was relieved to learn that the day's rest had very much improved it. She excused herself at last on the score of cleansing the dust from her person and dressing for dinner. But once alone and free to indulge her thoughts, she found her mind numb, so that she had difficulty even in recalling what had been said that day, though the pale features of Henry Haverigg with his gleaming black eyes swam in and out of her thoughts.

She discovered, over the next day or so, that her caution had been justified. Mrs Polegate's tongue was not the only one to wag. Sir John Frinton even went so far as to slyly twit her on her new conquest.

'Ah, me! The perennial fate of such an ancient *prétendant* as myself. Cast aside by the explosion of youth!'

'If you will pardon the liberty, sir, you talk a great deal of nonsense!'

Sir John laughed gently. 'But then I have had many years of practice.'

'That I do not doubt.'

'Nevertheless, I am not so sure that this young popinjay is the man destined to steal you from me.'

Verity's startled eyes flew to his. 'What—what do you mean?'

Sir John's lips quivered on that tantalising smile. 'Miss Lambourn, I am neither so blind nor so gullible as the majority of our dear neighbours.' He grinned as the dismay spread over her features. 'Fear not, my dear. I shall not betray you. In fact, you may command my services at any time, should circumstances so arrange themselves that you stand in need of help.'

'Th-thank you,' stuttered Verity, dazed. 'You are very good.'

'I am very *old*,' he contradicted with a wink, 'else I should not so imperil my own interests!'

Verity was obliged to laugh. But she found it increasingly harder to smile as the days wore on with no word and no sign of the Marquis of Salmesbury. Admiring the boxes of Tunbridge Ware in secret had become her solace, as she recalled how he had said they were a memento until they should meet again. But they were no substitute for his presence, and she began to believe that she had misunderstood his urgent words. Surely if he wanted so much to see her, and speak his mind—oh, Lord, what was it he wanted to say?—he would have found a way by now? It was almost four whole days since that hurried parting on Monday.

For the first time, she could see the date of the end of this adventure at Tunbridge Wells looming large, though it was still over a week away. For they were to start for Tetheridge in their fifth week to allow for Lady Crossens' slow method of travel. Her patroness was so clearly feeling the strain on her delicate health that there could be little hope that she might postpone their departure. Suppose the Marquis failed to contact her before that time? She would go away from here, never to see him again! This melancholy idea possessed her mind to such a degree that she found it hard indeed to concentrate on the action going forward on the stage when she accompanied her patroness to the theatre that night.

Mrs Baker's company were performing *The School for Scandal*, a piece which appeared to afford the rest of the Wellsian audience with food for much laughter. In Miss Lambourn's present mood, she found little to divert her in the antics of Lady Teazle and her companions. Besides, the crowded theatre was insufferably hot. She felt quite faint, and at last turned to murmur to Lady Crossens.

'The heat is intolerable, ma'am. Do you object to it if I walk in the corridor a little?'

The old lady, who was much enjoying the play, merely nodded her assent, and Verity slipped thankfully and unobtrusively out of the box. Closing the door softly behind her, she took a couple of paces forward, vigorously plying her fan, when a shadow loomed up before her and she almost screamed.

'Don't be alarmed, Miss Lambourn,' said a familiar voice quietly. 'It is only I.'

Wordlessly, she reached out, and the Marquis of Salmesbury took her hand in a strong clasp.

CHAPTER EIGHT

'I HAD not dared to hope I might catch you alone,' Henry said softly, drawing her a step or two closer to one of the wall-sconces so that a number of candles threw light over them both. 'I was going to wait for the first interval and waylay your party then.'

'But what are you doing here?' Verity asked foolishly, unaware that her fingers clung still to his.

'Can you ask? I had to see you!'

'But to meet in such a way!' Verity exclaimed, pulling away and tugging her hand free. 'If anyone were to see us!'

'Don't distress yourself. I shall not keep you above a moment.' His eyes travelled over her features. A smile lifted the corners of his mouth, and he whispered, 'Though I confess I should wish to do so—*forever.*'

'What?' Verity said faintly, unable to believe that she had heard him correctly.

'Never mind.' He spoke hastily, even a trifle curtly. 'This is hardly the time or the place to discuss such matters. Miss Lambourn, I must see you. Not like this. Openly, so that we may be free to talk. There is so much I want to say to you. I beg you, appoint a day when I may come to visit you, correctly and freely——'

'But I cannot!' she broke in. 'You must know what it is like here. Nothing—but *nothing* occurs in the town but everyone is instantly aware of it.'

'No one knew of our earlier meetings, however.'

'Yes, but you were not known then. I was questioned, believe me, but I turned it off. *Now*, however——'

'Very well, then,' he interrupted impatiently, 'you must come to me.'

'But, Mr Haverigg—I mean, my lord——'

'*Don't* call me that!' he ordered tersely. 'I am not "my lord" to you.' He seized one of her hands and held it tightly. 'Am I? *Am I*, Verity?'

Dumbly she shook her head, mesmerised by the force of those dynamic eyes.

He hissed in a breath, and his other hand let go his cane and took hold of her. As he drew her closer, the cane clattered to the floor, startling them both.

'Oh, take care!' Verity uttered as he let her go abruptly, cursing under his breath. She cast a furtive glance over her shoulder. 'I must go back.'

'Yes, yes, you will do so directly. Only help me to retrieve that accursed cane of mine.'

Quickly Verity bent and picked up the cane. She gave it to him and would have sped away, but he grasped her arm.

'A moment. You could come on another outing such as we had the other day, could you not?'

'I—I suppose that would be possible,' Verity said doubtfully, too anxious to think coherently.

'Very well. Tomorrow, then.'

'Tomorrow? No, I cannot! There is to be a cotillion ball in the afternoon, and——'

'Would that I could still dance!' the Marquis interrupted. 'Or that you preferred *my* company to so energetic a pastime.'

Verity shook her head vehemently. 'It is not that, indeed it isn't! I would like nothing better than to—but it would look so particular if I was absent, don't you see?'

He captured the hand with which she emphasised her words and brought it to hold against his cheek for a moment.

'The only thing I see, Miss Verity Lambourn, is your clear, innocent orbs looking straight into my soul.'

Verity stared into the black depths of his eyes which glittered oddly in the gloom. Her heart skittered madly, and it was only at a distance that she heard his voice, matter-of-fact now.

'The next day is hopeless, of course, for a clergyman's daughter, so it will have to be Monday. How I will find the patience I do not know!'

'Monday?' she said vaguely.

'Our meeting.'

'Oh, yes.'

'Good. Monday it is. You will say Quainton has arranged it.'

'Quainton? Why did you not send him tonight?'

'He has gone to Brighton. That is why you did not hear from me sooner. I will send my coachman for you. At ten o'clock?'

'Ten o'clock,' she repeated.

He brought the hand he still held to his lips. 'Until then.'

Verity nodded and turned to go back into the box. She felt unreal still, as if she were in a dream. At the door, she stopped and quickly glanced back, afraid she had imagined the whole. But Henry Haverigg was there, standing under the light, still watching her. He raised a hand in farewell and she slipped back into the box in something of a daze.

From the chaos of her thoughts one thing grew clear. She would have to tell Lady Crossens the truth. The Marquis had said she should mention it as his cousin's scheme, but Verity knew she could no longer prevaricate. The situation had grown far too serious for that. She made up her mind to confess the full story to her patroness before she slept that night.

* * *

'And you are telling me this is the very same man with whom you quarrelled that first day?' demanded Lady Crossens, her intent gaze under its lace nightcap fixed upon her protégée's face.

'Yes, ma'am,' Verity admitted, and looked away to examine with apparent interest the quilted coverlet on Lady Crossens' bed.

She had crept into her patroness's room after the maid had departed, to make her confession. The old lady had listened to the tale with admirable restraint, refraining alike from scolding or exclamatory comment. Indeed, it seemed to Verity, shamefacedly recounting it all, that Lady Crossens was not even disapproving. At the end, however, she expressed herself as having received a severe shock.

'What your poor dear father would have to say I shudder to think! As for your mama——'

Lady Crossens broke off and, to Verity's alarm, seemed at first to cackle in a gleeful way and then fall into a fit of choking.

'Dear ma'am, are you all right? May I do anything for you?' Verity offered anxiously, jumping off the edge of the bed where she had been sitting and starting towards her.

The old lady waved her away. 'I am perfectly well,' she answered from behind her hand. In a minute or two she seemed to recover and patted the coverlet. 'Sit down again, child. I have not finished with you yet.'

Verity obeyed, sighing deeply. 'I cannot blame you, ma'am, if you mean to give me a scold. Truly, I had no wish to deceive you.'

'Tush! How could you do so when you were yourself deceived?'

'He—the Marquis—did not mean it, either. Indeed, it was all my folly that caused him to prevaricate.'

'And I suppose it was due to your folly that he chose to hover secretly in the theatre corridor, instead of approaching you decently, like an honest man!' snapped Lady Crossens tartly.

'Yes, it was!' Verity answered, unexpectedly firing up. 'At least, it was *not* folly, for I knew how everyone must gossip and I begged him not to seek me out.'

'God grant me patience!' ejaculated Lady Crossens in exasperated tones. 'Folly? I think you have taken leave of your senses, child! After all, he is *only* a Marquis!'

Impervious to the heavy sarcasm of her patroness's tone, Verity defended herself vigorously. 'That is just the difficulty! If he were only plain Mr Haverigg, as I at first thought him, I could have borne it better.'

'*Borne* it? Borne what?'

'Oh, everything! The disorder of my mind, the—the misunderstandings, the tragic history behind him.'

Lady Crossens' eyes suddenly narrowed, her ill-temper arrested. Her wayward protégée, it appeared, was touched by something far other than a coronet. It was better, far better than she could have hoped. But the girl was altogether too nice in her notions. If care was not taken, the whole affair could yet come to nothing. She knew she was prone to be crotchety, for in truth she was tired and would be quite glad to get home to peace and quiet. But she must try not to allow her tetchiness to overcome her and alienate the girl! She stretched out a hand to grasp the one agitatedly fingering the pattern on the coverlet.

'Come, my child. What is done, is done. No use crying over spilt milk. Now tell me. What is the expedition he speaks of for Monday?'

'Hardly an expedition, ma'am,' Verity said more calmly, grateful for her ladyship's change of mood. 'There was no time to arrange the details, but I imagine it will be much the same as the other day, when we were chaperoned not only by his children, but by the nurses and Braxted's tutor, as well.'

'Hm. A trifle irregular, but I cannot think the sternest critic could cavil at it,' judged the old lady, who had no intention whatsoever of putting a spoke in this wheel. 'I think you may go with a clear conscience.'

'Oh, yes, ma'am,' Verity agreed at once. 'I am not afraid of anything—I know *he* would not behave other than gentlemanly. It was only that I was obliged before to deceive you for I knew how it would be, and I allowed you to think——'

'Pish and tush! All that is behind us. No, no, you go along on Monday and enjoy yourself. Now you had best get to bed, for if you do not need your rest, I do.'

Verity dutifully went off, able, now that her patroness knew everything, to look forward with a singing heart to a whole day in the company of Henry Haverigg. Although how she would get through the next two days she did not know. Had she been able to see into Lady Crossens' mind, she might have been less tranquil.

It was long before the old lady obtained the sleep she needed, for her own heart was bursting with triumph. How Grace would stare! A Marquis, no less! Never, never had she thought to do so well by the child. Not that she had had anything to do with it, except to bring her here. But a Marquis! Gracious heaven, but they were all, *all* of them, taken care of now! For Verity, as Lady Salmesbury, would see to all her sisters' husbands; would arrange her little brother's education. Why, Salmesbury might stand patron even to dear Harry himself. She could not have been more delighted if the child had been her own flesh and blood. Such an odd little creature to have secured such a fortune, too!

Here her ladyship's heady triumph suffered a check. An odd girl, indeed. Pray heaven she did not allow some idiotic scruple to stand in the way! What was more, if she had not gauged what that scruple might be, her name was not Emilia Crossens!

Whether or not her ladyship had correctly identified what might stand in the way of a potential union between Miss Verity Lambourn and himself, the Marquis had every intention of sweeping that particular obstacle out of his path. He had offered another such outing as the one to High Rocks, but in fact he had no idea of burdening himself with a party. He therefore arranged to pack into the carriage on Monday only the children and one of the nurses, and drive the vehicle himself.

Kittle, informed of the plan by Inskip, who told her one of them must be ready to accompany his lordship on Monday, immediately pulled rank over the new nurse and insisted on making the trip herself. Bradshaw, aware of her jealousy of her threatened position, made no objection, although she would have liked to meet Miss Lambourn again.

Salmesbury's coachman had been instructed to collect Miss Lambourn and bring her to the ruins of old Haverigg Hall, the medieval manor that had stood on the other side of the forest on a high hill overlooking the valley where the gypsies were at present encamped. Braxted, the Marquis knew, would love to scramble among the fallen stones, and Peggy would follow him, so that Verity and himself might enjoy a period of peaceful privacy. That this plan would make nonsense of the business of chaperonage did not bother Salmesbury in the least. What he had to say to Miss Lambourn would, he hoped, obviate the need for a chaperon either now or at any future time.

The day began a little overcast, much to his lordship's consternation, and he determined that if it were to come on to rain he would simply transfer the engagement to the comfort of Braxted Place. But by the time the coach set Miss Lambourn down at the broken lodge gates of the old hall, where the Marquis was waiting to escort her, the sun had broken through the cloud with the promise of another hot day.

'Where are we?' enquired Verity after the first greetings, looking about her in some surprise after the coachman had handed her down.

'It is our old house, Miss Lambourn,' answered the Marquis, stepping forward to take her hand. He pressed it, adding softly, 'Thank you for coming. You look charmingly—as usual!'

She blushed a little, for she had, in a sentimental vein, chosen the pink gingham chemise gown and the flower-trimmed chipstraw hat which she had been wearing that far-off day when they had collided in the library doorway.

Realising all of a sudden that they were alone, she looked anxiously about. 'Where are the others?'

'The children have gone forward with Kittle. Wystan could not wait to explore the Hall. It is quite a ruin, you know, and normally he is not permitted to come here.'

He dismissed the coachman and offered his arm to Miss Lambourn, who hesitated a moment, watching the coach begin to rumble away.

'I am not sure this is right,' she said worriedly. 'I have told my patroness that at least the nurses would be here.'

'Kittle is here,' he said reassuringly, again holding his arm for her to place her fingers within it. 'Come, Miss Lambourn. Do you distrust me?'

'N-no,' Verity said doubtfully, 'only I—I have cleared my conscience, and I do not want to burden it with a new deceit.'

'Then the sooner we join the children, the better,' Salmesbury suggested bracingly.

This seemed sensible and Verity at last consented to

place her hand into the crook of his elbow. They began to stroll very gently along the rutted driveway.

'It is very much pitted, Miss Lambourn, so take care,' warned his lordship, as if it were she who stood in more danger of tripping than he with his halting step. But his cane stood him in good stead, and, although their progress was slow, it was secure enough.

'The Hall, you know, belonged to our forebears of the Middle Ages, and has been going to rack since the time of Elizabeth.'

As the Marquis talked on of the ancestors who had inhabited the ruined structure they could see ahead, pointing out landmarks as they went by, a sense of unreality began to pervade Verity's mind. That impassioned little exchange at the theatre the other night seemed as remote as something she might have wrought with her own pen. The man beside her, so far from exhibiting the loverlike ardour that had apparently consumed him then, appeared as calmly controlled as if the meeting were indeed a simple party of pleasure.

That she was herself obliged to conceal an uneven heartbeat and a certain shortness of breath did not occur to her. She thought only that her too active imagination had betrayed her into reading too much into that night's hurried exchange.

As they came close to the ruins, Braxted, poised on a fragment of wall, saw them and waved. In a moment he came running up, closely followed by Kittle with the shrieking Peggy in her arms.

'Wystan, how do you do? And Peggy! I am so happy to see you both!' exclaimed Verity, as the dreamlike feeling at once drained away.

'This is a capital place, Verity!' Braxted shouted. 'You must come and 'splore it with us.'

'Pore it! Pore it!' squeaked Peggy, although she had no idea what her brother meant.

'Well, if you like,' Verity began, but was interrupted.

'Thank you, Braxted, but I think Miss Lambourn had better keep pace with me rather than you. We don't want her dashing about in your neck-or-nothing style. She will end by breaking a limb or something, and then how should we feel?'

'Oh!' said Braxted, eyeing Verity thoughtfully. 'She don't look that feeble to me, but if you say so.'

Verity laughed. 'I dare say your papa is right. Besides, it is growing a little too hot to run around.'

'Pooh!' exclaimed Braxted disgustedly. 'Not for me. Tally ho!'

Then he was off, charging away, and hopping nimbly from rock to rock over the fallen masonry.

'Tay-o, tay-o,' echoed Peggy, as she attempted to emulate him. 'Peddy comin'!' she called as Kittle quickly lifted her and hurried after Wystan.

Verity stood looking after them, a smile on her lips, and was almost startled when the soft voice spoke behind her.

'I hope you do not mind. After having gone to all this trouble to get you to myself, I could not allow my son to take you away from me.'

Verity turned, her heart fluttering, and saw in his face that Friday night had been no dream.

He pointed with his cane to where a clump of trees encroached on the ruin. 'There is some shade over there, and we may sit on the remains of the wall.'

They made their way through the thickly growing weeds in silence and sat, a little apart, on the low stone that jutted from the ancient foundations. Both pairs of eyes contemplated the distant figures of the children and the nurse, as they clambered about the old stones which marked out the rooms that once were there.

'You asked me a little while back what I owed you,' the Marquis said, suddenly breaking the silence. He gestured with the cane he still held, idling between his hands, towards the children. '*That*, Miss Lambourn, is what I owe you. That I am sitting here, able to watch my children at play, learning to know them again. All that is directly attributable to you.'

Verity looked at him. 'If that is so, I am glad,' she said quietly. 'Though I cannot imagine what words of mine can have brought it about.'

He turned to her then, a little rueful smile curving his lips. 'You rebuked me finely, did you not? And, not content with that, you made, in your innocent and quite understandable assumptions, such comments as made me see how selfish I had been. Very well to punish myself, but I had no right to punish my children.'

His voice had grown harsh and Verity's heart shrank within her. She put a hand on his arm. 'Pray, sir, don't, *don't* distress yourself so!'

'Distress myself! Do you think I would not suffer twice—no, a hundred times—the distress, could I but wipe out that one moment of ill-conditioned temper?'

'Oh, Mr Haverigg—my *lord*, please——'

His eyes, as they turned on her, were almost wild in their passion. '*Henry*,' he grated angrily. 'Call me Henry!'

Verity stared at him, nonplussed. She did not know what to say, much less do, but her whole heart went out to the tortured storm within him. Without conscious thought, her fingers reached up to touch his cheek.

'Poor Henry,' she whispered involuntarily, 'don't be sad!'

In one violent movement, he caught her fingers and pressed them to his lips, shutting his eyes. Then he almost flung her hand away and pushed himself to his feet, limping some few paces off in a series of jerking steps.

Verity stayed where she was, watching him doff his

beaver hat and wipe the back of his hand across his brow. She was no longer afflicted with those nervous flutterings of the heart, for her heart ached. Blindingly, as if she had not suspected it before, the knowledge came to her that she loved him. She did not know if she had the power to assuage the tempest in his soul, but at that moment she knew that she would give her life to do it.

Presently he turned and came back to reseat himself beside her, in control once more. He placed his hat on the wall beside him and rested his cane by it. Verity said nothing as he did so, waiting, willing to follow his lead, to spare him any way she could.

'I have to beg your pardon,' he said calmly. 'I brought you here to talk of that very matter, but I had no business to hurl my uncontrolled emotions at you!'

'Quite like a Gothic monster,' Verity said lightly.

He smiled. 'It must have seemed so indeed. I am so sorry.'

'Oh, do not mind it. Only consider how useful it will be to my next story!'

He laughed out at that. 'My God! A model for the villain, no less.'

'Naturally. Did you expect to play the hero?'

He looked at her. 'In this story, yes.'

Verity coloured a little, but she did not look away. 'But I thought I had explained how much of a bore I found all the virtuous heroes.'

Henry grinned suddenly, and his black eyes gleamed mischief. 'As well, then, that you have seen the worst of me!'

'Have I?' she asked shyly.

The grin faded. 'My angel, I sincerely hope so!'

A rosy glow invaded Verity's heart at this endearing form of address, but she was well aware that its use was premature. Before she could think of a suitable way to express this, however, the Marquis had begun to speak again.

'Verity, I want you to know the worst of me. That is the real reason I needed to talk to you. I want you to have no illusions about what happened here. I want no rumours, no half-truths to come between us.'

'Oh, no,' Verity protested, suddenly afraid. 'No, Henry, no! You need not tell me. It is quite unnecessary. What I have already heard is quite enough. No, I beg you, say no more!'

'I *must*,' he insisted. 'Please understand. I have no desire to distress you with a tale of horror. And it is horrible. But I cannot, will not, go further with what there is between us, unless you have heard the truth from me.'

'Well, if—if you must, then——' Verity faltered. She stopped and smiled at him. 'I'm sorry. I was being stupidly fearful. Tell me anything you wish.'

He drew a breath. 'Thank you.'

There was a pause, during which Verity could see him struggle with himself. She was tempted to say again that he need tell her nothing, but she saw, with a wisdom born of her discovered love for him, that he needed to unburden himself; that he was in fact conferring upon her the greatest privilege he could by imparting to her what had probably never wholly been confided to anyone.

'It began with a quarrel,' he got out, in a light tone at variance with the turmoil of emotion this story had cost him. 'Margaret, you see, was a social butterfly. She loved nothing better than to go into company, while I—well, we need not go into that. Suffice it that our tastes on this matter were widely divergent.'

'There is nothing in that,' Verity commented with a laugh. 'I could name you as many as a dozen subjects upon which my sisters and I are at variance.'

'I dare say. But between husband and wife it can be——'

Again he shied away from revealing too much, and Verity guessed that the quarrel he had mentioned had not been the first to be provoked between them.

'Yes, I take your point,' she said.

'Don't misunderstand me,' Henry said quickly. 'Though I did not care for the same sort of pursuits as Margaret, and would as lief have avoided them for the most part, I put no bar in the way of her enjoyment. I trust I was neither so selfish, nor so unkind. But on this particular occasion I confess I was recalcitrant. It seemed so pointless an expedition. Some party at a neighbour's place—to relieve the tedium of those few unoccupied weeks at the end of summer and before the London little season, I suppose. I knew she had missed much of the previous season, for little Margaret was born then. But she had been to Bath for most of the summer to recuperate, and I would have thought—however, that is neither here nor there! She wanted desperately to go and I did not. Oh, I had a reason, though to be sure Meg thought it petty. Perhaps it was.'

He stopped, biting his lip, and Verity, watching him, thought that he had gone over this argument with himself many times. At the back of her mind she noted, almost in passing, his use of a pet name for his dead wife, and an involuntary pang shot through her.

'What was the reason?' she prompted quietly.

A short, mirthless laugh escaped him. 'My one fatal conceit! A race. If I have a passion, it is for driving. I flatter myself I am a dab hand at the ribbons. Nothing, it seems, has the power to curb it, not even——'

'Why should you wish to curb it?' Verity broke in, unable to bear the bitter self-accusation in his tone. 'Every man must have a hobby.'

'I should wish to,' Henry grated through clenched

teeth, 'because the—the *accident* was directly attributable to that *hobby*!'

There was a momentary pause. Verity could feel his tension. Her own pulse was uneven. Her voice shook a little.

'Go on, Henry.'

Henry did not look at her. His eyes fixed themselves on a point in space, where the pictures in his mind paraded before him.

'I had arranged to run a race the following day. A friendly affair with a fellow addict, over by Faversham. I wanted to retire early, but Margaret was bored and very insistent.' He drew a breath, as if the story was becoming more painful to relate. 'We quarrelled.' He shook his head. 'A stupid affair. In the end Meg insisted she should go alone. I could not permit that, of course, and so, with a very ill grace, I gave in.'

His voice went flat. 'The party was quite as insipid as I had expected, and did nothing to improve my temper. Worse, Meg sparkled like the diamonds about her neck, and took—or so I thought—a deal of pleasure in demonstrating her enjoyment to me. I was determined to leave early and so get my rest in spite of her. She was furious and we had more words while the coach was being fetched.'

Again he paused, his breathing ragged. Verity, her own heart shrinking at what was to come, dared not utter a word.

'It was then that I—I took a false step. I could not bear the thought of a journey plagued by recriminations. I told the coachman to get up behind and took the reins myself. It was a—a *criminal* act. The act of a lunatic! For I was the worse for drink and my judgement was impaired.'

The dull ache in Verity's heart sharpened into acute pain. She longed to reach out, to hold him, to *silence* him. But she could not. Horrific as the tale was, she had to hear it.

'There was little moon that night and I drove recklessly, taking out my ill-temper on the horses and the road. Trying, I think, to give Meg the most uncomfortable ride of her life. *Which I did, God help me.*'

His voice throbbed with anguish, but he went on, jerking out the words in a disjointed way.

'There was a bridge—I was going too fast—scarcely saw it. I swerved the horses—and misjudged it. The coach swung wide. Smashed through the barrier.' He was gasping now. 'I was—thrown off. Flung to the—other side of the bridge. I hit the stone and fell—badly. Couldn't get up. I knew the coach was in the water. Meg—they told me later—hit her head. She was unconscious.' He flung his hands over his face. 'She drowned before the coachman could get to her.'

He was shuddering, his breath coming short and fast, while Verity, chilled to the marrow, sat as if turned to stone. Her befogged mind was incapable of registering anything other than the ghastly picture conjured up by the shocking events he had related. Almost as if she was a part of him, she could feel his anguish, and the mental lash with which he scourged himself.

Presently, the warmth of the hot sun penetrated the icy blanket that enwrapped her. A little shiver shook her, and she opened her clenched hands to find them clammy with perspiration. She turned her head and looked at the profile of the man beside her.

Henry was so still now, so remote, as if that iron control of his had him once more in its grip. But Verity, sensitively attuned to his emotions, felt the grief he had reawakened in the telling of the tragedy that had overtaken him. Beneath it, her own fears lurked, strengthened by this new knowledge. But she had no time now to deal with these. Henry was hurting. Henry must be comforted.

Verity reached out and took his hand, cupping it between her own as his head turned and the black eyes at last dared to look into hers again. She could not keep the quaver from her voice, nor the moisture from her eyes, but she spoke with a simplicity that touched him deeply.

'Dear Henry, it is for God to judge. For Him to decide whether there shall be retribution. If He can forgive you, can you not find it in your heart to forgive yourself?'

Slowly Henry's hand turned within her grasp and his fingers laced with her own. The black eyes were tender.

'Oh, Verity,' he uttered softly, 'what manner of girl are you? Have you no words of reproach? Do you not shrink from me in horror?'

Her lips trembled on a smile though her eyes were luminous with those unshed tears. 'I think I could never do that.'

Henry's eyes swept down to caress the smile, and back up to gaze into her own. Then he leaned towards her and swiftly pressed a light kiss on her lips.

Verity's bones turned to water and she felt oddly light-headed. On a gasp, she said, 'I d-don't think you should have d-done that.'

His face hovered still so close but she only just heard his murmured reply. 'How can I help it if you will look at me so?'

'W-what do you mean? How do I look at you?'

'Like a sleeper waking from a beautiful dream. . .to *this*.'

His mouth came down hard on hers and his arms encircled her body, crushing her to him. Something exploded in Verity's head and she was aware only of sensation: of his hungry lips drawing on hers; of the unexpected warmth of his pale cheek; of the firm muscular strength of the body locked against her chest, and moving under her hands as they groped involuntarily about his back.

She felt as if she were drowning, while at the same time a force was growing deep inside her. A force so strong that it brought a tide of heat hurtling through her veins, so that her own lips clung and moved in unison with the mouth locked with them, and she strained towards his body as if she would meld with it.

But when at last he released her, awareness came rushing back and she sprang up from the wall, and as suddenly sat down again as she discovered her knees were too weak to support her. She turned to look at the perpetrator of this devastating assault, and found him obviously equally discomposed, his chest heaving, his pale features tinged with unusual colour, and his fingers trembling as he half held his hands out to her.

'I most certainly do *not*,' she said, in a voice redolent with shock and with one hand at her palpitating bosom, 'think you should have done *that*!'

Henry's inevitable tension found relief in a burst of laughter, and Verity's blushes increased.

'I beg your pardon,' he said, valiantly trying to compose himself. 'It is uncivil of me to laugh at such a moment, I know, but—oh, Verity, you are adorable! So refreshingly innocent!' He took her hand and brought it to his lips. 'Forgive me! I had no intention, truly, of going so far before declaring myself.'

There could be no mistaking his meaning and Verity was struck dumb. The hazel eyes looked with a mixture of anticipation and apprehension into the black.

Henry smiled, retaining his clasp on her hand. 'Don't look at me so worriedly. It is rather I who should be afraid. I, who am no hero, and yet—I trust!—no villain either.'

'Don't speak of that!' Verity said quickly, suddenly finding her tongue. 'I spoke in jest.'

'Don't you think I know that? I am just a man,

Verity, who has made a serious error, with tragic consequences. You asked me if I could not find it in my heart to forgive myself. More to the point, and infinitely more important, can you find it in your heart to——?'

'*Papa*! *Papa*!'

Braxted's voice, with a note of urgency that instantly took the couple's attention, broke in on them.

Verity, acutely conscious of the compromising activities in which she had been engaged, leaped up, her cheeks aflame, and turned to the boy as he came running towards them.

'What is it? What has happened?'

The Marquis seized his hat and, leaning to grope for his cane where it had fallen in the grass, he also pushed himself painfully to his feet as Braxted's jumbled explanations reached them.

'She's hurt! Fallen down. Fainted, I think. I had to leave Peggy with her.'

'Oh, thank God!' gasped Verity. 'For a dreadful instant I though you were talking of Peggy.'

'No, it's Kittle. Kittle's gone and hurt herself.'

'Where?' demanded his father, preparing to move.

'No, Henry, I'll go,' Verity said quickly. 'Show me, Wystan!'

She was gone on the words, seizing the boy's hand and running in the direction he tugged her.

'For God's sake, take care!' called Salmesbury after them, as he saw her lift her skirts and jump her way across the ground made uneven by the profusion of fallen ancient stones under the weeds. He limped gamely forward himself at an unaccustomed pace.

But Verity, already in a state of high tension, was swept by this fresh excitement into near panic, racing like the wind towards the spot where Peggy's wails pinpointed the scene of the accident.

Kittle was lying between two narrow juts of broken

wall, but as they reached her they saw that she had recovered sufficiently to be able to raise herself on one elbow.

'Take care of your sister, Wystan!' ordered Verity tersely, going at once to kneel by the woman's side. 'How are you hurt?'

'It's my ankle, miss,' uttered the nurse in a faint voice. 'Twisted it, I did, as I come over the wall.'

She was struggling to sit up, and Verity moved so that she might support her from behind.

'Here, lean on me a little.'

Braxted, having collected his sister and quieted her yowls, had returned to stand by the nurse.

'I thought you were dead, Kittle!' he said, on a slightly disappointed note.

'No, Master Wystan,' she replied, 'but I did seem to lose my senses a moment.'

'Tittoo! Tittoo!' muttered Peggy plaintively.

'Only fancy if you had been dead!' said her brother, unheeding. 'We'd have had the devil of a job to get you home.'

'Be quiet, Wystan!' said Verity severely. 'Come here, please, and take my place so that I may have a look at poor Kittle's ankle.'

Braxted came, protesting, 'How can I hold Kittle and Peggy at the same time, I should like to know?'

'Sit with your back to Kittle, and she may rest against you.'

Matters were so arranged, in spite of the boy's arguments, delivered against his sister's interjections, and Verity moved to examine the injured part.

'At least there is no swelling,' she commented, as she gently moved the foot.

Kittle cried out. 'Ooh, miss, it do hurt!'

'I'm sorry. Well, it does not seem to be a bad sprain, thank God. Let us see if you can stand.'

With a good deal of puffing and blowing and groans

on the part of the patient, which caused Peggy to break out in tears again, crying, 'Tittoo, Tittoo,' so that her brother had his work cut out attending to her, Verity managed to get the woman on to her feet. By this time the Marquis was seen to be coming up with them.

'Can she walk?' he asked without preamble.

'We have not yet tried,' Verity responded, adding to the nurse, 'See if you can put your foot to the ground.'

Kittle did so, but raised it again, wincing.

'Very well, you must lean on me and hop,' Verity instructed practically. 'We will go this way to avoid the stones.'

'Let me lead,' Salmesbury advised. 'You will not go faster than I in that condition, and I know the way out of this labyrinth of a ruin.'

By a circuitous route, they came out of the ruin itself and traversed its environs to arrive at the trees where the Marquis had left the phaeton with its horses tethered so they might crop the bushes.

Kittle was very apologetic and expressed herself as feeling extremely foolish and low at having spoiled the party of pleasure.

'Stuff!' scoffed Verity. 'We will take you back home and have this ankle seen to.'

'Oh, no, miss! Oh, please, miss,' begged Kittle. 'I couldn't never forgive myself if you was to go to such trouble. No, indeed.'

'It is no trouble, I assure you. His lordship will not mind driving us all, I am sure.' She threw a smile at Henry as she spoke. 'Driving is his passion, after all.'

He smiled back, but, before he could respond, Kittle was off again.

'Oh, no, miss. His lordship is very kind. But I don't want to spoil the day, miss. If only his lordship might consent to take me up, the children could stay with you, miss, couldn't they? At least until Bradshaw comes back with his lordship.'

'Now that,' put in Henry in a pleased tone, 'is an excellent notion.' He gave Verity a meaning look. 'I think there is no need to end our day out so soon.'

Realising that he meant to continue their interrupted tête-à-tête, Verity felt the colour steal into her cheeks. But she made no comment, merely falling in with the plan, helping Kittle into the carriage and making sure she was comfortable.

'I'll be back in no time,' Henry promised. His eyes signalled to Verity a fleeting intimate message that this reassurance was meant for her. Then he drove away.

Verity, her heart fluttering, turned to find Braxted trying to stifle a fit of the giggles as he held little Peggy back from trying to run after the vehicle.

'What is the matter?'

He grinned. 'I was only thinking, now there are two old crocks!'

Verity could not help but laugh, but said, as she stooped to pick up Peggy, 'Yes, very well, I know it is amusing, but it is not at all a proper sentiment, so don't repeat it, I beg of you!'

'I won't. Can I go off again now? I haven't finished my 'sploring.'

'Very well, but keep within sight.'

Peggy, stunned into silence by these rapid events, remained so for a few moments in the novelty of finding herself in a strange embrace. But as she noticed Wystan darting about the ruins, she wriggled, signifying her desire to be released in no uncertain terms.

'Peddy go down! No 'old Peddy. Peddy want to pay. Down! Down!'

Verity, unable to keep hold of the wriggling bundle, was obliged to put her on the ground. Peggy immediately stumbled off after her brother, but Verity was easily able to keep within a few feet of her.

Her mind once more at leisure, she found her thoughts flowing back to the memory of Henry's kisses.

A sharp tug inside her brought back the feel of his passion and she found herself longing to feel it again. It seemed as if her wish was to be granted—if he had really been about to offer. She had been so sure at the time, but now——

An alien sound, coming in above Braxted's muted shouts and Peggy's shrill responses, broke into her absorption. Hoofbeats, muffled by the grassy ground.

She looked about, trying to identify where they were coming from. Suddenly a pair of horsemen erupted from the trees beyond the ruins, coming out of the forest that ran through the whole estate.

Verity stood watching them come for the space of a few seconds. Then, spurred by an intangible sense of danger, she closed the gap between herself and the little girl, lifting the infant as Braxted came running towards her, impelled no doubt by the natural curiosity of childhood.

The horsemen were trotting directly towards them and Verity called out to the boy. 'Wystan, hurry! Come here to me!'

The two horses slowed to pick their way over the stones and Verity grasped the boy's hand and held it tightly.

'Who are they? What do they want?' asked Braxted, a touch of fear overlaying the excitement in his voice.

'I don't know,' Verity replied, eyeing them nervously.

Without quite knowing why, she began to back away. Her heart was thudding and she could feel Peggy stirring uneasily as her fright communicated itself to the little girl.

Then everything happened so fast that she was never able afterwards to recall exactly the sequence of events.

The horses suddenly speeded up. With one accord, she and Wystan turned to run and Peggy set up a whimper. Verity let go the boy's hand and he dashed headlong for safety among the ruins. He was not quick enough.

With a cry of alarm, Verity saw one rider lean down and scoop up the child with one hand, hoisting him, kicking and screaming, across his saddle, while the other swung his leg over his mount and prepared to leap down.

Next instant, she was knocked to the ground and Peggy torn from her arms. Dazed, she scrambled up. Too late! The brute had remounted and was already away, the infant clutched in one strong arm.

Verity ran screaming after the horses in a fruitless, desperate attempt to catch them, hearing still Peggy's mournful wails and Braxted's shrill cries as the horsemen crashed back into the forest and disappeared among the trees.

CHAPTER NINE

SOBBING for breath, Verity came to a halt, clinging on to the nearest tree as her brain signalled the utter futility of this insane chase.

She must think! The children were gone. Kidnapped. Henry could not return for some time, but she would do better to wait. Oh, Wystan! Little Peggy! What in the world would Henry say? All he had endured, and now this! Tears dripped unnoticed down her cheeks as she dropped to her knees, desperately trying to think clearly in spite of her bursting lungs.

In a few moments she had recovered sufficiently to get up again, and with the recovery of her physical strength her faculties began to function more coherently. One thought emerged clear and strong. Help. She must get help. There must be a dwelling hereabouts, estate people or forest workers. Something!

Her frantic gaze searched the surrounding area, and, finding nothing, focused further afield, beyond the immediate confines of the ruins, over the trees and down into the valley.

A plume of smoke curling into the distant air impinged itself on her consciousness. The gypsy encampment! Her heart contracted. Gracious heaven, could the men have come from there? Into her mind's eye came the image of the gypsy she had first seen the day she met the children. Could he have meant to take them then? Had she thwarted his design?

Her too ready imagination presented her with a horrific, impossible picture: the gypsies, knives aloft, greedily gazing upon the two small bodies, lashed to a makeshift spit which turned over the leaping flames of an open fire. And riding around them all, the triumphant horsemen she had just seen.

Instantly she snapped out of the picture. Fool! she scolded herself. To allow her absurd realms of Gothic fancy rein at such a time! *Those* men were not gypsies. The mental image imprinted on her mind proved that. Old slouch hats and frock-coats, gaiters over their shoes. They were rustics, working men, not gypsies! And the gypsies, she remembered, common sense reasserting itself, were camped on the Marquis's land. It would be sheer suicide for them to attempt a crime of this nature, even if they had the inclination—which she refused to believe. Time and past that such stupid prejudice was set aside.

She looked towards the valley, straining her eyes, almost unconsciously beginning to move in the direction of the gypsy camp. From here she could see over the trees to gauge the right path to take. The forest was thin above the valley and the distance did not appear very great. But Verity hardly thought of all this as she began to walk purposefully towards the dipping edge of the land. The children were in her mind, and suddenly it seemed that the gypsies were the nearest available source of help.

The sun had risen high by now and even in the light cotton gown, Verity was uncomfortably hot. Strands of hair under the now lopsided chipstraw hat clung damply to her flushed cheeks, and in her scrambling haste she stumbled once or twice on the uneven ground. By the time she came out of the forest the pink gingham gown was dirtied over, ripped in several places, and she had scratches on her face and her ungloved hands from the swishing greenery she had thrust carelessly aside to clear her path.

From here she could clearly see the little clutch of gaily painted caravans a little below where she stood. But she was still some way off and a sigh escaped her.

She wondered, with an involuntary pang, if Henry had returned yet, and what he would do when he found them all gone. She thought, as she plodded on, that he might at first suppose them to be playing a trick, and waste a deal of time hunting fruitlessly about.

Could she but have known it, the Marquis was at that very moment staring from the seat of his phaeton in utter perplexity at the distant figure he could just glimpse, moving at a jogtrot in the direction of the gypsy camp, her hat bouncing on her shoulders, held on only by the ribbons about her neck.

There was a spot on the route from Braxted Place to the ruined manor of Haverigg Hall where the forest dipped so low that a clear view of the valley was obtained. Salmesbury's idle gaze had been caught by something familiar about the hurrying figure and he pulled up, uttering a shocked expletive.

'Good God! What in the world——?'

Bradshaw, the second nurse, who was up beside him, pleased to find herself a member of the expedition after all, glanced enquiringly up into his face. 'My lord?'

The Marquis pointed. 'See there! That is Miss Lambourn.'

The woman peered, frowning. 'But she don't have the children with her, my lord!'

'Exactly. She would never have left them. Damnation! They must have run away.'

'Oh, no, sir, surely not!' protested Bradshaw. 'Master Wystan thinks that highly of Miss Lambourn, my lord. He's talked of her often. I'm sure he'd never serve her such a trick. And with Miss Peggy, too!'

'You're right,' agreed Salmesbury, a heavy frown descending on his brow. 'He could never have outrun Verity while carrying the babe.'

'What does it mean, my lord?' asked the nurse anxiously.

'I don't know, but I have a fearful suspicion. We must go back at once!'

So saying, he began to turn the horses to face in the direction of Braxted Place again, revolving plans in his head, while his heart ached with dread.

They were waiting for her when she got to the camp. She had seen them gathering at the edge of their circle of caravans, one by one as the word passed round of a stranger on the way, intrigued no doubt by her haste and her unkempt appearance.

A knot of nervous tension settled in the pit of Verity's stomach as she searched among the tanned, impassive faces for some sign of warmth. Even the few ragged children who ventured out of the camp towards her exhibited a surly, silent hostility.

No one spoke as Verity came up, slowing her pace the last few yards, to come to a faltering halt before the seemingly solid phalanx of humanity that barred her progress. In fact there were less than a dozen, men in breeches and waistcoats with colourful handkerchiefs knotted about their necks, women in simple layered skirts and light embroidered tops. No bright scarves in evidence here, for this was everyday and they must keep them for best, like the villagers with their special Sunday clothes for church.

Verity looked from one to the other, and proffered a tentative question. 'I need help. The Marquis's children. They've been taken. . .kidnapped. . .please, can you help me?'

The faces were blank, shut in. They merely stared at her and said nothing.

Verity swallowed on a dry throat. Dear Lord, make them understand! she prayed silently. Desperation entered her voice.

'I'm not your enemy. I was alone with the children for a very short time. Two horsemen came out of the forest and took them. I saw your camp and ran down to see if you could help. *Please.*'

Not a flicker. As a clan, these people were so oppressed, so isolated, that even this innocent appeal failed to break through the wall of prideful, silent enmity they had learned, through bitter experience, to present to strangers.

Verity wanted to run away. She wished she had after all waited for Henry. But she was here, and the thought of the fear and horror that the children must be experiencing even now drove her to hunt her mind for inspiration. It came.

'There's an old woman who tells fortunes. I met her at Tunbridge Wells, at the fair. Is she here?'

There was a sudden change. Here and there the gypsies exchanged glances, shifted position.

'You know her?' Verity went on eagerly. 'I can't recall her name. An old gypsy. . .yes, something like *Mary*, was it?'

The relaxation could be felt. The stern poses eased and even a few mutterings could be heard. Verity caught one and it jogged her memory with the errant name.

'Mairenni!' she said triumphantly. 'That was it. Old Mairenni, she called herself. Oh, please, take me to her! She told me there was trouble and sorrow ahead. Now it has come. She'll help me. I know she will!'

One of the men stepped forward a pace and jerked his head, signifying that she should accompany him. He waited only to see that she understood, and then turned to stride off into the circle of caravans. As Verity followed, the tableau the gypsies made began to break up and shift. In a moment the little group had dispersed about their various businesses, and Verity was more or less alone with her guide.

Old Mairenni must have been waiting for them, apprised by some earlier messenger of the advent of this stranger. She came out of her caravan as they approached and stood on the top step, peering down.

'And is it we'm suspicioned, dearie? Will ye find yon childer stowed away in one o' we wagons, eh?'

'You know?' Verity asked, amazed.

The crone cackled. 'Aye. But there ain't nothing in that, dearie. Young 'un here brought yer tidings.'

She clicked her fingers and an urchin crept out from under the wagon, grinning cheekily up at Verity. She smiled at him automatically, but went to the steps, closer to the old woman.

'Will you help me?' she begged urgently.

'How? Is it the likes o' we be knowing anything worthwhile? How be we going to help?'

'I don't know how,' Verity confessed. 'But I feel sure you could—if you wished to.'

Mairenni stared down at her for a moment, her old eyes inscrutable as she scanned the face below her. Then she broke into her cackling laugh, and swinging a gnarled hand, called out in a cracked voice.

'Peneli! Ho, there, boy!'

Verity looked round to find that the man who had led her here had retired to stand some distance away, not quite out of earshot. Now he came forward, and an abrupt realisation jolted Verity's mind. It was that very same gypsy!

'Upon my word!' she ejaculated. 'It was you!'

His mouth curled sardonically, marring his handsome features. His voice was rough and deep, his accent as thickly overlaid with the west-country twang as was that of the old woman. 'Is it I took the Markiss's childer, then?'

'No, no, I didn't mean that,' Verity said hastily. 'But I have met you before. At least, it was you, was it not, that day I found the children on the road?'

'Aye,' he agreed, his dark eyes roving insolently over

her face and figure. 'Thought I meant 'em harm then, you did.'

Verity could not deny it. 'I admit that I was afraid. But I later repented of such a hasty conclusion. It was wrong of me, very wrong, and I beg your pardon.'

He shrugged. 'Can't be blaming ye. It's like yer kind. What do ye know of us Romanies?'

'Nowt she knows,' interrupted Old Mairenni. 'Enough now, Peneli. Come to we for help, she has. Is it our way to refuse? Go now. Take her. Likely news to be found at yon thievin' ken.'

Mairenni was evidently a person of some power, for the man Peneli merely nodded, and once again jerked his head to Verity and moved off. She paused to smile up at the old woman.

'Thank you. I hope you will allow me to come here again to visit you.'

The woman showed her gapped teeth in a grin. 'You'm welcome, dearie. Fortune smiles on ye, don't she?'

Then she waved the girl off with a sweep of her hand and turned away. Verity could hear her cackling as she turned to hurry off after Peneli.

The man led her to a spot behind one of the caravans where a clutch of ponies was grazing in a makeshift corral. He laid a hand on the roped gateway and turned to the visitor.

'Ye ride?'

Verity sighed. 'I'm afraid not.'

The Reverend Harry Lambourn kept but two horses, one to draw the gig and another for his own use. His purse did not run to mounting his bevy of girls.

The gypsy's lip curled in that disparaging way, but he merely said, 'It'll have t'be donkey. And fix you'm hat. Hot, it be.'

Verity obeyed, retying the ribbons, but without bothering to prettify the bow. In a few minutes she found herself sitting rather precariously on the blanketed back of an overfed creature, who plodded behind Peneli's pony at the end of a leading rein. The position was ignominious, to say the least, but Verity did not mind that. Her whole preoccupation was with the children, and she could only hope that wherever Peneli was taking her would bring her closer to finding them.

She was glad, nevertheless, to see that, once out of the valley, they very quickly left the main road and travelled crosscountry via a series of byways. She was in no fit state to be seen by chance wayfarers. She would have liked to converse with her dour companion, ask where they were going, but their relative positions made speech impossible.

They had been travelling for what seemed an age when Peneli slowed the pony's pace, allowing the donkey to come up alongside. His dark face looked down at Verity, expressionless.

'Can ye tell me why I should help ye to find yon Markiss's childer?'

A wild pulse began to pump in Verity's heart, but she met his gaze unflinchingly. 'You are camped on his land.'

'Be it we owe him a favour, then?'

'Perhaps.' Verity drew a resolute breath and went on firmly. 'But I think you will rather help me from out of a warm heart. The same impulse of charity that led you to approach his children that day we met. For you knew who they were, and you were going to help them then, were you not?'

'Aye,' he agreed, his voice devoid of any expression that might give her a clue to his thoughts. 'Would've took 'em home.'

'Why didn't you *say*?' Verity burst out.

He shrugged. 'Who'd believe a gypsy? Blame us first, ask questions after.'

She was obliged to admit the truth of this. A stupid

prejudice, and she had fallen victim to it herself. But there was little point in discussing it. She turned the subject.

'Where are you taking me?'

'Inn up yonder. Fiddler's Haunt, they calls it. Place of thieves and vagabonds.' He grinned maliciously. 'The likes of we.'

Verity ignored the taunt, but put an anxious plea. 'I beg you will not leave me there.'

'Don't fear on't. Mairenni sent me with ye. Mairenni's word is law.'

'Is she the—the chieftain?'

Unexpectedly, he gave out a loud guffaw. 'Nay. She'm me mam. We be all her childer, or her childer's mates.'

Verity was silent, thinking how odd it was that one should think differently and fearfully of a people whose core of life was in fact very similar to one's own. Old Mairenni, the matriarch, living among her own close-knit family, just as her own and her sisters' lives revolved closely around her father.

Their arrival minutes later at the Fiddler's Haunt put paid to such idle whimsy. It was a disreputable establishment, dilapidated and dirty, a place at which no respectable person would choose to bait. Scrawny livestock roamed its yard, scratching for food, and a slatternly maidservant scoured pans under the pump.

Peneli tethered the mounts and led the way into the dark interior. The large taproom stank of stale drink and tobacco, and a haze of smoke from a dozen pipes dimmed what little light filtered through the grimy windows.

Verity, sticking close to her guide, felt the eyes that appraised her from the shadows hunched on benches in dark corners. She was thankful that her own dirt and disorder allowed her to blend into the scene.

She would have been more fearful still had she

known that those unseen eyes easily saw beyond a few mere rips and smears of dirt. The indefinable quality that characterised her was obvious to those whose callings demanded an ability to sum up all chance strangers encountered in the course of their dubious careers.

Peneli moved to the counter, found a chair and bade his fair companion sit and be silent. Verity obeyed, feeling lonely and exposed as he left her to saunter from one group to another, muttering in a low tone with those he met.

As Verity watched him, her fear erupted in a dreadful vision: the shadows in the corners creeping forward, surrounding the shrinking heroine, their grimy, sweat-shining faces flickering evilly in the lanterns held in one or two hands, closing in on her, lasciviously smiling, licking their lips in anticipation at the thought of their evil intent. One filthy paw reached out to the beautiful young girl's face and she opened her mouth to scream.

'Don't fear!' said Peneli's deep voice, his rough tone low and soothing.

With a start, Verity came to herself to see the gypsy regarding her intently, beside him a thick-set man who was eyeing her with undisguised interest. She caught herself up on a gasp, annoyed with herself for having once again given way to her propensity for daydreaming. She felt clammy and cold, and realised that she was allowing fear to rule her.

She drew a steadying breath, threw a glance of reassurance at Peneli, and boldly stared back at the man he had brought, taking in the heavy jowls and the broken nose. Something clicked in her brain.

'Gracious heaven!' she ejaculated. 'Why, you are Sam Shottle!'

He looked taken aback. 'How come you knows me name, missie?'

'You were pointed out to me at the diversions. The fair, you know, the other day.' She got up, her voice eager. This was the man who had been talking with the children's nurse that day, the man who had been identified by the boy Jed.

'This is fortuitous, for you are acquainted with Kittle. And you've seen the children. Surely, surely, you can help me? Has he told you? They've been taken, but they can't have gone far. And perhaps you know people who will have information. The Marquis will pay well, I know that.'

Sam Shottle scratched his chin. 'Well, I don't know, missie. Did hear talk of summat o' the kind. No notion they meant the Markiss's children, mind.'

'You know something? Oh, pray tell me!'

'Not to say *know* exactly,' Shottle said cautiously. 'Heard talk, I did. That's all.'

'But *who*? Who talked? Can we not consult them?' begged Verity, oblivious now to the unsavoury surroundings.

Shottle looked dubious. 'Don't know as how——'

'*Please*.' Driven to desperate measures, Verity seized on the most persuasive argument she could think of. 'I can guarantee you a reward, for I am—I am to *marry* the Marquis.'

She was aware of a concerted reaction through the stuffy room. Murmurs and movement rippled from man to man. Sam Shottle's keen eyes gleamed with a new light.

'Are you, now?' he said in a ruminating tone. 'That's different, that is. Reckon I'd better take you to see Olly Hargate. 'Tis him and Jim Brigg as I hear a-gabbling o' them there nippers.'

'Do you mean you know where they might be found? Oh, thank heaven!'

'I don't say as I *know* exactly,' pointed out Shottle

with his usual caution. 'I'm saying as how I can take you to Olly Hargate, that's all.'

Verity smiled in relief. 'That will do for a start.'

She was thankful to come back out into the bright sunshine, for the foul air of the Fiddler's Haunt was more overpowering than the heat outside. Peneli the gypsy accompanied them for a little way, and then handed the donkey's rein to Sam Shottle.

'You're leaving us?' Verity asked, disappointed.

Peneli turned his impassive stare upon her. 'B'ain't fitting. Remember, blame first, questions after.'

Verity sighed. She understood. There was trouble brewing. The gypsies could not afford to become involved. Especially when it concerned the man whose land they were currently occupying.

Peneli told her she could borrow the donkey. 'When you'm done with he, let he go. Him'll find his own way.'

'Nothing of the sort!' Verity said indignantly. 'I shall bring him to you. Or at least send him with a messenger.'

She thanked the gypsy warmly for his help, but as he rode off in the opposite direction her heart sank and she looked with growing apprehension at the burly back of her new guide as he plodded on foot, the leading rein grasped firmly in his hand. The words of young Jed, Wystan's friend the climbing boy, came back to her unpleasantly. 'He beginned by thievin' and poachin'... Reckons to make his fortune... *He'll end in Botany Bay.*' Into what hands had she delivered herself?

The way to the establishment inhabited by this Olly Hargate appeared to Verity even more circuitous than the journey she had taken to the Fiddler's Haunt. But at last they came to a cottage. Shottle led the donkey around to the back and Verity was able to see that it was practically derelict and, she realised with a quickening of her heartbeat, extremely isolated.

There was a species of small barn off to its rear and to this Shottle turned his steps, pointing ahead, and saying gruffly over his shoulder, 'You better hide in there, missie, while I finds out if Olly knows summat.'

Verity eyed the barn with misgiving. 'Why should I do that? If he's here, he must have seen us arrive.'

'Likely he's asleep. Or drunk,' said Shottle sapiently. 'Else he'd have come out by this.'

He was still leading the donkey towards the ricketylooking barn, and, quite suddenly, a sound like muffled crying came to Verity's ears.

'What's that?' she demanded suspiciously, and, without waiting for aid, pushed herself sideways and slid off the donkey's back.

She landed awkwardly, but was up in a second, running to the barn as another, more distinct sob reached her.

'Wystan! Wystan! Are you in there?' she called out, frenziedly rattling the locked door.

There was silence from within. Then a muffled, hoarse shrieking broke out. Eyes blazing, Verity turned on Sam Shottle.

'Open this door! *Now.*'

With a nonchalant air, Shottle dug into a deep pocket and, smiling, brought out a key which he twirled ostentatiously.

'Open it,' Verity repeated, in a voice trembling with rage, far too upset to take in the implications of his actions.

The man unlocked the door and tugged it open with a flourish. Verity ran inside, peering in the sudden gloom. On a heap of sacking at the far end Wystan was lying, hands and feet bound, a scarf about his mouth, while near him was Peggy, peacefully asleep.

'Oh, my poor darlings!' Verity cried out in distress, and dashed forward.

The door behind her slammed shut, and the key turned in the lock.

'My lord, I beg you to listen to reason!' the secretary said urgently, going so far as to lay a restraining hand on the Marquis's arm.

'Reason?' Salmesbury repeated, a dull agony in his black eyes. 'My children are gone, and Miss Lambourn after them, and you talk to me of *reason*!'

'My lord, Miss Lambourn's visit to the gypsy camp was to seek help. I am sure of it.'

'Then why won't they *answer*? Damn them all to hell!'

Henry shook off Inskip's hand and threw his arm across his forehead. The headache was blinding and he could not think. On his return to Braxted Place, he had raised the alarm, and would have gone on to the gypsy encampment immediately, had not Inskip persuaded him that a groom on horseback would travel faster—and perhaps glean more information, though that thought he kept to himself. But Hoff, the only groom Salmesbury would trust, had met with the same wall of silence that had greeted Verity. The gypsies responded equally to either pleas and threats with nothing but blank stares. Hoff had been obliged to concede defeat.

Meanwhile, from the headquarters of the massive office, the secretary had organised a comprehensive search of the estate, and the news of the kidnap had spread like wildfire through the district.

It was oddly disquieting to watch the distress accumulating in his employer's face in these opulent surroundings. The green and gold décor, the gilt ornamentation to the mantel and the ceiling, and the elegant proportions of the furnishings seemed incongruous set against the dark shadow of anguish that was the Marquis of Salmesbury.

Inskip exchanged concerned glances with the chaplain, Eastleigh, as their master staggered blindly to his chair, and, leaning his elbow on the rich wood desk, dropped his aching head into his hands.

'My lord, can I get you anything?' Eastleigh asked anxiously, coming forward.

Salmesbury raised his head and shook it briefly, his pale features drawn, his eyes haggard as he sat kneading his brow. 'I have the headache.'

'I am not surprised, my lord,' Eastleigh said sympathetically. 'Shall I send for a composer, perhaps? Laudanum?'

'*No*,' Henry snapped. Then, recollecting himself, he summoned a brief smile and said more gently, 'No, thank you. I have no intention of returning to that particular slavery.'

He had taken so much of the pain-killing substance during the worst of his nightmare experiences that he had almost become an addict. It had been Hoff, that bluff, scolding nursemaid of a groom, who had saved him, dashing the glass from his hand, forcing him to do without it and learn to overcome by sheer force of will both his physical and mental agonies.

'Will you not lay down a little on your bed?' pursued the chaplain. 'Mr Inskip and I will——'

'Eastleigh, I know you mean well,' interrupted his lordship, 'but I pray you to bear with me. How could I possibly rest in these circumstances?' He turned, with determined calm, to his secretary. 'Inskip, what do we do next?'

'I am still waiting for all the men to report in, sir. Someone may have gleaned information by now that may give us a lead.'

Salmesbury nodded. 'Very well. But if there is nothing——'

A knock at the door broke into his thoughts and he automatically called out permission to enter. A head poked round the door. It was Bradshaw, the gaunt-looking nurse Inskip had hired with the intention of supplanting Kittle once Lady Margaret had become accustomed to her presence.

'I beg your pardon, my lord, for disturbing you at such a time,' she said diffidently.

'Well, come in, come in!' said the Marquis impatiently. 'What is it?'

The nurse edged into the room and carefully shut the door. 'I'm not sure as it's anything important, my lord, only——' She stopped, biting her lip.

'Well? Out with it!'

'It's Miss Kittle, sir. I can't find her!'

'Oh, my God, not another one gone!' Inskip muttered under his breath. Then, more loudly, 'What do you mean, Bradshaw?'

'Well, sir,' she said, turning with obvious relief to relay her story to this less intimidating auditor, for the Marquis's haggard aspect was daunting, 'she was laid up with this ankle, sir, as you know. One of the maids was with her in her room, applying cold compresses like you instructed, sir. Then the maid left her to sleep as Miss Kittle begged her to do. But when I went up to tell her as how the children were gone, sir, she weren't there. And no sign of her in the house.'

All three men stared blankly at her, as if they could not fathom why she should come bothering them with such a matter at such a time. Bradshaw looked from one to the other, and then addressed herself once more to the secretary.

'I just thought it odd, sir, that's all.'

Inskip frowned. 'Foolish, anyway. I dare say she has got wind of the present situation some other way. She would be naturally anxious. Perhaps she has got up to help search.'

'But she couldn't hardly walk, sir!' protested the nurse. 'Leastways, that was what it looked like.'

The black eyes, suddenly keen, looked across at her. 'What do you mean?'

Bradshaw ventured a little closer to the desk, her intelligent eyes searching his face. 'My lord, it ain't my place, perhaps, as I'm only the junior, but I can't say as I've been easy in my mind.'

'Go on,' Salmesbury said, one hand still pressed to his heavily frowning brow.

'It's just that I overheard Master Wystan one day, talking with that little friend of his. They were saying as how——'

'Just a moment, madam,' interrupted the cleric, in a voice that suddenly made him appear very much the stern tutor. '*What* friend? Master Wystan has no friends his own age.'

He did not see the spasm of sudden pain that crossed his employer's face, or the understanding look in the secretary's eyes as they rested briefly on Salmesbury and noted this reaction to the fresh arrow in his touchy conscience. But then both men lost this fleeting instant of recognition in interest at what the nurse was saying.

'It's a village boy called Jed. I think he's the sweep's lad, for I've seen him with the man. But he is certainly very well known to Master Wystan by their conversation. For they were discussing Miss Kittle's personal affairs, my lord, and laughing over what they thought was—well, a-*courting*, sir—with this terrible *bad* fellow. The boy Jed referred to him as one Shottle.'

Three sets of puzzled eyes exchanged glances.

Inskip shrugged. 'The name means nothing to me, my lord, but I could make enquiries.'

'Good God, what is the use of that?' exclaimed Salmesbury impatiently. 'No, no. Send someone to find this sweep's boy and bring him to me at once. Let us go to the horse's mouth, for God's sake!'

'Certainly, my lord,' the secretary said smoothly and left the room at once, pleased to find that with the possibility of a lead his employer's faculties were rising out of the despair that gripped them.

When he returned to the office, he found the Marquis on his feet and coldly determined. He handed a sealed note to Inskip.

'Have Hoff deliver that at once to the captain of the district militia. Whatever may come out of this boy's testimony, there is one thing we do know. Miss Lambourn went to the gypsies and subsequently disappeared. If they will not volunteer the information we seek, then let them be persuaded by other means. We will see how they answer to the barrel of a gun.'

CHAPTER TEN

WYSTAN talked non-stop as Verity wrestled with the bonds about his wrists and ankles. It was as if the pent-up fear was released by this outpouring of the tale.

'I couldn't breathe 'cause he had me hunged over the saddle, head down, and that was the worst of it. But when he tried to right me, I screamed and kicked him. And I shouted him Papa would have him throwed in prison an' transported if he didn't let me go! That's why he put the scarf round my mouth, and then I kept on kicking and he had to tie me up.'

'Gracious, how brave you were!' Verity exclaimed, pulling loose the final knot and setting his legs free.

But Wystan did not jump up as she had expected, only leaning down to rub his sore ankles.

'Yes, but I was afraid,' he admitted. ''Specially when they put us in here, 'cause Peggy had stopped crying by then, and——' his voice faltered a little ' – and they hadn't tied anything round her mouth and—and she didn't wake, and——' A sob tore from his throat and he suddenly hurled himself into Verity's arms, crying out into her shoulder, 'Oh, Verity, I—I th-thought Peggy was d-*dead*!'

He broke into a storm of weeping, while Verity held him close, her own eyes wet as she remembered with a bursting heart that he was only a little boy, with no mother, and no one to comfort his little distresses. Only this major disaster had had the power to break through his enforced reserve, and show that death held real terror for him, for he knew its merciless rule at first hand.

'There now, my darling,' she crooned, rocking him

gently. 'There now, my love. Verity's here, sweetheart. Verity's here now. There, darling.'

But it was only a sudden loud wail from his little sister that brought Wystan's head up from her shoulder, and turned his tears to laughter. The baby had got on her feet and was standing beside them, mouth wide, little face screwed up in the way infants had, ready to let out another protest if she did not get instant attention.

'*She* ain't dead!' he gurgled, letting Verity go and brushing the wet from his cheeks. 'Are you, Peggy?'

But Peggy wanted her turn on the comforting bosom. 'Peddy sit. Vetty 'old Peddy now!' She held up her little arms to be lifted.

'Come along, Peggy,' Verity said, smiling, and taking the child on to her lap. 'There, is that better?'

Peggy did not bother to reply, only signifying her deep content by shoving a thumb in her mouth, and snuggling against the soft breasts. Verity looked up to see Wystan surreptitiously wiping his eyes with his handkerchief, and tactfully refrained from comment. Instead she adopted a brisk, though playful tone, designed to keep fear at bay.

'Now, Wystan, we cannot stay here. We must think. If we were writing this as a story, how would we procure our escape?'

Braxted's eyes lit with interest, and he jumped up to examine their prison. 'We have to 'splore first.' He ran to the door. 'Locked. That's no good.'

He looked up and his eye brightened. His voice held a note of excitement. 'Verity, there's a kind of window up there!'

Verity got up, still holding Peggy, and came to join him. The sacks they had been sitting on were under a kind of loft which covered one end of the small barn. From the door they could see above it a square hole, open to the outside.

'Gracious, I believe it is a hayloft, and that is how they load the stacks. You see, they throw them from that opening straight on to the cart below. It saves a great deal of carrying.' Her eye ran across the edge of the loft. 'There should be a ladder.'

'There is,' exclaimed Wystan, 'only it looks broked.'

From one end of the hayloft two parallel lengths of wood ran down to the floor, but there were only a couple of crossbars at the bottom to show that it had ever been a ladder. The rest were missing.

'So that is why they did not concern themselves over the window,' sighed Verity. 'We cannot get up there.'

'Yes, we can! At least, I can.'

'Wystan, you can't climb a ladder without steps.'

'Yes, I can,' insisted the boy, dashing off to test the two wooden struts. 'Jed taught me to climb the chimbleys. This is just the same. You brace yourself each side and pull up.'

Without more ado, he jumped up those first two cross-bars and set his feet either side, bracing against the struts.

'Oh, take care!' cried Verity anxiously, darting forward.

'S'all right. I'm good at this.'

In only a few moments he had proved his boast, moving with remarkable swiftness up between the two parallel struts, pushing himself higher, gripping with his hands and sliding his feet up again. It hardly seemed any time before Verity's jumping heart was steadying and he was perched on the loft, grinning down at her.

'See?'

'Excellent!' applauded Verity, and did not spoil his triumph by asking the questions in her mind. How in the world was she to get up there herself? Though perhaps she might somehow lift Peggy. At least the children could get away. But how could they find their way alone?

Wystan, flushed with success, was already moving across the hayloft. 'I'll have a look through the window.'

Verity moved back so she could see him as he crossed over to look out of the hole.

'It's a long way down,' he began dubiously, and then Verity saw him stiffen. He ducked down and began crawling back towards the edge.

'What is it?' Verity asked, her pulse quickening.

'There's a man out there!' hissed Wystan fearfully.

'Oh, gracious heaven! Did he see you?'

'I don't know.'

'Why Wissen up dere?' asked Peggy suddenly in a piercing voice.

'Ssh!' Verity begged, quickly putting a hand across her mouth. Then to the boy, she asked, 'Is it one of the men who brought you here?'

'No.' His voice took on a note of puzzlement. 'He looks like a gypsy.'

Hope sprang up in Verity's breast. Peneli! He had not deserted her.

'Quick, Wystan!' she said urgently. 'Go to the window and call to him. If I am not mistaken, he has come to help us.'

'Why should he?' Wystan demanded suspiciously. 'I don't trust gypsies.'

'Do as I say!' Verity ordered, anxiety sharpening her voice. 'You trust me, don't you? He is not here to harm us, I promise you! He has already helped me today. Without him, I would never have found you. I thought he had gone home, but he must have followed us here.'

Dubious still, Braxted crept back to the window and cautiously looked out. The gypsy was right below him.

'Ho, young master! Is the lady in there?' he asked without preamble, his tone low.

'Yes, she is,' Wystan answered back. 'She says you've come to help us.'

'Aye,' agreed the man, phlegmatic as usual. 'Be there any rope in there?'

'Wait, I'll look.' He was soon back. 'No, there ain't. Nor downstairs, Verity says.'

The gypsy looked up. 'Mebbe some cloth we can tear?'

'There's lots of sacks,' Wystan offered.

'Aye, that'll do. Get it, young master. Many as ye can.'

Verity had by this time deposited Peggy on the floor, and she gathered up sacks and threw them to the boy, glancing frequently at the door and listening for the sound of footsteps. Peggy contributed her mite, dragging a sack laboriously from under the loft. Verity thanked her and threw it up.

'Tell Peneli,' she instructed Wystan as she continued with her own efforts, 'that I cannot get up there because of the broken ladder, and we cannot get Peggy up either.'

Peneli listened as the boy relayed this problem, meanwhile ripping the sacks apart, nicking them with the point of a knife produced from some recess in his boot, and tearing down their seams with all the strength of his brawny arms. He made no comment on Wystan's words, but threw up the end of his improvised rope of knotted sacking.

'Now, young master, see if ye can find a beam low enough for ye to get this over.'

Eager to do everything he could, and fairly blazing with mingled apprehension and excitement, Braxted searched the roof above him. But to his disappointment he could not reach high enough, and a couple of attempts to throw the heavy rope produced so much thumping that Peneli told him to desist.

'Ye'll bring yon bad 'uns out on we, boy! Look ye, take rope and tie it side o' yon ladder ye spoke of.'

Crestfallen at his failure, but sufficiently frightened of his captors to refrain from argument, Braxted took the end of the rope around one of the wooden struts and tied it with one of the useful knots Jed had taught him.

'Tight, is it?' Peneli asked, testing the pull with all the nonchalance of his race, as if they had all the time in the world.

'Tight as I could,' the boy confirmed, and watched in fascination as the gypsy climbed up to him, his feet literally walking up the outer wall as he pulled himself to the window. In a moment he was standing in the loft, half bent under the sloping roof.

'Oh, Peneli, thank heaven you are come!' called Verity from below, in accents of heartfelt gratitude. 'Did you follow us?'

'Aye, but you hush now!' he admonished her sternly. 'Yon thievin' coves'll hear!'

'I'm sorry,' Verity whispered contritely. 'What do you want us to do?'

He slung his lengths of sacking over a beam and threw them down to her. 'Tie up yon babe, quick.'

Verity did so, slipping the rope under Peggy's arms and tying it tight.

'*No.* Peggy no like!' shouted the infant, pulling at the bonds which were all too reminiscent of the times Kittle had tied her between two trees. 'Off! Off!'

'Ssh!' Verity begged hastily, crouching down to put a restraining hand over the child's mouth. 'Wystan's waiting, Peggy. Don't you want to go up to Wystan?'

Peggy turned her little face up, staring the long, long distance from her tiny height to where she could see her brother's face hanging upside-down over the edge of the loft.

'Wissen?' she asked uncertainly. 'Peddy up?'

'Come on, Peggy!' he called softly, knowing his exhortations would move her. 'Come up here, Peggy. It's good up here. Let the man bring you up now.'

Peggy beamed. 'Peddy up. Dood up 'ere. Man bing Peddy up *now*.'

'All right,' Verity said, nodding to Peneli.

'Lift 'er high,' instructed the gypsy.

Verity held the infant up as high as she could, feeling the weight taken out of her hands as Peneli drew in the slack. Then with a sudden, swift tug he swung the child up above the level of the loft, and, loosing the rope, grabbed her out of the air with both hands.

'Gracious heaven!' Verity gasped, her own hands automatically stretching up as if she would catch the infant from a fall.

'A capital catch!' Braxted cried, and received a light cuff for his pains.

'Hist, will ye? And take 'er while I get the missie.'

'Sorry,' muttered Wystan, abashed, hastily relieving the man of his sister and undoing the knots about her little body.

Now it was Verity's turn. As Peneli was preparing, she ran to the door and listened, trying to peep through the keyhole, convinced that some sound of their activities must reach the cottage nearby. But there was complete silence.

'I suppose they haven't gone away somewhere?' she suggested as she came back to below the loft.

'Nay,' the gypsy decided. 'Seen 'em, I would. Now, missie. Take yon rope and tie a loop around ye, and hold tight as ye can.'

Obeying, Verity began a silent prayer, unable to see Peneli as he braced himself against the wall at the back of the loft. Without warning, she felt the sacking tighten about her back, and her arms stretched as the improvised rope began to rise. Her feet left the floor, and she held on for dear life, suspended precariously in the air, as each jerk on the rope dug into her back and under her arms and pulled her a few more inches towards the loft and safety.

She closed her eyes briefly, opening them again as she remembered that she would be close to the edge of the wooden platform. If she didn't look she might easily hit her head. There was no room in her thoughts now for the captors who might burst in any second to prevent this extravagant and complex escape. All her mind was concentrated on the effort of remaining calm, refusing to look down, and waiting for the end of this dreadful ordeal.

In reality, the passage to the loft occupied the space of a few brief moments, but they felt to Verity like hours, and as she came up above the surface of the platform she scrambled with unseemly haste to swing her legs to safety. Rolling on to the planks, she lay there a moment, breathing raggedly, her heart sickeningly loud.

'Well done, Verity!' she heard Braxted say. 'Isn't this the most 'citing thing ever to happen to you?'

Verity had barely strength to shake her head, but she looked up to find the gypsy's expressionless eyes upon her. That gave her courage, and she forced herself to sit up.

'What now?' she asked in a far from steady voice.

It seemed to her there was a gleam of mischief in his eyes. It reminded her poignantly—and unbearably!—of the amusement that showed so often in Henry's black eyes, and she was obliged to swallow on a rising lump in her throat. Poor Henry! Whatever must be his feelings now? The thought spurred her to urgency, and she did not even protest in silence to herself when the gypsy spoke.

'Ye to go first. Down t'other side.'

Gritting her teeth, and keeping Henry's pale, haunted features firmly in her mind, Verity hoisted her petticoats indecorously high and climbed out to sit on the ledge of the opening. She felt the slack pull up behind her and, easing her rear forward, let herself go.

The sharp tug under the arms was painful, but she made no sound, only pushing herself away from the wall as she was lowered down to the ground. In fact the descent was far easier than the appalling lift. Or perhaps, she thought, as her feet touched safely on to terra firma, familiarity lessened the giddying sensation of helplessness.

Once she was freed of the rope, it proved a simple task for Peneli to lower the infant down to her. Wystan shinned down the rope like a monkey, and Peneli himself made as easy a job of it as he had of climbing up.

They left the rope hanging down the back of the barn and, creeping to the edge, peered round to see if there was as yet any sign of pursuit.

'Well, I don't suppose they would open the door unnecessarily,' Verity guessed in a soft voice, once they had ascertained that their captors were still ensconced in the cottage. 'For they neglected to tie me up and they don't know but what I might prove troublesome.'

Nevertheless, she held her hand over Peggy's mouth as, following Peneli's lead, they entered the undergrowth behind the barn and crept through it, well hidden by trees as they skirted the cottage. They could see a light within the dim interior and in front of it were two horses tethered close by.

'Let's hope they don't take it into their heads to check on us too soon,' Wystan said.

'Better waste no time,' Peneli advised, and set off.

Neither Verity nor the boy could resist several furtive glances behind them, but the gypsy did not look back once, and seemed to know by the sound that his little band of runaways was still with him. He led them deeply into the shelter of the trees for some little time, but at length they came across his pony, quietly standing, and realised he knew exactly where he was.

'Gracious, there is your donkey!' Verity exclaimed, catching sight of the animal. 'How in the world did you come by him?'

'Man Shottle let he go after locking ye up. I called he by special whistle.'

'Then you saw it all?'

'Aye. Saw his eye when ye told him ye meant to wed Markiss. Knew he meant harm.'

Braxted turned round eyes upon her. 'Are you going to *marry* Papa, Verity? Why, that is a capital notion!'

'Hush, Wystan,' Verity begged, blushing. 'Nothing is settled as yet.'

'Yes, but I think you ought,' said the boy, unheeding. 'Then you could come and live with us at the Place.'

'Yes, yes, but it is not at all certain. I only said it was to induce that horrid man to take me to find his associates.'

'Aye, and filled him's mind with more schemes to bleed yon Markiss,' put in Peneli roughly.

'It was stupid, I realise that now,' Verity said apologetically. 'But I cannot regret it, for we have the children safe.'

Soon she was seated on the donkey again, a delighted Peggy tucked before her, supported by her arm, while Wystan sat in a similar position with the gypsy on the pony.

The boy had evidently been turning her words over in his mind, for he suddenly demanded, 'Verity, if you and Papa were to be married, would you be our new mama?'

'Only if you wished it,' Verity replied, adding anxiously, 'but I repeat, Wystan, it is not a settled thing at all. You should not know anything about it, and I absolutely forbid you to speak of it again—to *anyone*.'

'But shan't I tell Papa how Peggy and I would like it? That would make him——'

'*No!*' Verity cried, alarmed. 'Upon my word, if you repeat *one word* of this conversation to your papa, I declare I shall never speak to you again!'

'Oh, very well,' consented the child reluctantly, 'but I——'

'*Wystan.* If you will not do as I ask, I shall think you unable to keep a secret, and I shall never be able to share one with you—*ever.*'

'I *can* keep a secret!' he objected indignantly. 'I never telled no one about Jed, did I?'

'No,' agreed Verity, trying for a calmer note, 'and of course I know you will respect my secret, too.'

''Course I will,' Wystan said importantly. 'Only if you *do* decide to marry Papa, will you tell me?'

Verity laughed. 'I should have to, shouldn't I? Now pray don't mention the matter again.'

Fortunately, or perhaps intentionally, he was diverted then by Peneli, who asked him how he had been captured and if he knew the people who did it.

'I should say I do! At least, not eggzackly, but I'd wager I know who made the plot. It was Kittle!'

'Tittoo!' cried Peggy, catching the name. But the others were too involved in discovery to heed her.

'Upon my word, Wystan, I believe you are right! There was not even a swelling on her ankle. She had no more sprained it than I had.'

'But she pretended so as to give those men a chance to get us.'

'And Sam Shottle is Kittle's sweetheart, according to young Jed. That proves it, for it was certainly he who captured me,' Verity agreed. 'I never did like the sound of that Kittle. What a dreadful thing for such a trusted servant to do!'

Dissecting the supposed ramifications of the plot, they hardly noticed the journey. But by the time they came to the gypsy encampment they had begun to feel tired and hungry and Peggy was whimpering incessantly, in spite of both Verity's and Wystan's efforts to distract her. It must be many hours since any of them had eaten, Verity realised, her own stomach acknowledging the fact.

As they descended into the valley, however, bodily wants were once more swept aside when Peneli suddenly brought his mount to a standstill and uttered an imprecation in the Romany tongue.

'What is it?' Verity asked.

Even as Wystan answered for him, she saw for herself the band of redcoated soldiers surrounding the huddled group of gypsies, while to one side, slightly in front of a number of people who were recognisably of his entourage, stood a familiar figure, leaning on a cane.

'Papa's called out the militia!' Raising his voice, Braxted yelled, '*Papa*! *Sir*! We're here! We're back!'

Faces turned towards them as Peneli clicked his tongue and the little cavalcade began to move again, faster now. Faces of surprise and delight. Except for those of the gypsies, which remained sullen and shut in. Except also for that of the Marquis himself, who stared in shocked disbelief, his pain-racked mind capable only of registering that his children and Miss Lambourn were accompanied by the gypsy, without taking in the fact that they were safely restored to him.

His overwrought nerves were discharged in a blast of invective delivered in a voice of molten rage.

'You *villians*!' he began, launching himself forward to burst through the ranks of soldiery, to confront the band of gypsies. 'You knew all the time! You lying, vicious nest of evil! You knew, you *knew*. How *dared* you deceive me?'

He swung himself about and flung out an arm to point at the man who sat behind his son, and did not even see the way the boy's big blue eyes gazed at him in horror and fear.

'Captain, arrest that man! Arrest them *all*. Shoot them! Do what you will with them. But *get them off my land*!'

He stopped, breathing hard, his black eyes wild.

Into the breathless hush that followed his words came Verity's voice, deeply shocked. 'Henry, are you mad? You cannot mean that!'

She slid from the donkey's back, still clutching the infant Peggy, and ran forward.

'I'll take the babe, ma'am,' said a voice, and, turning, she found Bradshaw in her way.

Relinquishing the child at once, Verity moved to where the Marquis still stood, his wild glance roaming over gypsies and soldiers alike, seeing no one. Verity's face swam into focus before him, but her anxious words did not reach through the fog in his brain.

'Henry!' Verity was saying urgently. 'Peneli saved us! Don't you understand? He helped us to escape.'

Recognition flickered briefly in the dark eyes, and he half put out a hand. Then he staggered a little, dropped his cane, and in an anguished voice cried out, '*Hoff*!'

Verity leapt forward as he reeled, but the faithful groom was before her, catching him as he fell.

'*Henry*!' Verity shrieked, as his eyes rolled and closed. 'Oh, my God!'

'It's all right, miss,' Hoff said soothingly. 'I'll see to him. Been too much for him, that's all.'

So saying, he lifted the unconscious man in his brawny arms as if he had been a child, and walked towards the phaeton. Verity, tears in her eyes, would have followed, but was intercepted by the secretary.

'Leave him, Miss Lambourn,' he said, low-voiced. 'Hoff knows exactly what to do for him.'

'You are his secretary?' Verity asked, her voice shaking.

He bowed. 'Inskip is my name.'

'Will Henry—will he be all right?'

'There is no cause for alarm,' he assured her. 'His lordship has had a stressful day. To lose the children was, I think, too severe a reminder of the past.'

'Yes. . .yes, of course.' Struggling to control her agitation, she looked to where the soldiers still guarded the gypsies. The need to right a wrong gave her courage. 'Mr Inskip, you must have the soldiers set the gypsies free! But for them I would never have found the children, and but for Peneli we might still be immured in that wretched barn.'

'I understand, ma'am, but unfortunately I have not the power to countermand his lordship's orders,' said Inskip apologetically.

'Oh, stuff! His lordship was not himself. Anyone can see that. Besides, the soldiers would be far better employed in getting after the villain Shottle and his gang.'

'Shottle? So young Jed was right!'

'Telled you so!' piped up a new voice, and the climbing boy pushed in, accompanied by a rather subdued Lord Braxted. 'Wys been tellin' me as how you come'd after 'em, bold as brass. A right one you are, missie, and no mistake!'

Verity smiled as Inskip chimed in, 'We all echo that sentiment, Miss Lambourn! What we should have done without you, I dare not think. Now I had better see the captain.'

When appealed to, pleadingly by Verity and eagerly by Wystan, the captain of the troop scratched his chin and demanded the full story. He was told it by Braxted, with footnotes added by Verity to clarify several points that became muddled in the telling.

'Seems we'd better get after this enterprising fellow

Shottle,' he said good-humouredly when they were done. He cocked an eye at Verity. 'Think your gypsy friend would consent to show us the way?'

'You mean you are not going to arrest them, nor throw them off his lordship's land?' she demanded, her heart lifting.

'In view of your evidence, ma'am, I can't do that. At least, I can't arrest the man. As to seeing the gypsies off, well, I'd need a *written* authority from the Marquis,' explained the captain, with a broad wink. 'I'll ask him again when he's recovered from his—er—illness.'

'Thank you!' Verity said, from the heart, for she knew that Henry would not repeat his request once he knew the full story. Besides, she would ask him not to. That is, she thought fleetingly, if, after today's telling exhibition, Henry and she were ever to talk again. She pushed the idea aside and turned back to the captain.

'Wait! I will ask Peneli if he will take you to the cottage.'

She swung about to look for the gypsy and found that, with the soldiers' guns no longer trained upon them, the clan had backed up to stand in a ragged line across an opening between two wagons, as if in readiness to defend their very small island against the threatening storm.

Searching for her saviour's tall person, Verity's gaze went from face to face and found nothing.

'Where is Peneli?' she asked of the blank countenances giving her back look for look. 'You need not fear me. Tell me, pray!'

A racked voice called out from behind the barrier. 'Ho, there, dearie! Come ye in.'

It was Mairenni, her clawed palm beckoning. Smiling in relief, Verity pushed through the unresisting gypsies, realising that it was the matriarch rather than their possessions they sought to protect. She thought suddenly, with a wave of tenderness for their loyalty, that Mairenni had not been among the group herded by the militia.

Peneli was beside his mother, his dark face brooding and sullen. 'Yon Markiss don't deserve ye.'

'Don't judge him too harshly,' Verity begged quickly. 'He has suffered greatly, and is still not truly recovered. He did not mean it and will be sorry presently, I promise you.'

Old Mairenni's knowing eyes twinkled up at her. 'Excuses for he ye'll be making, if he do chase us off the valley.'

'He won't,' Verity said confidently. 'I *know* him.'

'Aye,' Peneli nodded. 'Likely ye do, seeing as how you'm to wed he.'

Verity coloured. 'That is another matter.'

The cracked old voice of his mother intervened sharply. 'Don't ye pay no mind to them visions o'yourn, dearie! Leading ye false, they be. Mark old Mairenni's words.'

Biting her trembling lip, Verity put out a hand to take the old one held out to her in kindness and friendship, but she avoided the subject. 'I owe you both so much, but I must ask yet one more favour.'

Peneli nodded as if he read her mind. 'Take yon redcoats to cottage, is it?'

'Would you?'

'Aye. Finish job proper like. Mind, if it weren't for ye——'

She smiled tremulously. 'I can't thank you enough.'

'Enough it is,' interrupted old Mairenni. 'Get ye gone, Peneli, boy! And as for ye, dearie, go on home. Eat, sleep.' She wagged a finger in Verity's face. 'And enough o' setting you'm head alight, eh?'

'I will try,' Verity promised, and left her, but unfortunately, she could have said, her head was already very much alight.

When she rejoined Inskip, she discovered that both Wystan and Peggy had been taken home to be fed and rested, and only the secretary was waiting for her. She realised suddenly that she had not even seen Hoff the groom drive his master away.

'His lordship would never forgive me, ma'am,' Inskip told her, 'if I did not see you safe home, so I have called for the carriage to take us.'

'That is kind,' Verity said, adding, 'but I will not trouble you to escort me. I can quite well go alone.'

Inskip smiled. 'I have no doubt of that, Miss Lambourn. But you will appreciate that I am very happy in his lordship's employ, and would not care to find myself summarily dismissed!'

Verity did not laugh. She stared up at him, trouble in her face, but said nothing more until they sat in the privacy of Salmesbury's coach. She was near sick with hunger and fatigue, and, with the sun just beginning to sink, a chill was seeping into her bones and she was glad of the rug which the secretary tucked about her. But now that all need for action was past, the apprehensions that she had kept at bay came creeping in, wreathing her tired mind in a whirling onslaught of questions.

She sought in the dimming light for the secretary's profile and spoke with a quaver in her voice. 'Mr Inskip, will you tell me something?'

He turned his head, but she could not see his eyes, for which she was thankful.

'If I can, Miss Lambourn.'

'The—the Marchioness. Was she. . .very beautiful?'

There was a pause. Verity held her breath.

'I would not have said,' Inskip began carefully, 'the Lady Margaret was a beauty exactly. She was extremely pretty. The children are very like her, you know.'

'Then she must indeed have been pretty,' commented Verity in a neutral tone. 'He must have counted himself a very lucky man.'

Inskip said nothing. There was much he could say, but he had no idea how far matters had gone, although he could hardly fail to be aware of his employer's interest in Miss Lambourn. He did not want to prejudice the situation by any untoward comment. But all of a sudden, Miss Lambourn turned to him, speaking fast, almost as if she *must* speak.

'It is evident, even had he not told me, how distressed he has been! But his agony of mind, this *passion*—is it all since the accident? Was he—was he *happy*. . .before?'

It was a moment before Inskip said anything, but again his voice was careful. 'I think he was *contented*.'

To his surprise, Verity gave a rather hysterical little laugh. 'Upon my word, Mr Inskip, you are the perfect secretary! You answer my questions and yet you tell me *nothing*!'

'What would you have me say, Miss Lambourn? I am groping in the dark.'

'I would have you say that I may exorcise a ghost!' Her voice cracked. 'Oh, Mr Inskip, what am I to do? It has all happened so very fast, and I thought—up until tonight I thought it would all be well. I thought I had the power to *recover* him. But the hurt runs so very deep! It is much, much worse than I had imagined. And I am afraid. . . I am so afraid!'

Not knowing what else to do, Inskip put out a hand to grope for her arm and press it sympathetically. He felt for her distress, but was unable to offer a single word to assuage her fears. He had seen all too clearly for himself, and many times, the anguish that tormented his employer. How could he reassure this innocent young girl, brave and resourceful though she was, that her love—for he could not doubt that she loved the Marquis with her whole heart—would be enough?

Verity arrived back at the lodgings in Tunbridge Wells in a mood far other than that in which she had set out that morning. But it was still necessary to explain her sorry state to her patroness. Her hair was in a tangle, her hat on askew, and her pink gown in ruins.

'Good God in heaven!' ejaculated the old lady on catching sight of her. 'What in the world have you been doing, child?'

Maria Polegate, who had been dining with her friend, sat staring, her eyes nearly popping out of her head, bereft for once of words.

'It is a long story, ma'am,' Verity uttered, sinking into a chair. 'The children were kidnapped.'

'Mercy me!'

'Lord save us!'

'Tell us all about it at once!'

Neither old lady was prepared to waive her burning curiosity, in spite of Verity's plea of exhaustion.

'You may well be tired! And hungry, too, I dare say,' said Lady Crossens. 'You had better come to the table. I will tell the woman to bring the remains of dinner.'

'Oh, no, please,' Verity begged. 'I could not swallow a thing!'

'Pish and tush! You will take at least some cold meat and some bread and butter. A dish of tea, too. It will do you all the good in the world!'

'Yes, indeed,' corroborated Mrs Polegate, 'there is nothing like tea to refresh you after a fatiguing day. And after such adventures as you have had! You will feel very much more the thing after you have drunk it, I promise you.'

Fussed over and bullied into partaking of a little of the food that was presently brought, and thankfully gulping down a cup of hot tea, Verity found them to be right. She did feel a deal better, and was able to rouse herself sufficiently to deliver a fluent account of the day's adventures.

When she had finished, and the two elderly ladies had done exclaiming and blessing themselves, they drove her to bed and tucked her up, confident in the belief that she would drop asleep in minutes. Verity was so tired that she thought so herself.

But the instant she was alone, the doubts that had been relegated to the back of her mind came flooding in to plague her. And Henry's eyes, wild and anguished, just before he sank unconscious into his groom's arms.

Verity turned her face into her pillow and wept.

Could she have been transported by some magical means to Braxted Place, it might have resolved all her doubts. For her beloved Henry Haverigg, threshing in his huge four-poster bed in an agony of mind which sent shivers of fear through the heart of the faithfully attendant Hoff, uttered such words as must have brought welcome balm to her heart.

CHAPTER ELEVEN

'WHAT did I *say*?' begged the Marquis, his grip demanding about his faithful henchman's wrist.

Hoff eyed him uncertainly, unwilling to trigger off another such storm as he had witnessed last night.

The black eyes burned at him. '*Tell* me.'

The man sighed. He never had been able to resist that dynamic, compelling look. 'You were calling for that there Miss Lambourn something pitiful, me lord.'

It was the simplest way he could think of to describe the harrowing groans of his master as he called out for the girl as if she had been a goddess, empowered to *deliver* him—as he had begged—from the torture of his own mind.

But Henry stared at the groom, his expression perplexed. Then he shook his head angrily and gripped the wrist he held more tightly.

'Not that, fool! Do you think I can't remember that? My God, she walks in my mind day and night, and if I talk to her in my semi-delirium it is not to be wondered at!'

'Talk!' echoed his henchman scoffingly. 'Aye, if you want to call it that. But I never heard no conversation like it, nor I never will!'

The Marquis reared up in bed, releasing his grip on the man's wrist only so that he might grasp him by the shoulders, the better to bellow into his face.

'Because I know that if *she* were here beside me I could be *calm*! *Don't you understand*?'

He released the man and fell back upon his pillows, closing his eyes. His voice came tiredly, wretchedly. 'No matter how monstrous my actions, how bizarre, she, like you, dear friend and comforter——' with a flicker of a smile to the groom as those eyes flew briefly open and shut again '– she will not blame me. She knows me. It is as if she has always known me. And I her.'

His eyes opened and the energy mounted in his voice. 'Whatever I may have said, Verity knew I did not mean. But not so the gypsies, Hoff!' He was leaning up on his elbow now. 'What did I say to the gypsies? That is what I am asking you.'

'Ah!' said Hoff heavily, and nodded his head. 'You tried to have that there capting of militia arrest 'em. Said as how you didn't care if he shot 'em, only so as he got 'em off of your land.'

Salmesbury sighed, covering his eyes with one hand. 'And to them I owe the safety of my children and of Verity herself. Oh, *God*!' He sat up, preparing to throw off his covers. 'I must see them. God send the captain did not obey me!'

'That he didn't, me lord,' soothed his henchman, but put out a hand to prevent him from leaving the bed. 'But you'll not get up today, me lord!'

Salmesbury sank back, for he was indeed fatigued. He must see the gypsies, however. A picture of the previous evening was in his mind, and abruptly he saw again his son's face where he sat on the pony before the gypsy. Oh, God! *Wystan*. What had he thought?

'Hoff!' he said urgently, his hand going out. 'The children! How are the children?'

'Don't you worry your head over them, me lord. Fit as fiddles, both of 'em!'

'I must see the boy,' muttered Henry, once more attempting to rise.

'No, me lord, no! Stay put and rest, I beg you. You know Dr Claughton said as how you didn't ought to get up.'

'To hell with Dr Claughton! I shall certainly get up.'

He paused, an odd look in his black orbs. 'No, wait. I shall rest then, Hoff, and rise a little later. But first be so good as to fetch the children to me.'

This was so unprecedented that even Hoff could not forbear a shocked gasp. '*Here*, me lord?'

'Yes, here,' responded the Marquis, and grinned suddenly. 'Let them see another side of their father for once, and realise that he is but a mortal man.'

Hoff privately thought that what they would see, coupled with what they had witnessed last night, was more likely to convince them that their father was demented. For besides his crumpled nightshirt, and the blue smudges under his eyes, Henry's motions of the disturbed night had rid him of his nightcap, leaving his long brown hair falling about his shoulders in disarray.

Nor was the groom entirely mistaken. A few minutes later, he returned to his master's chamber with the infant Peggy in his arms, and Wystan lagging a little in his wake. The boy stopped short at sight of his father's dishevelled state and his jaw dropped open.

His eyes goggled a moment. But the slight figure in the bed leaned forward from the bank of pillows, and smiling, held out his arms. In instinctive reaction, Wystan gasped, '*Papa*!' and then ran to the bed to find himself enfolded, for the first time he could remember, in this man's strangely comforting embrace.

His sister Peggy, needless to say, no sooner saw her brother locked in those unfamiliar arms than she set up a jealous shriek.

'Me too, me too! Peddy want 'ug. 'Ug Peddy *now*!'

Both father and son burst out laughing, breaking apart. Soon both children were ensconced on the bed, a fatherly arm about each, while Wystan poured out the tale of their adventures the day before. Verity's name figured largely, and at last Henry became aware that every time his son mentioned it, he looked sideways at his father.

Had the boy guessed, then? Henry wondered. Well, why not? He was no fool. But Henry had no intention of discussing his plans as regards Verity Lambourn until he had settled everything with the lady herself. For although he could not doubt but that she reciprocated his affection, he was by no means certain of his acceptability as a husband.

There were the strange views she had expressed on marriage, and her wish to work at this writing—although she could as well pursue *that* married to him as not. More easily. Moreover, could she be expected to overlook the past? The dark shadow of Meg's accident would always be there, even when not in mind, in the legacy of his physical punishment. It was very well to know and respect the integrity Verity possessed, but might it not lead her to discard him? For he was unworthy, God only knew! And she was too honest a soul not to recognise the shoals ahead.

Inwardly sighing, he refocused his attention on the boy's face, realising that he had stopped speaking.

'I'm sorry, Wystan. What were you saying?'

Braxted frowned. 'You went away. In your head, I mean.'

The Marquis tightened his hold about the child's shoulders. 'I did. I beg your pardon.' He paused, looking into the blue eyes, in which he recognised uncertainty. 'Wystan, if you find me sometimes strange. . .distanced. . .or perhaps a little as if I have lost my senses, I pray you don't ever think it means I love you less. You and Peggy. You see, when your mama. . .died——' bringing out the word with difficulty '–I was very much at fault. I am still learning to live with that. Do you understand at all?'

The boy nodded solemnly. 'I think so. You get a bit broody-like.'

'That is it exactly.'

Wystan looked at him a moment longer, and then,

so abruptly that it startled Henry, his face broke apart in a wide smile. 'Well, you won't much longer. *She'll* see to that.' Then before his father could respond, he turned to his sister. 'Won't she, Peggy? She'll see to that.'

'Wissen see to dat,' shouted the infant.

'Not Wissen, silly! Ssh, it's a secret. Peggy not to tell.'

'Issa seekit. Peddy no tell.'

In a moment, the two of them were jumping on the bed, both shouting Peggy's version, 'Seekit! Seekit!' at the tops of their voices. Called to order by Hoff, who was afraid they might land on his master's injured leg, they tore round the room in boisterous spirits while the Marquis lay against his pillows, laughing, all the gloom vanishing from his features.

A couple of hours later, having partaken of a belated breakfast together, the Marquis and his son, with Hoff aboard at his own insistence, were perched in the phaeton, driving down into the valley towards the gaily painted caravans.

They must have seen him coming, for as he brought the carriage to a standstill, he saw them gathering in knots, coming from inside the circle, to stand, arms folded, presenting him with the same hostile silence that had greeted Verity.

The Marquis refused to be intimidated. He climbed unhurriedly from the phaeton, took up his cane and limped towards them. Stopping a few yards before them, he looked from face to face as if he sought to memorise them. They stared back impassively, but he could feel the vibration of loathing directed towards him. At last he began to speak, not in the manner of one addressing an audience, but looking first at one and then at another, appealing directly to each.

'I am come to retract the words I spoke to you last night. I do not seek your friendship, for I know that is impossible. But perhaps I may at least mitigate your hatred, and pray you to try to understand.'

There were the faintest flickers of the eyes, one to another, in silent communication. Salmesbury had evidently chosen an acceptable tack.

He held out his hand to Braxted, and the boy put his own into it. 'But for one of your number, this child, together with my daughter, would not be here with me today. For that you have my everlasting gratitude, and you may ask of me what you will.'

One of the gypsy women spat suddenly. 'We don't want no reward o'yourn, Markiss.'

'I don't blame you,' Salmesbury sighed. 'Very well. I will make no excuses, and I will offer you nothing. Believe me only when I say that what I spoke last night came from my distress of mind, and from nothing else. And accept also my assurance that as long as I am alive you and yours will ever be welcome on my land.'

With that, he turned away and began limping towards the carriage. A shout from behind stopped him.

'Ho, there, Markiss!'

He turned, and saw that one of the men had come forward. He was a tall, burly fellow with thick black hair waving down to his shoulders.

'That's Peneli,' whispered Wystan. 'The one who helped us escape.'

'You want me?' Henry asked of the man.

'Not I,' Peneli said proudly. He jerked his head. 'It's me mam.'

A hand reached up and clipped him smartly across the ear. Old Mairenni pushed past him, muttering, 'Keep civil tongue in you'm head, boy!'

She came on and Wystan backed away, for she was odd enough and sufficiently witch-like to frighten a little boy. She paid him no attention as he went to the phaeton to seek refuge with Hoff, but came up to the

Marquis, standing before him and squinting up into his face, her lined features questioning.

Henry frowned. 'We have met before, I think.'

'Aye, at fair,' she answered.

'Why, you are the woman who told fortunes!'

'That I am, master,' she nodded. 'Don't ye pay no mind to these 'un.' She gave that characteristic gypsy jerk of the head to indicate the gypsies behind her.

The Marquis flicked a glance at them and found they had begun to disperse. 'They have every right to be angry with me.'

'B'ain't angry, master. Glad they be as to find ye don't mean to throw we off you'm land.'

'They have a strange way of showing it,' Henry said with a brief smile.

'Ah, master! Ye don't understand Romany ways. Besides, knowed it we did, what ye say. She told we.'

'She?' he repeated, knowing very well what the woman meant.

'Don't ye judge he too harshly, she say,' the matriarch went on, without answering his question directly, but with her watchful eyes studying him covertly. 'He have suffered, she say. Sorry he'll be when he'm back to his senses.'

'She said that?'

'Aye. And she be right.'

Henry nodded. 'She usually is.'

Old Mairenni frowned, and her clawlike hand reached out to pluck at his sleeve. 'Aye, but she be all wrong now, mark my words!'

'What do you mean?' he said quickly, his black eyes staring into the crone's beady ones.

'I mean as how you'm at crossroads, Markiss! Wrong turn now, and—whisht!' She drew a thumb swiftly across her throat to indicate an end.

As Salmesbury stared at her, his heart began thumping oddly, as if some echo of his own fears were put here into words. His voice was unsteady. 'Fortune could not be that unkind.'

'Aye, but she can,' argued Mairenni, and her cracked voice took on heat. 'Only it *ain't* fortune, master. She be feared. Seeing them pictures in her head, she be. Told her to pay them no mind, I did, but she be stubborn. Ye be warned!'

She turned to go, but Henry reached out a hand to restrain her. 'No, wait!'

Halting, she looked back. 'Aye?'

There was a pause, but then he laughed a little and shrugged. 'You're bewitching me, old woman! And I have no notion what all these nonsensical omens and warnings of yours mean.'

She cackled at him. 'Ye'll pay them no mind anyhow! But don't be a-feared, master. Promised her all, I did—*after* the tears.'

Then she left him standing, snaking away, her bent old bones carrying her in a kind of zigzag path to the caravans, as she sang a snatch of some unknown song in a high-pitched voice that cracked with every other word.

The Marquis watched her go, still smiling, but oddly disquieted by the possible significance of her discourse, for he felt as if something important had slipped away from him in the jumble of her words.

Two days after Monday's ill-fated expedition to Haverigg Hall, the humdrum life of Tunbridge Wells had forced on Verity an appearance of outward calm. It was obvious that the wagging tongue of that inveterate gossip, Maria Polegate, had made her the cynosure of all eyes. Besides, the story of the kidnap had already made its way to the genteel circles of that avidly curious little town before ever Verity had arrived home at the end of that fateful day.

Verity could see the whispering behind fans, the

nods in her direction. But somehow it had ceased to be so important set against the juggling, the see-saw imbalance of her mind and heart. Coupled with the worry over how Henry was after that dreadful collapse, the indecision into which she had been thrown was almost unbearable. She knew that Lady Crossens was narrowly watching her, but she had shut herself in from any attempt to divine her trouble.

'Papa always says,' she told her image in the mirror, 'if you have doubts, *don't*. But oh, Henry, can I *bear* to refuse you?'

She watched in fascination as her hazel eyes in the mirror brightened, and the moisture crept down her cheek as the picture came to her mind of his wild eyes closing as he fainted into his groom's arms. She wondered how, if at all, she would hear news of his present health.

'Perhaps I will not have to refuse him. Perhaps he will not ask me. Perhaps he is. . .*incapable* of asking me—of *remembering* me! Perhaps it is only the image of her, Lady Margaret, that fills his mind, and I—I have no longer a place there.'

Her face in the glass blurred and she searched her sleeve for a handkerchief.

'Verity! Verity, we shall be late!'

The voice of her patroness calling from the corridor caused her quickly to wipe away the giveaway tears.

'Coming!' she replied, hastily patching over her damp cheeks with a dash of Hungary Water, and checking the mirror for reddened eyes.

They were engaged with Richard Cumberland, who was to read to them his latest play.

'Not that I wish to hear it,' as Lady Crossens had confided to her friend, 'for it is sure to be tedious in the extreme. But it may serve to take the poor child out of herself.'

'Oh, yes, indeed, Emilia,' nodded Mrs Polegate. She

sighed deeply. 'Such an unhappy state as she has got into. Just when we thought all was in train for the brightest of futures!' For it had not been long before the lady had wormed her old crony's secret hopes from her. 'What can have happened, do you suppose?'

'I am not going to speculate, Maria,' her ladyship said sharply, 'and nor are you! When she is ready, she will doubtless confide in me.'

If Mrs Polegate thought otherwise, she did not say so, but continued to wonder and suggest, in spite of her friend's prohibition. When she saw Verity come into the Assembly Rooms with her patroness, however, making for the corner where the playwright and his prospective audience was awaiting them, she thought perhaps Emilia had exaggerated, so well in hand did Verity have herself.

But if she fooled Mrs Polegate, there was one other whom she decided had seen through her, for surely it was not chance that led Sir John Frinton into an impish attempt to draw her into laughter?

'Now, Miss Heroine,' he said gaily, coming up to the group and rudely pushing past the bulk of Richard Cumberland, who had been about to offer Miss Lambourn a seat. 'Don't you think you had better entertain us with an account of your great adventure?'

Verity, who wanted nothing less than to talk about the kidnap, at once put in an objection. 'Oh, no. Here is Mr Cumberland who has been so kind as to invite us to hear his play. I am sure it will prove entertainment enough.'

'Oh, do you think so?' asked Sir John blandly, eyeing Cumberland with one eyebrow raised. 'For myself, I should have thought *anything* else—I mean——' correcting himself in so clumsy a fashion that no one could doubt that his slip was deliberate ' – of course, I should have thought *your* real-life adventure might prove of more general interest, and—er—stimulation.'

Cumberland was swelling with indignation, as people began to snigger around him. 'I will have you know, sir, that Miss Lambourn herself expressed an interest——'

'Quite, quite!' agreed Sir John, silencing him effectively, and noting with a pleased glance round that several of those within earshot had gathered about the group, ready to enjoy his wit. He would not disappoint them, even if his real object was to divert one particular young lady.

'But really, now, Cumberland, I think you are missing an excellent opportunity. Only consider, my dear fellow! Here is Miss Lambourn, the prettiest little heroine you could hope to find, full of a wonderful tale of romance and adventure—complete, I may say, with the innocents she managed to rescue, which as you must know is *always* a dead cert with audiences—and all you have to do is seize the story and fashion it into a play.'

There was a ripple of amusement, and Sir John's eye gleamed. He pursued his quarry relentlessly. 'Not that I mean to suggest, dear Cumberland, that your own plots are in any way devoid of excitement. Nor, of course, that you are in the habit of stealing ideas from others.'

As this was precisely the opinion of everyone present, most of whom had at some time or another been subjected to the unutterable boredom of the gentleman's productions, it provoked a deal of suppressed hilarity.

'How dare you, sir?' demanded the author, outraged.

'But my dear fellow, have I said anything amiss?' enquired Sir John innocently, glad to see a tiny smile on Verity's lips.

But Mr Cumberland had had enough. Turning his back on his tormentor, he addressed the prospective audience. 'If you are ready, ladies? Perhaps if you would sit here, Miss Lambourn.'

She was very glad to do as he asked, for although she was amused by Sir John's reprehensible behaviour she had no wish at all to relate the story of her adventures.

'Yes, do let us begin,' she said with an assumption of eagerness. 'Pray go away, Sir John, if you do not want to hear the piece.'

He bowed. 'Your wish is my command.'

Behind him Mr Cumberland portentously cleared his throat, and began, 'The scene is set in the Roman forum. . .'

Sir John and his group of admirers beat a hasty retreat, but Verity dutifully remained sitting to listen to the play with every evidence of enjoyment. The fact was, however, that she scarcely heard a word of Mr Cumberland's piece, and could not even have said what it was about had she been questioned. She came to herself with a start when the master of ceremonies, Richard Tyson, gently touched her arm.

'There is a young gentleman to see you, ma'am,' he said in her ear. 'Lord Braxted, he says he is.'

Verity sat up with a jerk, forgetting to lower her voice. 'What? Where?'

She realised the playwright had ceased speaking and was gazing at her in a pained way.

'Forgive me, Mr Cumberland,' she said quickly, 'but I am obliged to leave you for a space.'

He looked annoyed. 'I will await your return.'

'No, no, pray don't,' she begged. 'Do let the others hear it. I am sure Lady Crossens and Mrs Polegate——'

She broke off, as glancing at each lady in turn, she discovered both to have nodded off, their heads sinking on to their chests. 'Oh, dear! Oh, I am so sorry. But I *must* go.'

She rose on the words and followed Mr Tyson to the entrance of the Assembly Rooms where she at once saw Wystan standing with the secretary, Mr Inskip.

'Verity!' called the boy, grinning delightedly at her. 'I am come to ask you to take tea with us.'

Her heart beat rather fast and she glanced at Inskip. 'Is this by—by his lordship's invitation?'

'No, it isn't, it's by mine,' cut in Wystan. 'Mine and Peggy's. At least, 'course Papa knows about it.'

'His lordship begs you to honour the children with your company,' Inskip said with a smile, 'in order that they may express their thanks for what you did for them on Monday.'

'Eggzackly,' agreed Braxted, grinning. 'Do say you'll come.'

'Oh, Wystan, I don't know. I am actually engaged at this present, and——'

'Oh, *Verity*,' groaned the boy, looking crestfallen. 'You *must*. I even told Peggy and she wants you, too. She said, "Vetty come tea".'

Verity smiled. 'Did she?' She hesitated. Well, she must face it—*him*—sooner or later. 'Very well, I will come. Allow me a moment to let Lady Crossens know and I shall be with you.'

As she hurried back, weaving through the knots of people sitting and standing about in the Assembly Rooms, she instinctively glanced down at her person and remembered that the floral chintz had already been worn in Henry's presence. Well, it would have to do!

She was diverted then as she was intercepted in her path by Sir John Frinton.

'Miss Lambourn! Don't tell me you have deserted poor Cumberland? Upon my soul, I did not look for such usage from you to our illustrious playwright!'

She could not forbear a smile. 'For shame, Sir John! You behaved abominably to the poor man.'

'Alas!' he uttered, a hand exaggeratedly placed upon his heart. 'I have offended you, and I meant only to bring a smile to your sweet face, dear Miss Lambourn.'

'I wish you will not be so absurd!' Verity scolded. 'And do pray let me go. I am in a dreadful hurry.'

His eyebrows flew up. 'Don't dare to tell me you are dying to return to listen to that nauseating claptrap!'

'No, indeed. But I am waited for, and I must make my excuses to Mr Cumberland.'

Sir John's eyes lit with that mischievous gleam. 'Ah! Here is my chance to make amends. I shall carry your excuses to Cumberland, thus saving you a tedious and unpleasant task.'

'Would you indeed?' said Verity, relief flooding her face. 'And Lady Crossens, too, if you please. Tell her I have gone to Braxted Place. It is just that I am in a hurry, and——'

'And Cumberland will keep you as he bores on forever about lost opportunities, et cetera, et cetera.' He held up a hand. 'Have no fear! I will see to it on the instant.'

Verity thanked him and half turned to go, throwing him a doubtful glance. 'Yes, but you will not say anything wicked to him, will you?'

'I shall be discretion itself,' he assured her, bowing. But as she hurried away, his mouth curled into a smile of unholy glee and he turned to go on his self-appointed errand.

Verity, relieved to have got by so lightly, resolved to make a point of offering her apologies in person the very next time she saw Mr Cumberland. But he could not long occupy her mind, when she was on her way to Braxted Place where the object of all her thoughts awaited her.

The journey was beguiled by Wystan's account of the aftermath of the kidnap.

'The militia went after those brutes, but 'course

they'd runned off by then. Kittle ain't been seen since and they guess she's gone with them. Jed says Shottle was thick as thieves with Jim Brigg and Olly Hargate in any event. Seems they've done lots of bad things together.'

'But are the militia not continuing to search for them?' asked Verity, diverted from thoughts of the Marquis and the coming meeting. 'They surely can't mean to let such criminals get away?'

'Oh, they're after them all right. They got good descriptions and they reckon to run them to earth in a day or two.'

'They will certainly catch them,' Inskip put in, 'and they have evidence enough to throw them all in prison for a long time to come.'

'How is that?' Verity asked. 'I mean, we are witnesses, of course, but Wystan is a minor and I only saw Shottle.'

'They found a ransom note in the cottage,' the secretary told her. 'It was in the man Olly Hargate's hand, for it seems he was the only one who could write. They apparently had the intention of demanding ten thousand pounds for the children.'

'Yes!' chimed in Braxted in indignant tones. 'But when they had you, they started to write another, for they thought they could get another ten thousand for you alone!'

'How very stupid of them!' said Verity instantly. 'To suppose that I must be more valuable than the two of you!'

'Well, I don't know about that,' Braxted said, mollified. 'I dare say Papa would have paid handsomely to get you back.'

There was a short, embarrassed silence. Inskip broke it, tactfully veering off the subject of ransom notes.

'We suspect that the plot had been laid a long time

ago, for the militia have done some thorough questioning. It seems that Kittle is in fact Shottle's wife.'

'What?' gasped Verity. 'Are you saying she had this planned since she came to nurse Peggy?'

'We think so.'

'But her references?' protested Verity. 'Surely you checked them.'

'By letter only. It is quite usual, you know. But I sent grooms to check the addresses of the two people who recommended the woman, and it transpires that the impression of respectable households was false. For instance, Tannery Lodge proved to be Tannery Cottage, and the inmates—no longer in residence, I may add—common people who could no more afford a nurse than they could a maidservant.'

'How very dreadful!' exclaimed Verity, shocked. 'To think that such deceits may be practised so easily!' A sudden thought struck her. 'Gracious heaven, I do trust you have double-checked on the woman Bradshaw?'

'Have no fear,' Inskip said, smiling. 'I did so before we hired her. You see, his lordship had meant in any event to get rid of Kittle, just as soon as little Lady Margaret should have become sufficiently acquainted with Bradshaw.'

'Oh, so that's what was in the wind, is it?' interposed Braxted importantly. 'I thought Papa gave in over that one too easily.'

'Then all unwittingly,' Verity guessed, 'you precipitated the kidnap, for she must have guessed your intention.'

'Yes,' agreed Inskip. 'Which I dare say is why it was so badly executed. Evidently they had no time to lay their plans sufficiently well.'

'No,' Verity said in a subdued tone. 'I'm afraid they would certainly have succeeded if it had not been for my stupidity—though it all turned out for the best in the end!—for it was something I said that led Shottle to expand his scheme to include me. That must have thrown them out, for I cannot think they expected to have to contend with an adult.'

'That's true,' Wystan said eagerly. 'For with Peggy and me they could have travelled much further and gone a lot quicker.'

Inskip laughed suddenly. 'The wretched villains must have thought Christmas had come early!'

They all erupted into the laughter of relief which came to those who recognise how close they have been to disaster. Not that Verity's lightened mood enabled her to face with equanimity the prospect before her. Her yearning to see Henry, to know he was himself again, warred with the fears evoked the other night by his unprecedented outburst and the collapse that followed it.

Unlike his father, it seemed as if the young boy was not a penny the worse for his adventure. And, by his conversation, it appeared that Peggy too had rapidly recovered. Verity longed to ask about Henry, and searched Inskip's face for a clue, but she could not say anything in Wystan's presence for fear of his asking awkward questions. He had already shown that he was too young to be trusted not to refer to it, if something should put it in his head.

In the event, Braxted led her straight up to the nursery and they did not encounter the Marquis at all. As Verity greeted Peggy and sat down to tea with the children, Bradshaw in attendance, she wondered if Henry was deliberately avoiding her, or whether he was merely keeping out of the way to allow the children time with her.

It was the first time she had seen Braxted Place, and the vast marbled hall and Italianate décor did nothing to ease the uncertainty of her mind. While they were in the relatively unimposing nursery, it did not trouble her, but when Braxted offered to show her around she began to feel more and more depressed.

What had she, Verity Lambourn of Tetheridge Vicarage, to do with all this grandeur? As if Henry's tragic past were not enough, here was his milieu to distance her further.

'And here are all the family portraits,' announced Wystan, turning into the long gallery.

Slowly they traversed the length of it, the boy pointing out his forebears, stopping at one that bore a marked resemblance to Henry.

'That's the one who built this place, my great grandfather. That was before they made him a Marquis, so he called it Braxted Place.'

There were the ancient earls, who had inhabited the medieval manor of Haverigg Hall, and the lords and ladies who had followed them to the Elizabethan pile which had been razed to the ground by the Earl of Braxted, who had become the first Marquis of Salmesbury, and rebuilt in the latest Palladian style at enormous expense on the same spot.

Verity began to feel crushed by the weight of Henry's ancestry, so that he seemed less and less the Henry Haverigg she had met and learned to love, and more and more the third Marquis of Salmesbury, a personage whom she did not know and to whom she never could be equal—in station, in stature, or in anything else.

Then they paused before a more recent portrait. It was of a woman, and Verity stared, her heart plummeting. For in the sweet face, with its gentle smile, its dreamy eyes of blue, and the frame of corn-gold hair, she recognised in an instant the ghost that haunted the man she loved.

'That's Mama,' Wystan announced, as if Verity needed telling. 'You see, both Peggy and me are like her, not Papa. I 'member her very well, you know. She always smiled like that. Like as if she was thinking of something secret, something nice.'

He paused, his head on one side, considering the portrait. Verity found herself unable to say a word. Face to face with the barrier that would stand forever between herself and Henry, she experienced such resentment as she had never known before. She wanted to drag her nails across the canvas, rip that lovely face to shreds.

Shocked at the ferocity of her thoughts, she stepped back from the picture, as if afraid the devil in her might take her over and make her perform that act of hideous desecration. She stood trembling and sick to the stomach while Wystan's light treble grew and jangled in her head as he began to speak again, the words echoing and re-echoing until she wanted to scream.

'I asked Mama once why she smiled as if she had a secret, and she said she smiled whenever she thought of Papa. She said whenever Papa laughed, it was because he thought of her. She said they had fun together, they enjoyed each other.'

'*Fun together*. . .fun together. . .enjoyed each other . . .enjoyed. . .fun. . .fun. . .fun. . .'

The word hammered in her ears and she saw them—Henry laughing, the ghost smiling, on and on. The lovely woman smiling that secret smile, smiling. Mouth opening wide, jagged as it began to laugh, turning into a jeering, sneering, undulating gash. The gold hair rippling, flowing about her head, flying high as she opened wide her arms and rose into the air, screaming her evil laughter as she drew the man up to tangle in the invisible web she wove about him to hold him there forever. And somewhere far away, a tiny voice, crying hopelessly, *Henry, Henry*. . .

'Ah, there you are!' said Henry's voice.

Verity snapped out of the vision and her head jerked round. Henry! He was smiling, moving, limping along the gallery towards them. He was speaking, but she did not hear the words. For behind him, her overwrought imagination painted the ghostly form of Lady Margaret, smiling in triumph over his shoulder. . .smiling her secret smile.

'No!' Verity cried out, shaking her head. 'I can't.' She was backing from him. '*Henry, I can't.*'

Spinning on her heel, she sped away, oblivious to the voices calling her.

'Verity, wait!'

'Verity, where are you going?'

'Come back, Verity!'

Away she ran, through the gallery to the great staircase that took her down to the hall below, past the marbled glories, over the mottled floors, to the front door where she very nearly collided with the butler as he hurried to find out the cause of the commotion.

'Miss?' Cradoc said. 'Can I assist you?'

'*Please*,' she begged breathlessly. 'Ask the coachman to catch me up. I must go.'

She went as if to wrench at the double doors, but Cradoc was before her, pulling them open. Out she ran, speeding across the stone patio and down the steps, past the statues that decorated each corner of the three shallow flights of the double stairway.

As she started down the sweeping driveway, she began to slow and discovered that tears were streaming down her face. They continued to fall as she stumbled on, waiting for the coach to take her up and whisk her away from this dreadful place that gave her so much pain.

Inside the mansion, the Marquis kept a tight hold on his son's shoulder.

'But shan't I go after her, sir? I can catch her easy.'

'Let her go, Wystan,' answered Henry wearily. 'Let her be.'

'But Papa——'

'Enough!' He summoned a weak smile. 'She will be back. I promise you. I will fetch her back.'

Braxted's lower lip drooped. 'What if she don't want to come?'

His father was looking at the portrait of his dead wife, quite unaware that this was the first time he had done so without the sliver of that pinprick in his heart. Was this the trigger? Poor Margaret. If he could have felt this for her, perhaps she would not have died that night.

Then he answered his son, as his hand tightened on the boy's shoulder. 'I don't think I could endure it, if she does not want to come.'

CHAPTER TWELVE

VERITY had pleaded a headache, sending a servant with a message to Lady Crossens, and hiding in her room until she could learn to master her emotion. Her patroness, however, when she showed her brave face at the breakfast table next morning, was not deceived.

'Is your headache better?' she demanded, looking at the girl from under lowered brows.

'A little, ma'am,' Verity answered, toying with a small helping of the ham and eggs with which she had been served.

Lady Crossens snorted. 'Pho! Don't tell me! You are at loggerheads with that Marquis of yours, I'll be bound!'

Verity bit her lip, looking away. 'It—it is not like that.'

'Well, how then is it? Come, child. Can you not tell me what ails you?'

'I would if I could, ma'am. Only there is nothing you can do. No one can do anything.'

'Except *him*, I dare say,' said her ladyship shrewdly.

Verity looked up at her. 'No. He—he cannot help it. The past is—is——'

'*Past*,' snapped Lady Crossens. 'Good God, girl, do you suppose a man will pine forever over a dead woman?'

'Please, ma'am,' whispered Verity, wincing.

'You are a fool, Verity! And you know nothing of men. Mark my words. If he is not beating a path to your door at this very moment, you may call me a dunderhead!'

At that opportune moment, there was a knock at the door and the maid came in.

'Well, Dawson?'

'Please, ma'am, there's a gennelman called for Miss Lambourn.'

'Aha!' rasped her ladyship triumphantly. 'Show him up, Dawson.'

'He's already up, ma'am,' grinned the girl.

Verity, who had sat like a stricken statue, now rose to her feet, pale but determined.

'Come along,' instructed Lady Crossens, and opened the door to the parlour.

The Marquis was standing by the window looking out, his brown locks, uncovered, neatly confined in a tie at the nape of his neck. He turned as the door opened, his eyes going past her ladyship to Verity's downcast face behind her.

'You're Salmesbury, I take it,' said the old lady, sailing across the room and grasping his hand. 'I'm Emilia Crossens.'

'How do you do, ma'am?' he said politely, bowing slightly over the hand he held.

'Very well, I thank you. But you have come to see Miss Lambourn, I apprehend, and so I shall leave you at once. Not that I approve of these free and easy modern manners, but circumstances, you know, alter cases!'

'You are so right,' agreed the Marquis, an irrepressible twinkle in his eye.

'At my age I ought to be!' she rejoined, and, marching to the parlour door, she hustled the open-mouthed Dawson before her.

Left to confront Verity, Henry's amusement faded as he searched her set features. The white gown of figured muslin emphasised her deathly pallor. Concern showed in his voice.

'You are almost as pale as I.'

Verity's eyes flew up to meet his, but she checked the response that rose to her lips. Instead she spoke in a quiet, polite manner quite unlike her usual tone.

'Won't you sit down?'

She took a chair herself, and he fidgeted a moment or two, looking at her with a frown in his eyes, then seated himself in a chair near the window. She would not meet his gaze and he found it hard to know how to begin. The silence lengthened and Verity at last looked up.

'I have to apologise, sir, for my abrupt departure from your house yesterday.'

'Verity,' he said in a hurt tone, 'you are addressing me as if we are strangers!'

'I *must*,' she whispered.

'But why?'

She was silent. Henry pushed himself up. At once she rose, too, and moved a step back from him. His face showed his feelings as he stood there, stiff, the black eyes challenging. Verity felt his pain at her rejection, and swallowed on the rising lump in her throat, forcing herself to speak calmly.

'Henry, I know why you have come. But I can't—you must not——'

Her voice failed. Her obvious distress touched him and his stiff pose relaxed, the green frock-coat sitting more easily upon his less rigid frame.

'Why have you turned against me? I want you to marry me, Verity. I thought—was I mistaken?—that we were of the same mind.'

I *was*, she wanted to cry. But she must not. She had decided. She must not weaken. She had doubts, and if in doubt, said the Reverend Harry Lambourn, *don't*. She drew a breath and as of instinct moved a little closer to him.

'Henry, I think we allowed ourselves to be carried away. I never looked for marriage.'

'No, I know,' he said quickly. 'You told me so. It is not, surely, this wish of yours to live by—what did you call it?—the writing of Gothic novels?'

'No, no, I——'

'Because, if so, there is nothing to stop you doing so,' he pursued anxiously. 'At least, not *live* by them. But *write* them, certainly. Indeed, I should take great pleasure in reading them.'

'You can't know that,' Verity protested with a faint smile. 'You may think them quite dreadful. But, Henry, it is not that. Upon my word, that would be *too* petty!'

'And you are certainly not that. *Tell* me.'

'Oh, Henry, it is so hard to explain. I am not of your world, for one thing.'

'What does that matter?' he said impatiently. 'I may be a Marquis, but I am also a man, Verity.'

'I know, I know, and I have never really thought of you in that light. To me you are, you will *always* be only Henry Haverigg.'

He smiled. 'I would not have it otherwise. But if not my rank, then——'

'I said *to me*, Henry,' she cut in quietly. 'To the world, you are the Marquis of Salmesbury. I think I am a poor candidate for his Marchioness. And—and yesterday——'

'Ah, yesterday! You saw my palatial residence, is that it? My God, I never thought to be sorry for the circumstances of my birth!'

'Don't, Henry! It was not that. At least, not *only* that. You see, we had not—*I* had not—properly considered all the implications. Now I have thought of them. Or rather,' she amended, with a twist in her face that cut him to the heart, 'they have been forced upon my notice.'

Henry looked struck. 'Oh, God! It is not my rank, nor my house, nor my estates, is it? That portrait of Meg—the accident—my insane behaviour.' He turned his face away. 'You are thinking of my outburst at the gypsy camp the other day.'

'That is a part of it,' Verity confessed, for she could not lie. 'Oh, don't think I blame you! Believe me, I don't. You were overwrought. I understood.'

'You understood,' he agreed low-voiced, 'and I know you would never blame me. But it frightened you.'

'No, not that,' she said quickly. 'Not in the way you think.'

But it was plain that he did not believe her. 'I can be very like the monster you once spoke of, can I not?' His mouth had a bitter curl to it. 'And a cripple to boot.'

'*No*!' Verity cried.

He shrugged. 'Why deny it? I will never walk with ease again. I will be lucky if I am not confined to a wheeled chair in middle age. Scarcely a satisfactory bargain.'

'Oh, Henry, that is a monstrous way to speak!' Verity scolded angrily, sweeping away from him and back again, as if she could not be still. 'You know your injury has never caused me the least discomfort. It is slighting to dare to suggest I could refuse you for such a reason as that!'

'Then if not that, *why*?' he demanded, matching her anger. 'Please, Verity, let me understand! These items you have mentioned—I don't believe you really care about them. They are excuses. Be truthful with me, I implore you, for I *know* you are not afraid of me, of what I am!'

'Oh, never that, Henry, never that!' she uttered, unguardedly stepping closer, her hands going out.

He grasped them strongly. 'Verity, this—this *thing* between us began that first day. Why do you suppose I came to Tunbridge Wells? Again and again. Oh, I didn't know it then myself, I grant you. But it grew and grew—and you know it!—until there was no gainsaying it. Damn you to hell, Verity, *why*?'

'*Because it is not enough*!' she threw at him wildly.

He stared at her blankly, his anger arrested. 'Not enough?'

'It can never be enough.' She said it quietly, thinking as she did so that it explained all.

To Henry, it was like a blow in the face. His hold on her hands relaxed and he released them. *Not enough*? What more could there possibly be? He shook his head as if to clear it of a fog. He felt empty, drained. Collecting his cane, he began to limp towards the door.

Verity watched him, her heart wrung. She had not meant to hurt him, though she had known she must. Only she had not realised how much, in doing so, she would hurt herself. She felt herself cruel and hated it, as if she had shown him a glimpse of Paradise and then snatched it away. She wanted very badly to run to him, tell him of her love, say she did not mean it. But the portrait rose in her mind. That fatal portrait of Lady Margaret Haverigg, whom Henry had loved and lost, whom she knew she could never replace.

Henry turned at the door. Like an afterthought, he said, 'I had hoped to bring home a new mother for my children. They love you, you know.'

Her throat ached suddenly. Through it, she managed to say, 'They will forget.'

He smiled, a wistful, tender smile. 'Perhaps they may. But will I?' After the briefest of pauses, in a quite ordinary voice, he added, 'The militia have apprehended the kidnappers. I thought you would wish to know.'

Then he passed from the room.

'I think you must have taken leave of your senses!' uttered the old lady fretfully. She had come back into the room on Salmesbury's departure, only to have all her eager expectations destroyed at a stroke.

'It must seem like it, I dare say,' Verity agreed wanly.

'Look at you! I declare, I have never seen such misery! And for what?'

'For *truth*, ma'am! It would not be fair to either he or myself to marry him.'

'Truth! Fair!' snorted Lady Crossens, tacking back and forth across the small parlour like a sail in a choppy wind. 'The truth, my girl, is that you don't know when you're well off! Here is the answer to every young girl's dream, handed to you on a golden platter, and you spurn it for a scruple.'

'Oh, ma'am, it is more than a scruple,' Verity said desperately. 'Much, much more. Must I spend my life in a welter of pain merely because the man who delivers it is a Marquis?'

'Pish and tush!' snapped her patroness crossly. '"Welter of pain"! I never heard such theatrical rodomontade! What more could you wish? Do you not love him? Does he not love you?'

Verity's lip trembled. 'He has not said so.'

The old lady's wrath was arrested in full flood. She stopped in mid-stride and stared at the girl. 'I beg your pardon?'

'He has not said that he loves me,' Verity repeated clearly, though her voice shook.

'But the man is obviously head over ears!' uttered Lady Crossens in a stunned tone.

'Still he has not said so.'

'Pah! *Men*. What a set of brainless idiots they are! You'd think they would realise that all a young girl wants to hear is a lot of romantical whispering. I could wring the ninny's neck!'

'Oh, ma'am!' protested Verity, half laughing. 'You are quite mistaken! I know that he *cares* for me, of course I do. But you don't understand. Perhaps if his wife had died in some other way, some manner that might not have involved him, it would be different. I might hope, in time, to supplant her in his affections. But as things stand—oh, can you not see how impossible it would be? Never to know, never to be sure of his affections. Always to see him sad and grieving any time something happens to remind him of her, of his first, his truest love. Then to see him, at last recognising that he cannot, will *never* forget her in loving me, trying not to show it, perhaps even living a *lie*. Oh, I could not endure it! Better by far we should never begin, than end in such *coldness*.'

Lady Crossens stood transfixed for a moment, caught up in the tragic voice, the pictures conjured up by the vivid words. Then she shook her head fiercely.

'Pish! Pish! Pish! Your trouble, my child, is an overactive imagination. Dear Lord in heaven, anyone would suppose you think to find yourself living in the pages of a three-volume novel!'

Verity coloured, but said in a low tone, 'I know I am apt to exaggerate life, ma'am, at least in my head. But you have not seen him when he speaks of her. God knows I would give anything to be his wife, could I only be first with him! But I cannot compete with a *ghost*.'

The old lady threw up her hands. 'Well, I've done with you! I've no patience. But when you have thrown away your chance beyond recovery, I trust you will remember your family and the future you have denied to them! When I think of all they might have enjoyed under such patronage—your sisters, your little brother, and dear Grace! Yes, and your father, for even he would scarcely applaud such pig-headed stupidity! And if he cannot think of a suitable penance, you may come to me, for I *can*!'

With which valedictory utterance, her ladyship

stalked from the parlour, shutting the door behind her with unnecessary force. Verity was left to the doubtful comfort of a hearty bout of tears, but still holding tight to her convictions. For opposition had only strengthened them. Had Lady Crossens had children of her own, she might rather have seen more wisdom in painting the dismal picture of Verity's lonely future, at home with her broken heart—a picture she was desperately keeping at bay for fear that it would break her resolution. Just as she refused to think about Wystan and infant Peggy, unable even to cherish the glad tidings in Henry's last words—that the wicked Shottle and his gang had been captured—because they *were* Henry's last words.

It hardly seemed possible that only a few short weeks ago the sum of her ambition had been to live in a cottage and indulge her taste for the Gothic to her heart's content. Now, with *only* that prospect before her, she remembered old Mairenni's prediction: 'Looking for you'm heart's desire, ye'll find ye have it in yer hands.' Only her hands were empty now, and there was nothing she desired less than to take up her pen and write!

More with a forlorn hope of appeasing her patroness, than with any real wish to seek company, Verity made an appearance in the Assembly Rooms the same afternoon. She was glad to think that there were only a few days remaining to them before they must start for home, for her situation was unenviable.

The story of the kidnap was still talked of, and it had, by some means unknown to her, become common knowledge that she was sought after by the Marquis of Salmesbury. She was obliged to turn off several prying questions with a light laugh, as if it was all a piece of nonsense. But her patroness's smouldering temper was enough to inform everyone of the contrary. So it was that in Sir John Frinton Verity found her only sympathiser.

'A turn along the Pantiles, Miss Lambourn?' he offered, crooking his elbow invitingly, and with such a wealth of understanding in his impish old eyes that Verity was hard put to it to keep from bursting into tears.

'Th-thank you,' she managed to say, and was grateful for the tact that kept him silent until they were strolling along the paved walkway.

'You poor child!' he said then, laying his hand on hers where it rested on his own and squeezing her fingers.

'Oh, don't, please, Sir John,' she begged. 'It is difficult enough to keep my countenance as it is.'

'I see it is. Then I will refrain from such unhandsome comments, and merely inform you that you have certainly made an enemy for life!'

Her startled eyes flew to his. 'An enemy? Not you, I hope?'

'By no means.' He sighed in an exaggerated way. 'But poor Cumberland! You have offended beyond forgiveness, you know.'

'Oh, dear, poor man,' said Verity contritely. 'I did leave him so rudely, I know.'

'Now, Miss Lambourn, you are not going to tell me you were not glad of the excuse? Mind you, he did not take kindly to your having been seized by a fit of nausea in the middle of——'

'A fit of nausea! Gracious heaven, is that what you told him?' demanded Verity, aghast.

'I had to think of some plausible reason,' Sir John said blandly.

'Plausible!'

'Well, you had not found his rhetoric soporific, unlike Emilia and poor, dear Maria Polegate, so I assumed——' Then he began to laugh as Verity broke into voluble scolding.

'I have never in my life heard such——'

'Ah, but here is dear Maria herself,' he interrupted smoothly, successfully diverting his companion's attention as he added, 'And, if I am not mistaken, she is big with news!'

Verity followed the direction of his gaze to find Mrs Polegate hurrying towrds them, her eyes signalling a frantic message.

'Well, Maria?' drawled Sir John as she came puffing up. 'What earth-shattering titbit have you got hold of this time?'

'So dreadful!' gasped the lady, one hand holding her expansive bosom, which was rising and falling comically. 'Horrible! Poor, poor man!'

'Come, come, Maria!' chided Sir John, gently mocking. 'Get your breath back, my dear, or we shall never comprehend a word.'

'Oh—dear!' she got out. 'Yes—but it can't wait.' She looked at Verity. 'You will wish to know *at once*, I am sure.'

Verity went still, her hazel eyes fixed on the lady's face in painful enquiry. Her heart seemed to stop, and the world about her coalesced and became a hazy cloud.

'Dreadful! History repeats itself, you see,' said Mrs Polegate, not without a certain relish. 'A terrible accident, they say. Took a fall from his phaeton and taken up for dead!'

There was a buzzing in Verity's ears, and she did not hear her own voice croak out the question to which she already knew the answer.

'Who? *Who*?'

'Why, the Marquis, of course!'

Verity was unaware of her own scream as the world went black. The next thing she knew was a spinning in her vision that steadied into faces looking down at her. Voices made themselves heard.

'Thank God, she is coming round!'

'Verity, child! Verity, can you hear me?'

'Give her room, there! Let her breathe!'

A deeper voice bade her lie still, and she came fully to her senses to find herself lying at full stretch on a sofa in the Assembly Rooms, an object of a general curiosity, while beside her knelt an elderly man in whom she recognised one of the resident physicians.

'Rest, please, Miss Lambourn,' he said, one hand encircling her wrist to feel her pulse.

For a moment she was glad to do as he bid her, for she felt quite sick and her head ached dully. She closed her eyes. There was a murmur of voices about her, but she did not question what had happened until she recognised her patroness's testy muttering.

'I don't know how you came to be so foolish, Maria! Could you not have come to me first?'

The image of Mrs Polegate's face sprang into Verity's mind, and, with it, the appalling news she had brought.

'Henry!' she uttered distressfully, and struggled to sit up.

'No, no, Miss Lambourn,' protested the physician, trying to push her back. 'Lie still, I beg of you.'

'I can't, I can't,' Verity cried, pushing away his restraining hand and impelling herself up.

The action caused her a sudden nausea and she was obliged to grip tightly to the back of the sofa, forcing it down. The ladies' voices were again heard, this time directed at her.

'No, Verity, you will remain there.'

'Oh, Miss Lambourn, you must forgive me! Do pray stay where you are a little.'

'Be quiet, Maria! She will certainly stay here.'

Unheeding, Verity willed herself to overcome the

waves of sickness and swung her feet to the ground, fighting the many hands that sought to keep her here.

'*Henry*,' she uttered desperately. 'I must go to him!'

'No, no, Miss Lambourn!'

'Please stay, ma'am. You can do no good to yourself.'

'What does that matter?' Verity demanded, her ravaged features going wildly from face to face. 'I must go to Henry! I *must*.'

'Verity, listen to me——' began Lady Crossens in a scolding tone.

But Verity was on her feet, swaying a little, but with a set determination in her face that one at least of the surrounding well-wishers recognised.

'Let her be, Emilia,' said Sir John, laying a restraining hand on Lady Crossens' shoulder. 'Can you not see? Nothing less will satisfy her.'

He pushed through and, with an air of authority that made all give way before him, he took possession of Verity's hand and drew her within a protective arm.

'Come, child,' he said gently. 'I will take you to your Henry.'

'Thank you!' gasped Verity. 'Oh, thank you!'

Sir John turned to Lady Crossens. 'I will bring her safely back, Emilia, whatever the outcome.'

Her ladyship nodded, but her eyes, suspiciously bright, were on Verity's pale cheeks. 'You may as well sit down again, my dear,' she said gruffly, 'until the carriage is called for. I will send someone to fetch you a wrapper.'

Verity only nodded, sinking obediently down on to the sofa again, her mind rapidly numbing as it shied away from the dreadful images conjured up by Mrs Polegate's tale. She was well able to fill in the gaps with her own vivid imagination, but for once the ready visions were shut off, as being too painful to be contemplated at all.

Even so, she hardly heard the doctor, who still hovered over her, proffering a glass of some mixture which she dutifully drank as he instructed. She scarcely noticed how nearly the whole of the Wellsian visiting population took an interest, and how many of them accompanied her as Sir John Frinton led her out to the waiting carriage. Vaguely, as from some distant place, she heard the messages of goodwill, and felt the hands that pressed and the scented cheeks laid against her own. Dimly she recognised that they wished her well and so she smiled a little and whispered words of thanks.

But all her thoughts were of Henry, and she could no more understand now the confusion and fears of but a few hours before that had led her to refuse his suit than had her patroness at the time. If only he were alive and well, she would marry him in the teeth of twenty such Lady Margaret ghosts! What had she been about, to send him away so unhappy, so wretched that he let his ungovernable passion ride him to some hideous doom? For she knew, just as surely as if she had been there, that this was what had occurred. Must she now take poor Henry's burden of guilt upon her own shoulders? God could not be so cruel!

She was grateful for Sir John's calm flow of trivial remarks that kept such thoughts a little at bay. Whether he spoke of the weather or the scenery she did not know, but his voice was soothing. Though her nails dug into her own hands and the knot in her stomach hardened with every turn of the carriage wheels, that calm voice kept her from screaming aloud the fear that welled and welled within her as the miles went by.

It seemed to take forever, but at last the carriage turned into the long drive that led to Braxted Place. Verity leaned forward in her seat, staring intently out of the window, as if she might will the Marquis to appear there before her eyes.

As Cradoc opened the vast double doors to an imperative knock, two small hands seized him by the coat.

'Cradoc, where is he? Where have they taken him?'

'Miss?' asked the man in a puzzled voice.

'*Where is he*?'

Then the frantic hands released him, and Verity was speeding through the hall, calling out, 'Henry! Henry! Where are you?'

Cradoc made to follow her, but was halted by the man who had accompanied the girl. 'Let her be, man. She will find him for herself.'

The butler stood still, but stared after the girl as she flew up the grand marble stairway, her feet making even lighter work of the journey back over the way she had trodden only twenty-four hours ago, when she had run from this house like one crazed.

'Henry! Henry!' echoed her voice, carrying across the hall.

She did not hear the doors that opened, nor see the heads that popped out. Inskip came quickly into the hall to join the butler and Sir John.

'What is it, Cradoc?'

'I don't know, Mr Inskip. It's Miss Lambourn. Ripe for bedlam, I reckon! This gentleman brought her.'

Inskip glanced at Sir John, who bowed slightly and gave his name. 'She heard of the accident. Nothing would do for her but to come and see for herself how it was.'

'Good God!' ejaculated the secretary, and started off after her up the stairs. But by the time he reached the gallery, and opened his mouth to call, Verity was already approaching its other end. He stopped, watching her gravely, but there was the tiniest of smiles at the back of his eyes.

Verity did not know where to go, where to look. She paused uncertainly, her anguished gaze fluttering to the corridor ahead, and then up the next flight of stairs above her as she heard someone clattering down them.

'Wystan!' she cried out, as she recognised Braxted flying towards her.

'Was that you shouting, Verity?'

She did not answer, only seized his shoulders and shook him. 'Take me to your papa!'

The boy gazed up at her in perplexity. 'He's in his room.'

The grip left his shoulders, and she dashed a hand over her heated brow. 'Take me there!'

'But, Verity——'

'No questions!' she begged hoarsely. 'Take me, Wystan, for the love of God!'

'Come on, then!' he shouted, catching a little of her excitement, and sped off down the corridor that led from the long gallery.

Verity was in no mood to take in the labyrinthine route, nor to realise that her frantic calling would not have been audible on this side of the house. She only urged Wystan to hurry, every time he tried to ask her what was the matter.

It did not occur to her that the calm of the household argued against the tale she had heard, so urgent had become her need to reach Henry. Only when Wystan stopped at a door to knock, and she impatiently thrust him aside and flung it open for herself, did she pause to think.

For there, standing in his shirtsleeves before a dressing-table, with his valet in attendance, miraculously unharmed, stood Henry Haverigg, his startled eyes turned towards the door.

'Henry!' she cried out, and the wrapper dropped from about her shoulders as she ran across the room, her arms stretched out. 'You are alive! Oh, *Henry*!'

Henry received her in a comprehensive embrace that almost knocked him off his legs. Incredibly he kept his balance, holding tightly to the body that had unexpectedly descended upon him.

'Verity! My angel!' he uttered in tones of astonishment and delight. 'What in the world brings you? My God, my God, have you changed your mind?'

'They s-said you were dead!' Verity sobbed, raising her head from his shoulder and gazing adoringly into his face. 'Oh, Henry, it was all my fault! I should never have been so utterly, utterly foolish. But I was so confused! Oh, Henry, Henry, say you forgive me?'

Henry's black eyes searched her face. 'My darling, I am all too ready to forgive you anything at all, but I don't know what you are talking of!'

Verity drew a little away so she could the more easily stare at him. 'But the accident! They said you had fallen from your phaeton and been taken up for dead!'

'Oh, that.' He laughed in relief. 'Is that all? Good God, that was nothing! I took a fall, yes. Into some very muddy ground, let me tell you. I have just taken a bath and changed my clothes, as it happens.'

'But they said——'

Henry smiled. 'Come, now, Verity. You know how pale I am. No doubt the countryfolk who saw Hoff heave me into the phaeton thought I was at my last prayers. My doctor, Claughton, was not at all pleased with me, but I am very much alive, as you can see. A little bruised perhaps, but nothing serious.'

'Oh, thank God!' Verity uttered, collapsing on to his chest and crying weakly.

She was obliged to stop, however, because the Marquis chose this moment to kiss her, having first signalled to his open-mouthed son and his disapproving valet that they would do better to leave the room.

'Come, lend me your arm, and we will sit down,' he

said presently, indicating a sofa that was placed before the window, from which an extensive view of the gardens was obtained.

'But where is your cane?' Verity enquired, slipping her arm about his back so that he might lean on her shoulders.

'You are my cane,' he told her caressingly, as he unselfconsciously gave her his weight.

She thrilled to the words, and to the feel of his hip as it thrust against her in its forward pull, the intimacy more dear even than the tender kiss with which he thanked her.

When they were settled in comfort, Henry removed her bonnet and gave her his handkerchief.

'I can only say thank God for the exaggeration of countryfolk,' he told her happily, 'since it had the effect of bringing you here to rescue me.'

Verity dried her eyes. 'It is very well for you to make a joke of it, but I know you were driving carelessly, for you were in one of your black moods!'

Henry grinned. 'Miss Lambourn, if you wish to be an arbiter of my conduct, there is a penalty to be paid, you know.'

She bit her lip, but the smile crept out. 'I dare say I may guess what *that* is.'

'I dare say you may, since you are far from stupid. And,' he added, the black eyes wickedly quizzing her, 'although you may not have noticed in your agitation, you are now hopelessly compromised by your presence in my bedchamber!'

Startled, Verity looked about her, becoming aware for the first time of the opulence of her surroundings, the huge four-poster bed that dominated one side of the room. She made an instinctive move to rise and was firmly restrained.

'No, you don't! We will remain here until I have your promise to marry me.'

Verity turned to him, her eyes moist. 'Oh, Henry, of course I will marry you! I can't think why I was making such a fuss. When I thought you were...' Her voice failing, she could only seize his hand and hold it tightly.

'My darling, I think I must have a very ignoble soul,' Henry told her ruefully. 'To have you restored to me is like—like being released from an iron cage! Yet I can find in myself a perverse satisfaction that you felt something of the devastation I experienced this morning, when I believed I had lost you.'

'Devastation!' echoed Verity in staring disbelief. 'Dear Lord, I thought they had *torn out my heart*! Henry, Henry, I love you so desperately!'

Henry's eyes blazed with passion, and he seized her in his arms again in a kiss so forceful that the thought flitted through her dizzying brain that she would swoon again. Flame seemed to erupt inside her and she clung to him, responding to the violence of his lips with a longing deep within her for that which she now knew would soon be fulfilled.

When at last he let her go, he was smiling at her with so much tenderness in those black eyes that Verity wondered how she could ever have supposed he did not care enough. His next words confirmed that he did.

'Verity, do you know that you are the most wonderful thing that has ever happened to me in my whole life?'

'No,' she said baldly.

Henry blinked. 'What? Don't you know how I love you?'

Verity shook her head. 'No. You never said so.'

He looked blank. 'Did I not?' A little laugh was surprised out of him. 'Perhaps you are right. To me it was so obvious.'

'Not to me,' Verity said firmly. She lifted a finger to trace a line down that pale cheek, no longer afraid to speak of the thing that had driven her into such deep despair. 'You see, I had *Margaret* to think of.'

He frowned as if the name meant nothing to him. 'Margaret?'

'Yes, Meg. Your *wife*.'

Recognition flashed in his eyes, but he drew her closer within his embrace and put up a hand to caress her cheek. 'Yes, I see.'

'I could not believe you might love me as intensely as you had loved her. It seemed as though the manner of her loss would always keep you from me.'

Now he stared at her in amazement. 'Good God, now I don't see at all! Are you telling me that is why you refused me?'

Verity nodded, a little shame-faced. 'I was silly, I know, but——'

'No, you were not silly,' Henry interrupted. 'It was a natural conclusion for you to make. It is I who was the fool, not to see how it must appear!' He seized her hands, holding them tightly between his own, and his black eyes locked on to hers as if by this he might convince her better of what he was about to say. 'My darling, you don't understand. Meg and I were never *in love*. I cared for her, yes, of course I did. But not like *this*.'

Verity gazed back at him blankly. 'What do you mean? You were *married*.'

He smiled. 'My innocent, Meg and I were destined for one another almost before we were out of our cradles. It was all *arranged*, long before either of us knew anything of the matter.'

'What?' uttered Verity faintly, as ignorant of this aspect of aristocratic affairs as she was of the rest of his public life.

'*Yes*,' he insisted. 'She was the daughter of the Earl of Templand and Lady Margaret in her own right. Rank and birth are of the first consequence in these matters, and we both had wealth, too. It was an admirable match and we were both very dutiful. Fortunately, our respective parents saw the wisdom of allowing us to become acquainted and we saw much of each other as children. They took no chances, nevertheless, for our engagement was announced at Meg's début and we were married soon after. She was only just seventeen. I was little more than a year older.'

'I think that is terrible!' Verity said, appalled.

He shrugged, faintly smiling. 'Perhaps. It is quite usual for persons of our order, however, and we saw nothing amiss. We had no choice, but we made no objections either. It was duty.' He grinned suddenly, and kissed the hands he still held. 'But I already have an heir, and I am now at liberty to please myself.'

Verity was too much caught up in this revelation to be diverted by the pleasantry. She released her hands only so that she could grasp his arms.

'Then, Henry, when she died——'

The pale face shadowed a little. 'When she died, I was responsible. I grieved for her, more perhaps for her loss to the children than to myself. But it was for the *waste* that I suffered most! It was I who cut her off in the flower of her youth, and I must ever live with that knowledge. If I had not found you, I cannot think I would long have survived it.'

'Don't speak that way!' Verity scolded, but she softened the words with a kiss, raising her hands from his arms to cup his face between them.

'I love you,' he said softly, putting his lips to hers and with them gently caressing her mouth.

But in a moment Verity pulled a little away. Still she was not entirely satisfied, not entirely convinced.

'But Henry, had Meg lived. . .what then?'

An expression of faint distress flickered over his face. 'There, my sweet, you have perhaps one of the unkindest twists of fate. Or perhaps the kindest. Who knows? For if Meg had lived, we would have gone on in quiet content, accepting each other's vagaries, sometimes with impatience perhaps, even growing a little apart as we grew older.'

He slid his arm about Verity's back and with his other hand cupped her head, tipping it back so that her dark curls rioted about her while he roved her features with his eyes.

'And then I should never have known what it is to love a woman to the point of screaming madness, to love her to the depths of my soul, and to know that in all the world there is nothing I could desire more than to walk with her beside me through the remainder of my life.'

'Oh, Henry!' Verity whispered, and closed her eyes as she leaned forward to receive his kiss.

Behind them the door burst open. They came apart as if sprung, turning their heads to see who had caught them so indecorously entwined.

'You're going to be married!' yelled Braxted from the doorway, hitting the air with a triumphant fist. 'Inskip told me, and anyone can see it's true!'

Held in his other hand was his little sister. Tugging her along, he skipped towards the sofa.

'I brunged Peggy to see for herself. See, Peggy, they're going to be married, and I knowed it.' He began to chant. 'I knowed it! I knowed it!'

'I no-dit! I no-dit!' sang Peggy, her little face beaming as she reached the couple on the sofa, putting up her arms in mute invitation.

'I hope you will like it, Peggy,' Verity said, lifting the infant on to her lap, her countenance wreathed in smiles.

Wystan looked from one to the other of them. 'It is true, isn't it, Papa?'

Henry could not keep the happiness out of his face.

'Yes, it's true. Verity has consented to be my wife—and your new mama.'

'Hurrah!' Then the boy put his arms akimbo, staring at his father with an air of great seriousness, and added, 'And about time too!'

Instantly, Peggy swivelled about on Verity's lap and poking her father in the ribs, summed it up neatly.

'Time *too*. . .time to 'ug?'